PENGUIN BOOKS

THE BROTHERS HAWTHORNE

Also by Jennifer Lynn Barnes

The Inheritance Games

The Inheritance Games

The Hawthorne Legacy

The Final Gambit

The Brothers Hawthorne

Coming next: *The Grandest Game*

The Debutantes

Little White Lies

Deadly Little Scandals

THE BROTHERS HAWTHORNE

JENNIFER LYNN BARNES

PENGUIN BOOKS

PENGUIN BOOKS

UK | USA | Canada | Ireland | Australia
India | New Zealand | South Africa

Penguin Books is part of the Penguin Random House group of companies
whose addresses can be found at global.penguinrandomhouse.com

www.penguin.co.uk
www.puffin.co.uk
www.ladybird.co.uk

First published in the USA by Little, Brown and Company,
a division of Hachette Book Group 2023
This edition published in the UK by Penguin Books 2023

002

Cover design by Karina Granda
Interior design by Carla Weise

Printed and bound in Great Britain by Clays Ltd, Elcograf S.p.A.

The authorized representative in the EEA is Penguin Random House Ireland,
Morrison Chambers, 32 Nassau Street, Dublin D02 YH68

A CIP catalogue record for this book is available from the British Library

HARDBACK ISBN:
978–0–241–63849–1

INTERNATIONAL PAPERBACK ISBN:
978–0–241–63850–7

All correspondence to:
Penguin Books
Penguin Random House Children's
One Embassy Gardens, 8 Viaduct Gardens, London SW11 7BW

For Judy Eshelman

TWELVE AND A HALF YEARS AGO

Grayson and Jameson Hawthorne knew the rules. You couldn't get around rules if you didn't know them. *On Christmas morning, you may not step foot outside your rooms before the clock strikes seven.*

Beneath his blanket, Jameson lifted a military-grade walkie-talkie to his mouth. "You set the clocks forward?" He was seven to his brother's eight—both plenty old enough to spot a loophole.

That was the trick. The challenge. The game.

"I did," Grayson confirmed.

Jameson paused. "What if the old man set them back after we went to bed?"

"Then we'll have to go to Plan B."

Hawthornes *always* had a Plan B. But this time, it proved unnecessary. Hawthorne House had five grandfather clocks, and they all struck seven at the exact same time: 6:25.

Success! Jameson flung down his walkie-talkie, threw back the covers, and took off—out the door, down the hall, two lefts, a right, across the landing to the grand staircase. Jameson *flew.* But Grayson was a year older, a year taller—and he'd already made it from his wing halfway down the stairs.

Taking the steps two at a time, Jameson made it seventy percent of the way down, then launched himself over the banister. He hurtled toward the ground floor and landed on top of Grayson. They both went down, a mess of limbs and Christmas morning madness, then scrambled to their feet and raced neck and neck, arriving at the Great Room doors at the exact same time—only to find their five-year-old brother had beaten them there.

Xander was curled up on the floor like a puppy. Yawning, he opened his eyes and blinked up at them. "Is it Christmas?"

"What are you doing, Xan?" Grayson frowned. "Did you sleep down here? The rules say..."

"*Can't step a foot,*" Xander replied, sitting up. "I didn't. I *rolled.*" At his brothers' unblinking stares, Xander demonstrated.

"You log-rolled all the way from your bedroom?" Jameson was impressed.

"No stepping." Xander grinned. "I win!"

"Kid's got us there." Fourteen-year-old Nash sauntered over to join them and hoisted Xander up on his shoulders. "Ready?"

The fifteen-foot-tall doors to the Great Room were closed only once a year, from midnight on Christmas Eve until the boys descended on Christmas morning. Staring at the gold rings on the door, Jameson imagined the marvels that lay on the other side.

Christmas at Hawthorne House was *magic.*

"You get that door, Nash," Grayson ordered. "Jamie, help me with this one."

Grinning, Jameson locked his fingers around the ring, next to Grayson's. "One, two, three . . . pull!"

The majestic doors parted, revealing . . . *nothing.*

"It's gone." Grayson went unnaturally still.

"What is?" Xander asked, craning his neck to see.

"Christmas," Jameson whispered. No stockings. No presents. No marvels or surprises. Even the decorations were gone, all except the tree, and even that had been stripped of ornaments.

Grayson swallowed. "Maybe the old man didn't want us to break the rules this time."

That was the thing about games: Sometimes you lost.

"No Christmas?" Xander's voice quivered. "But I *rolled.*"

Nash set Xander down. "I'll fix this," he swore in a low tone. "I promise."

"No." Jameson shook his head, his chest and eyes burning. "We're missing something." He forced himself to take in every detail of the room. "There!" he said, pointing to a spot near the top of the tree where a single ornament hung, hidden among the branches.

That wasn't a coincidence. There were no coincidences in Hawthorne House.

Nash crossed the room and snagged the ornament, then held it out. A sphere made of clear plastic dangled from a red ribbon. The plastic had a visible seam.

There was something inside.

Grayson took the ornament and, with the precision of a neurosurgeon, broke it open. A single white puzzle piece fell out. Jameson pounced. He turned the piece over and saw his grandfather's scrawl on the back. *1/6.*

"One out of six," he said out loud, and then his eyes widened. "The other trees!"

There were six Christmas trees in Hawthorne House. The one in the foyer stretched up twenty feet overhead, its boughs wrapped in sparkling lights. The dining room tree was strung with pearls, the one in the Tea Room bedecked in crystal. Cascading velvet ribbons danced through the branches of an enormous fir on the second-story landing; a white tree decorated solely in gold sat on the third.

Nash, Grayson, Jameson, and Xander scoured them all, obtaining five more ornaments, four with puzzle pieces inside. Opening those four ornaments allowed them to assemble the puzzle: a square. A *blank* square.

Jameson and Grayson reached for the final ornament at the same time. "I'm the one who found the first clue," Jameson insisted fiercely. "I *knew* there was a game."

After a long moment, Grayson let go. Jameson had the ornament open in a flash. Inside, he found a small metal key on a little flashlight keychain

"Try the light on the puzzle, Jamie." Even Nash couldn't resist the lure of this game.

Jameson turned the flashlight on and angled its beam toward the assembled puzzle. Words appeared. *SOUTHWEST CORNER OF THE ESTATE*.

"How long will it take us to walk there?" Xander asked dramatically. *"Hours?"*

The Hawthorne estate, like Hawthorne House, was sizable.

Nash knelt next to Xander. "Wrong question, little man." He looked up at the other two. "Either of you wanna tell me the right one?"

Jameson's gaze darted to the keychain, but Grayson beat him to speaking. "What exactly is that a key *to*?"

The answer was a golf cart. Nash drove. As the southwest corner of the estate came into view, an awed hush swept over the brothers as they gaped at the sight before them.

This present *definitely* wouldn't have fit in the Great Room.

A quartet of ancient oak trees, all of them massive, now hosted the most elaborate tree house any of them—and possibly anyone in the world—had ever seen. The multi-level marvel looked like something out of a fairy tale, like it had been called from the oaks by magic, like it *belonged* there. Jameson counted nine walkways stretching between the trees. The house had two towers. Six spiraling slides. Ladders, ropes, steps that seemed to float midair.

This was the tree house to end all tree houses.

Their grandfather stood in front of it all, arms crossed, the barest hint of a smile on his face. "You know, boys," the great Tobias Hawthorne called, as the golf cart came to a stop and the wind whistled through branches, "I thought you'd get here faster."

CHAPTER 1

GRAYSON

Faster. Grayson Hawthorne was power and control. His form was flawless. He'd long ago perfected the art of visualizing his opponent, *feeling* each strike, channeling his body's momentum into every block, every attack.

But you could always be faster.

After his tenth time through the sequence, Grayson stopped, sweat dripping down his bare chest. Keeping his breathing even and controlled, he knelt in front of what remained of their childhood tree house, unrolled his pack, and surveyed his choices: three daggers, two with ornate hilts and one understated and smooth. It was this last blade that Grayson picked up.

Knife in hand, Grayson straightened, his arms by his side. Mind, clear. Body, free of tension. *Begin.* There were many styles of knife fighting, and the year he was thirteen, Grayson had studied them all. Of course, billionaire Tobias Hawthorne's grandsons had never merely *studied* anything. Once they'd chosen a focus, they were expected to live it, breathe it, master it.

And this was what Grayson had learned that year: Stance was everything. You didn't move the blade. You moved, and the blade moved. Faster. *Faster.* It had to feel natural. It had to *be* natural. The moment your muscles tensed, the moment you stopped breathing, the moment you broke your stance instead of flowing from one to the next, you lost.

And Hawthornes didn't lose.

"When I told you to get a hobby, this isn't what I meant."

Grayson ignored Xander's presence for as long as it took to finish the sequence—and throw the dagger with exacting precision at a low-hanging branch six feet away. "Hawthornes don't have hobbies," he told his little brother, walking to retrieve the blade. "We have specialties. Expertise."

"*Anything worth doing is worth doing well,*" Xander quoted, wiggling his eyebrows—one of which had only just started to grow back after an experiment gone wrong. "*And anything done well can be done better.*"

Why would a Hawthorne settle for better, a voice whispered in the back of Grayson's mind, *when they could be the best?*

Grayson closed his hand around the dagger's hilt and pulled. "I should be getting back to work."

"You are a man obsessed," Xander declared.

Grayson secured the dagger in its holder, then rolled the pack back up, tying it closed. "I have twenty-eight billion reasons to be obsessed."

Avery had set an impossible task for herself—and for them. Five years to give away more than twenty-eight billion dollars. That was the majority of the Hawthorne fortune. They'd spent the past seven months just assembling the foundation's board and advisory committee.

"We have five more months to nail down the first three billion in donations," Grayson stated crisply, "and I promised Avery I would be there with her every step of the way."

Promises mattered to Grayson Hawthorne—and so did Avery Kylie Grambs. The girl who had inherited their grandfather's fortune. The stranger who had become one of them.

"Speaking as someone with friends, a girlfriend, and a small army of robots, I just think you could do with a little more balance in your life," Xander opined. "An *actual* hobby? Down time?"

Grayson gave him a look. "You've filed at least three patents since school let out for the summer last month, Xan."

Xander shrugged. "They're recreational patents."

Grayson snorted, then assessed his brother. "How *is* Isaiah?" he asked softly.

Growing up, none of the Hawthorne brothers had known their fathers' identities—until Grayson had discovered that his was Sheffield *Grayson*. Nash's was a man named Jake *Nash*. And Xander's was Isaiah *Alexander*. Of the three men, only Isaiah actually deserved to be called a father. He and Xander had filed those "recreational patents" together.

"We're supposed to be talking about you," Xander said stubbornly.

"I should get back to work," Grayson reiterated, adopting a tone that was very effective at putting everyone *except* his brothers in their place. "And despite what Avery and Jameson seem to believe, I don't need a babysitter."

"You don't need a babysitter," Xander agreed cheerfully, "and I am definitely not writing a book entitled *The Care and Feeding of Your Broody Twenty-Year-Old Brother.*"

Grayson's eyes narrowed to slits.

"I can assure you," Xander said with great solemnity, "it doesn't have pictures."

Before Grayson could summon an appropriate threat in response, his phone buzzed. Assuming it was the figures he'd requested, Grayson picked the phone up, only to discover a text from Nash. He looked back at Xander and knew instantly that his youngest brother had received the same message.

Grayson was the one who read the fateful missive out loud: "Nine-one-one."

CHAPTER 2

JAMESON

The roar of the falls. The mist in the air. The feel of the back of Avery's body against the front of his. Jameson Winchester Hawthorne was *hungry*—for this, for her, for everything, all of it, *more*.

Iguazú Falls was the world's largest waterfall system. The walkway they were standing on took them right up to the edge of an incredible drop-off. Staring out at the falls, Jameson felt the lure of *more*. He eyed the railing. "Do you dare me?" he murmured into the back of Avery's head.

She reached back to touch his jaw. "Absolutely not."

Jameson's lips curved—a teasing smile, a wicked one. "You're probably right, Heiress."

She turned her head to the side and met his gaze. "Probably?"

Jameson looked back at the falls. *Unstoppable. Off limits. Deadly.* "Probably."

They were staying in a villa built on stilts and surrounded by jungle, no one around for miles but the two of them, Avery's security team, and the jaguars roaring in the distance.

Jameson felt Avery's approach before he heard it.

"Heads or tails?" She leaned against the railing, brandishing a bronze-and-silver coin. Her brown hair was falling out of its ponytail, her long-sleeved shirt still damp from the falls.

Jameson brought his hand to her hair tie, then worked it slowly and gently down—and off. *Heads or tails* was an invitation. A challenge. *You kiss me, or I kiss you.* "Dealer's choice, Heiress."

"If I'm the dealer..." Avery placed a palm flat on his chest, her eyes daring him to do something about that wet shirt of hers. "We're going to need cards."

The things we could do, Jameson thought, *with a deck of cards.* But before he could voice some of the more tantalizing possibilities, the satellite phone buzzed. Only five people had the number: his brothers, her sister, and her lawyer. Jameson groaned.

The text was from Nash. Nine seconds later, when the satellite phone rang, Jameson answered. "Delightful timing, as always, Gray."

"I take it you received Nash's message?"

"We've been summoned," Jameson intoned. "You planning to play hooky again?"

Each Hawthorne brother got a single nine-one-one a year. The code didn't mean *emergency* so much as *I want you all here,* but if one brother texted, the others came, no questions asked. Ignoring a nine-one-one led to... consequences.

"If you say *one word* about leather pants," Grayson bit out. "I will—"

"Did you say *leather pants*?" Jameson was enjoying this way too much. "You're breaking up, Gray. Are you asking me to send you a picture of the incredibly tight leather pants you had to wear the one time you ignored a nine-one-one?"

"Do not send me a picture—"

"A video?" Jameson asked loudly. "You want a video of yourself singing karaoke in the leather pants?"

Avery plucked the phone from his hands. She knew as well as Jameson did that there would be no ignoring Nash's summons, and she had a bad habit of *not* tormenting his brothers.

"It's me, Grayson." Avery examined Nash's text herself. "We'll see you in London."

CHAPTER 3

JAMESON

On a private jet in the dead of night, Jameson looked out the window. Avery was asleep on his chest. Near the front of the plane, Oren and the rest of the security team were quiet.

Quiet always got to Jameson, the same way stillness did. Skye had told them once that she wasn't made for inertness, and as much as Jameson hated to see any similarity between himself and his spoiled, sometimes homicidal mother, he knew what she meant.

It had been getting worse these past weeks. *Since Prague.* Jameson pushed down the unwanted reminder, but at night, with nothing to distract him, he could barely resist the urge to remember, to *think*, to give in to the siren call of risk and a mystery that needed to be solved.

"You've got that look on your face."

Jameson ran a hand over Avery's hair. Her head was still on his chest, but her eyes were open. "What look?" he asked softly.

"*Our* look."

Avery's brain was just as wired for puzzles as his was. That was exactly why Jameson couldn't risk letting the silence and stillness close in, why he *had* to keep himself occupied. Because if he let himself really think about Prague, he'd want to tell her, and if he told her, it would be real. And once it was real, he feared no amount of distraction would be capable of holding him back, no matter how reckless or dangerous pursuing this might be.

Jameson trusted Avery with all that he had and all that he was, but he couldn't always trust *himself* to do the right thing. The smart thing. The safe thing.

Don't tell her. Jameson forced his mind down a different path, banishing all thoughts of Prague. "You got me, Heiress." The only way for him to hide anything from Avery was to show her something else. Something true. *Misdirection.* "My gap year is almost over."

"You're restless." Avery pulled back from his chest. "You have been for months. It wasn't as noticeable on this trip, but on all the others, when I'm working..."

"I *want*..." Jameson closed his eyes, picturing himself back at the falls, hearing the roar—and eyeing the railing. "I don't know what I want. *Something.*" He looked back out the window, into blackness. *"To do great things."*

That was a Hawthorne's charge, always—and not *great* as in *very good. Great* as in vast and lasting and incredible. *Great* like the falls.

"We *are* doing great things," Avery told him. Giving away his grandfather's billions was *it* for her. She was going to change the world. *And I'm right here with her. I can hear the roar. I can feel the spray.* But Jameson couldn't shake the gnawing sense that he was standing behind the ropes.

He wasn't doing great things. Not in the way she was. Not even in the way Gray was.

"This will be our first time back in Europe," Avery said quietly, leaning forward to look out into the black, same as him, "since Prague."

Very perceptive, Avery Kylie Grambs.

There was an art to the careless smile. "I've told you, Heiress, you don't need to worry about Prague."

"I'm not worried, Hawthorne. I'm curious. Why won't you tell me what happened that night?" Avery knew how to use silence to her advantage, wielding each pause to command his full attention, to make him *feel* her silence like breath on his skin. "You came home at dawn. You smelled like fire and ash. And you had a cut"—she brought her hand to the place where his collarbone dipped, right at the base of his neck—"here."

If Avery had wanted to force him to tell her, she could have. One little word—*Tahiti*—and his secrets would have been hers. But she wouldn't force this, and Jameson knew that, and it killed him. Everything about her *killed him* in the best possible way.

Don't tell her. Don't think about it. Resist.

Jameson brought his lips within a centimeter of hers. "If you want, Mystery Girl," he murmured, heat rising between them, the name a remnant of another time, "you can start calling me Mystery Boy."

CHAPTER 4

GRAYSON

It had been years since Grayson had stepped foot in London, but the flat looked just the same: same historical facade, same modern interior, same twin terraces, same exquisite view.

Same four brothers taking in that view.

Beside Grayson, Jameson cocked an eyebrow at Nash. "What's the situation, cowboy?" Grayson had been wondering the same thing. Nash almost never used his yearly nine-one-one.

"This." Their oldest brother plunked a velvet box down on the glass-top table. A *ring* box. Grayson found himself suddenly unable to blink as Nash flipped it open to reveal a remarkable piece: a black opal wrapped in intricate diamond leaves and set in platinum. The flecks of color in the gemstone were electric, the workmanship without peer. "Nan gave it to me," Nash said. "It was our grandmother's."

Nash was the only one of them with memories of Alice Hawthorne, who'd died before the rest of the Hawthorne brothers were even born.

"It wasn't her wedding or engagement ring," Nash drawled. "But Nan thought it would suit Lib." Nash bowed his head slightly. "For that purpose."

Lib as in *Libby Grambs*, Nash's partner, Avery's sister. Grayson felt a breath catch in his throat.

"Our great-grandmother gave you a family ring for Libby," Xander summarized, "and that's a problem?"

"It is," Nash confirmed.

Grayson expelled the breath. "Because you're not ready."

Nash looked up and cracked a slow and devious grin. "Because I already bought her one myself." He plunked a second ring box down on the table. One by one, the muscles over Grayson's rib cage tightened, and he wasn't even sure why.

Jameson, who'd gone unnaturally still the moment he'd seen the first ring, snapped out of it and flicked open the second box. It was empty.

Nash already proposed. He and Libby are already engaged. The realization hit Grayson with startling force. *Everything is changing.* That was a useless thought, obvious and overdue. Their grandfather was dead. They'd all been disinherited. Everything had *already* changed. Nash was already with Libby. Jameson was with Avery. Even Xander had Max.

"Nash Westbrook Hawthorne," Xander boomed. "Prepare yourself for a bracing, celebratory hug of manly joy!"

Xander did not, in fact, give Nash time to prepare before crashing into him—hugging, grappling, wrestling, attempting to hoist Nash into the air, it was all the same. Jameson joined the melee, and Grayson forced everything else to fade away as he clapped a hand on Nash's shoulder—then pulled him backward.

Three on one. Nash didn't stand a chance.

“Impromptu bachelor party!” Jameson declared when the four of them finally broke apart. “Give me an hour.”

“Stop.” Nash held up a hand, then followed his first *who’s-the-oldest-brother-here* order with a second. “Turn.” Jameson obliged, and Nash fixed him with a look. “You planning on breaking any laws, Jamie? Because you’ve been on quite a kick lately.”

To Grayson’s knowledge, there had been an incident in Monaco, another in Belize…

Jameson gave a little shrug. “You know what they say, Nash. No charges filed, no harm done.”

“Is that what they say?” Nash replied, his tone deceptively mild. And then, inexplicably, Grayson found himself on the end of Nash’s *look*.

What did I do? Grayson’s eyes narrowed. “You didn’t bring us here for your own sake.”

Nash leaned back. “You accusin’ me of a being a mother hen, Gray?”

“Them’s fighting words,” Xander said happily, altogether too pleased at the prospect.

Nash cast one last look at Grayson, then turned back to Jameson. “Impromptu bachelor party,” he agreed. “But Gray and Xan will help you plan—and tree house rules.”

What happened in the tree house stayed in the tree house.

CHAPTER 5
GRAYSON

Their night ended at three in the morning. "Ice-climbing, skywalk, speedboat, mopeds . . ." To Grayson's ears, Jameson sounded very satisfied with himself. "Not to mention clubbing."

"I thought the medieval crypt was a nice touch," Xander added.

Grayson arched a brow. "I suspect Nash could have gone without being duct-taped."

The man of the hour took off his cowboy hat and leaned against the wall. "What happens in the tree house stays in the tree house," he reiterated, his quiet tone reminding Grayson that Avery and Libby were asleep upstairs.

A lump rose in Grayson's throat. "Congratulations," he told his brother. He meant it. Life *was* change. People were supposed to move forward, even if he could not.

Jameson and Xander stumbled to bed, but Nash held Grayson back. When it was just the two of them, he placed something in

Grayson's hand. *The ring box.* The one with their grandmother's black opal ring.

"Why don't you hold on to this?" Nash said.

Grayson swallowed, the muscles in his throat tight. "Why me?" Jameson would have been the obvious choice, for obvious reasons.

"Why not you, Gray?" Nash leaned forward, putting his gaze level with Grayson's. "Someday, with someone—why not you?"

The ring was still in its box on his nightstand when Grayson woke up hours later. *Why not you?*

Grayson pushed himself out of bed and briskly tucked the box into a hidden compartment in his luggage. If Nash wanted the heirloom ring kept safe, he'd keep it safe. Protecting things that mattered was what Grayson Hawthorne did, even when he couldn't afford to let them matter too much.

Out on the terrace, Avery was already up, helping herself to an impressive breakfast spread. "I hear last night was the stuff of legends." She handed him a cup of coffee—black, hot, and filled to almost overflowing.

"Jamie has a big mouth," Grayson replied. The mug warmed his hand.

"Trust me," Avery murmured, "Jameson knows how to keep secrets just fine."

Grayson studied her, the way he wouldn't have allowed himself to months earlier. It didn't hurt quite the way it would have then. "Is he spiraling?"

"No." Avery shook her head, and her hair fell into her face. "He's just looking for something—or trying not to look for something. Or both." She paused. "What about you, Gray?"

"I'm fine." The response was automatic, rote, and brooked no argument. But he could never quite seem to stop there with her. "And for the record, if Xander shows you a 'book' he's been writing, you *will* destroy it, or there will be consequences."

"Consequences!" Xander jackrabbited onto the terrace, wriggled between them, and snagged a chocolate croissant. "My favorite!"

"Who among us doesn't love the taste of consequences in the morning?" Jameson ambled out, helped himself to a croissant, and waved it in Grayson's general direction. "Avery tell you about her new meeting schedule? London officially knows the Hawthorne heiress is in town."

"Meetings?" Grayson picked up his phone. "What time?" A call came in before Avery could reply. When Grayson saw who was calling, he abruptly stood. "I need to take this." He strode back inside, closed the door, and made sure hc hadn't been followed before he answered.

"I assume we have a situation."

CHAPTER 6

JAMESON

"Fascinating." Jameson stared in the direction Grayson had gone. "Was that a hint of genuine human emotion on his face?"

Avery gave him a look. "Worried?" she asked. "Or curious?"

"About Grayson?" Jameson replied. *Both.* "Neither. It's probably his tailor calling to make fun of him for being a twenty-year-old who has a tailor."

Xander grinned. "Should I creep inside and eavesdrop on that phone call?"

"Are you implying that you're even remotely capable of stealth?" Jameson retorted.

"I can be stealthy!" Xander insisted. "Clearly, you're just still bitter at the extent to which my legendary dance moves blew everyone's mind at the club last night."

Refusing to take the bait, Jameson glanced at Oren, who'd joined them on the terrace. "Speaking of our little celebration," Jameson said, "how bad is the paparazzi situation this morning?"

"British tabloids." Oren's eyes narrowed to slits. Avery's head of security was former military and frighteningly capable. That he'd narrowed his eyes at all told Jameson that the paparazzi situation wasn't *good*. "I've got two of my men patrolling out front."

"And I have meetings," Avery replied firmly. Clearly, she wasn't planning to change her plans because of the paparazzi. Oren was too smart to ask her to.

"I could distract them," Jameson offered devilishly. Trouble was a specialty of his.

"I appreciate the offer," Avery murmured, stopping on her way inside to brush her lips lightly and teasingly against his. "But no."

The kiss was brief. *Too brief.* Jameson watched her go. Oren followed. Eventually, Xander went to take a shower. Jameson stayed on the terrace, taking in the view, letting a decadent, buttery croissant melt on his tongue, bit by bit, as he tried not to think about how *quiet* it was, how *still*.

And then Grayson reappeared, a suitcase in hand. "I have to go."

"Go where?" Jameson said immediately. Being challenged was good for Grayson's god complex, and challenging him was rarely boring. "And why?"

"I have some personal business to attend to."

"Since when do *you* have personal business?" Jameson was officially intrigued.

Grayson didn't dignify that question with a response. He just turned and began to walk back through the flat. Jameson went to follow, but then his phone buzzed—*Oren*.

He's with Avery. Jameson came to an immediate standstill and answered. "Problem?" he asked the bodyguard.

"Not on my end. Avery's fine. But one of my men just intercepted the porter." As Oren made his report, Grayson's retreating form disappeared from Jameson's view. "It appears the porter has a delivery. For you."

In the hall, the porter held out a silver tray. On the tray sat a single card.

Jameson cocked his head to the side. "What is this?"

The porter's eyes were bright. "It appears to be a card, sir. A calling card."

His curiosity piqued, Jameson reached for the card, grabbing it between his middle and index fingers—a magician's hold, like he might make it disappear. The moment his gaze landed on the words embossed on the card, the rest of the world faded away.

The front of the card bore a name and an address. *Ian Johnstone-Jameson. 9 King's Gate Terrace.* Jameson flipped the card over. In handwritten scrawl, he found no instructions, only a time. 2 *PM.*

CHAPTER 7

JAMESON

Hours later, Jameson ducked out of the flat, with Nash, Xander, and the security team none the wiser. As for the British paparazzi, they weren't used to tracking Hawthornes. Jameson arrived at 9 King's Gate Terrace fashionably late and alone.

If you want to play, Ian Johnstone-Jameson, *I'll play.* Not because he needed or wanted or longed for a father, the way he had as a kid, but because these days, doing *something* to keep his mind occupied always felt less dangerous than doing nothing.

The building was white and vast, stretching up five stories and running the length of the block, luxury flat after luxury flat, an embassy or two mixed among them. The area was posh. Exclusive. Before Jameson could press his finger to the call button, security strode down the walk. *One guard for several units.*

"May I help you, sir?" The man's tone suggested that *no, indeed he could not.*

But Jameson wasn't a Hawthorne for nothing. "I was invited. Number nine."

"I was unaware that *he* was in residence." The man's reply was smooth, but his eyes were sharp. Jameson brandished the card. "Ah," the man said, taking it from him. "I see."

Two minutes later, Jameson was standing in the entry of a flat that made the Hawthorne London abode look modest. White marble inlaid with a glistening black *B* marked a foyer that seemed to stretch back forever, cutting all the way through the flat. Glass doors offered an undisturbed view of the impeccable artwork lining the stark-white hall all the way down.

Ian Johnstone-Jameson pushed through one of those glass doors.

This family is prominent enough, Jameson could hear his mother saying mockingly, *that any of the men I slept with would have to live under a rock not to know that they had a son.*

The man striding toward him now was mid-forties with thick brown hair kept just long enough that he couldn't pass for your typical CEO or politician. There was something achingly familiar about his features—definitely not his nose or jaw, but the shape and color of his eyes, the curl of his lips. The *amusement*.

"I had heard that there was some resemblance," Ian commented in an accent as posh as his address. He cocked his head slightly to one side in a habitual motion Jameson recognized all too well. "Would you like a tour?"

Jameson raised an eyebrow. "Would you like to give me one?" Nothing mattered unless you let it.

"Tit for tat." Ian's lips twisted into a smile. "That, I can respect. Three questions." The British man turned, strode back the way he'd come, and pushed open the first glass door. "That's what I'll give you in exchange for your answering one of mine."

Ian Johnstone-Jameson held the glass door open, waiting. Jameson let him wait, then languidly strolled forward.

"You'll ask your questions first," Ian said.

Will I? Jameson thought, but he was far too Hawthorne to fall into the trap of saying that out loud. "And if I don't have any questions for you, I wonder what you'll offer me next."

Ian's eyes glinted, a vivid green. "You didn't phrase that as a question," he noted.

Jameson flashed his teeth. "No. I didn't." Down the long hall they went, through more glass doors and past a Matisse painting. Jameson waited until they wound their way to the kitchen—all black, from the countertops to the appliances to the granite floors—before giving voice to his first question. "What do you want, Ian Johnstone-Jameson?"

You couldn't grow up Hawthorne without realizing that everyone wanted something.

"Simple," Ian replied. "I want to ask you my question. It's more of a favor, really. But as a show of good faith, I'll go ahead and offer up an answer to your question in the general sense as well. As a rule in life, I want three things: Pleasure. Challenge." He smiled. "And to win."

Jameson hadn't expected anything this man had to say to hit him hard.

Focus. He could almost hear his grandfather's admonition. *Lose focus, boys, and lose the game.* For once, Jameson leaned into the memory. He was Jameson Winchester Hawthorne. He didn't need a damn thing from the man in front of him.

They were nothing alike.

"What does winning look like to you?" Jameson chose a question that was meant to give him the measure of the man. *Know a man and know his weakness.*

"Different things." Ian seemed to relish his answer. "A lovely night with a beautiful woman. A yes from men who love to say no. And often . . ." He put special emphasis on that word. "It looks like a winning hand. I'm a bit of a gamesman."

Jameson saw straight through that statement. "You gamble."

"Don't we all?" Ian replied. "But, yes, by profession, I'm a poker player. I met your mother in Las Vegas the year I won a particularly sought-after international title. Frankly, my family would prefer that I'd chosen a more respectable pastime, like chess—or better yet, finance. But I'm good enough at what I do that I generally don't have to drink from the family cup, so their preferences—my father's and eldest brother's in particular—are irrelevant." Ian drummed his fingers lightly on the countertop. "Most of the time."

You have brothers? Jameson thought the question but didn't say it. Instead, he offered up a statement. "They don't know about me." Jameson raked his gaze over Ian's face. "Your family."

Everyone had a tell. It was just a matter of finding it.

"That wasn't a question," Ian replied, his expression never changing. *And that's the tell.* This was a man whose face had a thousand different ways of conveying that life and everyone in it were naught but amusements. A thousand ways—and he'd just locked into one.

"Not a question," Jameson agreed. "But I got my answer."

Ian Johnstone-Jameson liked to win. His family's opinions of him were irrelevant *most of the time*. They didn't know he had an illegitimate son.

"For what it's worth," Ian said, "it was a few years before I realized myself, and at that point, well . . ." *Why bother?* his little shrug seemed to say.

Jameson refused to let that sting. He had one question left. The smart move was to go for leverage. *What's your eldest brother's cell phone number? Your father's direct line? What is the question you're most hoping I don't ask?*

But Jameson wasn't the Hawthorne known for making the *smart* choice. He took risks. He went with his gut. *This might be the only conversation we ever have.* "Do you sleepwalk?"

It was such an inane question—trivial, could be answered in a single word.

"No." For an instant, Ian Johnstone-Jameson looked a little less above it all.

"I did," Jameson said quietly. "When I was a kid." He gave a little shrug, as careless as anything Ian could manage. "Three questions, three answers. Your turn."

"As I said, I find myself in need of a favor, and you..." There was something knowing in the way that Ian said that word. "Well, I think you'll find my offer enticing."

"Hawthornes aren't easily enticed," Jameson replied.

"What I need from you has very little to do with the fact that you're a Hawthorne and a great deal to do with the fact that you're my son."

It was the first time he'd said it, the first time Jameson had ever heard any man say those words to him. *You're my son.*

Point, Ian.

"I find myself in need of a player," the man said. "Someone smart and cunning, merciless but never dull. Someone who can calculate odds, defy them, work people, sell a bluff, and—no matter what—come out on top."

"And yet..." Jameson summoned up a smirk. "You're not playing the game in question yourself."

And there it was again—Ian's tell. Point, Jameson.

"I have been asked not to tread on certain hallowed ground."

Ian made that confession sound like yet another amusement. "My presence is *temporarily* unwelcome."

Jameson translated. "You were banned." *From where?* "Start at the beginning and tell me everything. If I catch you holding anything back—and I will catch you—then my response to your request will be no. Clear?"

"As glass." Ian braced his elbows against the glittering black countertop. "There's an establishment in London whose name is never spoken. Speak it and you may find yourself on the end of some very bad luck courtesy of this country's most powerful men. Aristocrats, politicians, the extraordinarily wealthy..."

Ian studied Jameson just long enough to make sure he *really* had an audience, and then he turned, opened a black cabinet, and removed two lowball glasses made of cut crystal. He set them on the island but didn't retrieve a bottle.

"The club in question," Ian said, "is called the Devil's Mercy."

The name stuck to Jameson, emblazoned on his brain, beckoning him like a sign declaring that no one was allowed past.

"The Mercy was founded in the Regency period, but while the other elite gambling houses of the day aimed for renown, the Mercy was a different sort of enterprise, as much secret society as gaming hell." Ian ran a finger lightly over the rim of one of the crystal glasses, his gaze still on Jameson's. "You won't find the Devil's Mercy mentioned in history books. It didn't rise and fall alongside the likes of Crockfords or compete with famous gentlemen's clubs like White's. From the beginning, the Mercy operated in secrecy, founded by someone so high in society that a mere whisper of its existence was enough to guarantee that anyone offered a chance at membership would give nearly anything to obtain it.

"The location of the club moved frequently in those early days, but the luxury on offer, the proximity to power, the challenge… there was nothing like the Mercy." Ian's eyes were alight. "There *is* nothing like it."

Jameson didn't know anything about Crockfords or White's or the Regency period, but he recognized the story beneath the story. *Power. Exclusivity. Secrets. Games.*

"There's nothing like it," Jameson said, his mind churning. "And you were banned. The name must never be spoken, but here you are, telling me its entire secret history."

"I lost something on the tables at the Mercy." Ian's eyes went flat. "Vantage—my mother's ancestral home. She left it to me over my brothers, and I need to win it back. Or rather, I need *you* to win it back for me."

"And why would I help you?" Jameson asked, his voice low and silky. This man was a stranger. They were nothing to each other.

"Why indeed?" Ian walked over to a different set of cabinets and pulled out a bottle of scotch. He poured an inch of it in each glass, then slid one across the black granite to Jameson.

Father of the year.

"There are only a handful of people on this planet who *could* do what I'm asking of you," Ian said, his tone electric. "In two hundred years, only one person that I know of has ever set out to gain entrance to the Mercy and succeeded. And getting in is just the beginning of what it will take to win Vantage back. So why would I hold out any hope your answer would be yes?"

Ian picked up his glass and raised it in toast.

"Because you love a challenge. You love to play. You love to win. And no matter what you win"—Ian Johnstone-Jameson lifted the glass to his lips, the unholy intensity in his eyes all too familiar—"you always need more."

CHAPTER 8

JAMESON

Jameson said no. He left. But hours later, Ian's words still haunted him. *You love to play. You love to win. And no matter what you win, you always need more.*

Jameson stared out into the night. There was something about rooftops. It wasn't just being high up or the way it felt to go right up to the edge. It was seeing everything but being alone.

"I don't own this entire building, you know." Avery spoke from somewhere behind him. "Pretty sure the roof belongs to someone else. We could be arrested for trespassing."

"Says the girl who always manages to slip away *before* the police arrive," Jameson pointed out, turning his head to see her step out of shadow.

"I have survival instincts." Avery came to stand beside him at the roof's edge. "You never learned to want to stay out of trouble."

He'd never had to. He'd grown up with the world as his

playground—with Hawthorne looks and the Hawthorne name and a grandfather richer than kings.

Jameson took a breath: night air into the lungs, night air out. "I met my father today."

"You what?" Avery wasn't an easy person to take off guard. Surprising her always felt like a win, and though Jameson would have denied it, he needed a win right now.

"Ian Johnstone-Jameson." He let the name roll off his tongue. "Professional poker player. Black sheep of what appears to be an extremely wealthy family."

"Appears to be?" Avery repeated. "You haven't searched the name?"

Jameson caught her gaze. "I don't want you to, either, Heiress." He let the rooftop go silent. And then, because it was *her*, he said the words he'd thought far too many times since Ian had asked for that favor. "Nothing matters unless you let it."

"I remember that boy," Avery said quietly. "Shirtless in the solarium, drunk on bourbon after we saw the Red Will, determined that nothing would hurt him." She let that penetrate his shields, then continued: "You were angry because we had to ask Skye about your middle names. About your fathers."

"In retrospect," Jameson quipped, "I'm impressed Skye didn't give away the game right then." They'd asked about middle names—not first.

"Your father mattered to you then." Avery didn't pull her punches. Ever. "He matters now. That's why you're up here."

Jameson swallowed. "I told myself after Gray met his asshole father that I never wanted to meet mine."

He'd known his father's last name was Jameson, but he hadn't looked. He hadn't even let himself wonder—until that card.

"How was it?" Avery asked.

Jameson looked up. *Not a star in the sky.* "He hasn't had you kidnapped yet or killed anyone so that's a plus." Grayson's father had set the bar low. Making light of that let Jameson really answer Avery's question. "He wants something from me."

"Screw him," Avery said fiercely. "He doesn't get to ask you for anything."

"Exactly."

"But..."

"What makes you think there's a *but*?" Jameson retorted.

"This." Avery let her fingertips brush his face just above his jawline. Her other hand went, feather-light, to his brow. "And this."

Jameson swallowed. "I don't owe him anything. And I don't care what he thinks of me. But..." She was right. Of course she was. "I can't stop thinking about what he said."

Jameson stepped back from the edge of the roof, and when Avery did the same, he bent to murmur in her ear. "There's an establishment in London whose name is never spoken...."

Jameson told her everything, and the more he said, the faster the words came, the more his body buzzed with the rush of adrenaline pumping through his veins. Because Ian Johnstone-Jameson had been right.

He liked to play. He liked to win. And now, more than ever, he needed *something*.

"You want to say yes." Avery read him like a book.

"I said no."

"You didn't mean it."

This didn't have to be about what Ian Johnstone-Jameson deserved. This didn't have to be about him at all. "The Devil's Mercy." Jameson felt a thrill just saying the name. *A centuries-old secret. An underground gambling house. Money and power and games with stakes.*

"You're going to do it, aren't you?" Avery asked.

Jameson opened his eyes, stared into hers, then lit the fuse. "No, Heiress. *We* are."

CHAPTER 9

GRAYSON

Grayson stepped off the plane to eight voicemails, seven of them from Xander. By the seventh, his youngest brother had taken to singing what appeared to be an opera-style epic about brotherly concern and cheesesteak.

The one remaining message was from Zabrowski, only minutes old. "I did some digging. The girl is still in custody, but nothing's been filed yet. No arrest paperwork. No charges. You ask me, someone else already has a finger on the scales. Let me know how you want to proceed."

Grayson deleted the message. *If they haven't truly arrested her, they have no legal right to keep her in custody.* That would certainly make things simpler.

Per the arrangements Grayson had made on his way to the airport in London, a car was waiting for him in long-term parking, the key under the mat. Grayson hadn't inherited the Hawthorne billions, but the Hawthorne name was still worth something, and he wasn't without financial resources—the same resources he'd been using to pay Zabrowski's retainer.

It was because of the private investigator that Grayson knew that Juliet went, inexplicably, by Gigi, that she was the younger twin by seven minutes, and that her sister, Savannah, was far less likely to find herself in a situation in need of interference.

His interference.

Grayson started up the Ferrari 488 Spider his contact had provided. As far as vehicles went, it was more Jameson's style than his, but some situations required making an entrance. Turning his mind to strategy kept Grayson from thinking too hard about the fact that Juliet and Savannah Grayson didn't even know he existed.

Just like they didn't know that the father the three of them shared was dead.

Sheffield Grayson had made the mistake of attacking Avery. It hadn't ended well for him. As far as the rest of the world knew, the wealthy Phoenix businessman had simply disappeared. Popular theory seemed to be that he'd taken off for some tropical tax haven with a much younger woman. Grayson had been keeping an eye on Juliet and Savannah ever since.

In and out, he reminded himself. He wasn't in Phoenix to forge relationships or tell the twins who he was. There was a situation to be handled. Grayson would handle it.

When he walked into the Phoenix Police Department, he let one and only one thought rise to the surface of his mind. *Never question your own authority and no one else will, either.*

"Anyone see that Ferrari out front?" A twentysomething patrol officer rushed in. "Holy sh—" He cut off and stared at Grayson, who, like the car, had a way of making an impression.

Grayson didn't let a hint of amusement show on his face. "You have Juliet Grayson in your custody." That was not a question, but Grayson's demeanor demanded a response.

"Gigi?" Another officer joined the two of them, craning his neck, like he somehow expected to be able to see Grayson's Ferrari through the walls. "Oh yeah. We have her."

"You'll want to rectify that." There was a difference between telling people what you wanted and making it clear that it was in their best interest to give it to you. Explicit threats were for people who needed to assert their power. *Never assert what you can assume, Grayson.*

"Who the hell are you?"

Grayson knew without turning that the person who had just spoken was older than the other two officers—and higher ranked. A sergeant, perhaps, or a lieutenant. That, in combination with the way that the name *Juliet Grayson* had gotten his attention, told Grayson all he needed to know: This man was the reason that arrest paperwork hadn't been filed.

"Do you really have to ask?" Grayson replied. He knew the power of certain facial expressions: the kind without a hint of aggression, the kind that made a promise nonetheless.

The lieutenant—Grayson could see his badge now—took measure of Grayson, the cut of his very expensive suit, his absolute lack of nerves. It was easy enough to see the man debating: Had Grayson been sent by the same person who'd called in a favor with him?

"I can call our mutual friend, if you like." Grayson, like all Hawthornes, was an excellent bluffer. He slipped his phone from his pocket. "Or you can have one of these officers take me to the girl."

CHAPTER 10

GRAYSON

They were keeping Juliet Grayson in an interrogation room. She sat cross-legged on top of the table, her wrists resting on her knees, palms up. Her hair was chocolate brown to Grayson's light blond, wavy where his was straight. She wore it cut just below her chin, the waves buoyant, gravity-defying, and a little wild.

She was staring at an empty coffee cup, her eyes—brighter and bluer than his—unblinking.

"Still no telekinesis?" the cop who'd led Grayson back here asked.

The prisoner grinned. "Maybe I need more coffee?"

"You definitely do not need more coffee," the cop said.

The girl—Grayson's flesh and blood, though she couldn't know that and he wouldn't dwell on it—hopped off the table, her hair bouncing. "*Matilda* by Roald Dahl," she told him by way of explanation. "It's a children's book in which a neglected kid genius develops the ability to move objects with her mind. The first thing she ever knocks over is a glass of water. I read it when I was seven, and it ruined me for life."

Grayson found himself almost wanting to smile, perhaps because the girl across from him was beaming like it was her default state. Without turning back toward the police officer, he spoke. "Leave us."

The trick to making people do what you wanted was absolute certainty that they would.

"Wow!" the human ray of sunshine across from him said once the cop was gone. "That was great!" She adopted a deep and serious voice. "*Leave us.* I'm Gigi, by the way, and I bet *you* never have to break into bank vaults. You just look at them, and boom, they're open!"

Break into bank vaults? Grayson had known the location where she had been taken into police custody, but the details had been vague.

"Impressive eyebrow arch," Gigi told him cheerfully. "But can you do this?" She let her blue eyes go very round, her lower lip trembling. Then she grinned and jerked a thumb toward the table, where the empty coffee cup she'd been trying to knock over was surrounded by five others. "Read 'em and weep. I make that face, and they just keep bringing me coffee! And chocolate, but I don't like chocolate." Out of nowhere, she produced a candy bar and held it out to him. "Twix?"

Grayson had an urge to tell her that this wasn't a game. That she was in police custody. That this was *serious*. Instead, he tamped down on the protective instincts and opted for: "You haven't asked who I am."

"I mean, I did say *I'm Gigi*," she said with a winning smile, "so the lack of introduction here is kind of on you, buddy." She lowered her voice. "Did Mr. Trowbridge send you? It's about time. I called him last night as soon as they brought me in."

Trowbridge. Grayson filed the name away and decided the most prudent course of action was to leave the premises before someone realized that no one had, in fact, sent him. "Let's go."

Gigi practically vibrated out of her skin when she saw the Spider. "You know, full disclosure, I have not historically been the best driver, but blue really is my color and—"

"No," Grayson said. By the time he made it to the driver's side, Gigi was already making herself comfortable in the passenger seat. *Never get in a car with a stranger,* he wanted to tell her, but he stopped himself. *In and out.* He was here to deliver her home, make sure the legal situation was fully taken care of, and that was it.

"You don't work for Mr. Trowbridge, do you?" Gigi said, after they'd been on the road for a few minutes.

"Does Mr. Trowbridge have a first name?" Grayson asked.

"Kent," Gigi supplied helpfully. "He's a family friend. And our lawyer. Lawyer-friend. I used my phone call to call him instead of my mom because she isn't a lawyer and also there's a slight chance she's under the impression that I spent last night and today at a friend's house, where I committed no crimes and wholesome fun was had by all."

The more Gigi talked, the faster she talked. Grayson was beginning to develop the sense that she should not be given caffeine. At all.

"If Mr. Trowbridge didn't send you..." Gigi's voice went quiet. "Was it my dad?"

Grayson had been raised to push down his emotions. Control was not and had never been optional. He kept his mind in the present. He didn't think about Sheffield Grayson at all.

"It was, wasn't it?" Gigi leaped to the conclusion like a ballerina across the stage. "Can you make sure Dad knows I wasn't *really* breaking into that bank? I was just kind of moseying my way back to where they keep the ultra-secure safe-deposit boxes. But not in a bad way!"

"Moseying?" Grayson let his skeptical tone speak for itself.

The seventeen-year-old next to him grinned. "It's not my fault I have a really sneaky mosey." She paused. "Seriously, though, have you talked to my dad recently?"

You father is dead. "I have not."

"But you do know him?" Gigi didn't wait for a response. "You worked for him or something? Secretly. On something that totally explains his disappearance?"

Grayson swallowed. "I cannot help you."

The energy she'd exuded up to that point seemed to retract. "I know that he must have had a good reason for leaving. I know that there's not another woman. I know about the box."

Clearly, Gigi believed that he understood what she was talking about. That he did, in fact, work for her father. Telling her the truth—any part of it—would have been a kindness, but it was a kindness he could not afford.

I know, she'd said, *about the box.* "The safe-deposit box." Grayson made the obvious inference, given her earlier confession about the events that had led to her arrest.

"I have the key," Gigi said earnestly. "But it's not under his real name, and I don't know what name he used. Do you?"

Sheffield Grayson had a safe-deposit box under another name. It took Grayson less than a second to process that—and the possible implications. "Juliet, your father didn't send me. I don't work for him."

"But you do know him," Gigi said quietly. "Don't you?"

Grayson flashed back to a conversation, a cold exchange. *My nephew was the closest thing I will ever have to a son, and he is dead because of the Hawthorne family.* "Not well."

He'd met Sheffield Grayson only that once.

"Well enough to know he didn't just leave?" Gigi asked, a note of hope in her voice. "He wouldn't have," she continued fiercely. Blinking back tears, she looked down, her riotous waves falling into her face. "When I was five, I had my tonsils out, and my dad filled the entire hospital room with balloons. There were so many the nurses got mad. He sits front row at all of Savannah's games—or at least, he used to. He would *never* cheat on my mom."

Grayson felt each sentence out of her mouth like a slice into bare skin. *He did cheat on your mother.* He couldn't tell her that. *I'm the result.*

"So this whole 'he ran off to the Maldives or Tunisia for some tax-free hanky-panky' thing? I don't believe it," Gigi said vehemently. "My dad didn't just leave. And I'm going to prove it."

"With whatever is in that safe-deposit box." Grayson heard the way his tone must have sounded to her: calm and cool. But his mind was on Avery and what she stood to lose if the truth about Sheffield Grayson's disappearance came out.

He pulled his car to a stop in front of a large stucco house. The design was Tuscan, striking and tasteful. If Gigi wondered how he knew where she lived, she gave no sign of it. Instead, she pulled a delicate chain out from beneath her aquamarine shirt.

On the end of the chain, there was a key. *A safe-deposit box key.*

"I found this *inside* my dad's computer." Gigi gave Grayson a beseeching look. "I'm a computer person. I think he wanted me to find it, you know? To find him."

"You should get some sleep."

"After six cups of jailhouse coffee?" Gigi tossed her hair. "I'm pretty sure I can fly."

Grayson eyed the height of the roof on the Grayson family's abode. "You cannot." He brought his gray eyes to meet her bright blue ones. This might well be good-bye. "You cannot fly. You cannot keep breaking into banks. You can't, Juliet."

She closed her eyes. "My dad called me that, you know. He was the only one. I declared myself Gigi at age two and brought everyone else over to my side by sheer force of will." Blue eyes opened again, bright and clear and full of steel. "I'm like that."

She's not going to stop. Grayson sat with that thought for a moment.

"Will you at least tell me your name?" Gigi asked.

Clearly, she hadn't recognized him. *Not a fan of celebrity gossip sites, then.* He gave her his first name only. "Grayson."

"Your first name *just happens* to be the same as my last name?" Gigi gave him a look. "Don't take this the wrong way, 'Grayson,' but I think you could use some lessons on being sneaky."

If only she knew.

CHAPTER 11

GRAYSON

Twenty minutes later, Grayson pulled the Ferrari up to the Haywood-Astyria and let the hotel valets fight over his keys.

"Name?"

In lieu of replying to the desk clerk's request, Grayson slid a black card rimmed in gold out of his wallet. He placed it flat on the counter.

"Your name, sir?" the clerk prompted again, but he barely got the question out before an eagle-eyed woman with her hair in an elegant bun approached.

"I'll take care of this one, Ryan." She picked up the card—not a credit card, but a key to a designated suite in this and every hotel under the same ownership in the country. If the suite was occupied, it would be vacated shortly, unless its occupant had the same card Grayson had just displayed.

Hardly likely.

"Will you be staying with us for the week?" The inquiry was polite, discreet. She did not ask his name.

"Just a night," Grayson replied, but he wasn't as sure of the answer as he sounded. His encounter with Gigi had given him much to consider—and very little of it good. "Is the pool open?" he asked evenly.

"Of course," the woman replied.

Grayson calmly met her gaze. "What would it take for it not to be?"

Swimming, like the violin, longsword, knife fighting, and photography, had been one of Grayson's selections in their grandfather's yearly birthday ritual. He'd been on the track for the Olympics once. Now all he wanted was to swim until his body gave in—faster, harder, cutting through the water, his pace punishing, unsustainable.

He sustained it.

With his lungs and muscles burning, Grayson didn't have to think about Gigi, about hospital rooms full of balloons and fathers who sat in the front row at games. About the safe-deposit box. About the key Gigi wore around her neck.

Most people considered power and weakness opposites, but Grayson had learned early in life that the real opposite of weakness was *control*.

He wasn't sure how many times his phone rang before he heard it. His body screaming, he swam to the side of the pool and checked his messages. He had three new voicemails and two texts from Xander. The first text said: *Call me back in ten minutes, or I'm going to fill your voicemail with yodeling.*

The second text was a reminder: *I do not excel at yodeling.*

In the black-card suite, Grayson took a brief, scalding shower. He wrapped a towel around his body, then bit the bullet.

"I'm fine," he said immediately, once Xander had picked up the call.

"You're in Phoenix," Xander replied cheerfully.

Grayson made a mental note to scan his electronics for tracking software.

"You know that I know who lives in Phoenix, right?" Xander prodded. "Allow me to remind you that I am a good listener. A very good listener who has not told Jameson, Avery, or Nash where you are. Yet."

The *yet* was as much of a threat as the yodeling had been. Grayson knew that neither would have been effective if he hadn't, on some level, wanted to talk.

"Sheffield Grayson was married when I was conceived." Grayson started with facts, the obvious ones. "He slept with Skye to spite our grandfather, whom he blamed for the death of his nephew Colin."

"The fire on Hawthorne Island," Xander said quietly.

Grayson bowed his neck. "The fire on Hawthorne Island," he confirmed. Grayson had never held any illusions that, if only his mystery father knew about his existence, he would be wanted. But he hadn't expected to be *hated*, either.

"Several years after Colin's death," Grayson told Xander calmly, "my father and his wife had twins. Girls."

"You have sisters," Xander said cheerily. The twins' existence wasn't news to him. None of this was.

"I have responsibilities," Grayson corrected. "Their father is dead." In the mirror, the muscles over his collarbone had gone tight. "The twins don't know what kind of man he really was or what happened to him." Grayson swallowed. "They can never know."

"Why are you in Phoenix, Gray?" Xander said softly.

"One of the girls ran into trouble. I was tipped off about the issue and came here to resolve it."

He could practically hear Xander turning that information over. "And did you?"

Grayson's entire body ached. "No."

Gigi was no longer in police custody. Given the way Grayson had been allowed to walk out of the precinct with her, he doubted paperwork would ever be filed. But the true situation? That was far from resolved.

Grayson told Xander what he had learned. "I don't know what's inside that safe-deposit box," he finished, "but if there is *any* chance it implicates Sheffield Grayson in the bombing of Avery's plane or her kidnapping..."

"That could then implicate Avery," Xander filled in, "in his disappearance."

"I can't let Gigi open that box," Grayson said, the words coming out with the force of a vow. He'd failed to protect Avery once. *More than once.* He wouldn't fail her again.

"So what's our play?" Xander asked.

"There's no *we* here, Xan." Grayson turned away from the mirror. "Just me."

"Just you." Xander was being far too agreeable. "And your sisters."

We share nothing but blood. The thought was deliberate, measured, but its purpose was entirely undone when Xander spoke next. "What's she like, the one you met?"

Grayson kept his answer short. "In some ways, she reminds me of you." Maybe that explained how protective he felt of the girl already.

"You're going to have to lie to her." The warning in Xander's tone was clear. "Sabotage her. Gain her trust and betray her."

Grayson ended the call before he replied. "I know."

Without giving himself even a second for guilt or second-guessing, he picked up the hotel phone and called down to the lobby. "As it turns out," he said, his voice like stone, "I'll need this room for at least a week."

ELEVEN YEARS AND TEN MONTHS AGO

There were thirteen different ways to enter the tree house—officially. Unofficially, if a person were willing to risk falling, there were many more. Grayson wasn't surprised when he looked out and saw Jameson dangling precariously off a branch, nor was he surprised when his younger brother managed to somehow catapult himself in through the window.

"You're late," Grayson said. Jameson was always late. Jameson was *allowed* to be late.

"Tomorrow, when we're the same age, I'm going to tell you to loosen up." Jameson punctuated that statement by jumping to catch one of the beams overhead, swinging back and forth, and launching himself feet-first at Grayson, who jumped out of the way.

"I'll still be older than you tomorrow," Grayson retorted. Had Jameson been born one day later, the two of them would have been exactly a year apart in age. Instead, his *younger* brother had arrived on August twenty-second, one day before Grayson's first birthday.

That meant that for one day each year, they were technically the same age.

"Are you ready?" Grayson asked quietly. "For your birthday?" *First yours, then mine.*

"I'm ready," Jameson said, his chin jutting out.

Ready to turn eight, Grayson translated. *Ready to be called into the old man's study.*

Jameson swallowed. "He's going to make me fight you, Gray."

Grayson couldn't argue with that conclusion. Each year on their birthdays, their grandfather greeted them with three words. *Invest. Cultivate. Create.* They were given ten thousand dollars to invest. They got to choose a talent to cultivate for the year—anything in the world they wanted to learn to do. And they were given a challenge to be completed by their next birthday.

For the past three years, Grayson and Jameson had chosen martial arts forms for the *cultivate* side of things. *Of course the old man is going to make Jameson fight me.*

"And then the next day," Grayson muttered, "on my birthday, he'll make me fight him."

It was a horrible thing to spend a *year* on something and then lose.

"You can't go easy on me, okay?" Jameson's expression was fierce.

The old man will know if I do. "Okay."

Jameson's eyes narrowed. "Promise?"

Grayson drew a line down his face with his thumb, starting at his hairline and going all the way to his chin. "Promise."

There was no taking back *that* kind of promise. It was theirs and theirs alone.

Jameson expelled a breath. "What was your challenge this year? What did you have to create?"

Grayson's heart rate ticked up at the question. In two days, he would be expected to both demonstrate the skill he'd cultivated over the last twelve months and present his grandfather with his response to his last birthday challenge. "A haiku."

Jameson wrinkled his forehead. "A what?"

"A poem." Grayson looked down. "Haiku is a poetic form of Japanese provenance, wherein each poem is three lines long, a total of seventeen syllables, broken down into five syllables in the first and last lines and seven for the line in between."

The definition was burned into his mind.

"Seventeen syllables?" Jameson was outraged. "Are you kidding me? That's it?"

"They have to be perfect." Grayson forced his eyes up to meet his brother's. "That's what the old man said. No room for error. When you only get three lines, every word has to be the right word." He swallowed. "It has to be beautiful. It has to mean something. It has to hurt."

Jameson frowned. "Hurt?"

Grayson's hand found its way to his pocket, to the medallion inside. "When words are real enough, when they're the exact right words, when what you're saying matters, when it's beautiful and perfect and true—*it hurts*."

Grayson slipped the medallion out of his pocket and handed it over.

Jameson examined it. "Did you have to engrave the words on the metal yourself?"

Grayson shook his head and swallowed. "I just had to be sure that they were perfect first." He took the medallion back from Jameson. "What about you? What was your challenge?"

"A card castle." Jameson's expression was murderous. "I had

to use five hundred cards. No glue. No adhesives *at all.* Nothing but cards." Jameson disappeared out the tree house window again. Grayson heard him moving around up in one of the towers, and when he came back, he was a holding a fancy camera in his hand. "I had to take a photograph every time it was going well and every time I failed."

Seven years old. Five hundred cards. Grayson was willing to bet Jameson had failed a lot. He held out his hand for the camera, and to his surprise, his brother handed it over. Grayson scrolled through picture after picture. Jameson had started trying to build tall towers, then switched to wide.

Every time something beautiful emerged on the camera, the next shot showed the ground littered with cards. *So many times.* There were hundreds of pictures on this camera.

Grayson skipped to the last shot. Jameson had built his castle in the shape of an L, five stories tall, flush against the walls of one of his rooms.

"When did you finish?" Grayson asked, still staring at that last picture.

"Last night," Jameson said. "I cut slits in the floor."

No adhesives. Nothing but cards. But using the room? Grayson could see how that would be more of a gray area—but still! "You carved slits in the wood floors?" he asked, half-horrified, half-awed.

The old man loved Hawthorne House. Every floorboard, every light fixture, every detail.

"And the walls," Jameson added, completely unrepentant. He crossed his arms over his chest. "Did you decide what you're going to do with your ten thousand dollars this year?"

Invest. "Yes," Grayson told his brother. "You?"

Jameson nodded. By the rules of the game, their choices on

that front were not to be discussed. "I guess that just leaves deciding what talent we're going to choose to cultivate next year. I was thinking..." Jameson assumed a ready position and slashed his hands through the air. "Knife fighting!"

Grayson's eyes were drawn back to the camera. He thought about some of the shots Jameson had taken—the successes and the failures—and something in him itched to reframe them or, better yet, to catch the cards *while* they fell.

"Photography."

"No way!" Jameson retorted immediately. "I never want to take a picture again."

Grayson didn't put the camera down. "Do what you want, Jamie. No one ever said we had to pick the same thing."

"Fine," Jameson declared. "Then I'm picking rock climbing." He jumped back up on the windowsill. "Because unlike certain other people in this tree house, I'm not afraid to fall."

CHAPTER 12

JAMESON

This time, Jameson was the one who set the place for the meeting. Beside him, Avery took in the location he'd chosen: a medieval crypt the size of a ballroom, an eerie, elegant underground chamber hidden away from the world.

"You rented it for Nash's bachelor party?" Avery guessed—correctly.

Before Jameson could reply, Ian stepped through the doorway and made a show of raking his gaze across the cavernous space: dark stone columns stretching up into an arcing stone ceiling, stained glass letting in the only hints of natural light from the world above.

"Interesting meeting place."

Jameson gave a little shrug. "I've always been just a little bit much."

"Hmmm." Ian made a noncommittal sound, then allowed his gaze to land on Avery. "And I see you brought company."

Avery fixed Ian with a look. "Jameson told me everything."

"Did he now?" Ian's lips curved.

Jameson mirrored that smile. "Two minds are better than one. Tell us about Vantage."

"What would you like to know? It's not a castle, exactly." The word *exactly* did the heavy lifting in that sentence. "It sits high on an isthmus in Scotland overlooking the water. It's been in my mother's family a very long time."

In America, *a very long time* could mean forty years. But on this side of the pond? They were probably talking centuries, plural.

"We spent summers there when I was child," Ian continued. "Far more than my father's properties, Vantage is home."

"Who's *we*?" Avery pressed.

"I have two brothers," Ian said. "Both older, both horribly irrelevant to this story."

"What story?" Jameson retorted.

"The one," Ian replied, "that you and I are writing right now." There was intensity buried in those words. "And Avery, of course," the man added.

I never introduced her by name. Jameson wasn't surprised that Ian knew who Avery was. The whole world knew the Hawthorne heiress. "Returning to our *story*," Jameson said, "you bet your mother's not-a-castle-exactly on a hand of cards?"

"In my defense, I was very drunk, and it was a very good hand." There was a flash of something dark in Ian's eyes. "The deed to Vantage is, as we speak, in the hands of the Proprietor."

"The man who runs the Devil's Mercy," Jameson inferred. Anticipation began building inside him. This was *something*. "Does this Proprietor have a name?"

"Several, I'm sure," Ian replied. "None that he has given me. Control of the Mercy passes every fifty or so years, once the Proprietor has chosen an heir. When that heir ascends to Proprietor himself, he leaves everything else behind, including the name he was born with. The Proprietor of the Devil's Mercy may never marry, may never have children, may not maintain familial ties of any kind."

Jameson let that information work its way through his mind. "The Proprietor is the one we'll need to approach for membership?"

Ian let out a bone-dry laugh. "That would be impossible. You must get one of the Proprietor's many emissaries to approach you."

"And how do we do that?" Avery beat Jameson to the question.

"I have some ideas." Ian turned to look at one of the stained-glass windows. "But first, ask me what you will need to do *after* you're invited into the hallowed halls of the Mercy."

"Ask you about step two," Jameson replied skeptically, "before we've figured out step one?"

Ian flashed him a grin. "Once you've obtained membership and won access to the Mercy, you will need to get the Proprietor's attention. Not his employees'. Not his right-hand man's. *His.* Once a year, there is a special game of highest stakes, played by invitation only." Ian's tone took on the same energy and depth with which he'd first spoken to Jameson about the Mercy. "The Game may take any form. Some years it's a race. Sometimes it's a physical challenge, sometimes a mental one. There are years when it has been a hunt."

Something about the way that Ian said the word *hunt* was unsettling.

"If the Mercy is exclusive," Ian continued, his voice low and as rich as chocolate, "the Game... well, it's really something else, and clearly, I won't be getting an invitation this year."

Because whatever you did when you lost Vantage got you banned from the club. "You won't be getting that coveted invitation," Jameson replied, "but you expect me to?"

He was nineteen, an outsider. *Seems like a damn tall order to me.*

"An existing member would be the more obvious choice," Jameson noted. "But that would require a chip you could call in—or a friend to ask." Sometime, needling a person made them show their hand. "Short on friends, Ian?"

"I'm asking *you.*" Ian came to stand toe-to-toe with him, making it impossible for Jameson to look away. "Impress the Proprietor. Tempt him. Make yourself impossible to refuse."

For a split second, Jameson felt like he was back in Tobias Hawthorne's study. "And if I gain entrance to this game," he said, "if I play and win it..."

"The winner may claim any prize won by the house in the prior year." Ian's mouth settled into a grim line. "I doubt that you will be the only one after Vantage."

Jameson rolled that around in his mind. "So, by my count, all I need to do is get invited to join the world's most exclusive secret gambling club...." He lifted one finger with those words, then a second as he continued. "Then somehow persuade its leader to invite me to an even more exclusive private game, which"—a third finger—"I'll then need to win."

"Give the boy a prize," Ian said.

Jameson's eyes narrowed. "That leads us back to the start. How exactly am I supposed to get invited to join the Devil's Mercy?"

"Do they even let Americans in?" Avery asked. "Or teenagers?"

"Historically," Ian said, "no. Membership is only extended to those in the highest echelons of British society, based on a combination of power, status, and wealth."

"So why," Jameson said shrewdly, "would the Devil's Mercy be interested in me?" He was an American teenager who *used* to be rich, but the power, the connections, the knowledge, the influence, the institutional backing—those had never been *his*.

Unlike Grayson, he hadn't been raised to assume they ever would be.

Maybe that was what let Jameson answer his own question. "They wouldn't."

Ian had said that Jameson was more useful to him as his son than as a Hawthorne, but Jameson saw now that wasn't the whole truth. *He knows who Avery is.* Maybe it hadn't mattered that Jameson was a Hawthorne, but the fact that he was in a relationship with the Hawthorne heiress?

He suspected that mattered very much.

"You wanted me to bring her in on this," Jameson accused. "She's the one you were after." He refused to let that hurt.

"You're my player, Jameson," Ian replied. "But she's your way in. Draw the Proprietor's attention. Make yourself a package deal."

"No." Jameson's muscles turned to stone. He could feel the explosion coming.

"Jameson." Avery laid a hand on his shoulder.

"I'm not using you, Heiress."

"You said it yourself on the roof: You're not doing this. *We* are." Avery looked past him to Ian. "If we start asking around about the Mercy, will that draw the Proprietor's attention?"

"One way or another," Ian replied.

Jameson didn't like the sound of that.

"Think about it, Hawthorne." Avery stepped closer toward him. "I'm one of the most famous and infamous people in the world."

"Powerful," Jameson said, looking at her and only her. "And rich.

Through your multi-billion-dollar foundation, very connected. And you and I—we can make a lot of noise."

"Which," Ian added, "the Devil's Mercy does not want."

Jameson turned back toward Ian and channeled the formidable Tobias Hawthorne at his most terrifying. "You played me. It won't happen again."

Ian placed a fatherly hand on Jameson's shoulder. "I'd be disappointed if it did."

CHAPTER 13
JAMESON

Slowly, the sound of Ian's footsteps receded. Oren appeared in the doorway and gave Avery a nod. They were alone. Jameson looked up at the crypt's soaring ceilings, allowing his mind to sort through potential next moves. Then he looked back at Avery. "Feel up to making a call?"

Avery knew exactly which call he meant. They exited the crypt, and she pulled the trigger. "Alisa? You know that event you were trying to talk me into? I've had a change of heart. It would be good for the foundation for me to see and be seen while I'm in London."

Alisa Ortega was Avery's lawyer—and the foundation's. In reality, Alisa's services extended far beyond legal matters. She was part publicist, part fixer, wholly terrifying.

When Avery hung up the phone, Jameson brought his gaze to hers. "Dare I even ask?"

If Alisa had a social event she wanted Avery to attend, it was sure to be a prominent one. *The kind,* Jameson thought, *that attracts the rich, the powerful, the connected, the famous.*

Avery sauntered up to Jameson, a distinctly *heads or tails* look in her eye—and then she brushed past him. "Come on, Hawthorne," she called back over her shoulder. "What's life without surprise?"

Wherever they were going, it apparently had a dress code. A *very* formal one. Jameson put on the long-tailed navy morning jacket Alisa's people had provided and examined the fit of his pale-green waistcoat. Turning his attention to the three top hats he'd been given to choose from, Jameson felt a familiar buzz of energy humming beneath his skin.

Step one, get the Proprietor's attention. The more impossible the challenge laid before him, the more it brought the world into magnificent focus.

"I'd go for the hat on the left," Nash drawled behind him. "Nice sheen."

Jameson glanced back at his brother. "You wouldn't go for any of them." *Formal* wasn't exactly the oldest Hawthorne brother's style.

"I'm not you," Nash replied. The words were plain enough, but Jameson heard layers of meaning buried there—and ignored them. Unfortunately, Nash wasn't one to be ignored. "I met Jake Nash and walked away just fine," he said quietly. "But you're not me, Jamie."

Jameson's eyes narrowed. "I take it Avery told you about Ian."

"It's real cute," Nash replied, "that you think I need anyone's help keepin' tabs on you." Hazel eyes ringed in amber met Jameson's green ones, head on.

Jameson looked away. "Blood doesn't make family. I have Avery. I have all of you. I don't need anything else." Setting his jaw, Jameson turned his attention back to the top hats and chose the one on the left. "You're right," he told Nash. "Nice sheen."

This conversation is over. Jameson sauntered past, daring Nash to say one more thing, and made his way to the dressing room. The twin doors were already opened a crack. Jameson knocked, pushing one door inward. He saw the stylists first, then Avery, and once he saw Avery, it was like he couldn't see anything else.

They'd styled her in white lace. The dress looked modest at first glance: It fell below her knee, came up nearly to her collarbone, and had sleeves that covered her from shoulder to elbow. But *the fit*. Jameson knew her body—every inch of it—but if he hadn't, that dress would have had him wanting to, *dying* to. The tailored fabric showed the swell of her chest, the exact location of the smallest part of her waist. A thick black belt split the top half of the dress from the bottom—and that part wasn't exactly loose, either.

There was just enough left to the imagination to make Jameson *want* to imagine it. The way her hair had been swept back from her face made her neck look long and graceful. Inviting.

Who am I, Jameson thought, *to turn down an invitation?*

"And finally . . . ," one of the stylists said, holding out an imperious hand. The other stylist placed a hat in it: white, with a wide, asymmetrical brim and a black rose, its petals kissed with tiny jewels, attached to the underside. Pinned in place, the hat sat on Avery's head at angle, the sparkling black rose drawing the gaze to her eyes.

"Figured out where we're going yet?" Avery said.

Jameson held out a hand and waited for her to take it. He anticipated her touch, then felt it through every inch of his body when the pads of her fingers brushed his palm, electric.

This was the beginning.

"Are we, by any chance," he said, answering her challenge, "off to the races?"

CHAPTER 14

JAMESON

"Like the Kentucky Derby," Jameson murmured in Avery's ear as they stepped onto a fabulously green lawn, "but make it royal."

There was no press on racecourse grounds and no personal security allowed. Oren had grudgingly signed off on Avery's attendance, primarily because, for once, she wasn't the biggest target in the vicinity. *The rich. The famous. The connected. The royal.*

"Ready to make some noise?" Avery murmured back.

Jameson swept his gaze over a sea of men in top hats and long-tailed jackets and impeccably dressed women vying for a spot in *Vogue*. "Always."

An hour in, the champagne and Pimm's were flowing freely, and word of the Hawthorne heiress's appearance had spread. In other circumstances, with literal royals in attendance, that might have mattered less. But Avery was in the beginning stages of giving away twenty-eight billion dollars. And then there was the fact that she literally had a horse in this race.

Actually, she had *two.*

"Thamenold had a good showing yesterday." The lordly gentleman currently holding court around them was one of many who'd made a similar comment. "Is there any truth to the rumors that you're looking to part with him, Ms. Grambs?"

Thamenold. Jameson's mind automatically rearranged the letters in the horse's name. *The old man.* As with everything his grandfather had ever done, there were layers of meaning.

"You must know better than to listen to rumors," Avery replied coyly.

That was his cue. "Although," Jameson said, lowering his voice, but pitching it so that everyone in the vicinity could still hear, "I have to say that you certainly have some interesting rumors on this side of the pond. Legendary, even."

You aren't going to ask what I'm referring to, but you won't forget I mentioned it, either.

"What about Lady Monoceros?" another older gentleman asked. "She's running today, is she not? Have you placed a bet on your own horse, Ms. Grambs?"

Avery met the gentleman's gaze. "Jameson and I are interested in a different kind of wager. We hear that London offers some very intriguing…options." The spacing in her last sentence spoke volumes.

"Sorry, Heiress." Jameson brought a champagne glass to his lips. "But my money isn't on Lady Monoceros." He waited for one of the men to take his bait and wasn't disappointed.

"Who did you put your money on, then?"

Jameson flashed a smile. "Devil's Mercy." He counted the beats of silence that followed.

"You mean Devil's Duel?" a third man said abruptly. "He's had some nice showings."

Jameson let another beat pass before he lifted his glass once more. "Of course. Devil's Duel. My mistake."

And so it went, encounter after encounter, comment after comment, glass after glass. Someone here had to be a member. Someone here would recognize the name *Devil's Mercy* and realize that he hadn't misspoken. Someone would understand what they were really looking for when they talked of rumors and legends, wagers and intrigue and *options.*

And it's anyone's guess, Jameson thought, *how that someone will respond.*

CHAPTER 15
JAMESON

The hats came off at the after party. In the upper floors of a private club, Jameson and Avery mixed with the younger set—and requested that every photo posted online be accompanied by the same hashtag: *TDM*.

There was more than one way to make noise, and the more they made, the more alive Jameson felt. Hyper-alert, he missed nothing as he and Avery made their way back through the throng of socialites.

"Did you see the way he kissed her on the stairwell earlier?"

"I heard he overdosed in Morocco a few months ago."

"You know there are four brothers, right? Do you think they all look like *that*?"

"If you ask me, she's not nearly as pretty in person."

"Can you believe—"

Jameson tried to filter out what people were saying about him, about Avery. He tried to focus on hearing something *more*, and one comment bubbled up over the rest. "It looks like *That Duchess* decided to grace us with her presence."

Jameson followed the speaker's haughty gaze and saw an elegant woman in her twenties. She was tall and lithe, her skin a deep brown, the cut, length, and fit of her bright yellow dress exquisite. Beneath a petite yellow hat, thick braids of varying sizes adorned her head. Those braids were gathered at the base of her neck and streamed down her back, all the way to her hips. More than one person seemed to watch as the woman closed her fingers around the stem of a champagne glass.

Jameson caught Avery's hand and traced a symbol onto her palm. It was a game they played late at night, each touch a message to be decoded—in this case, an arrow.

Avery subtly turned her head in the direction he'd indicated—toward *That Duchess.* By the time they'd wound their way toward her, she'd taken up position with her back to a wall.

"Can I get you anything else, madam? Sir?" The waiter who'd been assigned to Jameson and Avery the moment they'd entered the club, obvious VIPs, appeared once more.

Jameson decided to use that as an opening and looked to his target. "What are you drinking?" he asked *That Duchess.*

"Prosecco and the tears of my enemies." Her voice was wry, her British accent crisp, refined, aristocratic. "With a splash of elderflower liqueur."

"Do you have a lot of enemies?" Avery asked.

The duchess—assuming she really *was* a duchess—looked out over the club. "You know how it is," she told Avery. "Some of us exist just a little too loudly for the comfort of those who would prefer we did not exist at all."

Midnight came and went.

"I have an idea, and you're not going to like it," Avery said. She traced letter after letter onto the palm of Jameson's hand. *S, P, L...*

He closed his fingers around hers. "You think we should split up."

"I'm either the bait or I'm not," Avery told him. "And I won't be alone." She nodded her head toward the discreet position Oren had taken up nearby. "Give me ten minutes, and if none of the mysterious Proprietor's emissaries seek me out, we'll call it a night."

Jameson wasn't wired to step back, to let anyone else play in his stead. But she wasn't just *anyone*. "Ten minutes," he murmured. "I'll be outside."

Leaning against the building, Jameson slipped his hand into his pocket. His fingers closed around a pocket watch. Three turns of the minute hand to specific numbers, and a spring would release, the face of the watch popping away, revealing a hidden compartment. Jameson thought of the small object currently nestled there, an object he should have gotten rid of weeks ago. *Right after Prague.*

Resisting the urge to trigger the release was harder than it should have been. *Six minutes.* That was how long Avery had left.

"Hit your limit with that lot in there?"

Jameson looked up to see a boy dressed in a black trench coat. It took a moment for Jameson to place him. *The waiter.* "Something like that."

The waiter hunched over his phone, a posture that very clearly said *I'm on break*.

"You off work for the night?" Jameson asked. "Or just taking a breather?"

The waiter straightened, his face cast half in shadow and half in the light from a lone streetlamp nearby. "Actually," he said, seeming suddenly taller and broader through the shoulders as he took a step forward and pocketed the phone, "my work is just getting started."

Instantly, Jameson's mind took in a dozen different things—about his opponent, about the fact that they were alone on the street, about the way the streetlight suddenly flickered.

The guy was younger than Jameson had taken him for inside. Seventeen, maybe? Eighteen at most. But his eyes—they didn't look young. They were a rich, deep brown, the pupils nearly disappearing into the irises. Based on his speech, he was British; based on his appearance, he was likely of Indian or Pakistani descent. The collar on his trench coat was popped. His features were angular and sharp, his black hair thick and just long enough to curl.

Long enough to grab in a fight. Jameson's gaze went to the door to their right.

"It's locked," the guy told Jameson, his accent shifting, still British but markedly less posh than it had been a moment before.

"You came after me," Jameson noted. "Not Avery."

His opponent somehow gave the impression of shrugging without moving an inch. "All eyes are on her, and my employer was under the impression that you might be the bigger liability."

Jameson adjusted his stance—slightly, subtly. "I've been called worse."

"My employer asked me to have a chat with you."

Jameson had wanted the Proprietor's attention. Apparently, he had it. *We've had it all night*, he realized, thinking back to the attentive waiter seemingly assigned to the VIPs.

"We want in." Jameson decided to cut to the chase "Avery. Me. What would it take for us to join the Devil's Mercy?"

"I'm afraid *he* isn't terribly concerned with what you want."

The streetlight went out. *Darkness.* "Where did you hear about the Mercy?" The words came out low, threatening.

Jameson stalled, letting his eyes adjust to the dark. "Avery and I just want a taste of what the club has to offer. Just a few days. There must be something your employer wants."

"I wouldn't know. I'm just the messenger."

And what kind of message were you sent to impart? Jameson had never shied away from danger. His body settled into a ready stance, soaking up the adrenaline the way a sunbather basks in the sun. *If you want to dance, messenger, let's dance.*

Light flooded the street. Avery stepped out of the building. Oren was right behind her. He propped the door open, ensuring the street stayed lit.

"Just a messenger," Jameson repeated. That was all the recap of the situation that Avery would need.

"And not the only one whose acquaintance you'll meet if the two of you keep this up, I'm afraid," the messenger replied, slipping back into the waiter's upper-crust accent with disturbing ease.

"I'm not scared," Avery said.

The messenger looked at her, and the way his expression shifted made Jameson grind his teeth. Whoever this particular emissary was, whatever he was capable of, the set of his lips suggested a deep appreciation for beautiful women.

"There's a list, love," the messenger told Avery. "You don't want to be on it."

Jameson gave a small, affected shrug. "We're on a lot of lists. I'll have you know that most celebrity gossip sites rank me as the second-hottest Hawthorne."

Avery rolled her eyes. "I thought you were going to stay away from those sites."

Jameson brought his eyes back to the messenger's. "I've never been very good at staying away when I should." *Your employer was right,* his tone promised. *I am the liability here.* He lowered his voice. "Just a taste."

That was all they were asking for, all they needed—for now.

The Proprietor's emissary looked from Jameson to Avery, and his gaze lingered there. "I'll convey your message." *Avery's, not mine.*

Without warning, the door Oren had propped open slammed shut, drowning their surroundings in darkness once more. Two seconds later, the streetlight came back on.

The messenger was gone.

CHAPTER 16
JAMESON

The drive back to the Hawthorne flat seemed to take an eternity, and the foyer was dark and quiet when they arrived. Jameson flipped on a light and was greeted by four sticky notes affixed in a straight line to the closest wall. There was a single word written on each one in Xander's haphazard scrawl.

"*Neck*," Avery read out loud. "*Gotcha. Ringy. Goo.*"

This was either Xander's way of warning them that there was a prank involving bells and slime in their future... or a code. Fueled by the lingering buzz of adrenaline from the night's endeavors, Jameson's mind sorted rapidly through the letters, switching up their order. *ING* was a common combination, so he started there.

"*Going*," he guessed. "Probably followed by *to*..."

"Sub in the *c-h* from *gotcha* for the *n* in neck?" Avery murmured beside him.

Jameson's pulse ticked upward. This was practically their

version of dirty talk. "*Going to check . . .*," he murmured back, his body listing toward hers. "*On . . .*"

Four letters left. *A, G, R, Y.* Jameson's phone rang just as the meaning of Xander's message clicked into place. "Leaving London so soon?" he answered.

Nash spoke on the other end of the line. "We're trusting you, Jamie."

"To take care of myself?"

"To remember that you don't have to."

The muscles in Jameson's throat unexpectedly tightened. "You have absolutely nothing to worry about," he said. *I have Avery. I have the Devil's Mercy. I'm going to be just fine.*

"Make good choices!" Xander yelled in the background.

Jameson ended the call, and the next moment, Oren spoke. "We have company on the terrace."

Company. Jameson was suddenly keenly aware of his surroundings. Every sound. Every shadow. Every element of security that Oren had put in place.

"My men will take care of it," Oren said, but Avery shook her head.

"No," she said. Jameson took that as his cue to move toward the terrace, his steps silent, his stride long, Avery right behind him.

The door was open. Jameson stepped out onto the terrace before Oren could stop him.

The messenger lazed in one chair, his feet propped up on another. "Your neighbor has excellent taste in wine," he declared, swirling a bit of it in a wineglass and nodding toward the bottle on the table. "Horrible taste in cats, though," he added. "Hairless, two of them." He gave Avery a little wink. "I've always been more of a dog person myself."

The waiter persona. The fighter cloaked in darkness. And now this. Jameson felt like he'd met three different people. But the dark brown eyes, the artful mess of barely curling black hair, the sharp features—they were all the same.

"You broke into the neighboring flat." Avery stated the obvious.

"I break nothing." Holding his wineglass between his thumb and his middle finger, the messenger tapped his other three fingers lightly along the stem. "Except hearts."

Breaking into the flat next door was child's play for you. Jameson was suddenly sure of that. *You're a chameleon. A conman. A thief.* With that thought came a disturbing possibility. "How do we even know that you work for the Mercy?"

What if they were being conned?

"Because"—the chameleon swung his feet off the chair, turning slightly and leaning forward, his elbows on his knees—"your message was received." He let those words hang in the air, then leaned back again. "Or at least," he told Avery, "*yours* was." He set down his glass of wine and reached into his trench coat.

In a flash, Oren was standing in front of Avery. Their visitor slowly withdrew his hand, brandishing a black-and-silver envelope and dropping it onto the table, the motion graceful and smooth.

Jameson was at the table in an instant. The envelope was square and large. The paper was black matte, embossed with an elaborate design: a silver triangle embedded in a silver circle in a silver square. Within the triangle, there was another square, inside it, another circle. The pattern repeated over and over.

That's not silver, Jameson realized up close. *It's platinum.*

"Satisfied?" the messenger asked with an arch of a thick and angled brow. He didn't wait for an answer; instead, he returned his gaze to Avery. "One week, all access." He picked up his wineglass and swirled the red liquid inside it again. "And all it will cost you is two hundred thousand pounds."

Avery still couldn't hear a number like that without blanching. But she set her jaw. "It has to be both of us."

"It doesn't *have* to be anything, love." There was a note of warning in the response Avery received. "Do you know how rare what you're being offered is? How many men would kill for it?"

"That begs a question, doesn't it?" Jameson tossed out.

"Not the correct usage of that phrase" came the arch reply, "but do go on."

Jameson's eyes narrowed. "I'm guessing the Proprietor of the Devil's Mercy isn't hard up for cash. So why offer Avery anything for a measly two hundred thousand?"

"You misunderstand." The messenger's voice went low and silky. "It's not a fee. The levy to join the Devil's Mercy is much steeper. But you"—he swung his gaze back around to Avery—"won't be joining or paying the levy. You'll be a visitor, and the Factotum wants you playing at the tables." There was a calculated pause. "He wants you to lose."

"The Factotum." Jameson latched on to the title. "Not the Proprietor."

"I'm afraid neither one of you rises to the level of meriting the attention of the Proprietor. The Factotum is his second-in-command. He runs much of the Mercy, day to day."

"He's the one you report to?" Avery said.

"The one," Jameson added, "who wants us to lose."

"Wants *her* to," the messenger corrected. "However, the Factotum anticipated your request regarding Mr. Hawthorne, Ms. Grambs. If you want your very temporary visiting membership status extended to a second party, it's going to cost you. Five hundred thousand pounds lost on the tables at the Mercy over the course of three nights."

That was the kind of number that even Jameson couldn't shrug off. "Why would she agree to that?"

The chameleon smiled. "Why indeed?" *I know,* that tone said, *that you want more than you've asked for. I know that you have ulterior motives. I know you aren't showing your hand.*

"You said I have to lose the money in three days," Avery noted. She spoke slowly, but Jameson could see her mind moving fast. "But we'd have access to the Devil's Mercy for a week."

Jameson heard what she was really saying, what she'd realized. "We can win it back." That statement received no pushback, no correction, and Jameson ran the scenario out in his head. *Get in. Lose money. Win it back. Gain the Proprietor's attention—and an invitation to the game.*

"What's in it for the Factotum?" Jameson had been raised to ask the right questions.

"I wouldn't know."

Jameson looked for a tell of some kind on his quarry's face and saw nothing.

"But if I were speculating," the messenger continued lightly, "I'd say that the Factotum is on the hunt."

"The hunt for what?" Avery asked.

"A new member," Jameson guessed, daring their visitor to tell him that he was wrong. "You're the lure, Heiress." The conclusion wasn't much of a leap. "Lots of money. Young."

"A brash, overconfident little girl." Avery's eyes narrowed. "What happens if we need more than a week?"

"*Need* is an interesting choice of word." The messenger let that observation hang in the air, then he nodded to the platinum-marked envelope. "Inside, you'll find a nondisclosure agreement. You'll want to sign it." He reached into his trench coat again and withdrew a pen. Like the envelope, it appeared to be made of platinum. Its surface was ornately engraved, the design as incomprehensible to Jameson as hieroglyphics.

Avery opened the envelope. She read the document inside—a single page. "This just covers the nondisclosure. What about the rest of the terms?"

"Five hundred thousand pounds lost on the tables over the course of three nights, in exchange for one week's access. Those are the terms, on your honor—and his."

His. There was emphasis on that word, like the Factotum was as much larger-in-life to his errand boy as Tobias Hawthorne had been to his grandsons. *If the Factotum demands that kind of respect...exactly how powerful is the Proprietor?*

Jameson opted to shelve that question and ask a different one. "Do you have a name?"

"Rohan." There was something sharp and knowing on his face as he spoke. "Not that it matters."

"Well, Rohan," Avery said, "you can tell your boss he has a deal." She picked up the pen and signed.

Rohan shifted his gaze to Jameson. "You'll be signing, too, if you want to play."

Avery slipped the pen into Jameson's hand. He turned it in his fingers, taking in every element of the design, committing it to memory.

And then he signed.

CHAPTER 17

GRAYSON

Grayson knew that every problem had solutions, plural. Falling into the trap of assuming there was only one could keep you from seeing the optimal combination. Complex problems were fluid, dynamic.

Gigi was a complex problem.

Having spent the twenty-four hours since he'd dropped her off biding his time and considering all angles, Grayson knew that the most obvious solution was for him to see to it that she lost the key she wore around her neck. No key, no safe-deposit box access, no inconvenient evidence or revelations. But there were other possible courses of action given that Gigi also had no idea which safe-deposit box was her father's.

Keep an eye on her. Assess the best strategy for stealing her key. Stop her from figuring out what name the box is under. All of those actions required reaching back out. Luckily, the internet made that easy. It was simple enough to find the social media platform on which Gigi Grayson was most active, create an account, and begin to compose a direct message.

@OMGiGi. Grayson stared at the username and debated the best approach. *I need to see you again.* That was direct, straightforward—but what if she saw it as having romantic undertones? Grayson shuddered. *Did the coffee finally wear off?* seemed more benign, but could that be seen as flirting, too?

There were some significant downsides to subterfuge.

Have you heard from Kent Trowbridge? Grayson typed the words—no disturbing undertones whatsoever—into the message box and hit Send. While he waited for a reply, he decided to do a bit of research on the man that Gigi had called for help.

The man who had left her at the police station overnight and for much of the following day, seemingly without so much as informing her mother that she was in police custody.

With trademark efficiency, Grayson skimmed the search results. As Gigi had indicated, Kent Trowbridge was indeed a lawyer. A prominent one. Before Grayson could dig any deeper, Gigi returned his message.

Grayson opened it and stared at the screen. She'd sent him... a picture of a cat? A fat orange cat lying on its back with its paws on its face. Chunky lettering on the bottom of the picture spelled out *WHO DIS?*

Grayson typed back a single word: his first name.

Still going with that, huh? came Gigi's reply. Before he could start typing again, a barrage of other messages arrived.

@OMGiGi: *Ask me about my master plan, "Grayson."*

@OMGiGi: *On second thought, I'll tell you in person.*

@OMGiGi: *You are coming over, right?*

@OMGiGi: *My dad would want you to.*

Grayson focused on the fact that she had extended the invitation, not on her reference to their father. Before he could accept, she sent a picture of another cat: white, fluffy, yowling.

@OMGiGi: *This cat wants you to come over.*

@OMGiGi: *Fair warning: I have an unlimited supply of cats.*

Grayson snorted. *I hope you are referring to pictures of cats,* he typed back.

@OMGiGi: *Perhaps! Perhaps not. Come over and find out.*

Grayson felt a jab of guilt, as Xander's warning came back to him. *You're going to have to lie to her. Sabotage her. Gain her trust and betray her.* Gigi's trust really didn't seem difficult to gain. Grayson halfway wanted to sit her down and impress upon her that she needed to be more careful.

She never should have gotten into a car with him.

She shouldn't be inviting him over now.

But the most Grayson could allow himself was two messages, sent in quick succession. Two warnings.

@NonErrata575: *You are far too trusting.*

@NonErrata575: *I have my own reasons for looking for your father.*

@OMGiGi: *That sounds nefarious! But I don't care! All that matters is that you're looking.*

Grayson stared at the screen, a muscle in his jaw tensing. It was to his advantage for Gigi to believe they wanted the same thing. It shouldn't have hurt. *You shouldn't believe in me,* he thought, and then, on the off chance that she found nefarious males a little *too* intriguing, he sent another message for good measure.

@NonErrata575: *You should know that I have a girlfriend.*

There. That lie should ensure that Gigi Grayson didn't start to get any unfortunate ideas about the dark and mysterious stranger willing to join her on this search.

In response, Grayson received thirteen pictures of cats.

@OMGigi: *By the way, do you want to be Sherlock or Watson?*

CHAPTER 18

GRAYSON

Grayson pulled the Ferrari past the open gate onto the long drive leading up to the Grayson mansion. The stark-white stucco design was almost obsessively symmetrical, the terra-cotta tiles on the roof matched exactly to the clay-red bricks that lined the drive.

Grayson slowed as he passed an enormous fountain. He clocked the height to which it sprayed and the bronze sculptures rising out of the water: an eagle and a swan. Stepping out of the Ferrari, Grayson found himself thinking about Sheffield Grayson—and the one and only time they'd met. *I've built three different companies from the ground up*, the man had declared. *You don't achieve what I have achieved without an eye to potential eventualities. Potential risks.*

That was what Grayson had been to his father—all that he had been. A risk.

"So I've been thinking!" Gigi popped out from behind a palm

tree like it was the most natural thing in the world. "You asked about Mr. Trowbridge, right? And you know how I called him when I got arrested and he did pretty much nothing—like, he didn't even tell my mom?"

Gigi's tone and the speed with which she talked simultaneously made everything sound like a question and left absolutely no time for a response. "What if he knows about the safe-deposit box? What if he has record of the name my dad used to open it?"

Grayson was certain that Trowbridge had, in fact, done *something* when Gigi was taken into police custody, because she hadn't actually been arrested. But right now, he focused on pushing the conversation in another direction. "*If* your father indeed had a safe-deposit box under a fake name, what makes you think Trowbridge would know that name?"

"I don't know." Gigi issued the words like they were a dismissal of Grayson's query, rather than an admission that she hadn't thought this through. "My dad was obviously taking precautions." Gigi lowered her voice. "Maybe it has something to do with the guys in the suits."

Only show surprise if it's to your advantage to do so. "What guys in suits?"

"Who's to say?" Gigi gave an adorable little shrug. "I only saw them once when they came to talk to my mom. I was supposed to be in school, but I'm a firm believer in unschooling and also I had cramps, so..." Another shrug.

"Men in suits came to your home?" Grayson pushed her to focus. "And spoke with your mother."

"After they left, I heard her crying. I told Savannah, and she said it was probably nothing, but aliens could land on top of the portico and Savannah would still tell me that it was nothing."

There were a limited number of possibilities for the scenario that Gigi had described with the "men in suits"—none of them good. *Note to self,* Grayson thought, *fire Zabrowski.*

"And if aliens did land on the portico," Gigi continued buoyantly, "do you know who the Grayson family would call? *Mr. Trowbridge.* So I say we get up close and personal with his files. If we find the name, *boom!* We go back to the bank and finagle our way into that box. And don't tell me we can't because I'm pretty sure *you* can."

Steal her key. Subvert her search for the name.

"Assume everything goes according to this plan of yours," Grayson instructed. "You intend to go back to the bank where you were very recently arrested?" He used a tone designed to make her squirm, but she was, apparently, immune.

"We'll mosey across that bridge when we come to it. In the meantime, our next move is obvious."

Talk to Trowbridge, Grayson filled in silently.

"Party!" Gigi declared.

"I do not think *obvious* means what you think it means," Grayson informed her.

"Trust me," Gigi said, then she tugged him onto the porch. "Come on!"

Grayson let himself be led but balked when she threw open the front door to reveal a vast foyer with marble pillars. Compared to Hawthorne House, the Grayson mansion was nothing. The extravagance shouldn't have intimidated him in the least.

The *extravagance* didn't.

My nephew was the closest thing I will ever have to a son. Grayson could hear the words like Sheffield Grayson was standing right beside him.

"Look, 'Grayson,'" Gigi said cheerfully, "we could stand here debating whether or not you're going to come in or whether or not my plan is pure genius, or we could jump straight to the part where you give in." Gigi ducked out of view and popped back up a moment later holding what appeared to be a very large housecat that resembled a small leopard. "This is Katara. She's a sexy beast that loves cuddles but *will* scratch you if the situation calls for it."

Grayson banished the memory of his father's voice. The second he stepped across the threshold, the cat leapt out of Gigi's arms and took off in one direction, while Gigi bounded off in another.

"Where are you going?" Grayson called after her.

"Party!" she called back, like that was an answer. "I know some-one who can help."

CHAPTER 19

GRAYSON

As he followed Gigi, Grayson committed the house's floorplan to memory. A pair of bold, abstract paintings hung in the hall to the left of the foyer. As he and Gigi passed them, Grayson noted the small bronze plaques affixed to the wall beneath the massive canvases.

Savannah, age 3, one read. And the other: *Gigi, age* 3.

Not abstract paintings, then. Children's paintings. Up close, it was clear there was no method to the brushstrokes, no mastery of white space or visual metaphor. The paintings simply *were.*

Grayson ripped his gaze from the wall.

"Two things," Gigi declared when she stopped in front of a door at the end of the corridor. "Don't interrupt. And don't comment on the music." She threw open the door.

The first thing Grayson saw was himself. *Mirrors.* Three of the four walls of the massive room were lined with mirrored panes, ceiling to floor. The music Gigi had referenced was classical—and loud. At first glance, it would have been easy to mistake the space for a dance studio, if not for the markings on the floor and the hoop.

This was a half-court. *Basketball.* A girl stood on the free-throw line. Pale blonde hair braided back from her face framed her head like a wreath. *Or a crown.* She wasn't dressed for sports. A pleated silver skirt hit just below her knees. She was barefoot, a pair of black heels beside her on the line. On her other side, there was a rack of balls.

As Grayson watched, the girl—presumably Gigi's fraternal twin—sank three shots in a row.

Don't interrupt, Gigi had advised him. *And don't comment on the music.* It seemed to be blasting from all sides. *Tchaikovsky,* he recognized.

When there were four balls left, the girl in the silver skirt took three steps back. She picked up a ball and sent it arcing high, straight into the basket.

Three balls left. Two. By the last shot, she was back past the three-point line, and the music had built to a painful crescendo. *Nothing but net.*

Abruptly, the music cut off. And just as abruptly, Savannah Grayson stalked toward them—and past them—without a word.

"Her room's this way," Gigi announced helpfully.

They followed Savannah all the way back down the long hall, only to have the door to her room shut in their faces.

"She'll be out in a minute," Gigi translated. "And she says it's very nice to meet you."

"Patio." That word was issued from the other side of the door. Savannah's voice was high and clear, but her intonation was almost...familiar. "Ten minutes."

"So it has been spoken," Gigi intoned beside Grayson in a stage whisper. "And so it shall be."

The patio was covered, tiled, and larger than most homes. Grayson counted seating for thirty. There was a full outdoor kitchen despite the fact that the *actual* kitchen was visible through four sets of double glass doors. Twin tile staircases stretched up to a second story of outdoor seating.

To his own annoyance, Grayson caught himself staring at the pool. It was wide in some parts, narrower in others, and curved like a river around twin palm trees, each of which sat opposite a firepit. The water was dark blue, the pool lit, even in the daytime.

A treacherous part of Grayson's mind conjured up the image of his younger self swimming. He tried to direct his attention elsewhere, but his gaze caught on the pool's edge—and two sets of tiny handprints immortalized in cement.

"Let me do the talking," Gigi advised as the sound of heels clicking against tile announced her twin's arrival.

Savannah's braids were gone now, her long, pale hair held back by a silver headband. Where Gigi was dimples and animated features that looked almost too big for her face, Savannah was angles carved out of ice. She had Grayson's high cheekbones, his sharp jawline, and eerily familiar eyes that straddled the line between silvery gray and unforgiving ice blue.

She'd looked softer in the pictures he'd seen of the twins together. *Less like me.*

"I see we have a visitor." Savannah stayed standing long enough to cast him an assessing look, then sank into one of the many outdoor dining chairs.

"Sav, this is 'Grayson.' He's helping me look for Dad." The air quotes Gigi put around his name did not go unnoticed, but Grayson was more focused on Savannah's response.

"Is he?" Savannah returned. Her eyes locked on Grayson's, and though her expression was perfectly pleasant, it was the kind of pleasant that called to mind his aunt Zara: a sharply feminine smile that said *I could kill you with a strand of pearls.* Having taken Grayson's measure and found him wanting, Savannah turned back to her twin. "I told you, Gigi. Dad left."

Gigi blew at a piece of hair that had settled over her eyes. "He wouldn't just leave," she said mutinously.

"Yes. He would."

Undaunted, Gigi shot her sister the same round-eyed look she'd used to obtain all that coffee from the cops. "How much do you love me?"

"That question never bodes well," Savannah replied.

"Grayson and I are throwing a party, but the thing is . . . we kind of need Duncan's help."

"And Duncan would be . . . ," Grayson prompted.

"Savannah's boyfriend," Gigi explained. "Duncan Trowbridge."

Suddenly, Gigi's insistence that a party was the obvious next step made more sense. If she could talk the Trowbridge boy into hosting at *his* house . . .

Savannah laid her left hand on her knee and her right on her left wrist. *Poise. Elegance.* "Sure, Gigi. I left my phone in my room if you want to grab it."

Gigi beamed at her sister then jackrabbited off, leaving Grayson with her twin. Savannah sat in her chair like a queen on her throne, letting the silence stretch out between them.

It was almost endearing, the way she thought she could intimidate him.

"You'll be gone by the time she gets back," Savannah decreed.

"That doesn't sound like a request," Grayson noted.

Savannah turned her gaze toward the pool. A slight wind caught her hair, but not a strand ended up in her face. "Do I look like the kind of girl who makes *requests*?"

Grayson thought back to watching her sink shot after shot. Something twisted inside of him, and he felt an inexplicable desire to save her from herself. *If you never give, Savannah, someday you'll break.*

"My twin is a people person who's never met a bad idea she didn't immediately embrace like a long-lost friend. Restraint is not her strong suit."

"So you protect her." Grayson kept his own voice even by sheer force of will.

Savannah stood and took a step toward him, her heels audibly striking the tile. "I know who you are, Grayson Hawthorne."

Somehow, that didn't surprise him. He had a feeling Savannah Grayson knew far more than most people gave her credit for.

"Do you understand me?" Savannah's crystal-clear voice went low, her silvery eyes locked on to his. *"I know."*

Grayson felt comprehension wash over him. She didn't just know who he was. She knew who he was to *her*. And even though Grayson could have stood in a glass elevator in the middle of an earthquake without ever letting his heart rate speed up, he couldn't shrug that off. He didn't allow his expression to shift. He didn't allow a single crack in his iron-clad control—on the surface. But he *felt* the sting of her words.

Savannah knew, and she clearly didn't consider him . . . anything.

"Your sister was arrested," Grayson told her. Not an ounce of emotion showed in his tone. He made sure of that. "She spent the night before last in jail. I'm the one who got her out."

"It is not your job to take care of *my* sister."

It wasn't news to him that nothing here was *his*. "She seems hell-bent on making trouble for herself." Grayson said that like an observation, nothing more. "She believes your father didn't just leave."

"She believes," Savannah countered, her chin held high, "that our father would never cheat on our mother. But here you are." She looked him up and down and gave a single, regal shake of her head. "Like I said, you'll be gone by the time she gets back."

That can't happen, Savannah. Grayson had no intention of leaving until the situation with Gigi had been dealt with.

"I am not going to tell you again," Savannah said slowly. *"Get out."*

"Never announce what you're not going to tell someone," Grayson advised. "That keeps the focus on you and a bluff you may or may not be able to carry through. Focus on the other person."

"You don't want to make me repeat myself."

Grayson inclined his head. "Better."

"You are not wanted here." Savannah sold that statement, wholly and completely. And all Grayson could think was that she had his eyes.

"That's enough."

Savannah's head whipped toward the now-open glass doors to the kitchen and the woman who stood there. "Mom." Cracks appeared in Savannah's icy facade: a slight widening of her eyes, a subtle down-turning of her lips. "What did you hear?"

"Nothing I didn't already know, baby." Acacia Grayson turned calmly toward her husband's son. "Why don't you go check on your sister, Savannah, and give our visitor and me a moment alone?"

CHAPTER 20

GRAYSON

Acacia closed the patio doors behind them, sequestering herself and Grayson in the kitchen. She had blonde hair the same light shade as Savannah's. She was taller than his own mother and wispy thin.

Thinking of Skye had a way of opening old wounds, so Grayson didn't. "How long have you known?" Grayson hadn't planned to seize control of this conversation with his father's wife, but some habits were hard to break.

"About you?" Acacia walked to take a seat at a round glass table. "Not nearly long enough. I would like to think that if I had known earlier, I could have influenced Sheff to do the right thing." She closed her eyes, just for a moment, and Grayson found himself inexplicably thinking of children's paintings and tiny handprints in cement. Both had, in all likelihood, been her doing. "I would like to believe," Acacia continued softly, "that I'm the kind of person who would never hold a child responsible for the actions of his parents."

Betrayal. An affair. Those were the actions she spoke of. Pushing down all other thoughts, Grayson took a seat across from Acacia. "I wouldn't judge you if you despised me."

"I don't." Acacia looked down. "Twenty-two months. That's the straight answer to your question. I found out about you the day of my mother's funeral, twenty-two months ago."

Grayson did the math for himself. Twenty-two months ago, Sheffield Grayson had still been alive—and so had the old man. *Who would tell a grieving daughter something like that on the day she buries her mother?*

"I am not here to disrupt your family," Grayson said. It felt important to make sure she understood that.

"If you want to get to know the girls, Grayson, I won't stop you."

That's not what I'm here for. That isn't what this is about. "Gigi doesn't know who I am."

Acacia let out a shaky breath. "I shouldn't be grateful about that, but children look at you differently after they know." She let her gaze go back to the patio, where Savannah no longer stood. "And once they know that you know."

Clearly, Acacia's awareness had been news to Savannah, but the fact that Savannah knew about Grayson's existence hadn't surprised her mother. "How long has Savannah known about me?" he asked.

"Since the summer she was fourteen." Acacia's voice was steady. "I didn't know what had changed at the time, but it's obvious now."

Grayson's jaw hardened. "He made her keep his secret?" Grayson didn't say his father's name. He wouldn't inflict the phrase *your husband* on the woman across from him. But what his words lacked in specificity his tone made up for.

"I doubt Sheff had to make Savannah do anything." Acacia's

voice was almost too calm. "From what I understand, my parents knew for much longer. Since before..." Her hand trembled slightly on the table. "Since before you were born. I don't know the details, but I suspect my mother had a word with Sheff. I can just hear her telling him that affairs were one thing, but for goodness' sake, be discreet, the way my father was."

Getting your affair partner pregnant was not discreet, especially when her last name was Hawthorne.

"The money was theirs, you know." Acacia went quiet. The silence was heavy. "All of this, the seed funding for all of Sheff's ventures..." She swallowed. "If my mother confronted Sheff, it's likely she issued some very pointed threats."

Grayson processed that. "He gave me the impression that he was a self-made man."

"I was unaware that the two of you had met." Acacia looked down again.

Grayson felt a stab of sympathy but knew he had to preempt any questions she might ask about that meeting. "My grandfather had just passed away...."

"Yes. Of course." Acacia blinked rapidly. "I'm very sorry."

She's trying not to cry. "Not as sorry as I am," Grayson told her. His father's wife wasn't what he'd expected. She hadn't lashed out at him once. There was something so...*maternal* about her.

"You're welcome here, Grayson." Acacia's voice was hoarse, but she raised her head, setting her jaw. "For as long as you want."

Grayson couldn't afford to let that mean much. "I suspect Savannah would disagree."

"Savannah lived to make Sheff proud," Acacia said softly. "She was a colicky baby, quiet and serious as a toddler. And Gigi was... not." Grayson suspected that was an understatement. "I used to worry that Savannah would get lost. Her sister looked—*looks*—quite a bit like my husband's late nephew."

Colin, Grayson thought. *The reason your husband was out for vengeance.*

"Between the resemblance and Gigi being such a cheerful little thing, she had Sheff wrapped around her finger from day one. Savannah always seemed keenly aware of that, even as a baby. But she found her way. She shot her first basket when she was five and never looked back."

Grayson remembered something, then. "Colin played basketball." After his death, Sheffield Grayson had founded a nonprofit sports charity in his nephew's honor.

"So did Sheff, in college. He drove Colin so hard, had such hopes for him...."

And then Colin died. Because of the Hawthorne family. "Savannah let him recapture some of that," Grayson inferred. It was the logical conclusion, and he was nothing if not logical.

"As much as any daughter could." Acacia drew in another breath. "Savannah is going to judge me for staying with her father once I knew. To her, that will seem weak." She brought her gaze back to Grayson's. "But I assure you, I am not."

No. You are not. "Gigi told me that you were recently visited by gentlemen in suits."

To Acacia, that would seem like it had come out of nowhere, but that was the point. Less time for her to cover, less opportunity to manage her reaction.

"Gigi is mistaken."

"If you need anything...," Grayson said.

Gigi skidded into the kitchen. "I texted Duncan from Savannah's phone. Party's on for tomorrow night! In the meantime, who's ready for step negative one?"

"Step negative one?" Grayson repeated.

"Two steps before step one," Acacia clarified, and she met Grayson's eyes with a clear, silent message: Their heart-to-heart was over.

"Gigi got herself arrested." Savannah didn't come all the way into the kitchen as she let that bomb drop. *Keeping her distance from her mother—and me.*

"Et tu, Brute?" Gigi said to her twin, then she turned to Grayson, her eyes narrowing as she realized where Savannah must have gotten her information. "And et *tu*, Brute?" she repeated, then cocked her head to the side. "What's the plural of Brute?"

"It's a name," Grayson told her. "Not typically pluralized."

"Fascinating!" Gigi declared. "Much more interesting than anything that may or may not have resulted in my calling the family lawyer—who, by the way, left me in jail overnight and most of the next day!"

Acacia held up a hand. "Back up. Jail?"

"It's taken care of," Grayson cut in.

Acacia gave him a look: part admonition, part warning, *motherly.* But she let the interruption slide. "Well, then. I'll let the three of you get to step negative one. Savannah?" Acacia met her daughter's eyes. "Be nice."

CHAPTER 21

GRAYSON

"This is Dad's office," Gigi told Grayson. She gestured to a sleek desktop computer. "I found the key to the safe-deposit box in there last week, affixed to an index card that was affixed to the inside of the computer, near the cooling fan."

Grayson assumed that Gigi would, at some point, explain what they were doing in the study. For the time being, she'd given him an entry. He took it. "May I see the key?" he asked, nodding to the chain around her neck.

Steal the key. Subvert her search for the name.

Gigi reached back to unclasp her necklace, then handed it over to Grayson. He examined the key. Making it disappear was one option, but the better option might be making and swapping in a duplicate—and not a perfect one. *Just flawed enough that it won't open the safe-deposit box.*

"May I take a picture of the key?" Grayson asked. "I want a closer look at the etchings here." He rubbed his thumb over the head of the key, which bore the name of the bank. "There's some chance that the key identifies the number of the box that it opens."

"And if we had *that*," Gigi said, thrilled to her bones, "we wouldn't have to figure out the name dad used to figure out which box this key goes to!"

Steeling himself against her beaming smile, Grayson took a series of photographs of the key with his phone. Not just of the head of the key—and not just from one angle. If he could create a 3D rendering, he could easily have a decoy made.

For show, he pulled up one of the photos and zoomed in on the etchings.

"You're really doing this," Savannah stated sharply beside him. "With her." Savannah knew how to weaponize silence, even if it was brief. "Because you don't believe that my father would leave. You don't believe there could possibly be another woman, because Sheffield Grayson would never cheat on his wife."

The utter ice in those words was clear. Grayson didn't let it bother him. Savannah had a right to be angry, and her instincts were good: He *couldn't* be trusted.

"I believe," Grayson told her calmly, "that Gigi is going to do this with or without my help."

"Affirmative." The girl in question grinned. "Chaotic good, thy name is Gigi. Let's talk about step negative one."

Savannah gave Grayson one last, piercing warning look, then turned to her sister. "Enlighten us."

Gigi held out a hand to Grayson. "My key, if you please."

"It's clean," Grayson told her, as he handed the necklace back to her. "No number."

"But we will not be deterred!" Gigi declared. "And before we ransack Duncan's dad's office and look through *his* files—you can yell at me about that later, Sav—I figured we should make sure we've covered our bases here."

"You haven't already searched this place?" Grayson said mildly.

"I have." Gigi smiled. "You two haven't."

If there was anything to be found here, the easiest way of keeping it out of her hands was finding it himself. "You said that the key was affixed to an index card." Grayson rolled that over in his mind. "Do you still have the card?"

Gigi's eyes grew saucer round, then she practically dove for the trash can. Victorious, she popped back to her feet. "Here."

She handed him the card. Grayson noted that it had been cut down from the original size, possibly to fit inside the computer. *But why use a card at all?* He shrugged for Gigi's benefit. "It's just a white card."

But as soon as she wasn't looking, he pocketed it.

"Put your searching hats on, people." Gigi grinned.

"I am not helping you with this," Savannah told her sister emphatically.

Gigi patted her arm. "I believe that you believe that, but at a certain point, you have to ask yourself: Why are you here?"

"Because," the taller—and older—twin said, "I don't trust *him*."

"Don't take offense," Gigi told Grayson. "She only means it in the literal sense. And who among us doesn't have a few little deeply entrenched trust issues?"

Grayson felt the ends of his lips twitch, wanting to curl upward.

"Just look for anything that could indicate what name Dad might have used to register a secret safe-deposit box," Gigi instructed. "A fake ID, scrap paper, an external hard drive. Maybe paperwork signed in another name?"

"Did your father have an actual office, off premises?" Grayson put no special emphasis on that question—nothing to make it clear that if the answer was yes, he'd be doing some breaking and entering tonight himself.

"No," Gigi replied. "Dad sold his company a few weeks after Grammy went to the great Sunday brunch in the sky."

Not long before he came after Avery. Grayson filed that away.

"Did you try *Colin*?" Savannah asked Gigi. The question came out quiet. "For the name." That, more than anything that Acacia had said, told Grayson how much the twins had grown up in the shadow of their long-dead cousin.

"Too obvious," Gigi replied, her throat seeming to tighten around the words. "But yes."

Grayson knew what it was like to work and work and never be enough. To lose the person who'd *made* you and live forever thereafter with the knowledge that they'd preferred someone else.

"If you're starting with the computer," he told Gigi briskly, "I'll try the desk."

The desk was clean. So were the shelves. The chairs and side tables. The moldings on the walls. Grayson continued to search quickly and efficiently, keeping an eye on the girls as he did. He removed shades from lamps, examined every floorboard with military precision. Finally, he turned his attention to the art: two large landscape paintings on the walls and a bronze eagle that matched the two sculptures in the fountain outside.

Nothing hidden behind or in them.

That just left two framed photos. One was of a teenage boy midair, a ball arcing from his fingertips. His coloring matched Gigi's, his sweat-laden hair a mop of chocolate-colored curls. *Colin.* Grayson removed the picture from the wall and took off its backing. He searched, found nothing, and replaced it. Then he turned to the second photograph, a family portrait. Savannah was straight-faced, Gigi smiling, the two of them dressed in matching outfits. Grayson tried to place their age. *Four, maybe five?* Behind them, their mother leaned against their father.

They look like a family. They looked happy enough. *Normal.* There had been nothing normal about his own childhood.

Pushing back against that thought, Grayson removed the frame from the wall and the back from the frame, to no avail. And then he spotted a seam in the wood of the frame.

A seam that had no reason to be there.

Grayson ran his fingers along the side, prodding until he found the trigger. A small piece of wood popped out, revealing a compartment inside the frame—a very small one. Shifting to shield his actions fully from view, Grayson tipped the frame sideways. A small square fell out.

A USB drive.

He palmed it, and less than a second later, it was secured in the cuff of his dress shirt. One more smooth motion set the frame to right, but before he could set it back down, he felt one of the girls approach. *Savannah.* Without a word, she picked up the photo of Colin. "I don't know what game you're playing here, Grayson, and I don't care."

Had she seen him take the USB? Grayson didn't think so and proceeded accordingly. "If you're about to issue a warning," he told Savannah softly, "I take it you know your target? What do you have that I want? What do I have that I'm terrified to lose?" He brought his eyes to hers. It felt far too much like looking in a mirror. "What type of person," he continued, "am I?"

She raised a delicate brow. "Do you really want me to answer that?"

Answering a question with a question. Good.

"You two look cozy!" Gigi declared from across the room.

"Grayson was just about to call it a night," Savannah said. "We found nothing, Gigi. There's nothing to be found. Satisfied?"

"Always," Gigi replied emphatically. "Also, never! I am full of contradictions."

Grayson felt another tug toward her, toward both of them—and did his best to dismiss it. "I think we're done in here," he said. "What's step zero?"

"The step in between steps negative one and one!" Gigi beamed at him. "You catch on quickly, my pseudonymous friend."

"Not quickly enough." Savannah sidled between the two of them. "It's getting late."

Grayson waited for Gigi to object, but she didn't. "Totally. And step zero involves beauty sleep and outfit selection, because tomorrow night, we party."

CHAPTER 22

GRAYSON

Gigi saw him out but didn't follow him down the front steps. As Grayson paced toward the Ferrari, he heard a voice farther down the drive. *Acacia's.* "You left her there overnight? *And didn't call me?*"

Grayson could go still with a moment's notice. Complete control of his body made it that much easier to disappear into his surroundings.

"She has to learn sometime." That voice was male, unremarkable. "Do you know what would have happened if I hadn't intervened, Acacia?"

Pinpointing their location to be inside the portico, Grayson allowed himself two more steps in that direction. *Silent. Measured.*

"It is not your job to teach my daughters anything, Kent."

"And that's not the only thing that's bothering you, Mrs. Grayson."

Trowbridge. Given that the two of them were clearly on a

first-name basis, the fact that he'd chosen to address her as Mrs. Grayson felt pointed.

"Gigi saw the investigators," Acacia admitted in a hushed voice that Grayson could barely hear. "I'm trying my best to protect the girls, but—"

"We've been over this, Acacia. You don't have the resources to protect anyone. I'm doing the best I can, but you know—"

"I am going to handle this." Acacia's voice wasn't hushed now.

"Your parents aren't here anymore. Your husband is gone. And the money—"

"I know." Acacia appeared, pacing outside the portico.

"I'll do whatever I can." Kent Trowbridge stepped out after her. He was shorter than she was and moved like a guy who prided himself on being fitter than men half his age. "You know that I am here for you, Acacia. You just have to let me be here for you."

The moment Grayson saw the lawyer place a hand on Acacia's shoulder—far too close to her neck—he took three loud steps forward. Instantly, Trowbridge's hand dropped. Acacia stepped away from him, and they both whipped their heads toward the house.

"I hope I'm not interrupting anything." Grayson didn't raise his voice, but he had his grandfather's way of being heard. He walked, his pace unhurried, to a spot just short of the Ferrari, then paused and held out his hand, forcing his opponent to close the distance between them to take it.

"Grayson Hawthorne," he said, meeting the lawyer's eyes.

He saw a spark of recognition at his last name. "Kent Trowbridge."

Grayson let his lips curl slightly. "I know." There was power in those two words. *Make them wonder what you know.*

Trowbridge glanced back at Acacia. "We'll talk later," he told her.

Grayson didn't step into his own car until the lawyer was gone. He didn't press Acacia on what he'd overheard. Instead, as he pulled out of the drive, he made a call. "Zabrowski, you have exactly one chance to prove to me that you're worth continuing to keep on retainer."

CHAPTER 23

JAMESON

Twelve hours after Jameson and Avery signed the NDA, another black envelope showed up at the flat. This one featured only a single thread of shining platinum, encircling a black wax seal. The design imprinted on the wax was familiar. *A triangle inside a circle inside a square.* Jameson ran his thumb over the contours, his brain rotating the shapes, disassembling them, reassembling them. He broke the seal and opened the envelope to find an invitation—also black, with silver script. Affixed to the bottom of the card, there was a small but ornate key.

Jameson skimmed the instructions and plucked the gold key from the card, then turned to Avery, an electric smile spreading over his face. "It appears we're headed to the opera."

"Zip me up?" Avery's gown was black with gold embroidery, a delicate, complicated pattern that swirled down her torso, her hips, all the way to the floor. The sight of her in that dress, open in the back, brought Jameson right back to the edge of the falls, hungering for *more*.

"My pleasure." He gave himself a moment first, tracing his hand from her bare neck to the small of her back, then splaying his fingers outward, the warmth of her skin soft and scalding against his palm.

Avery's back arched. When she spoke, her voice was low and rough. *"Tahiti."* When one of them said that code word—*their* code word—the other had to let their guard down entirely.

Jameson was surprised it had taken her this long. He leaned forward, his lips brushing her ear. "You want me to *strip*?" He brought his thumb to a spot just below her jawbone where he could see her pulse.

"I want you to admit that this matters to you," Avery said, leaning into his touch.

Jameson wound his free arm around her, pulling her body back against his. "Winning always matters." Being with her like this—it felt like winning every damn time. "An impossible challenge," he murmured directly into her skin. "A hidden world. A secret game. It's all very me."

"And that's it? This is just a diversion?" Avery turned her head, and Jameson began slowly tracing her jawline. *Tahiti* meant being honest—with himself, with her. He let his hand drop from her jaw.

N-O. He drew the letters with his thumb on her back.

"No," Avery murmured. "This isn't just a challenge or a game or a diversion to you." She paused. "Is it Ian?"

The question cut into him, but beneath his touch, she was soft and warm and *there*. Five more letters etched onto her back, and he could barely breathe. *M-A-Y-B-E.*

"Maybe?" Avery asked softly.

"I know he's using us," Jameson told her, his voice catching in his throat. "Using me." She'd called *Tahiti*. He couldn't stop there. A deal was a deal. "Maybe, on some level, I want to prove Ian made a mistake staying away all these years. Maybe a small part of me wants to impress him. Maybe I want to *make* him want me, so that I can be the one who walks away."

Avery turned then, her dress still undone in the back, her hand coming up to his face. "You," she said, her voice as raw as he felt, "are a blazing fire." When she said it, he could believe it. "You're a force of nature who makes the impossible possible without batting an eye. You're brilliant and devious and *kind*."

It was the last description that he had the hardest time believing, the last one that undid him. "I'm also very handsome," he quipped, but the words came out thick.

"You," Avery told him, her voice reverberating through every bone in his body, "are everything."

She was. This was. "Is that all?" he murmured, with a crooked little smile.

She matched his smile like a poker player matching a bet. "Isn't that enough?"

Jameson leaned forward, reaching behind her to pull the zipper on her dress slowly, tortuously upward. "I'm a Hawthorne, Heiress. Nothing is ever enough."

CHAPTER 24

JAMESON

They went to the opera. Twenty minutes in, per the instructions they'd received, Jameson and Avery ducked out of their private box and made their way to the elevator.

"This is where we leave you," Avery told Oren. The invitation had been *very* clear.

"I don't like this." Avery's bodyguard folded his arms over his chest and surveyed his charge. "But threats against you are at an all-time low, and if the two of you are going to do this, you need to go before anyone realizes you've left your box."

Seconds later, Jameson and Avery were alone in the elevator. With his heart beating a little harder, a little faster, Jameson laid the gold key that had accompanied their invitation against the elevator's control panel.

Every button lit up emerald green.

Beside him, Avery pressed in the code they'd been given. The elevator went pitch-black. With a whoosh, they descended, past the ground floor, farther than one would go for a parking garage or basement. *Down, down, down.*

When the elevator doors opened again, Jameson was overcome with a sense of overwhelming vastness as he stepped out into some kind of cavern, the sound of his footsteps echoing. Avery followed, and a torch burst to life to their left.

Not a natural cavern, Jameson realized. *Man-made. A tunnel.* And cutting through that tunnel was an underground river. Even with the torchlight, it looked black.

As Jameson stepped forward, muted light sparked to life at the water's edge. *A lantern.* It took Jameson a moment to register the person holding the lantern. *A child.* Jameson put the boy's age at eleven or twelve.

Silently, the child turned and stepped out onto the water—onto a boat. It looked a bit like a gondola, long and thin. The child attached the lantern to the top, picked up a pole, and turned to the two of them, waiting.

Jameson and Avery walked the stone path to the boat. They stepped on board. The child said nothing as he began to row, the pole digging into the bottom of the canal.

Jameson went to take it from him. "I can—"

"No." The kid didn't even look at him, just tightened his grip on the pole.

"Are you okay?" Avery asked, concerned. "Is someone forcing you to do this? If you need help . . ."

"No," the kid said again with a tone that made Jameson wonder if he'd underestimated his age. "I'm fine. Better than fine."

The underground river bent. The boat took the turn, and Jameson realized that this part of the tunnel wasn't made of ordinary stone. The walls were black, but it seemed like light shined within them. *Some kind of quartz?* Silence descended until all Jameson could hear was the sound of the boat cutting through the water as the boy poled them onward.

"We're the only ones out here," Avery said quietly, her voice echoing on the water. "Down here."

"There are many paths," the boy said, something almost leonine in the set of his features. "Many entrances, many exits. All roads lead to the Mercy if you're welcome there—and none do if you are not."

Three more bends of the river, and then the boat ran up on some kind of beach. Torches burst into flame, encircling the boat, illuminating a door. Standing in front of the door was Rohan. He wore a red tuxedo with a black shirt underneath and stood like a soldier at attention, but torchlight showed the expression on his face to be utterly relaxed. Self-satisfied. *The way someone is when they've won.*

"You shouldn't be working at your age, let alone this late at night," Avery told the boy who'd brought them here. Her gaze darted toward Rohan. "If he made you think otherwise..."

"The Factotum didn't make me think anything," the boy said. His tone was fierce, his chin held high. "And someday, when he's the Proprietor, I'm going to be Factotum for him."

CHAPTER 25

JAMESON

Rohan didn't work for the Factotum. Rohan *was* the Factotum. *Not just a messenger.* As Jameson strode forward, words Ian had spoken came back to him. He'd said that Jameson needed the Proprietor's attention. *Not his right-hand man's.* And he'd said that every fifty years or so, the Proprietor of the Devil's Mercy chose a successor.

"Child labor?" Avery stood toe-to-toe with Rohan. "That can't be legal."

"A certain type of child knows how to keep secrets better than adults." There wasn't a hint of apology in Rohan's tone. "The Mercy can't save every child it finds in a horrific situation, but those it does save rarely regret it in the end."

Jameson heard layers of meaning in those words. *You were that child, weren't you?*

Rohan turned his back on them and placed his right hand flat on a black stone. It flared to life, reading his palm, and triggered the sound of a dozen locks being turned. Rohan stepped back, and the door opened toward them.

"Where angels fear to tread, have your fun instead." Rohan's voice was almost musical, but there was something dark in his tone. *A promise.* One that Jameson suspected that men in Rohan's position had been making for centuries. "But be warned: The house always wins."

With no hesitation—like a person *incapable* of hesitation—Jameson stepped through the door. The room beyond was round and domed, the ceiling at least two stories high, the architecture vaguely Roman. Other doors were barely visible in the walls.

Many entrances, many exits. Jameson thought briefly of Hawthorne House and its labyrinthine secret passages, and then he focused on his surroundings, on the parts of the domed room far more visible than the doors.

Five soaring marble arches marked larger openings in the curved wall at equidistant intervals around the room. Thick, rippling curtains hung down from the arches, all of them black, each made of a different fabric. *Velvet, silk...*

Avery came to stand beside him, and Jameson continued his assessment. The floor beneath their feet was made of golden granite. In the center of the room, there was a circle of columns. Half of them surged up to the domed ceiling; the other half were only as tall as Jameson's shoulder. On top of each of the smaller columns, there was a shallow golden pan filled with water.

Floating in the water in each of those golden pans was a lily.

Jameson strode inward, and as he did, he noticed the design on the floor, encircled by the columns. *A lemniscate.* The formal term came to Jameson before the common one. *The infinity symbol.* The pattern had been laid into the granite in sparkling black and white.

"Onyx." Rohan spoke directly behind Jameson. "And white agate."

Jameson whirled, expecting to see Rohan inches away, only to realize the Factotum was still by the door.

"Trick of the walls," Rohan said with a smile, then he turned to Avery and held out his arm. "I have business to attend to, but the Proprietor has given me leave to get you situated first."

The Proprietor. Jameson tried not to show his hand at the mere mention of the man, just like he tried not to glare at Rohan when Avery took his arm and the Factotum began to lead her around the room. *All part of the game.*

Jameson's stride was long enough that he caught up to them long before they made it to the first grand archway.

"The Mercy has five archways," Rohan said, his words seeming to echo all around them. "Each leads to entertainment of a different sort." Rohan said the word *entertainment* with a wicked sort of smile. A roguish one.

The kind Jameson was used to wielding himself.

"Each area is dedicated to a deadly sin. We are, after all, the Devil's Mercy." Rohan swept aside the curtain to their left. Beyond, Jameson could make out dozens of canopies, whatever was beneath them obscured by layers of chiffon.

"Lust?" Jameson guessed.

"Sloth," Rohan replied with a smirk. "We keep several masseurs on staff, if relaxation is what you're after."

Jameson doubted most members of this club came here to relax.

"Gluttony, next." Rohan led them to the next archway. "You'll find our chefs second to none. All beverages are, of course, top-shelf and complimentary."

Where angels fear to tread, have your fun instead. The warning came back to Jameson. *But be warned: The house always wins.*

Next, archway number three. Rohan pulled a velour curtain barely back. Inside, there was a spiraling staircase, the same shade of gold as the atrium's granite floor.

"Lust." Rohan let the curtain drop. "There are private chambers upstairs. What members use those chambers for"—he gave Jameson a moment to *imagine*—"is up to them." Rohan's eyes hardened. "But lay a hand on anyone who does not want a hand there or who is too inebriated to consent, and I cannot guarantee that you will still *have* a hand in the morning."

That just left two archways. As they approached the first, Jameson realized that its curtain was much heavier than the others. The moment Rohan pulled it back, they were hit by the roar of a crowd. Past the archway, Jameson could see what looked to be two dozen people, and beyond the crowd—a boxing ring.

"Some of our members like to fight," Rohan stated, lingering for just a moment on that word. "Some like to place bets on the fights. I would caution you against the former, at least as far as facing off against our house fighters is concerned. Those who fight for the Mercy never pull their punches. Blood is shed. Bones are broken." Rohan's lips pulled back from his teeth into something like a smile. "Caution must be exercised. If you end up in a disagreement with another player at the tables, however, you're welcome to take the disagreement to the ring."

"Wrath?" Jameson guessed with an arch of his brow.

"Wrath. Envy. Pride." Rohan dropped the curtain. "People end up in the ring for all kinds of reasons." Something about the way Rohan said that made Jameson think that the Factotum had spent time in the ring himself. "As you explore the Mercy, note that bets may be placed in four of the five areas. Members bet on fights and on the tables, of course, but the first two rooms I showed you each have a book, and those books hold more *unconventional* wagers. Any wager written into one of those books and signed for is binding, no matter how bizarre. And speaking of binding wagers..." Rohan produced, seemingly out of nowhere, a velvet pouch and handed it to Avery. "Your transfer came through, untraceable, just how we like them. You'll find five-thousand-pound, ten-thousand-pound, and hundred-thousand-pound marks inside. These chips *will* be handed over to me at the end of the night." His teeth flashed in another smile. "For safe-keeping."

The three of them made it almost full circle around the room, to the final arch. "*Greed*," Rohan said, his lips curving upward. "Beyond this curtain, you'll find the tables. We offer an eclectic selection of games. Ms. Grambs, you'll want to concentrate on those where you're playing against the membership, not the house. And as for you..." Rohan shifted his gaze from Avery to Jameson. "Don't wager anything you can't afford to lose, Jameson Hawthorne." Rohan leaned forward to speak directly into Jameson's ear, his voice a silky whisper. "There's a reason that men like your father aren't allowed back."

CHAPTER 26

JAMESON

Stepping into the gaming room was like stepping back in time to a ballroom from eras past. The towering ceilings made Jameson wonder just how far underground they were. He focused on that question, not the more obvious one: How long had Rohan known that Ian was Jameson's father?

And what else does he know? Jameson pushed back against the thought. He needed to focus on what mattered. *Let nothing escape your notice. Take it all in. Know it. Use it.*

The walls of the ballroom were made of pale wood. Gold moldings covered the ceiling, like something out of a Venetian palace. The shining white marble floor was partly covered with a massive, lush carpet, sapphire in color, struck through with gold. Ornate tables, obviously antique, were positioned strategically around the room. Different shapes, different sizes.

Different games.

At the closest table, a dealer dressed in an old-fashioned ball-gown handed a pair of dice to an elderly gentleman.

"Hazard," a voice said to Jameson's left. *That Duchess* stepped into his peripheral view. "The game you're watching? It's called hazard." The duchess's gown was jade green tonight, made from fabric that flowed with her movements, slit on either side up to her thighs.

Like Avery, she was holding a velvet pouch.

"It's the predecessor of dice—or what you Americans call craps," the duchess continued. "But a bit more complicated, I'm afraid." She inclined her head toward the man with the dice. "The person throwing is known as the caster. He picks a number no lower than five, no higher than nine. The number chosen dictates the conditions under which you win or lose. Fail to do either after the first throw, and the number thrown becomes a part of the game as well." She smiled. "Like I said, it's complicated. I'm Zella."

Jameson raised a brow. "Just Zella?"

"I've always been of the belief that titles tell you less about the player than the game." Zella gave a graceful little shrug. "You may use mine if you wish, but I do not—unless there's a reason to."

Every instinct Jameson possessed converged into a single thought: *There is a reason for everything this woman does.*

"And what about the two of you?" Zella said. "What would you like to be called here at court?"

"I'm Avery. He's Jameson."

The fact that Avery had answered the question let Jameson be the one to ask: "Court?"

"It's how some people refer to the Mercy," Zella said. "The bed of power and all that, just rife with politics and intrigue. For example . . ." Her dark brown eyes roved over the room—and the copious amounts of attention the three of them were now attracting. "Almost everyone here tonight is now wondering if we know each other."

Avery studied the duchess. "Do you want them to think we do?"

"Perhaps." Zella smiled. "The Mercy is a place where bargains are struck. Deals made. Alliances formed. That's the thing about power and wealth, isn't it?" she said, addressing the question to Avery. "Men who have a great deal nearly always want more."

The duchess held out an arm to Avery, who took it, and then and only then did Zella offer Jameson the other. He took it as well, and she led them through the room, a promenade that he knew with every bone in his body served her purpose—whatever that purpose was.

"Men," Jameson echoed. Aside from the dealers—all female, all dressed in old-fashioned ballgowns—there were very few women in this room.

"It's rarer for women to be granted membership," Zella said. She shifted her gaze to Avery. "You must be quite remarkable—or have something the Proprietor wants very much."

The Proprietor. Jameson could almost taste the thrill of his next impossible task. *Get his attention. Win entrance to the Game.*

"Woman to woman," Zella said to Avery, "let me help you become a bit more acclimated." She nodded to tables as she passed. "Whist. Piquet. Vingt-et-un."

Jameson didn't recognize the first two games, but he was able to quickly figure out the last one. "Twenty-one," he translated. "As in blackjack."

"In the era in which the Devil's Mercy was founded, it was known as vingt-et-un."

Jameson took that as an indication that the Mercy was *supposed* to feel like leaving the world's present reality behind.

"I don't suppose there's a poker table?" Jameson said dryly.

Zella nodded to a set of ornate stairs. "Poker is played on the balcony. A recent addition. Seventy years ago, perhaps? As you'll discover, most games played here go back much further."

Jameson had the feeling that when the duchess said *games*, she wasn't referring only to those being played on the tables.

"And the Proprietor?" Jameson asked. "Is he here tonight?"

"I've found it best to assume he's everywhere," Zella said. "We are, after all, in his domain. Now," she continued, having finished their little promenade, "if the two of you will excuse me, I have an eidetic memory, a reputation at the tables, and a plan." The duchess turned her head toward Avery. "If anyone here makes you uncomfortable or does something they should not, know that you have an ally in me. Outsiders should stick together—to a point. Bonne chance."

Jameson watched Zella walk away and mentally translated her parting words. *Good luck.* He scanned the room, taking it all in: so many games, so many possibilities, one task at hand. Feeling like an electric charge through his veins, Jameson turned to Avery and nodded to the staircase to the balcony overhead.

"What do you say, Heiress?" Jameson whispered. "Ready to lose?"

CHAPTER 27

GRAYSON

Grayson imported the photographs he'd taken of Gigi's key the night before to his laptop. Using his hand in the photo for scale, he calculated the key's dimensions, double-checked those calculations, and used them, along with a ghost image of the key, to begin building a digital model. By the time the Haywood-Astyria's personal concierge came to check on him midday, he was nearly done.

"Is there anything we can get you, sir?"

For a black-card guest at this establishment, that question didn't refer only to hotel amenities. "I'm going to need a 3D printer," Grayson replied. He didn't have to provide a rationale for the request, so he did not. "Please."

The concierge left. Grayson finished his work. Saving it, he made a second, nearly identical file, altering the key's teeth just enough to render this one useless. *Sorry, Gigi.* Not allowing himself to wallow in that thought, he turned his attention to an equally unpleasant one. "What exactly does one wear to a high school party?"

Even when Grayson had been in high school, he hadn't ever needed the answer to that question. His brothers had attended such parties occasionally, but Grayson had never seen the point. And if he *had* gone, he wouldn't have wasted a single second deciding what to wear. A fine suit was like armor, and Grayson had been raised to walk into every room armed.

But not tonight.

Tonight, he needed to blend in. Unfortunately, Grayson Davenport Hawthorne knew nothing about blending. "Shorts?"

Thankfully, his phone rang before he could meditate too long on that possibility. "Zabrowski," Grayson answered, sliding smoothly into business mode. "I trust you have answers for me."

If you allow people to fail you, he could hear his grandfather lecturing, *they inevitably will. So don't give them the option.*

"I ran a basic background check on Kent Trowbridge," the private investigator reported.

"Do I pay you," Grayson said evenly, "for *basic*?"

"And then I fleshed it out," Zabrowski said hurriedly. "As you've probably gathered, the guy's a lawyer—and very connected. Comes from a whole family of lawyers. Or maybe *dynasty* is the better word."

"I take it they're financially... *stable*," Grayson translated.

"Very. And interestingly for your purposes, the guy grew up alongside Acacia Grayson née Engstrom. The Trowbridge and Engstrom families go way back."

Grayson filed that piece of information away. "Anything else?"

"He's widowed, one son."

Grayson was well aware of the son. "And the Grayson family's current financial situation?" The list of assignments he'd given Zabrowski after the conversation he'd overheard between Acacia and Trowbridge was lengthy.

The detective kept his reply short. "Not good."

The muscles in Grayson's jaw tightened. He'd kept Zabrowski on retainer to make sure that the girls were taken care of, and he had been given the distinct impression that finances were not an issue in the Grayson household—and never would be. "Explain."

"When the Engstrom matriarch passed away the year before last, everything was left to Acacia and her daughters—in trusts."

Grayson thought about Acacia saying that her parents were the ones who'd bankrolled her husband's companies. "And?" He had no intention of letting Zabrowski off that easily.

"Outside of those trusts, all of Acacia Grayson's assets were jointly held with her husband...who has since come under IRS and FBI investigation."

Grayson had never allowed himself a temper, so he didn't lose it. He didn't say *What the hell have I been paying your retainer for?* He didn't have to. "What kind of investigation?" he demanded with icy, unnatural calm.

That tone had put the fear of God and Hawthornes in better men than the detective. Grayson could practically hear him gulp.

"White collar, presumably," Zabrowski managed. "Tax evasion, embezzlement, insider trading—your guess is as good as mine."

"Do I pay you to *guess*?"

"Point is, the joint accounts are frozen." Zabrowski rushed the words. "Some have already been seized. Someone's keeping it out of the press, but—"

"And the money left to Acacia in trust?" Grayson asked. Those funds would have been hers and hers alone, not subject to seizure based on her husband's crimes unless she was implicated as well.

"Gone," Zabrowski said.

Grayson felt his eyes narrow. "What do you mean, *gone*?"

"Do you know how many laws I had to break to even get this information?" Zabrowski shot back.

"Let's assume none," Grayson said in a tone meant to remind the private investigator that if laws *had* been broken, he couldn't know about it. "Continue."

If Zabrowski resented being given orders by a person less than half his age, he was wise enough not to show it. "Acacia Grayson's trust was drained—presumably by her husband before he fled the country."

Sheffield Grayson didn't flee the country. "And the girls' trusts?" Grayson asked.

"Intact and substantial," Zabrowski assured him. "But the Engstroms must have had some reservations about their daughter and her husband, because neither were listed as trustees."

Grayson processed that in an instant and wasted no time with his reply. "Allow me to guess: Kent Trowbridge."

If the joint accounts were frozen and Acacia's trust was gone, that almost certainly meant Acacia was using her daughters' trusts to fund their living expenses—but as trustee, Trowbridge would have to sign off on those expenditures. Grayson thought back to the night before, to the way the lawyer had put his hand on Acacia's shoulder, far too close to her neck.

"Keep digging," he ordered Zabrowski. "I want a copy of the trust paperwork so I can read through the provisions myself."

"I can't just—"

"I am not interested in *can't*." Grayson lowered his voice. Making someone strain to hear you was one way of ensuring they were that much more motivated to listen. "I'll also need the details of the IRS and FBI investigations—but don't run afoul of either agency yourself."

"That all?" Zabrowski clearly meant that sarcastically, but Grayson chose to take the question at face value.

"You'll find a transfer in your account, twice the retainer I've been paying." That was another power move: transferring the money before the other person had a chance to decline your offer. "And I'll need a recommendation." Grayson pivoted to an easier ask, one to make the man forget for a second or two how tall the rest of the order was. "Who do you have who can discreetly make keys?"

CHAPTER 28
GRAYSON

The situation—*Gigi, the key, the party, the search*—had changed. That much was clear. Before, his objective had been to make sure that Gigi didn't find her way into their father's safe-deposit box. Now, however, he needed in that box himself.

Before the FBI realizes it exists. Grayson didn't have a guess about what white-collar crimes his father might have committed, but he *did* know that the man had paid money to have Avery followed, stalked, attacked, and kidnapped. Assuming Sheffield Grayson had covered his tracks, that suggested the existence of offshore accounts or otherwise untraceable funds. If the FBI somehow managed to find a trail, however slim, of those transactions—or any other proof of Sheffield Grayson's plot against the Hawthorne heiress—they might begin to view his disappearance through another lens.

They might start asking questions and pulling at threads that Grayson could not let unravel.

That in mind, Grayson picked up the small, discreet USB drive he'd taken from Sheffield Grayson's study. He plugged an adapter into his laptop, but when he went to plug the drive into the adapter, he realized that it didn't fit. *Not a USB*. It was slightly wider, slightly taller. He turned the end upward and examined it. *Definitely not a USB*. Grayson could make out what looked like small, wire-thin pegs inside. *So what is it?* He prodded at the casing, then set it down and reached into his pocket, withdrawing the index card he'd taken from Sheffield Grayson's office.

A fake USB. An index card, cut down in size. Grayson felt like he was back at Hawthorne House, playing one of the old man's Saturday morning games. A collection of objects would be laid out in front of Grayson and his brothers, but their purpose, their use, where to begin? Figuring that out was the challenge.

Sheffield Grayson is not the old man, and this is not a game. Grayson told himself that, but it did no good: He had to examine every inch of the card. There was a slight notch in one side and two on another, spaced about an inch apart.

Three notches in a white card. A fake USB drive. Before Grayson could puzzle over—and through—that, his phone rang, and Xander's name flashed across the screen. Deciding to save himself the trouble—and the yodeling—of ignoring the call, Grayson picked up. "Hello."

"What's wrong?" Xander demanded immediately.

Grayson frowned. "What would make you think there's something wrong?"

"You said hello."

Grayson's frown deepened. "I say hello."

"No, you don't." Xander's grin was audible in his voice. "Now say it in French!"

Grayson did not oblige. "I stole what appeared to be a USB drive from Sheffield Grayson's home office," he reported instead. "He had it hidden in a secret compartment in a framed portrait of his family."

Xander processed that. "Gray, would now be an appropriate time to talk about your feelings?"

Hands in cement, paintings on the wall. "No." Grayson didn't belabor that point. "Whatever the drive is, it's not a USB. I don't think it's digital at all. There was also an index card, apparently blank."

"Invisible ink?" Xander said.

"Possibly," Grayson replied. "I'll try the basics."

"Light, heat, blacklight," Xander rattled off, a grin audible in his voice. "Sodium iodide."

"Exactly." Grayson let his eyes go back to the card.

"And how is everything going with *the sister*?" Xander probed.

Still staring at the index card, Grayson corrected him. "Sisters." The word escaped him. He'd been careful not to think of the girls that way up to this point, but he could feel himself on a slippery slope.

They were his to protect, even if he wasn't *their* family.

"Sisters, plural? As in you met the other one?"

"She knows who I am and despises me on principle." Grayson gave a slight shake of his head. "I'm a threat to her family."

"And threats must be extinguished," Xander intoned. "Is she blonde?"

Grayson scowled. "What does that have to do with anything?"

"Does she like giving orders?" Xander asked excitedly. "What are her thoughts on suits?"

The point Xander was making did not escape Grayson. "The fact that she doesn't trust me is going to make my job more difficult."

"Gray?" Xander said gently. "That's not the difficult part."

Grayson thought fleetingly of the family portrait. Of the picture of Colin. Of Acacia saying that if she'd known about him earlier, things might have been different.

Damn Xander.

"Repeat after me, Gray: *My feelings are valid.*"

"Stop talking," Grayson ordered.

"*My emotions are real,*" Xander continued. "Go on. Say it."

"I'm hanging up on you now."

"Who's your favorite brother?" Xander called loudly enough that Grayson could still hear him even as he removed the phone from his ear.

"Nash," he answered loudly.

"Lies!"

Grayson's phone vibrated. "I'm getting another call," he told Xander.

"More lies!" Xander said happily. "Give my regards to Girl Grayson!"

"Good-bye, Xander."

"You said *good-b—*"

Grayson hung up before Xander could finish, switching over to take the incoming call. "Yes?"

On the other end of the line, there was silence.

"Hello?" Grayson tried. *See?* He aimed a mental retort at Xander. *I say hello.*

"Is this Grayson Hawthorne?" The voice that asked that question was female and unfamiliar. There was something about it—the tone, the timbre, the spacing in that question—that kept him from hanging up.

"To whom am I speaking?" Grayson asked.

"That doesn't matter." She said that like a simple truth, but the subtle rise and fall of her pitch and the way her voice sounded to his ears made him think that she was wrong.

Who this girl was mattered very much.

"To whom am I speaking?" Grayson repeated. "Or would you prefer I rephrase the question: On whom am I about to hang up?"

"Don't hang up." That wasn't a plea, but it wasn't quite an order, either. "You're speaking with someone from *whom* the Hawthorne family has taken a great deal."

The way she tossed the word *whom* right back at him did not go unnoticed—and neither did the way her voice got a little quieter and a little deeper.

"I presume that when you say *the Hawthorne family*, you mean my grandfather." Grayson kept his own tone even. "Whatever Tobias Hawthorne did or didn't do, it's none of my concern."

That was a lie, the kind that even Grayson couldn't will into being true.

"My father shot and killed himself when I was four years old." The girl's voice was calmer than it should have been. "I was the only one in the house with him when it happened. And do you know what the last thing he said to me was?"

Twin muscles in Grayson's throat tightened. "How did you get this number?" he demanded. In the back of his mind, he could see it. *A small girl. A man with a gun.*

"Shockingly, asshole, my father's last words were not *How did you get this number*."

Grayson waited for her to tell him what those last words had been, and when she didn't, he realized: She'd hung up.

I am not responsible for the things the old man did. Grayson stared at the phone for far too long, then put it down. The only things he was responsible for right now were testing that blank index card for invisible ink and getting dressed.

What the hell *did* people wear to high school parties?

CHAPTER 29

GRAYSON

You *have* worn shorts before, haven't you?"

Grayson narrowed his eyes at Gigi. "I don't want to talk about it."

Instead, he took in the scene around them. The Trowbridge abode had one of those modern, open floorplans. The only thing demarcating the foyer, dining room, kitchen, living room, and Great Room from one another was the decor. Overhead, a dozen teenagers leaned against a minimalist railing. At least three of them appeared to be trying to toss Ping-Pong balls over the railing and into plastic cups below.

Their aim was horrible.

A ball ricocheted by. Grayson didn't even blink. Instead, he assessed the partygoers on the ground floor—and those he could see through glass doors leading out back to the pool. There were perhaps fifty or sixty teenagers here total. *No adults.*

Grayson let his gaze return to Gigi, who smiled impishly. "Can you dance?" she asked Grayson. "If I can't sneak back to the private wing unassisted, I might need you to dance."

"You will not need me to dance," Grayson replied in a tone that very few people would have dared to question.

"My job is stealth," Gigi told him seriously. "Yours is distraction. I believe in you, Grayson." She flashed her phone's screen at him. "And so does this cat."

Gigi grinned, pocketed the phone, and then nodded toward a staircase in the back corner. The steps were made of glass, each one seemingly suspended midair. Savannah stood three steps down from the top. There was a boy beside her and one step up. Clearly, the two of them were holding court.

"That's Duncan," Gigi murmured. "He has the personality of a bagel, but around here, people go for that." Then, as if compelled to be fair to both Duncan and bagels, she continued, "He's not bad. Just... boring. Expected."

Grayson watched as the boy in question put an arm around Savannah's waist. She didn't stiffen, didn't blink, didn't give a single indication that she felt it at all. "And Savannah does what's expected," he noted. *Give my regards to Girl Grayson!* he could hear Xander saying.

"More or less," Gigi replied. Without warning, she bounded off and returned a moment later holding an open bottle, which she promptly thrust into his hand. "Hold this. Try to look normal. And watch for my signal."

Before he could ask *What signal?* she was gone. Grayson looked down at the bottle in his hand, which had a bright yellow label and appeared to be... alcoholic lemonade of some sort?

He looked back to the staircase, to Savannah—and she looked straight through him.

Grayson took a drink. *Too sweet.* He resisted the urge to make a face and returned to taking the measure of his surroundings: the people, the music, the place, all of it. While most of the furniture was clearly expensive, far too many of the pieces aimed to impress. The result fit the version of Kent Trowbridge that Grayson had seen the night before. Neither possessed any real finesse.

Moving through the party, Grayson kept his head down and his eyes open. He'd attended charity galas and business events, cocktail hours, professional sporting events, and the opening of the New York Stock Exchange.

He could handle one high school party.

"I haven't seen you at one of these before." A girl fell in next to him and smiled, and the next thing Grayson knew, he was surrounded by no fewer than three of her friends, all exits blocked.

"One of these . . . parties." Grayson tried to sound *normal*. He took a very normal swig out of the bottle in his hand. *Still too sweet.*

"If you went to Carrington Hall or Bishop Caffrey," the girl said coyly, "I'd know."

"I'm just visiting." Grayson gave up on attempting to seem normal and gave her a very Hawthorne look. "And I'm too old for you."

"I knew it!" one of the other girls declared. "See! I told you all." She grinned at Grayson. "You're Grayson Hawthorne."

Grayson didn't bat an eye. "No, I'm not."

"You totally are!" Still grinning, the girl turned to her friends. "He totally is."

"I am so sorry that Avery girl took all of your money," one of the others said seriously.

"And chose your brother," another one added.

"And broke your heart!"

"But not your spirit." The bravest of the girls reached out and laid a hand on his arm.

Grayson found himself wishing he had a suit jacket to button or sleeves to cuff. *Now would be a good time for that signal*, he told Gigi silently—to no avail. "Avery didn't take anything," he said stiffly. "And she didn't—"

"You don't have to talk about it," one of the girls assured him. "Can I get a picture?"

Grayson set his jaw. "I would prefer that you did—" *Not.* He didn't even get a chance to say the last word before she squeezed in next to him.

"One more!"

"Smile!"

"This is unreal!"

"Can I get you another... hard lemonade, Grayson?"

He was going to kill Gigi. For all he knew, she was already searching Kent Trowbridge's office while he served as distraction *just by existing.*

"Who are you here with?"

This time, Grayson summoned up a response. "Friends of the family." He looked back toward the staircase, where Savannah and the Trowbridge boy were still holding court.

"Oh," one of the girls said flatly. "Her."

"It's a good thing we saved you, then," another declared.

Grayson arched a brow. "And why," he asked crisply, "is that?"

"Savannah Grayson thinks she's so much better than everyone else."

"I mean, look at what she's wearing. This isn't brunch at the country club."

"And the *heels*—she's already, like, six feet tall!"

"And the way she just expects to win, to get *everything*."

"She's such a bitch! I'm surprised Duncan hasn't gotten frostbite."

"That's enough." Grayson didn't raise his voice. He didn't have to. And still, not a single one of them looked at him the way they'd looked at her.

"Friiiiiigiiiiiiid." A guy joined them. He'd apparently been close enough to hear the topic of their conversation, but not close enough to realize that he was, in fact, taking his life in his own hands with that comment.

Grayson took a single step forward, and then Gigi appeared at his side. "This wasn't what I meant," she whispered, as a vein pulsed in Grayson's temple, "when I said *dance*."

CHAPTER 30

GRAYSON

"So your name really is Grayson." That was Gigi's takeaway once the two of them had extricated themselves from the party. "And you're famous. That could complicate things, but as a rule, I'm in favor of complications." She led him to a door in another wing that definitely should have been locked. "I am also in favor of lock-picking." Gigi smiled serenely as she pushed the door inward. "Voilà."

Grayson glanced at the lock as he stepped into the room. It wasn't an easy model to pick. "Been planning on a life of crime for a while?" he asked.

"I get bored easily," Gigi informed him. "And when I'm bored, I learn things. All kinds of things." The emphasis she put on the word *all* was mildly concerning, but it wasn't his priority at the moment.

Grayson scanned Kent Trowbridge's home office with military precision and a Hawthorne's eye for detail. There were built-in shelves along three walls, and the spacing on two of them didn't match the third. The expensive rug covering the dark wood floors had a fringe that was tangled at one corner. All the cabinets and drawers had locks. There wasn't a single family photo, though there was a painting of Trowbridge himself, hanging just behind the desk.

Gigi made a beeline for the computer. She tapped at the keys, then began searching through papers on the top of the desk. "I've known Mr. Trowbridge my whole life. He *thinks* he's tech-savvy, but I would bet big money he has his passwords written down somewhere."

Leaving Gigi to her search, Grayson squatted to observe the tangled fringe on the rug. He flipped the corner back and was rewarded with the key to the desk.

"You are *magic*," Gigi declared. She slid across the desk, ballerina leapt to his side, snatched the key from his hand, and had the desk drawers open in three seconds flat.

"Victory!"

Grayson crossed to her side of the desk. There, taped to the bottom of the drawer, was a piece of paper containing at least forty passwords.

Gigi scanned them. "This one's labeled *DTC*." She pointed to a password three down from the top, which began with those three letters. "Desktop computer."

Grayson considered trying to get between Gigi and the computer but assessed his likelihood of success as poor. Instead, he slipped his phone out of his pocket, took a picture of the passwords, closed and locked the drawers, and returned the key to its original location under the rug.

"Covering our tracks," he told Gigi. *And assuring that I'm the one with the rest of the passwords.* As an attorney, tech-savvy or not, Trowbridge would almost certainly have privileged documents password-protected or saved to a secure server. For now, the computer would keep Gigi busy, allowing Grayson to tend to other matters.

One couldn't grow up in Hawthorne House without learning to spot a shelf that wasn't just a shelf. It didn't take Grayson long to locate a hinge—or the release. As soon as he'd triggered it, the shelf opened like a door. Behind it, built into a recess on the wall, was a safe.

Grayson glanced back at Gigi, who was so thoroughly immersed in searching the computer that she noticed nothing. *She's got an external hard drive.* Grayson registered that as he returned his attention to the safe. Unlike Gigi, he hadn't learned to pick locks out of boredom. The walls of his childhood playroom had been lined with them, each one a puzzle, a challenge. And when it came to challenges, a Hawthorne never really had a choice. All four brothers knew how to crack certain types of combination locks.

The only question was if this was one of them.

Grayson brought his hand up to the dial, and then he heard something. *Voices, out in the hall.* Without a moment's hesitation, he righted the bookshelf, obscuring the safe. He darted to the door, flipped the lock, then looked back at Gigi, who was staring at the shelves now obscuring the safe, which she had most definitely noticed.

The voices in the hallway drew closer.

Grayson met Gigi's eyes. She shook her head, then gestured emphatically to the computer and the external hard drive. Her meaning was clear: She wasn't done. He heard the distinct sound of a key being slipped into a lock. In a single motion, Grayson bounded across the room, grabbed Gigi, and sank with her to the floor behind the desk. She wiggled out of his grasp enough to dart a hand up and turn the monitor off just as the door to the office opened.

"You wanted privacy." That voice was male, but it did not belong to Kent Trowbridge. "You've got it."

"I just needed a moment to breathe." *Savannah.* Grayson recognized her voice instantly. *Which suggests the other belongs to a Trowbridge—just not the father.*

"You're breathing just fine, baby."

Grayson did not trust the boy's tone. He turned his head slightly, silently, leaning so that he could barely see past the edge of the desk. Duncan Trowbridge hooked an arm around Savannah from behind, placing a hand flat on her stomach. That hand creeped upward.

"You could be nicer to people, you know," Duncan murmured. "Including me."

Grayson's jaw tensed. He had no right to watch this, so he averted his eyes just as Duncan Trowbridge's hand made it to the strap of Savannah's top—and began working that strap down.

"I'm nice enough." Savannah's tone could have cut glass, but she didn't step away from the boy. Grayson would have heard it if she had.

"Show me how nice you can be."

"Come on, Duncan." Now there was a step, an audible click against the part of the floor that wasn't covered by the rug.

"You're my girlfriend, Savannah."

Grayson heard another step—this one, Duncan's. *Closing in on her. Bastard.*

"You're beautiful," the boy continued, and the words struck Grayson as accusatory.

"We should get back to the party." Savannah didn't sound distressed. She sounded like a person with an ironclad grip on control.

"You're the one who said you wanted privacy." Duncan seemed to be trying to make those words low and inviting, but they must not have had the effect he intended. "What, you wanted privacy from me, too?"

"No." Savannah spoke clearly. "Of course not."

Was Grayson imagining the strain in her voice? Now that Savannah and Duncan had moved, he couldn't see anything of either of them except for their feet. He looked to Gigi, whose eyes were wide.

"Then relax," Duncan murmured.

Was she okay?

"I am relaxed."

"Just let me touch you."

Savannah's heels sidestepped. "We should get back to the party. To your friends."

"Be nice. They're *our* friends." He stepped closer to her even than he'd been before. She didn't move. "*Be nice,*" Duncan Trowbridge murmured again, and whatever he was doing, Savannah just stood there.

Get your hands off my sister. Grayson could feel the words building inside him. It didn't matter that saying them would reveal his presence in a room where he was not supposed to be. It didn't matter that Savannah didn't consider him her brother or that Gigi didn't even know they were related.

Savannah had said—twice—that she wanted to go back to the party. She'd stepped away from her boyfriend. *Twice.* And all he'd had to say to that was *Be nice.*

Grayson stood, flowing to his feet with power and grace, but before he could say or do anything, Gigi popped up beside him. "Fancy meeting you two here!" she said loudly.

Duncan stepped abruptly back from Savannah, who righted her clothes.

"Gigi?" Duncan appeared confused—and possibly inebriated. *That shall make killing him easier.* "What the hell?" Duncan turned to Savannah. "Did you know she was back there?"

Savannah shot Gigi a withering look—and Grayson a worse one. "I did not."

Duncan suddenly remembered where they were and scowled. "What are you and this guy doing in my dad's—"

Grayson didn't wait for the kid to finish the sentence. "Walk away."

Duncan blinked. "Excuse me?"

Holding on to his fury by a hair, Grayson exercised steellike restraint in taking just one more step. "Walk. Away."

Duncan turned to Savannah. "Who the hell is this guy?"

You're about to find out, Grayson thought, but Gigi hopped in front of him and offered up her own answer to the question. "He's . . . my new boyfriend!"

Grayson was horrified. By the look of Savannah's expression, she was the same.

"Boyfriend?" Duncan repeated dumbly.

"I am not her boyfriend," Grayson said emphatically.

Gigi elbowed him in the ribs. "He doesn't like labels," she declared. "And we were here for the same reason as you two. Privacy."

"No," Grayson gritted out. "No privacy!"

"I'm going back to the party." Savannah looked to Duncan. "Are you coming?"

She brushed past him. Grayson didn't expect that to work, but Duncan Trowbridge was apparently less concerned with the intruders in his father's study than he was with his own frustration. As the two of them made it to the hall, Grayson heard the boy mutter, "You don't have to be such a bitch."

Grayson lunged forward, and Gigi popped in front of him again. Logically, Grayson knew that picking a fight with Duncan Trowbridge wasn't a good idea. Logically, he knew that Savannah wouldn't thank him for it.

"Breathe," Gigi advised him.

Grayson did. "I thought," he said, his voice razor-sharp, "you said he was boring." That wasn't the word Grayson would have used to describe what they'd just seen and overheard.

"I've never heard him talk to her like that," Gigi replied, her voice uncharacteristically quiet. "They're normally so...perfect."

The word hit Grayson like a slap. How many times had he heard himself described that way? How many times had he punished himself for being anything less?

Gigi walked back to the desk. She turned the computer monitor back on. "Transfer complete," she reported quietly. She glanced over at the bookshelves. "Any chance you know how we can get into that safe?"

There was a chance, a good one, but not as good as the chance that if anything went missing, Kent Trowbridge would talk to his son and demand to know who'd had access to his study. *I can always come back.*

Would it be legal? No.

Would it be easy? Likely not.

But neither of those things could stop a Hawthorne. "No," Grayson told Gigi. "And we should go before anyone else figures out we're in here. I've got the passwords." He nodded toward the hard drive. "What did you download?"

"All the PDFs, docs, and image files." Gigi paused. "I should check on Savannah. She likes to pretend that she doesn't have feelings to hurt, but..."

But. The muscles in Grayson's abdomen tightened. "I can take the hard drive."

"That's okay," Gigi told him. "I can store it in my cleavage."

Grayson blanched.

"Kidding! I don't have cleavage. But I do have a purse. And I fully intend to stay up all night going through files, once I convince my sister to bail on this party. Can you send me the passwords?"

After I make some alterations. As the two of them exited the office, Grayson scanned the hall and his gaze landed on a window. On the front lawn, near the street, he could make out a figure leaning lazily back against a truck.

The figure wore a cowboy hat.

"Grayson?" Gigi prompted. "You'll send me the passwords, right?"

"I will," Grayson confirmed. "But there's something I have to take care of first."

CHAPTER 31

GRAYSON

Nash rocked casually back on his heels as Grayson approached.

"What are you doing here?" Grayson asked flatly.

"I could ask you the same thing, little brother." Nash liked to perpetually remind Grayson who the older brother was in their relationship—and who was the kid.

"Xander told you where I was and what I'm doing," Grayson concluded.

Nash neither confirmed nor denied that statement. "You're playing with fire, Gray."

"Be that as it may, I do not recall asking for backup." Grayson gave Nash a hard look. His older brother offered him a knowing one in return. "Where's your fiancée?" Grayson asked pointedly. *Libby needs you, Nash. I don't.*

"Back at Hawthorne House getting ready for Cupcake-a-Palooza," Nash replied, his tone as casual as his posture. "Where's your brain at, Grayson?"

Grayson made a mental note to throttle Xander. "I have everything under control."

Nash cocked a brow at him. "If that was true, you would have noticed me tailing you on the way here."

Grayson hadn't noticed a damn thing. "I don't need your help," he gritted out.

Nash removed his cowboy hat and took a step toward him. "Then why haven't you noticed I'm not your only tail?"

Damn you, Nash. Grayson pulled the Spider onto the highway and let his gaze flick to the rearview mirror just in time to see another car do the same. The vehicle was black, nondescript. The driver knew how to hang back. But now that Nash had tipped him off, Grayson recognized that the driver *always* hung back by exactly two cars.

The black car was two cars behind him on the highway.

When Grayson pulled off, the car pulled off but managed to fall back. *Two cars.*

Grayson took three rights in a row, and by the time the car had taken the third after him, Grayson had already pulled the Ferrari onto the shoulder of the road. There was sufficient light here, a gas station ahead. Grayson told himself that confronting and identifying his tail was a strategy, but on some level, he knew that he was spoiling for a fight—the fight he hadn't gotten from Nash, the fight he'd very nearly picked with the boy who'd dared to tell Savannah to *be nice.*

The black car drove past. Grayson got a picture of its plates just before the car turned right again. A moment later, Nash pulled into the gas station down the road, but Grayson refused to let himself be distracted by backup he hadn't asked for and didn't want. Instead, he focused on his quarry. *Let's see if you come back.*

Three minutes later, the black car did. This time, it pulled onto the shoulder of the road next to him. Down the street at the gas station, Nash got out of his car. Grayson noticed but ignored him.

I have everything under control, he'd told his brother. *I don't need your help.*

The driver's-side door of the black car opened. A lone figure stepped out, clothed in shadow. The other three car doors remained closed. *Just one threat to contend with*, Grayson thought. *Good.* There was a certain satisfaction in taking care of threats.

His pursuer—now his target—advanced from the shadows into light, pace unhurried, steps silent. Grayson took stock of what the light showed: a male, at least six foot two, long and lean with dark blond hair that hung over one eye all the way down to his cheekbone. He wore a threadbare gray T-shirt that did nothing to mask the sinewy muscles underneath, and Grayson knew, just from the way his opponent moved, that he was armed.

"And who might you be?" Grayson asked.

Stillness, sudden and absolute. "Who I am is less important than who I work for."

Young. Utterly unafraid. That was Grayson's immediate impression. *Probably fast.*

"Trowbridge?" Grayson said, looking to his opponent's face, to eyes like midnight beneath thick, angled brows, one of them slashed through with a small white scar.

"Not Trowbridge." The guy took a series of slow steps, circling Grayson. *Young. Unafraid. Probably fast.* Grayson added two more descriptors: *Dangerous. Hard.* Dark eyes glittered as the guy came to a sudden stop. "Guess again."

Grayson bared his teeth in a smile full of warning. "I don't guess." *Power and control.* It always came down to power and control—who had them, who didn't, who would lose them first.

"She wasn't kidding," his opponent replied, the words cutting through the night air like a butcher knife, "when she said you were arrogant."

Grayson took a single step forward. *"She?"*

The guy smiled and began to circle him once more. "I work for Eve."

NINE YEARS AND THREE MONTHS AGO

Jameson stood at the base of the tree house and looked up. Scowling at the cast on his arm, he moved toward the closest staircase.

"Taking the easy way up?"

That wasn't Xander or Grayson, who were supposed to be meeting him here. It was the old man. Jameson fought the urge to whip his head toward his grandfather and kept his gaze locked on the staircase instead.

"It's the smart thing to do," Jameson said. The sound of footsteps alerted him to his grandfather's approach.

"And are you?" the old man asked, the question pointed. "Smart?"

Jameson swallowed. This was a conversation he'd been avoiding for days. His eyes darted upward, searching the tree house for his brothers.

"I'm not who you expected to find here." Tobias Hawthorne wasn't a tall man, and at ten, Jameson was already past his chin.

But it *felt* like the old man towered over him anyway. "I'm afraid that your brothers are otherwise occupied."

There was a moment of silence, and then Jameson heard it in the distance: the telltale sound of a violin, the notes caressed and carried by the wind.

"Beautiful, isn't it?" the old man said. "But that's to be expected. Perfection without artistry is worth very little."

From the tone in his voice, Jameson *knew* that his grandfather had said those exact words to Grayson before sending him away. *He wanted me alone.*

Jameson glowered at the cast on his arm, then raised his eyes—and his chin—defiantly. "I fell."

Sometimes, it was better to just rip off the bandage.

"That you did." How was it that Tobias Hawthorne's words could sound so nonchalant and cut so deeply? "Tell me, Jameson, what did you find yourself thinking, midair, when your motorbike went in one direction and you the other?"

It had been during a competition, his third this year. He'd won the first two. "Nothing." Jameson spoke the word into the dirt.

Hawthornes weren't supposed to lose.

"And that," Tobias Hawthorne said, his voice low and silky, "is the problem."

Jameson lifted his gaze without being told. It would be worse if he didn't.

"There are moments in life," his grandfather the billionaire continued, "when we are gifted with the opportunity to go outside ourselves. To see the world anew. *To see what other people miss.*"

The emphasis in those words made Jameson draw in a breath. "I didn't see anything when I crashed."

"You didn't look." The old man let that hang in the air, and then he reached to knock lightly on Jameson's cast. "Tell me, does your arm hurt?"

"Yes."

"Is it supposed to?"

The question caught Jameson off guard, but he tried not to show it. "I guess."

"In this family, we do not guess." The old man's tone wasn't harsh, but it was *sure*, like the words he'd just spoken were as certain as the rise and fall of the sun. "You're old enough now for me to be honest, Jamie. I see a great deal of myself in you."

Jameson hadn't expected that, not at all, and it let him focus on his grandfather fully, completely.

"But you must know there are certain...weaknesses." Now that Tobias Hawthorne had Jameson's full attention, he clearly had no intention of letting it go. "Compared to your brothers," he said, "your mind is ordinary."

Ordinary. Jameson felt like the old man had reached into his chest and ripped out his heart. The fingers on his good hand curled into a fist. "You're saying I'm not as smart as they are." The words came out angry and fierce—but deep down, Jameson knew it was true. He'd always known it. "Grayson. Xander." He swallowed. "Nash?" That one was less clear.

"Why are you asking about Nash?" the old man said sharply. "The truth, Jameson, is that you are indeed intelligent."

"But they're smarter." Jameson wasn't going to cry. He *wasn't*. He hadn't cried when his arm had snapped, and he wasn't going to now.

"Grayson's mind is more efficient than yours and far less prone to error." The old man placed no special emphasis on that statement, but he did nothing to gentle it, either. "And Xander—well, he's the brightest of all of you and certainly the most capable of thinking outside the box."

Grayson was perfect. Xander was one of a kind. And Jameson just . . . was.

"Their gifts are not yours." The old man placed a hand on Jameson's chin, preventing him from looking away. "But, Jameson Winchester Hawthorne, a person can train their mind to see the world, to really *see* it." Tobias Hawthorne gave his grandson a frank, assessing look. "I have to wonder, though, once you see that web of possibilities laid out in front of you, unencumbered by fear of pain or failure, by thoughts telling you what can and cannot, should and should not be done . . ." The intensity in the old man's words built. "What will you do with what you see?"

I don't have to be ordinary. That was what Jameson heard. *I won't be. I'm not.* "Whatever I have to."

That was his answer—the only possible answer.

Tobias Hawthorne bestowed upon him a slight nod and an even slighter smile. "When you have certain weaknesses," he said softly, rapping once on Jameson's cast, "you have to want it more."

Jameson didn't wince. "Want what more?"

"Everything." Without another word, the old man started climbing the stairs. Three steps in, he looked back. "I'll see you at the top."

Jameson didn't take the stairs. Or the ladder. Or the slide—or anything that could even remotely be considered the easy way up. *Forget your arm. Ignore the pain.* He tuned out the sound of perfect Grayson's beautiful music.

If he was going to be the best, he had to *want* it.

He began to climb.

CHAPTER 32

JAMESON

Night two at the Devil's Mercy had, thus far, passed much the same as the first: Avery losing at poker and Jameson winning down below—never too much, never at any one table for too long. Winning, after all, wasn't the point. Getting the lay of the land was. *Seeing.*

This was what Jameson saw in that underground palace of a gaming hall: mirrors that weren't just mirrors, moldings shaped to mask peepholes, triangular jeweled necklaces worn by the dealers that he deeply suspected contained listening devices or cameras or both. Jameson remembered the way that Rohan had thrown his voice in the atrium—*a trick of the walls*—and thought about Zella's response when asked about the Proprietor. *He's everywhere.*

And all Jameson had to do was impress him—or if not impress, intrigue.

A Hawthorne knew how to bide his time, so that was what Jameson did, playing at one table, then another, noting everything, including the fact that there were at least twice as many people here tonight as there had been the night before.

Word of the Hawthorne heiress's overconfidence at the poker tables was spreading.

Jameson stayed down below as Avery put on her show up in the alcoves, making his way through the old-fashioned games one by one. Hazard was easy enough to pick up but didn't require any real skill. Piquet was more interesting, allowing one player to face off directly against another. Points were awarded across multiple rounds. The deal alternated between the two players, with the strategic advantage to the non-dealer. The exact mechanisms of scoring were complicated.

Jameson was good at complicated. *"Quatorze."*

The man across from him scowled. *"Good."*

In the language of the game that meant the man couldn't best Jameson's set. "That gives me thirty," Jameson noted, leaning back in his chair. The man opposite him was, he had gathered, a power player in the financial sector—one who'd generously warned Jameson that he'd been a mainstay at the Mercy for longer than Jameson had been alive. "Thirty points on combinations alone," Jameson reiterated, and then he put the poor sod out of his misery. *"Repique."*

In other words: another sixty bonus points—and the game.

A velvet pouch was flung his way.

"Much appreciated." Jameson smirked, then looked back over his shoulder at the decorative mirror that stood far enough away from the tables to pose no danger of cheating.

Do you see me?

Do you see what I can do?

He stood and made his way to yet another table, ready to plunk his entire winnings down on a single hand if it meant drawing the attention of the Proprietor.

Don't wager anything you can't afford to lose. Rohan's warning came back to him. Fortunately, Jameson Hawthorne had a tendency to see warnings as a challenge, an invitation.

A single hand of vingt-et-un later, he'd doubled his winnings.

Will you notice if I start counting cards? With multiple decks in play, it wasn't a matter of remembering every card so much as assigning simple values to ranges of cards and keeping a running tally of those values, proportioned over the number of decks remaining.

What will you do, Jameson could hear the old man asking him, *with what you see?*

Rohan slid in for the dealer. Jameson didn't so much as blink, but the other men at the vingt-et-un table reacted visibly to the Factotum's presence. This was Rohan the charmer, handsome and wicked, his posture not threatening in the least, yet the other players radiated poorly masked unease.

"December fourth, nineteen eighty-nine." Rohan offered up a roguish smile as he began expertly dealing out the cards. "That was a Monday. Boxing Day, eighteen fifty-nine—also a Monday." With a single face-up card in front of each player, Rohan dealt a card to himself, facedown. "I've always had a mind for dates." He dealt five more face-up cards—one to each of them, including himself. "And numbers." Rohan looked to the man to Jameson's left and arched a brow. "January eleventh, March sixth, June first, all of this year. Shall I rattle off the days of the week?"

The man to Jameson's left said nothing, and Rohan shifted his gaze past Jameson to a second man. "Would you like to hear them, Ainsley?"

"I'd like to play," the man blustered.

"Play?" Rohan said, leaning forward slightly. "Is that what you call your recent activities?"

The question seemed to suck the oxygen out of the room.

"You know the rules." Rohan's smile relaxed, his eyes crinkling slightly at the corners. "Everyone here knows the rules. Since the two of you have been in this together, here's what we'll do. We'll play this hand I've dealt, *you* and *you* and me. If I win..." Rohan's smile fell away, like sand blown smooth by the wind. "Well, you know what happens if I win." Rohan nodded to the men's face-up cards. "If either of you win, I'll let you fight it out in the ring."

One thing that Jameson had learned early on about observing the world was to pay attention to blank spaces: pauses in sentences, what wasn't said, places where crowds should have been gathered but weren't. A blank face. An opening.

No one in this secret, underground lair of luxury and wagers was looking at the vingt-et-un table now.

"What if we both win?" the man to his left said. Jameson was fairly certain the guy was a politician—and even more certain he was sweating.

"The offer's the same." Rohan flashed another easy smile, but there was something unsettling about it. The Factotum was wearing another red suit this evening, with black underneath, an ensemble fit for the club's namesake. "Where angels fear to tread, have your fun instead," he murmured, his eyes flashing. "But remember..."

The house always wins.

Rohan shifted his gaze to the man on the right and waited. The man took another card. His friend did not.

Rohan dealt himself a card. He flipped the facedown one over. "Dealer wins."

The men said nothing, their faces ashen. The moment Rohan stepped away, the dealer slid back in, the jewel around her neck reminding Jameson that he was being watched.

They all were.

The dealer gathered the losing cards, then nodded to Jameson. "You still in?" she asked.

Out of the corner of his eyes, Jameson saw a man with thick red hair and features that looked carved from stone—and then he saw the space around the man. Other people got out of his way.

Jameson tracked the man's progression, then turned back to the dealer, in her old-fashioned ballgown. "Actually," he said, "I'm feeling like a game of whist."

"You'll need a partner."

Jameson turned to see Zella standing behind him. "Are you volunteering?" he asked her.

"That depends," the duchess replied. "How often do you lose, Jameson Hawthorne?"

Jameson was used to being the one who assessed other people, looking for the right play. It was interesting to him to see this woman do the same. *How often do I lose?* "As often as it takes," he told her, "to win the games that matter most."

Jameson could practically feel the duchess reading him the way *he* read people. "You have a specific opponent in mind," she noted. "For your game of whist."

Jameson didn't deny it. "Who is he? The red-haired man?"

In answer, Zella began to walk toward the whist table where the man in question now sat. *He appeared right after Rohan dealt with those men.* The timing seemed a bit too coincidental, as did the way people looked at—and avoided looking at—this man who dripped power.

The Proprietor?

"The answer to the question you're really asking?" Zella murmured beside him. "It's no."

She'd zeroed in on the question beneath the question with remarkable ease. "Who are *you*?" Jameson asked the woman beside him.

"I'm just a woman who married a duke." Zella gave a slight shrug, as elegant as the teardrop sapphire that hung around her neck. "A nonroyal duke, for what that's worth. Handsome. Young."

You love him, your duke. Jameson wasn't sure where that instinct came from, but he didn't second-guess it, and he didn't press for details about her marriage. "Just marrying a duke wouldn't get you membership here."

Zella smiled. "You could say I have a gift for turning glass ceilings into glass castles."

Glass castles? Jameson probed the phrase for meaning. *Beautiful, but still constraining.* They'd nearly made their way to the whist table.

With long, graceful strides, Zella came to stand behind the duo slotted to play against the red-haired man. "Would one of you gentlemen mind—"

Both men stood before the duchess even finished the request. Jameson wondered if they were that motivated to give Zella what she wanted—or if they simply didn't want to play against the man who'd claimed a seat at their table.

Whoever he was.

Zella took one of the vacated chairs and gestured toward the other. "Mr. Hawthorne?"

Jameson sat.

"Zella," the man said with an arch of his brow.

"Branford." Zella met Jameson's gaze again. "Shall we begin?"

CHAPTER 33

JAMESON

Branford played forcefully, efficiently, and with absolutely no chitchat. Whist was considerably simpler than piquet, and Jameson picked it up quickly.

But not quickly enough.

"You shouldn't be here." Branford eyed the cards Jameson had just played. "Boy." He laid down his next play—and just like that, Jameson's team lost.

Strangely, Zella didn't seem to mind.

Branford spared a perfunctory glance for his partner. "See that my half is credited to my account." He stood—and then abruptly sat back down in the wing-backed chair, inclining his head downward.

It took Jameson the span of a heartbeat to realize why: Avery stood at the top of the magnificent staircase—and she wasn't alone. A man with slicked-back white hair and a barely there salt-and-pepper beard stood next to her. He wore all black and held a shining silver cane.

Not silver, Jameson realized. *Platinum.*

Every single person in the room sat like Branford had, their heads angled toward the floor. *Like bowing before a king.* The man—*the Proprietor*—could have been seventy or ninety or anything in between. He put weight on the cane and held his free arm out to Avery.

She took it.

As they descended, Branford met the Proprietor's eyes and gave the slightest nod of his head.

Once you see that web of possibilities laid out in front of you, unencumbered by fear of pain or failure... What will you do with what you see?

Jameson didn't incline his head. In sharp contrast to the rest of the room, he didn't stay seated. He climbed to his feet and walked past Branford. Fully aware that every eye in the room was on him now, he strolled to meet Avery and the Proprietor at the bottom of the stairs. He lifted his gaze to the Proprietor's.

And he winked.

What was life without a little risk?

CHAPTER 34

JAMESON

The ride back through the underground canal was quiet. The boat had been left unmanned, leaving Jameson to pole. Avery was silent beside him.

Jameson looked at her out of the corner of his eyes, and he knew. Just from the set of her lips and the way she stared out at the water, he knew.

"*Tahiti*, Heiress."

Her chest rose and fell, one slow breath. "I've been offered entrance to the Game."

On some level, Jameson had known it the moment he'd seen the Proprietor standing next to her at the top of the stairs. "Tell me you accepted," he said, his voice low. "Tell me you didn't ask him to extend the offer to me, too."

Avery looked down, shadows rippling across her features. "Why wouldn't you want me to—"

"Damn it, Heiress!" Jameson bit out. Muscles tensing, he pulled the pole from the river. Water dripped onto the boards, onto him, but he barely noticed. He set the pole down then straightened and stepped toward her, the slight vessel rocking beneath his feet. "I didn't mean that."

"Yes," Avery said, her chin coming up and her hair falling away from her face. "You did. And my asking the Proprietor to include you didn't work, so clearly, it was the wrong call."

Jameson hated that he'd snapped at her, hated feeling like her win was his loss. Refusing to continue feeling that way, he brought his hands to the nape of her neck, his fingers curling gently into her hair.

"You don't have to be so gentle." Avery's voice was low, but it echoed through the canal, the two of them illuminated only by the lantern on the front of the boat and the slight glow from the stone all around them.

Jameson angled her head back. Her neck was bare, her face still cast in shadow. "Yes. I do."

The next instant, Avery's fingers were buried in his hair—and *she* wasn't gentle. There were times when the anticipation of their lips touching was as powerful as any kiss, but neither one of them was in the mood for anticipation right now.

He needed this. He needed *her.* Kissing Avery always felt *right.* It felt like *everything*, like *more*, like there was a purpose to his hunger, and this was it.

This was it.

This was it.

And still, he couldn't turn off the part of his brain that said he'd failed. That yet again, he wasn't enough. *Ordinary.*

Avery was the one who pulled back—but only slightly. Her lips grazed his as she spoke. "There's something else I need to tell you. It's about the man you were playing whist with."

Jameson's body pounded with the ghost of her touch, every one of his senses heightened. "Playing whist against," he corrected, recalling the tone with which Branford had called him *boy*.

"Did he tell you his name?" Avery asked.

"Zella called him Branford." Jameson knew Avery's tells, all of them. "You know something."

"I was informed that Branford is a title, not a name." Avery picked up his hand, turning it palm up "A courtesy title, which I guess means he hasn't inherited the big one yet."

Jameson looked down at his hand, held in hers. "And what exactly is the big one?"

Avery sketched a *W* on the palm of his hand, and Jameson felt her touch in every square inch of his body.

"According to the Proprietor," Avery murmured, "Branford is the eldest son and heir of the Earl of Wycliffe." Another pause, another moment when Jameson's body registered just how close to hers it was. "And that makes him Simon Johnstone-Jameson," Avery finished, "Viscount Branford."

CHAPTER 35

JAMESON

Ian had some explaining to do.

"Fancy meeting you here," Jameson greeted from the shadows as the man in question ambled into the hotel room, drunk or hungover or possibly both.

Ian's head whipped up. "Where did you come from?"

It was a reasonable question. After all, this room was on the fourth floor of a very nice, very secure hotel. Jameson glanced meaningfully at the window in response.

"I would have called on you at King's Gate Terrace, but we both know that flat isn't yours." It hadn't taken Jameson long to figure out that Ian wasn't in residence—or for the security guard to stiffly suggest he check this hotel. "King's Gate Terrace belongs to Branford," Jameson continued. "Or should I say Simon? The viscount?"

"So you've met my brother." Ian took a perch on the edge of the desk. "A real charmer, isn't he?"

Jameson thought briefly of his own brothers—of traditions and rivalries and history, of what it meant to grow up alongside someone, to be formed in contrast to them. "The charmer beat me at whist."

Ian took that in. For someone who had obviously been drinking, he'd sobered quickly. Jameson waited for a cutting comment about his loss, a dig, a lecture, *judgment*.

"I've never cared much for whist," Ian said with a shrug.

The oddest feeling seized Jameson's chest.

"And the King's Gate Terrace flat isn't Simon's, by the way," Ian continued flippantly. "If you recall, I have more than one brother."

Both older, Jameson remembered Ian telling Avery. "And a father who's an earl," Jameson added, focusing on that.

"If it helps," Ian offered lazily, "it's one of the newer earldoms. Created in eighteen seventy-one."

"That doesn't help." Jameson gave Ian a look. "And neither does sending me into the Devil's Mercy unprepared for what I'd find there." For *who* he'd find there.

"Simon is barely a member." Ian waved away the objection. "He hasn't shown his face at the Mercy in years."

"Until now."

"Someone must have informed my brother of my loss," Ian admitted.

"You think he's trying to procure an invitation to the Game." Jameson did not phrase that as a question.

"As a general rule," Ian replied, "my brother does not *try* to do anything."

He succeeds. The words went unspoken, but Jameson responded as if they had not. "You're saying that Simon Johnstone-Jameson, Viscount Branford, gets what he wants."

"I'm saying," Ian replied, "that you *cannot* let him win Vantage."

There was something raw and brutal in that *cannot*. Jameson didn't want to hear it—or understand it or recognize it—but he did.

"Growing up the third-born son of an earl," Ian said after a moment, his voice thick, "was, I'd imagine, a bit like growing up the third-born grandson of an American billionaire." Ian walked over to the window and looked down at the wall that Jameson had scaled to break in here. "One perfect brother," he continued, "one brilliant one—and then there was me."

He wants me to feel that we're the same. Jameson recognized the move for what it was. *He played me before. He doesn't get to play me again.*

But when Ian turned back from the window, he didn't look like he was playing. "My mother saw something in me," Ian Johnstone-Jameson said hoarsely. "She left Vantage to *me*." He took a step forward. "Win it back," he told Jameson, "and someday, I'll leave it to you."

That promise hit with the force of a punch. Jameson's ears roared. *Nothing matters unless you let it.* "Why would you do that?" he shot back.

"Why not?" Ian replied impulsively. "I'm not the settling down type. It'll have to go to someone, won't it?" The idea seemed to be growing on him. "And it would drive Simon mad."

That last sentence, more than anything else, convinced Jameson that Ian's offer was genuine. *If I win him Vantage, he'll leave it to me.* The Hawthorne side of Jameson recognized the obvious: He could win it for himself, cut Ian out.

But then it wouldn't be a gift from his father.

Jameson didn't linger on that thought for long. "Tonight, Avery received an invitation to the Game," he told Ian. "I haven't. Not yet."

Ian's bloodshot eyes focused on Jameson—and only on Jameson.

"Did the Proprietor appear at the top of the grand staircase and descend?"

Jameson gave a sharp nod. "With Avery on his arm."

"Then we must act quickly." Ian began pacing, and Jameson knew the man's mind was racing, knew exactly *how* it was racing. "The rest of the players will be chosen tomorrow evening. Tell me what you've done so far to win entrance to the Game."

Not enough, Jameson thought. "Tell me what you did to get banned first," he countered. "The Factotum knows that I'm your son."

Ian ran a hand roughly through his hair. "Little bastard knows everything."

Jameson shrugged. "That seems to be his job—that and keeping the membership in order." He thought back to the way Rohan had dealt with those men. "What did you do, Ian?"

What else don't I know?

"I lost." Ian turned his palms toward Jameson in an insincere mea culpa. "People who lose too much get desperate. The Factotum does not trust desperate men." Ian's lips curled into a smile, dark and wry. "And I may have upturned a chair or two."

So you have a temper. Jameson didn't dwell on that. This wasn't a time for dwelling on anything. "There were two men there tonight. I don't know what they did, exactly, but the Factotum—*Rohan*—he rattled off a series of dates, presumably ones on which they'd committed some kind of transgression. He offered them the chance to play him."

Ian tilted his head to the side, his body very still. "What were the terms?"

"If one or both of them won, they could fight it out in ring."

"Ah." Ian lifted a brow. "Loser in the ring takes the punishment for both. It would certainly make for motivated fighters—and a great deal of money wagered on the result. But that's not what happened, is it?"

"Rohan won the hand. He said they knew what would happen if he did." Jameson had a strong sense that everyone in that room had known. Everyone but him. "Were they banned the way you were?"

"Exile is considered a lighter punishment." Ian's characteristic air of detached amusement was back. "No, those poor sods, whoever they are, will pay a much steeper price." Ian rocked back on his heels. "It's not a coincidence the Factotum made an example of someone right before the Game."

Jameson's eyes narrowed. "What do you know that I don't?"

"Your heiress, she didn't actually join the Mercy, so I assume she didn't have to pay the levy."

Jameson thought back to Rohan's initial offer. *The levy to join the Devil's Mercy is much steeper.* "The cost of joining—how much is it?" When Ian didn't reply, Jameson amended his question. "*What* is it?"

Ian turned back to the window, and Jameson had the vague sense that he was checking to make sure they weren't being watched—or listened to. "There is a ledger in the Devil's Mercy, as old as the club itself. To gain membership, to pay the levy, you must provide fodder for the ledger. Blackmail material that could be leveraged against you."

Jameson felt his pulse speed up. "Secrets."

"Terrible ones," Ian agreed. "The Proprietor must have a way of keeping all those powerful men in line, after all." Ian spoke like he wasn't one of them. "A secret and proof. That's what the ledger contains. Those who cross the Proprietor quickly find themselves at his mercy."

The Devil's Mercy. Suddenly, the club's name held new meaning. "Does the Proprietor *have* any mercy?" Jameson asked.

"It depends on the offense. Occasionally, he'll ruin a man simply to remind the rest of us that he can, but more frequently, the punishment fits the crime. Men who risk the Proprietor's wrath find themselves at risk. Their levy becomes a prize to be won by their peers."

Jameson's mind raced as he put the pieces together. "The Game. It's not just for *assets* the house has won over the course of the year."

Ian's eyes locked on to his. "The winner may choose: a coveted prize or a forfeited levy, a disgraced member's page from the ledger."

A terrible secret, Jameson thought. *Blackmail material.* The kind that could ruin a person.

"The more powerful the member," Ian continued, "the more valuable his levy is to the rest. Tell me, who ran afoul of the Devil tonight?"

The Devil. Jameson wasn't sure if that was supposed to refer to Rohan or the Proprietor or the Mercy itself. "I don't know."

Ian stared at him hard, then looked away. "Maybe I'm asking too much of you."

Jameson felt like a needle had been stabbed straight through his chest. *Ordinary,* a voice inside him taunted. *Lesser.* He gritted his teeth. "Ainsley." Jameson pulled the name out of his memory. "Rohan addressed one of the men as Ainsley."

Ian cursed under his breath. "There's not a member of the Mercy that won't be grappling for an invitation to the Game now." The man stepped forward, an eerily familiar intensity in his vivid green eyes. "What have you done to earn one?"

Jameson didn't flinch, didn't hesitate, didn't blink. "I won at the tables."

"That won't be enough."

How many times had Jameson heard some iteration of those words? How many times had he said them to himself? *When you have certain weaknesses, you have to want it more.* "I issued a challenge."

"Tell me."

Jameson did.

"You *winked* at him? During the descent?" Ian threw his head back and laughed. It was so unexpected that Jameson almost didn't notice—*I have his laugh.*

Jameson was too much of a Hawthorne to dwell on that. "I was taught to see openings—and take them. For better or worse, the Proprietor will be keeping an eye on me now."

"If you're going to succeed," Ian replied, all trace of laughter gone from his tone, "you're going to have to do a hell of a lot more than win at the tables."

Know no fear. Hold nothing back. Jameson felt something unfurling inside himself. "Then I won't confine my winning to the tables." He could do this. He *was* this. "Tomorrow, I'll start the night in the ring."

CHAPTER 36

GRAYSON

Eve. Grayson felt nothing when he heard the name. He let himself feel nothing. "What do you want?" he asked Eve's spy.

"What *I* want," the dark-eyed boy replied, coming to a standstill, "is not your concern." The obvious implication was that what *Eve* wanted was.

Grayson was not prone toward forgiveness—not for himself, not for her. Betrayal tasted like failure still, bitter as a poisoned root, coppery like blood. Eve had used him to get what she wanted: the full power of her great-grandfather's fortune, his empire.

His employees, Grayson thought, assessing the spy who'd been tailing him through new eyes. Vincent Blake was dangerous. Anyone who worked for him was likely to be the same.

Raking his gaze over his adversary, Grayson saw flashes of ink on the spy's forearms. *Tattoos, obscured by his shirt.* A single back tendril was visible snaking out of his collar and climbing the side of his neck.

"Do you do everything Eve tells you to?" Grayson asked. He could have made that sound like an insult or a challenge. He didn't. The less you gave away with your tone, the more meaning you could extract from your opponent's response.

"You don't want to know what I've done." The guy didn't so much as blink.

"You'll have to tell her I spotted you." Grayson tried again, his tone just as neutral.

"You the kind of guy who likes to tell people what they have to do?" A question of that sort should have been accompanied by some sort of motion: a cock of the head, a narrowing of the eyes, a hardening of the muscles in the jaw. But the guy in front of Grayson was statue-still: unmoving, unmovable.

I don't have a word to say to you about the kind of man I am. "You can tell Eve that my stance hasn't changed. She made her choice. She's nothing to me."

Nothing except an error in judgment and a reminder of what happened when Grayson let his guard down. What happened when he made mistakes.

"If you think I'm going to tell Eve that, you're living in a dream world, rich boy." The spy shifted liquidly from stillness into motion, slowly circling Grayson once more, a predator playing with his prey—then he turned.

The spy spoke as he walked away but didn't look back. "For what it's worth, hotshot, *you* weren't the one she sent me to Phoenix to watch."

CHAPTER 37

GRAYSON

Eve had someone staking out the Grayson family. No matter how many times Grayson went over the facts, that was the conclusion he reached. And no matter how many times he came to that conclusion, as he drove back to the hotel, he couldn't banish the memory that wanted to come.

"I didn't mean to disturb you."

"Yes. You did." Grayson pulls himself out of the pool. The night air hits his skin like ice—or maybe that's a side effect of talking to a ghost.

The girl in front of him looks so much like Emily that he can barely breathe.

"My existence disturbs people." Her voice is like Em's, too, but with a different kind of sharpness, a more subtle blade. "Side effect of being an affair baby."

That statement reminds Grayson of who this girl really is—not a Hawthorne by name or blood but twisted in the branches of the family tree nonetheless, theirs to protect.

"What?" Eve demands, probably because of the way he's looking at her. She pushes her hair back from her face, and Grayson's gaze catches on the bruise on her temple—ugly, mottled edges pushing beyond the confines of a bandage. Someone hurt her.

And that someone will pay.

"Does it pain you?" He takes a step toward her, drawn like a moth to the flame.

"My existence?"

"Your wound."

Grayson finally wrenched himself from the memory and focused on what mattered: Eve had someone—a very dangerous someone—watching the Grayson family. Stalking them from afar. Given that Eve was one of the only people on the planet who knew that Sheffield Grayson wasn't *missing*, that was an utterly unacceptable risk.

She's got someone watching my father's family—and now that I'm here, watching me. Grayson was on high alert as he slipped the black key card into the door of his hotel room. He didn't so much as turn on the lights until he'd verified that the place was clean. No listening devices. No cameras.

No Nash.

When Grayson did finally turn on a lamp, the first thing he saw was the 3D printer he'd requested. He woke up his computer and was greeted by a circular red icon telling him the number of direct messages he'd missed from Gigi. *Seventeen.*

She wanted the picture he'd taken of Trowbridge's passwords, and she'd resorted to hairless cat pictures and all caps in her attempt to get it.

I WILL BUY YOU THIS TINY HAIRLESS KITTEN IF YOU DON'T GIVE ME WHAT I WANT.

Grayson felt a tug of affection. It was remarkable, really, how quickly she'd gotten under his defenses. *Don't get attached. You know what you have to do.*

Grayson transferred the photograph from his phone to his computer, then set about altering it. A 9 in one password became an 8, a 7 in another was changed into a 2. A *V* could be easily morphed to a *W*, an *L* to a *D*, a Z to a 7. Any digit could be deleted from the end of a sequence.

With every change Grayson made, he pictured Gigi's beaming smile, her bright, dancing eyes. He finished and sent her the photo, along with a message: *If you don't get anywhere tonight, I'll need a copy of the files tomorrow.*

He tried not to feel guilty about the fact that she wouldn't get anywhere—by design.

Set on his course, Grayson printed a copy of each of the keys he'd designed: one an exact duplicate of Gigi's and the other a decoy. Then he shot a message off to Zabrowski, with three directives.

The keys are ready for pickup.

You'll want to update me on your progress.

Attached you'll find a photograph of a car, complete with license plate. The driver was six foot two, approximately one-hundred-sixty-five pounds, blond hair, dark eyes, scar through his left eyebrow. Approximate age somewhere between sixteen and twenty, tattoos on upper arms and neck. I want identification and full background on him. Now.

Grayson made another transfer into Zabrowski's account as soon as the message was sent. Then he shut a door in his mind on everything related to Eve and her spy. His focus came to rest instead on the two items he'd brought home the day before: the not-a-USB-drive and the index card.

His earlier attempts at revealing invisible ink had gone nowhere, so this time, his gaze was drawn to the notches in the card: two on the top edge of the card, one on the right. The other two edges were unblemished. The notches were small. *Less than a centimeter, smooth, no distortion to the card.* If the card had been taped to the inside of the computer, could pulling it off—repeatedly—have caused the notches?

Am I seeing meaning where there is none?

Grayson picked up the fake USB and tested its resistance when he pressed it down on the card. *Nothing.* He thought of the altered photograph he'd sent Gigi, about the way he was setting her up to fail—and then he thought about Savannah and the way people talked about her, even as they fawned over him.

It's none of my business. Setting aside the items on the desk, Grayson put the keys he'd printed in an envelope and sent them to the front desk to await Zabrowski's pickup. Refusing to dwell on that action, he entered the largest of the suite's three bathrooms, flipped the shower on as hot as it would go, and stripped off his shirt.

Waiting for the steam inside the shower to build, he paced to the double doors that separated the bathroom from the attached bedroom. Pushing the doors open, he judged the frame to be just wide enough. With his arms in a V, he placed a palm flat on each side of the doorframe, and then he slowly lifted himself off the ground. Arms spread to either side, every muscle in them tense, every muscle in his chest and neck and abdomen the same, he held the position.

He watched the bathroom mirror fog over, watched his own image slowly disappear, and with it and the concentration it took to hold his position, thoughts and images bled from his mind one by one. First Gigi, then Savannah. Eve. Her spy. The girls at the party.

"I am so sorry that Avery girl took all of your money."

"And chose your brother."

"And broke your heart!"

His heart wasn't broken. It couldn't be when keeping himself aloft took every ounce of focus he had. When his thoughts finally stilled to silence, his arms gave out. He fell to the ground, to his knees.

He didn't stay down for long.

The shower was too hot, but Grayson didn't back away from the spray or turn down the heat. He wasn't sure how long he'd stood there when his phone rang. But when he turned the water off and stepped out of the shower, when he saw the call was incoming from a blocked number, he prepared himself.

Eve's spy would have reported back by now.

Grayson shouldn't have answered her call, but he did. "What do you want?"

"Answers." *That's not Eve's voice.* It was the girl who'd called before. Her register was lower than Eve's, not quite husky but only a hair's breadth from it. "Specifically, two of them."

"Two answers." Grayson's reply sounded haughty to his own ears.

"I was four." Within that lower register, her pitch rose and fell. "It was my birthday. I lived with my mom. I barely knew my father, but for some reason, I was with him that day."

Your father, Grayson filled in, but he didn't interrupt her, didn't stop her, forced himself to listen to every pause, every breath, every word.

"My father"—she said that phrase like she had to force herself to put those two words side by side—"gave me a candy necklace with just three pieces of candy left on it. I guess he ate the rest?" That only half sounded like a question. Her voice went husky, breaking at odd intervals like what she was saying broke her. "So. He gave me the necklace and a flower. A calla lily. And he leaned forward and whispered in my ear, *A Hawthorne did this.*"

She didn't pause, but Grayson's brain latched on to those words, forcing him to play catch-up as she continued speaking.

"And then he turned and started walking away, and that's when I saw the gun." *Now* she paused. "I couldn't move. I just stood there, holding what was left of that candy necklace and the flower, and I watched my father and his gun walk up the stairs."

There was something in the way she paced the words that made it sound like she was relaying something that had happened to someone else.

"And at the top of the stairs, he turned around, and he said words that didn't even make sense, gibberish. And then he disappeared. Less than a minute later, I heard the gun go off."

The deliberate lack of intensity in her voice hit him almost as hard as her words, as the mental image she'd given him.

"I didn't go upstairs." That sounded almost like a question. "I remember dropping the flower, and then, all of a sudden, my mom and stepdad were there, and it was over." This time, he heard her inhale, audibly, sharply. "I forgot about it. Blocked it out. And then a couple of years ago, I started hearing and seeing the name Hawthorne all over the news."

It wasn't a full two years ago. Grayson pushed down the urge to make that point. "My grandfather died."

"There was a new heiress. Mystery. Intrigue. A real Cinderella story. *Hawthorne. Hawthorne. Hawthorne.*"

Grayson thought about what she had said—what she had been told. *A Hawthorne did this.* "You remembered."

"In dreams, mostly."

For some reason, that hit him hard. *I almost never dream.* The words very nearly escaped him. "You said you had two questions." Grayson needed to keep this conversation on track.

"I said that I wanted two answers." Her correction was cutting and precise. She wasted no more time in specifying the first. "What did your grandfather do?"

Grayson could have argued with her, could have pointed out that Hawthorne was not an uncommon name. But instead, he thought of a room in Hawthorne House filled with stacks and stacks of files. "I could not say." He kept his voice just as curt as hers. "But probabilities being what they are, whatever Tobias Hawthorne did or did not do, it likely ruined your father financially." That was all he intended to say, but he couldn't shake the feeling that he owed her more.

Couldn't shake the thought of a little girl holding a single lily and a mostly eaten candy necklace. *Staring at an empty staircase. A gunshot ringing in her ears.*

"If you tell me your father's name..." Grayson started to say.

She cut him off. "No."

Annoyance surged. "What do you expect me to do without a name?"

"I don't know." She sounded...not vulnerable. Not angry, exactly. "The last thing he said, at the top of the stairs..."

"*Words that didn't even make sense,*" Grayson murmured.

"*What begins a bet?*" she quoted. "And then he said: *Not that.*" The girl waited for Grayson to speak, but impatience didn't let her wait long. "Does that mean anything to you, Hawthorne boy?"

What begins a bet? Not that.

"No." Grayson almost hated to say that to her.

"I shouldn't have called. I don't know why I keep doing this."

She was going to hang up. Grayson realized that simultaneously with another, more unexpected realization: He didn't want her to. "It might be a riddle." Grayson heard a little hitch of breath, then continued. "My grandfather was very big into riddles."

"What begins a bet?" The girl's voice took on a different tone now. *"Not that."*

And then she really did hang up. Grayson kept holding the phone to his ear for the longest time. He realized that he was dripping water onto the mat, that his skin, still pink from the punishing heat of the shower, was now chilled.

Grabbing a towel, he turned the riddle over in his head, and then he texted Xander. *Are you back at Hawthorne House?*

The reply came almost instantly: *Nope*, followed by a suspicious array of tiny illustrated symbols: a party popper, musical notes, a flame, and a crown. *But I have connections*, Xander's next text read. *What do you need?*

"Connections?" Grayson snorted—but that didn't stop him from replying to Xander's text. *I need someone to look back through the old man's List.*

CHAPTER 38

GRAYSON

That night, Grayson dreamed of a labyrinth. He stood at the center, glass shards suspended in the air all around him. He couldn't walk forward, couldn't step back without one slicing into his flesh. In the shining surface of each shard, he saw an image.

The black opal ring. Avery. Emily. Eve. Gigi and Savannah—

Grayson bolted up in bed, a phantom fist locked around his lungs. He tossed back the covers and reached over to hit a switch on the wall. The shade covering the bedroom window slowly rose, revealing that the sun was high in the sky.

He'd slept late.

Grayson checked his phone. No updates on the old man's List yet—and none from Gigi, for that matter. He considered reaching back out but fought the urge to do so. Patience was a virtue. He'd seen to it that she wouldn't get anywhere with her search of any password-protected files. That gave him time.

Once he had a decoy key...

Once he had a more thorough understanding of the situation with the FBI...

Once Gigi was ready to hand over the files...

Then Grayson would make his next move. In the meantime, if his presence in Phoenix had caused Eve to pull her spy off the Grayson family and onto him—and the night before suggested that she had—all the better.

The next morning, as Grayson was swimming his twentieth lap in the hotel pool, Zabrowski finally got back in touch.

I'm here.

The time for waiting was over.

Grayson changed into dry clothes and walked to meet Zabrowski in an alley two blocks away. The first thing the PI did was hand over two envelopes, each containing one of the models Grayson had supplied and a matching metal key. Grayson inspected the keys, ensuring a visual match between the color of the metal Zabrowski's contact had used and Gigi's key.

Finding the keys suitable, he slipped them into his suit pocket and brought his gaze back to rest on Zabrowski's.

"No luck on the paperwork for the twins' trusts," the man reported. "But I was able to get some answers about the investigation into Sheffield Grayson. They have him dead to rights on tax evasion and hiding significant streams of income offshore."

"No wonder the IRS is freezing accounts. And the FBI?"

"Very interested in where some of that income came from," Zabrowski replied. "It's looking like embezzlement."

"From his own company?"

"This is where it gets interesting. Turns out Sheffield Grayson only owned a thirty percent stake. His mother-in-law, who funded the thing, owned the rest."

Grayson rolled that over in his mind and remembered something Gigi had said. "He sold the company right after the girls' grandmother died. Assuming her interests in the company were included in one or more of the trusts she set up for her heirs, I'm guessing Sheffield Grayson was highly motivated to divest of the whole thing before the trustee started sniffing around."

The trustee. Trowbridge. The pieces of this puzzle were starting to fit together in Grayson's mind, but he didn't have enough information to see the whole of it yet. "How hard are the feds pushing the investigation?"

"Unclear."

"Have they had any luck locating him?" Grayson asked. That was as close as he could come to asking what he really wanted to know.

"None. Consensus seems to be that this guy is a slippery bastard."

As long as Grayson made sure that stayed the consensus, Avery would be fine. "Do you have anything else for me?" Grayson asked.

Zabrowski reached into his car and then handed a file to Grayson, who flipped it open to see a familiar face staring back. *Dark eyes. That scar through the eyebrow.*

"Mattias Slater," Zabrowski said. "Goes by Slate. Record is squeaky-clean, but his father's isn't—long list of charges, but only one set ever stuck."

Grayson skimmed through the file. "Expensive defense counsel," he noted.

"Until," Zabrowski said with a significant look, "that last set of felony charges."

The ones that stuck, Grayson thought. He wondered if Mattias

Slater's father had worked for the Blake family—for Vincent Blake. If so, that would explain the expensive lawyers. *Until he ran afoul of the boss?*

"What do we know about Mattias?" Grayson asked. "Personally?"

Zabrowski's eyes narrowed. "In a day? Not much. His father's dead. Mother filed medical bankruptcy last year."

Grayson thought back to his confrontation with Eve's spy. *You don't want to know,* Mattias Slater had said, *what I've done.*

"You want me to keep looking?" Zabrowski asked.

Grayson closed the file. "Prioritize the trust paperwork," he told Zabrowski. "But yes."

Grayson opened the door to the hotel lobby to find a very un-Haywood-Astyria scene in progress.

Gigi was standing on a wingback chair having a discussion with hotel security. "About yea tall," she was saying, "prone to eyebrow arching, very fond of imperative sentences, blond and broody."

"As you have already been informed by multiple parties, madam, we cannot provide information about guests."

"Would it help if I described his super sharp cheekbones or did a comedic impression of some kind?" Gigi asked winningly.

Grayson decided to intervene. "No," he said, striding to stand between Gigi and the guard. "That would not help. Please get down from that chair."

"*Eyebrow arch,*" Gigi told the security guard in a deep, dramatic voice. "*Followed by an imperative sentence.*"

Grayson could not help noticing the way the security guard's lips twitched. "I'll take it from here," he told the man.

Gigi hopped off the chair and grinned. "Ask me what I'm doing here, Grayson."

"What are you doing here?"

She rose up on her tiptoes. "We're in!"

"The files?" Grayson didn't show a hint of the surprise he felt. "The passwords?" He'd *changed* the passwords. She shouldn't have gotten anywhere with those files.

"Useless!" Gigi replied happily. "I spent the whole day on them and got nowhere. Buuuuuuut. . . ." Gigi's grin was broad enough to break her face. "Savannah found a fake ID hidden behind the electrical panel in the gym!" She practically vibrated with energy. "We know the name he used to open the box. We have the key. Next stop: the bank!"

Grayson thought about the duplicate key in his pocket and eyed the one around her neck. The clock was ticking now. He had to find a way to make the switch.

CHAPTER 39

JAMESON

The ring at the Devil's Mercy was smaller than a modern boxing ring and marked off with coarse, fraying ropes that whispered of another time.

"You shouldn't stay for this," Jameson told Avery as he clocked the way the first two fighters climbed up onto the platform: bare-chested, no shoes, no gloves.

"On the contrary." Rohan appeared beside them, dressed in black. The tuxedo should have looked formal, but he wore no tie, and the first four buttons on his shirt were undone. "She should stay." His dark eyes met Avery's. "Place a bet or two."

"Wouldn't I be wagering against the house?" Avery asked. Tonight was the third night, and she still had nearly two hundred thousand pounds to lose on the tables, per their deal.

"Consider your fee paid in full." Rohan smiled, his expression far too relaxed for Jameson's liking. "The third night was really more of an insurance policy on my part."

In other words: Whatever fish the Factotum had been after had already taken the bait. *Paid the levy,* Jameson thought, the words snaking their way through his brain. *Joined the club.*

And now, Rohan's concentration was elsewhere. *On the Game.*

The Devil's Mercy was even more crowded tonight than it had been the night before, as if the entire membership had turned out—men as old as their nineties and as young as their twenties, a few women but not many.

"Who should she bet on?" Jameson threw out the question to draw Rohan's attention away from Avery.

The Factotum turned toward the ring and the men inside it. "Can't you tell?" The two were evenly matched in size but moved differently. "I'll give you a hint: The one with the lighter step is one of our house fighters."

With those words, Rohan strode toward the ring, the crowd parting for him like magic. Rohan hopped up onto the platform but stayed outside the ropes. "You have two minutes to finish placing your bets," he announced. A trick of the space—or his voice—made the words seem like they were coming at Jameson from all sides.

He tracked Rohan's progression as the Factotum walked the outside edge of the ropes. *You never lose your balance, do you?* That was the impression that Jameson got, that Rohan would have moved with the same liquid grace across the edge of a skyscraper.

"For those who are joining us tonight for the first time or after a long absence," Rohan said with a flourish, "a reminder of the rules. Matches consist of an indeterminate number of rounds. A round ends when one of our fighters hits the floor." A cheer went up. "The match ends," Rohan continued, "when the person who hits the floor doesn't get up."

In other words, Jameson thought, his focus intense, his heart rate accelerating, *the only ways for a match to end are for a fighter to yield or be knocked unconscious.*

"No gloves." Rohan smiled again. *A warning smile.* "No rings. No weapons of any kind. No mercy."

The crowd echoed the words back at the Factotum. "No mercy!"

Rohan turned to the fighters in the ring. "As ever, if your face shows evidence of the fight, you'll be expected to find a way to recover discreetly. If you are unable to do so, the Mercy will be happy to provide assistance."

That sounded less like an offer than a threat.

Rohan jumped backward, landing on the floor below. "You may begin."

The first fight went three rounds, the second only one. The third match—between two house fighters—lasted the longest. Jameson ignored the bloodshed, the roar of the crowd, the raw brutality of the fighters and the mercenary glints in their eyes. He focused instead on the blank spaces.

The moves the fighters didn't make.

The openings they left.

The areas in the ring and around their bodies untouched by the blur of motion, by elbows and fists, feet and knees and heads.

The fractions of time that passed between moves.

Weaknesses—and the ways they compensated for them.

"You don't have to do this," Avery said beside him, her words lost to the noise of the crowd for everyone but him.

"On the contrary..." Jameson stole Rohan's turn of phrase. "I do. But you don't have to watch, Heiress."

She looked at him with one of those uniquely Avery expressions that made it hard for Jameson to remember life before her. "I'm not just watching, Hawthorne. I'll be placing a wager."

On him. She was betting *on him.*

In the ring, one of the two house fighters went down and didn't get up. The fresher of the two raised a fist in the air. *Victory.*

Rohan jumped back up to the edge of the ring. "We have a winner." The crowd roared its approval. "Do we have a challenger?"

Jameson raised his own fist into the air. Silence fell as the rich and the powerful turned to stare at him.

Jameson smirked a very Hawthorne smirk. "I'll give it a whirl."

CHAPTER 40

JAMESON

Jameson knew he didn't look like a fighter. He was the leanest of his brothers, his muscles sinewy, his limbs long. His default expression read as cocky. He looked like a privileged little prep school boy.

He didn't move like a fighter, either.

In the ring, Jameson stripped off his jacket and shirt, and if the audience noticed any of his scars, if anyone had the foresight to wonder how he'd gotten them or how high his tolerance for pain was, they gave no indication of it.

All except for Rohan, who cocked his head to the side and assessed him anew.

Jameson slipped his shoes off, then bent to pull off his socks. *Bare feet. Bare knuckles. Bare chest.* He stood staring straight ahead as blood and sweat were mopped off the floor of the ring.

The house fighter across from him took a swig of water and

shook his head. *Little fool doesn't stand a chance.* The guy couldn't have telegraphed the thought any more clearly.

Jameson didn't let himself smile. *Life's a game.* A familiar buzz of energy began to build inside him. *And all you get to decide is if you're going to play to win.*

"You may begin."

Jameson didn't circle his opponent. He mirrored the man's moves, anticipating each one with eerie accuracy, right down to the angle at which the guy held his head. Was mocking his opponent the smartest way to start a match?

Maybe not. But Jameson excelled at pissing people off, and he'd always been taught to play to his strengths.

He stopped mimicking the moment the house fighter threw his first punch and switched to dodging instead. The more times the guy tasted air, the angrier he got. Jameson slid into the white space on the man's weak side. Another punch came, thrown harder than the rest.

Hard enough to leave his opponent off balance.

When you see your moment, the old man's voice whispered all around him, *you take it.*

Jameson did. He spun, then went airborne, driving the lower part of his shin into the side of his opponent's head.

The house fighter went down and stayed down. Jameson straightened. He turned back to the crowd and hopped up to balance on one of the posts that held the ropes. "Looks like we have a winner," he said, preempting Rohan's line. "Do we have a challenger?"

Looking out at the crowd, his gaze found Avery's immediately. Behind her and to the left, making a concerted effort to blend into the crowd, was a man with slicked-back white hair. Gone was the salt-and-pepper beard, but he still held the cane.

The moment Jameson's eyes met his, the Proprietor stopped trying to blend. He hit his cane against the ground three times, hard.

I've got your attention now, Jameson thought. He stayed on the post, perfectly balanced, not even winded, as the crowd went silent. The Proprietor offered pointed applause. *One thundering clap. Two. Three.* And then he lifted his cane and angled the platinum handle toward the ring.

"Rohan," the Proprietor said pleasantly. "If you please?"

Jameson looked to the Devil's Mercy's number two. The expression on Rohan's face was impossible to read as he slipped off his black tuxedo jacket and began unbuttoning the rest of his shirt.

Jameson jumped back down into the ring, and as he did, he caught the look in the Proprietor's eyes and thought suddenly of his grandfather, of all the times he'd thought he'd earned the old man's approval and realized, almost too late, that what he'd earned was another lesson.

CHAPTER 41

JAMESON

Rohan didn't have a single scar that Jameson could see. Shirtless, there was no minimizing the breadth of his shoulders, the hyper-definition of muscles, sharpest where they met bone. There was no visible tension in the way the Factotum stood, and Jameson was hit with a sudden premonition that there would be no blank space with this opponent.

No weaknesses.

No openings.

No time between moves.

This should be fun. Jameson felt the adrenaline building inside him—the anticipation, the awareness that he wasn't going to get out of *this* fight unscathed.

This was going to hurt.

Blood dripped down his temple. The metallic taste of it was thick in his mouth. His body was mottled with bruises. But on the plus side, only three of his many bruised ribs felt cracked.

Rohan threw him face-first onto the rock-hard mat, and for the first time over the past nineteen rounds, the Factotum spoke. *"Stay down."*

Jameson laughed. It came out ugly and garbled, so Rohan could be excused for not recognizing the genuine humor in it.

Hawthornes didn't stay down.

Besides, it wasn't like Jameson hadn't gotten in some good hits of his own. Rohan's lip was split, his ribs as busted as Jameson's. The only advantage the Factotum had, really, was that neither of *his* eyes was swollen shut.

Jameson forced his knees to bend and got them underneath him. The heels of his hands dug into the mat. He breathed through the pain, focusing on it, drawing strength from it, then brought his head up, well aware that the expression on his face probably looked, to the crowd, a little manic.

One foot underneath him, then the other.

Rohan returned to his corner, an expression like regret in his deep brown eyes.

He's stronger, Jameson thought. *I was faster.* At this point, Jameson's speed was past tense. Where his own fighting style was a mix of those he'd mastered across his childhood, Rohan's defied description.

The Factotum fought every single round like he was fighting to survive.

There was only one way to counter instincts like that, especially with injuries slowing him down. *Stop trying to.* Jameson couldn't anticipate Rohan's next move. He couldn't match his strength—or his reach. *If I fight to survive, I'll lose.* The only thing that could beat *survival* was a death wish.

No fear. No pain. Less strategy—and more *risk.*

He ran straight at Rohan, his head down. *Get inside his reach.* Just before they collided, Jameson threw his right elbow up, catching the Factotum under his chin. Rohan weathered the blow and countered, but Jameson barely felt it, because the elbow to the chin had never been the point.

The point was his other arm, snaking around Rohan's neck from behind.

Rohan was down. To the crowd it might have looked like he was out, but Jameson knew better. He saw the tension in the back of the Factotum's hands, the ripple moving up his arms. Any second, Rohan was going to push back up.

But he didn't.

It wasn't until Jameson looked out at the crowd and saw the Proprietor holding his employee's gaze that Jameson realized. *He's giving an order.*

Rohan stayed down.

Jameson dragged himself from the ring, barely standing. Avery was there in an instant, propping him up on one side, and another figure slid in on the other.

Zella. "If you bleed on this gown," the duchess warned, "I'm dropping you."

"Bloodstains," Jameson slurred with a grin that set his face on fire. "The point at which outsiders no longer stick together."

On his other side, Avery's body pushed in closer to his. "I

told your brothers you were *fine*," she muttered. "I promised Grayson you weren't spiraling. And Nash? He's going to kill you—and me."

"Libby won't let him. Killing bad. Cupcakes good." Jameson ignored the pain and turned, looking for the Proprietor through the crowd—but the man was gone. And when Jameson swung his screaming head back toward the ring, so was Rohan.

CHAPTER 42

JAMESON

"It's an unwritten rule. If anyone goes twenty rounds with a house fighter, the house yields."

For someone who couldn't have been a member of the Devil's Mercy for long, Zella knew an awful lot about its unwritten rules. She'd escorted him and Avery into the atrium, then past a set of velour curtains—*Lust*—and up a winding, golden staircase. Now the three of them were in a room like Jameson had never seen. The bed was larger than king-sized. The ceiling was a deep midnight blue, just reflective enough that Jameson, lying prone on the bed, could catch the occasional glimpse of a ghost of their images. The floor on which Zella and Avery stood was made of round, smooth stones that had been warm under his still-bare feet.

The wall that Jameson could see when he propped himself up was seemingly made of water, falling into a basin below like a waterfall tamed.

The sheets beneath his body—the sheets he was bleeding on—were made of the softest silk.

"What are you doing?" Avery demanded, putting a hand on his shoulder and pushing him gently back down onto the bed. "You need to lay still."

"I need to do *more*." That word. It always came back to that word—needing more, wanting more, wanting to *be* more. "The Proprietor will choose the players in the Game tonight. I can't spend the rest of it up here."

"I'm not asking you to, Jameson." Avery brought her hand to his abdomen, just under his rib cage—his bruised and battered rib cage. "I am asking you," she continued fiercely, "to remember that *this* matters." His pain. His body. "*You* matter."

Once upon a time, he would have had a flippant response for that, would have deployed it like a grenade. But not now. Not with her. "I went to see Ian last night." The admission came out more pained than he would have liked—or maybe that was his jaw. "Don't look at me like that, Heiress. I know what I'm doing."

He knew—now and always—what it took to win.

"At least let us clean you up," Zella said, her voice no-nonsense. "Believe me, the Proprietor won't thank you for leaving a bloody trail across the Mercy."

Jameson let them tend to him, his body throbbing, his mind pulsing, his thoughts singular. *What's next?* He'd won on the tables. He'd won in the ring. That left two areas—besides this one—in the Devil's Mercy.

And each of those two rooms held a book.

Those books hold more. . . . unconventional *wagers. Any wager written into one of those books and signed for is binding, no matter how bizarre.* Jameson meditated on that bit of information as antiseptic and bandages were applied to his cuts, as his ribs were wrapped. As he pulled his shirt and jacket back on, his body screaming its objections now that the adrenaline of the fight was starting to ebb away.

"What would you do," Jameson asked Zella, his mind sorting through an array of possibilities, "if you wanted to get the Proprietor's attention?"

It wasn't just his *attention* Jameson needed.

"Surprise him." Zella turned and ran one hand lightly through the waterfall on the wall. "Or make him think that you have something he wants. Or if you have as little sense as it appears..." The duchess turned from the wall, her brown eyes settling on his. "Make him see you as a threat."

"You know about the Game," Avery said, and there was no question in her voice as she took a step toward the duchess. "You want in—if you're not *in* already. Why would you help us?"

Help me, Jameson thought.

"Because I can." Zella looked from Avery to Jameson. "And because the advantage to choosing one's competition is knowing one's competition."

Any help she gave him served her own ends. "And you know me?" Jameson challenged.

"I know risk-takers," Zella said. "I know privilege." The duchess let that word hang in the air, and then she looked from Jameson to Avery. "I know love."

You know a hell of a lot more than that, Jameson thought.

Zella smiled slightly then, almost as if she'd heard him clear as day. "I know," she said, "that there's more than one way to shatter glass."

And with that, the duchess made her exit.

"What did Ian say to you?" Avery asked him as soon as they were alone. "When you went to see him—what the hell did he say?"

Jameson didn't make her call *Tahiti*. "He offered to leave me Vantage when he dies, if I win it back for him now."

Avery stared at—and into—him. "You could win it for *yourself*."

That was true. It had always been true. But Jameson couldn't help thinking about Ian saying that he didn't care for whist. About the laugh he'd managed to surprise out of the man, so much like his own.

"I can't win anything for anyone," Jameson bit out, a ball rising in his throat, "if I don't get an invitation to the Game."

Every bruise on his body was a live wire, but the only thing that mattered was what was next. *Surprise the Proprietor. Tempt him. Threaten him.* "Time to get back out there."

To Avery's credit, she didn't try to talk him out of it—just handed him a quartet of over-the-counter pain pills and a bottle of water. "I'm coming with you."

Game on.

CHAPTER 43

JAMESON

The food smelled delicious—or so Jameson was informed, since he couldn't smell *anything* at the moment. Eating was also out the question.

"Could I get you some soup, sir?" The bartender looked more like a bouncer. Like the dealers in the gaming room, he wore clothes lifted straight out of another era. No jewels around his neck, but Jameson caught a thick ring on his middle finger.

A triangle embedded inside a circle inside a square.

"Or something a little stronger?" The bartender lifted a crystal goblet onto the bar. The liquid inside was a dark shade of amber, almost gold.

"Soup and spirits," Avery murmured into the back of Jameson's head. "Think they offer that to everyone who survives the ring?"

Jameson's body drank in the closeness of hers, allowing it to fuel his resolve, and then he cut to the chase with the bartender. "I'm after the book."

The bartender looked Jameson up and down. The man appeared to be in his forties, but Jameson thought suddenly of the boy in the boat that first night and wondered exactly how long this gentleman had worked at the Devil's Mercy.

Exactly how loyal to the Proprietor he was.

"Ah." The bartender reached below again, and this time, he withdrew a leather-bound tome that looked like it weighed too much to be so easily maneuvered with one hand. *One very large hand*, Jameson noted.

"Are the two of you looking to place any bet in particular?" the bartender asked.

Avery stepped back. "Not me," she said. "Just him."

Jameson knew how hard it was for her to sit this one out, just like *she* knew that he was the one who needed to impress. Ignoring the pang of the distance Avery had just put between them, Jameson flipped open the book. "May I?"

The bartender laid his massive hands flat on the bar, just behind the book, but said nothing as Jameson began to flip through it. The pages were yellowed with age, the dates beside the earliest bets written in script so formal it was difficult to read.

December 2. Jameson finally made out one date on the first page. *1823.*

Beneath each date was a single sentence. Each sentence contained two names.

Mr. Edward Sully bets Sir Harold Letts one hundred fifty that the eldest daughter of the Baron Asherton will not be wed before the younger two.

Lord Renner bets Mr. Downey, four hundred to two hundred, that Old Mitch will die in the spring (spring defined as the latter half of March, the whole of April, the whole of May, and the first week of June).

Mr. Fausset bets Lord Harding fifty-five that a man, agreed upon in confidence between the two, will take on a third mistress before his wife begets their second child.

No wonder the book was so large. It contained every random wager ever placed at the Devil's Mercy—or at least in this room. Political outcomes, social scandals, births and deaths, who would wed who and when and in what weather and with what guests in attendance.

Jameson flipped to more recent bets. "Are there any rules," he asked the bartender, "on what one may or may not wager?"

"This room is dedicated to longer-term outcomes, three months or more. If you're looking to place a bet on the shorter term, you'll require the book next door. Beyond that, you may wager on anything for which you have a taker, with the understanding that *all* wagers will be enforced."

Jameson looked up. Compared to the ring, attendance in this room was sparse, but every man—and the one woman—present was paying attention to his exchange with the bartender, some doing less to hide their interest than others.

One man, who looked to be in his thirties, stood and crossed the room. "I'd wager ten thousand that this lad gets himself killed before he's thirty. Any takers?"

"If you exclude illness and require the death be the result of his own actions?" Another man stood. "I'm in."

Jameson ignored them. He caught Avery's eyes, a silent warning for her to do the same. As the bet was written into the book and signed, Jameson let his gaze come to rest on the bartender's ring.

That and a mirror behind the shelves of liquor were the most likely points from which the Proprietor could observe.

What kind of bet will get me an invite to the Game? Jameson thought back to Zella's advice. He needed to be surprising, tempting, threatening—or a combination of the three.

At that exact moment, Rohan stepped through the black curtains. His face wasn't quite as battered as Jameson's, and he wore it better. He walked like his ribs weren't smarting at all.

It killed you, Jameson thought, with a slight twist of his lips, *to stay down.*

"Were I a member," Rohan said, his words carrying, though his voice wasn't loud, "I'd be wagering on the likelihood that Ms. Grambs breaks up with him within the year." He met Jameson's gaze. "No offense."

"None taken," Jameson replied.

"Lots taken," Avery told Rohan, her eyes narrowing.

Jameson smiled like his bruised jaw had never felt better. "I'll wager fifty thousand pounds that the Proprietor chooses someone other than his Factotum as his heir."

Sometimes, Jameson felt like he knew things without knowing how. The glint in Rohan's eyes told him he'd guessed correctly: Rohan hadn't yet been named heir.

He was still being tested.

"I'll take that bet," the man who'd wagered that Jameson was going to get himself killed said. "Assuming you're good for it."

"I am," Jameson replied, and then he looked back at the bartender's ring, back at the mirror. *Surprising. Tempting. Threatening.* "And I'll offer up another fifty thousand pounds that says the Proprietor is already dying. I'd give him . . . let's say . . . two years?"

The look in Rohan's eyes now made Jameson feel like the

two of them were back in the ring, like Rohan was standing over him, saying, *Stay down.* A threat and a warning—and something more.

"No one is going to take that bet," the bartender told Jameson. "Are you done here?"

Jameson could feel the clock ticking onward, feel the night slipping away from him. *I'm not done. I can't be done.*

He had to do something. He swallowed. "Short-term bets are kept next door?"

CHAPTER 44

JAMESON

This time, Jameson went alone. Chiffon canopies lined the walls. From beneath one of them, a woman stepped out. Like the dealers and the bartender, she was dressed in historical garb.

"You're hurt," the woman noted, the cadence of her voice almost lyrical. "I can help with that."

Jameson remembered what Rohan had said about having masseurs on staff. "I don't mind hurting. I was told you had a book? Short-term bets."

"And what will you be betting on?" the woman asked.

Surprising, tempting, threatening. Jameson wracked his mind for the right play for this exact moment, and his brain kept circling back to the same place.

To the same option.

Prague. Jameson Winchester Hawthorne thought back to that night—to what he'd heard, what he knew, what he wasn't supposed to know. And then he made a choice. Not the obvious one, not even a good one.

Not without risk.

But what was more tempting than knowledge—or more surprising than a bet that, from the Proprietor's perspective, he would have no reason, none at all, to make?

No fear. No holding back. "I'd like to wager on what's getting ready to happen to the price of wheat."

A single Hail Mary pass could be a sign of desperation. A series of them was strategy.

Jameson ended the night at the tables. This time, he didn't bother himself about winning too much or playing at any one game for too long. His blood was buzzing in his veins. His body was shot, but his mind was going at the speed of light, and he wasn't about to let anything slow him down.

When Branford and Zella sat down for a game of whist, Jameson lost no time taking one of the seats to play against them. Avery took the remaining chair at the table.

"Looks like I have a teammate." Jameson met her eyes. Branford and Zella didn't know what they were in for. "I'd offer to deal," Jameson continued, "but I'd hate to upset the control freaks among us." He handed the deck to Branford. "Uncle?"

Simon Johnstone-Jameson's poker face was immaculate. Ian had said that his family didn't know about his illegitimate son. Jameson couldn't tell, looking at Branford now, if that was true.

"Your presence has been requested." Rohan appeared above them.

Branford went to stand, and Zella cocked her head to the side.

"Not you," she told Branford. Jameson's gut said that was a guess—but hopefully, a good one.

Rohan's eyes narrowed almost imperceptibly, and a moment later, the rogue's smile was back, split lip be damned. "Not *just* you, Branford. The Proprietor will see all four of you in his office."

CHAPTER 45

JAMESON

The office in question wasn't grand. It wasn't large. It was empty but for a desk. On the desk, there was a book—bigger than either of the others that Jameson had seen that night, its cover made of shining metal.

Jameson didn't need to ask what that book was. He knew just from the way that Zella looked at it. Just from the way that Branford did.

"Ms. Grambs," the Proprietor said. "If you wouldn't mind joining Rohan in the hall?"

Jameson didn't like that idea, but he didn't object, either. Once the door closed behind Avery and Rohan, the Proprietor turned his attention to the three who remained. "You know why you're here."

Jameson was struck by how ordinary the man's voice was, how normal he looked up close. If you passed him on the street, you wouldn't look twice.

Jameson couldn't be sure that he *hadn't* passed him on the street at some point.

"I wouldn't dare to assume," Zella said demurely.

"We both know that's not true, my dear." The Proprietor leaned forward, his elbows on the desk that separated him from the three of them. "You wouldn't be here if you didn't dare much, much more." He shifted his weight again, slightly back. "Only one person," he commented softly, "has ever managed to break into the Mercy."

Jameson turned toward Zella and raised both eyebrows.

The duchess gave an elegant little shrug. "Glass ceilings and all that," she told Jameson.

"Your place in the Game is assured, Your Grace." The Proprietor reached into a desk drawer and withdrew an envelope, much like the one that had held Avery's initial invitation to the Mercy. He held it out to Zella, who took it, then the Proprietor's hand returned to the drawer. "While you're at it," he told her, "I would be most obliged if you'd take Avery's to her."

Avery this time, Jameson thought. *Not Ms. Grambs.*

Zella closed her fingers around both envelopes and made her way to the door. "Bonne chance, gentlemen."

And then there were two.

"Luck." The Proprietor snorted. "If you're going to compete against that one, you'll need it."

The word *compete* had Jameson's pulse quickening. This was it.

Branford, however, latched on to a different word. "*If*," he repeated.

"Your places in the Game, I'm afraid, are not assured," the Proprietor said. "Simon, you're well aware of the cost to join the Mercy." The use of Branford's given name seemed deliberate, a reminder that here, his title did not matter. Here, he wasn't the one with power. "What more might you be willing to pay in exchange for an invitation to the Game?"

Branford's jaw tightened—slightly, but it was there. "Another levy." That wasn't a question or an offer. That was the Viscount Branford cutting to the chase.

The Proprietor's smile didn't look like any that Jameson had ever seen. "It need not concern yourself this time," he said. "But you must, as I'm sure you realize, make it worth my while." The Proprietor drummed his fingers lightly over the top of the desk, a sign, Jameson thought, that he was enjoying this. "And it must be something you would rather not come out. After all, these things are always more interesting when at least a few players have 'skin in the game,' as the Americans like to say."

The Proprietor turned his head toward Jameson. "And that, my boy, leads us to you. There's a bit of a resemblance to your brother, don't you think, Simon?"

Branford didn't so much as flick his eyes toward Jameson. "In rashness, if nothing else."

Jameson chose not to take that personally. All his focus remained on the Proprietor.

"You're bold, young man." The Proprietor stood and caught his cane between his thumb and forefinger and swung it lightly back and forth, like a metronome or a needle on a scale. "If I'd encountered you when you were younger, if your last name wasn't Hawthorne . . . ," the Proprietor told Jameson, "you could have had an interesting future at the Mercy indeed."

Jameson thought about the young boy who tended the boats, about the bartender, the house fighters, the dealers. About Rohan.

"But here you are," the Proprietor mused. "Not a member of the Mercy and not in my employ." He nodded toward the desk. "Do you know what this book is?"

"Am I supposed to?" Jameson replied, the barest hint of challenge in his tone.

"Oh, most assuredly not." There was something dark and serpentine buried in the Proprietor's tone as he studied Jameson's face. And then he smiled. "Your grandfather trained you well, Mr. Hawthorne. Your face gives away very little."

Jameson shrugged. "I'm also fairly skilled at motocross."

"And fighting," the Proprietor added. He went silent for a moment longer than was comfortable for anyone in the room. "I respect a fighter. Tell me..." The cane was still going back and forth in his hands, though the older man gave no sign of moving it at all. "What makes you think that I am dying?"

So that was the move—or one of them, anyway—that had paid off.

The Proprietor's fingers tightened suddenly around the cane. "This?" he said, nodding toward it.

"No," Jameson replied. He debated withholding an explanation but decided that might register as one insult too many. "You remind me of my grandfather." The words came out quieter than he meant them to. "Before."

There had been weeks when the old man was ill, when he'd been planning his final hurrah, and none of them but Xander had known.

"The way you tested Rohan," Jameson continued. "In the ring."

"I was testing you," the Proprietor countered.

Jameson shrugged. "Three birds with one stone."

"And the third would be...?"

"I don't know," Jameson replied honestly. "I just know that there is one, just like I know that you have a *presumptive* heir." He paused. "Just like my brothers and I now know to never presume." Jameson met the Proprietor's gaze. "And there was a tremor—a very slight one—when Avery took your arm last night."

"She told you that?" the Proprietor demanded.

"She didn't have to," Jameson said. At the time, he hadn't even noticed, but he'd long ago trained himself to be able to play a scene over and over again in his mind.

"Why," the Proprietor said, after a long and pointed silence, "did you place a bet on thc price of wheat?"

Jameson's mouth felt suddenly dry, but he had no intention of letting the old man across from him see that. "Because I'm not a fan of corn or oats."

Another lengthy silence, and then the Proprietor dropped his cane flat on the desk with an audible clunk. "You are interesting, Jameson Hawthorne. I'll give you that." The Proprietor walked around the desk—without the cane. "And I think it would be somewhat entertaining to watch you lose the Game." He turned toward Jameson's uncle. "It would feel a bit poetic, don't you think, Branford? Ian's son?"

He called him Branford this time, Jameson registered. *Not Simon.* Because this time, the Viscount Branford was not the one that the Proprietor was attempting to put in his place.

"But there is a balance to these things," the man continued, his lips curving, eyes just beginning to narrow. "Weights on the scales."

Nothing worthwhile, Jameson could hear his grandfather saying, *comes without a cost.*

"I'll pay the levy," Jameson said.

"In a fashion." The Proprietor walked closer to him still. "I want a secret, Jameson Hawthorne," he said, his voice low and silky. "The kind men would kill and die for. The kind that shakes the ground beneath our feet, the kind that must never be spoken, the kind you wouldn't dare share even with the lovely Avery Grambs." The Proprietor reached out, grabbing Jameson's chin, turning his head to get a good look at every cut and every bruise. "Do you have a secret like that?"

Jameson didn't pull back. Again, his mind went to Prague. *Resist.* Jameson didn't. "I do."

CHAPTER 46

GRAYSON

Gigi drove. It did not take Grayson long to ascertain that Gigi should not drive.

"You're over the line," he said mildly.

"So the car keeps informing me!" Gigi swerved to correct the problem. "But let's talk about *you*. Do you know what Savannah said after the party last night?"

"I can only imagine."

"Nothing," Gigi replied. She turned to give Grayson a look. "That's weird, right?"

"Eyes on the road."

Gigi obligingly looked back at the road but wasn't deterred from making her point. "And you just disappeared. Also weird. And the way the two of you reacted to my thinking-on-ye-old-feet subterfuge when Duncan asked what we were doing in his dad's office?"

Gigi paused, and Grayson gathered that he was supposed to reply. "Weird?" he suggested dryly.

"Extremely!" Gigi came to a stop at a light and turned to look at him once more. "You two have a history, don't you? That's why Savannah has been in cat-with-an-arching-back mode since you got here. That's why you're here." Gigi's voice grew almost tender. "You still love her."

"What?" Grayson squeaked. He had never squeaked in his life, but some things could not be helped. "*No*," he told Gigi emphatically. "I told you—"

"You have a girlfriend," Gigi said with a roll of her eyes. The light turned green, and she accelerated. "Fine, then. What is this imaginary girlfriend like?"

"Smart," Grayson said, and there was still a part of him—a fainter part now, like an echo or a memory or a shadow—that had to fight to keep from seeing Avery's face when he said it. "Not in a predictable kind of way." He paused. "Maybe that's a good word for her. Unpredictable. Unexpected."

"In what way?" Gigi asked.

Echoes faded. Shadows receded in light. And some memories were meant to stay in the past. So this time, Grayson didn't think about Avery. Instead, he thought about the black opal ring, about Nash holding his gaze and saying, *Why not you?*

"I am not a person who's easily surprised or easily defeated," Grayson said, his voice coming out thicker than it should have. "My partner..." That make-believe impossibility of a girl. "She can do both. She *does* both, frequently. She's not perfect." He swallowed. "And when I'm with her, I don't have to be, either."

"How did you meet?"

I am making her up as I speak. "Grocery store. She was buying limes." *Limes?* Grayson cursed himself.

"Was it love at first sight?" Gigi asked with a little sigh.

"I don't believe in love at first sight. Neither does she." Grayson swallowed. "We just...*fit*."

Gigi held up a hand, which was mildly terrifying since she was turning left at the same time. "Okay, you've sold me on the existence of the mythical girlfriend. But can you at least admit that you've been playing pretend since I met you?"

Grayson felt a twinge in his stomach. *What exactly does she know?* He didn't have time to consider that question. "Brake," he told Gigi. "Brake!"

She braked, and a moment later, pulled into the parking lot of the bank. Screeching to a stop and parking the car, she turned to look at him. "You're pretending to be Mr. Stoic, but I see straight through you." She grinned. "You like me. Not *that* way, obviously—which, *same*, buddy—but in a friendly kind of way. I'm growing on you. Admit it, we're friends."

She opened the door and jumped out of the jeep without waiting for a response. Grayson steeled himself. *We're not friends, Gigi.* He got out of the vehicle and walked around to the front, his mind on what had to be done next.

The decoy key was still in his pocket.

"Not a word about the fact that I'm not parked in the lines." Gigi expelled a breath, then she craned her neck up at the bank. "Let's do this."

Grayson stepped into her path. "You can't go in."

"You say *can't*, I hear *definitely going to*—"

"They'll recognize you." Grayson waited until he had her eyes before continuing. "It will be hard enough getting into the box without authorization. We don't want them calling the cops again." He gentled his tone, as much as he could. "You can't do this, Gigi."

She looked down. "But you can?"

"I'm a Hawthorne. I can do anything." Grayson waited, just a beat, timing his next move with precision. "All you have to do is give me the key."

Gigi pulled her necklace out from underneath her shirt, her eyes round, her fingers handling the necklace like it bore precious stones. "I guess you don't need the chain." She unclasped it.

Regret hit him with surprising force. "I'll take it anyway," he told her. "For good luck." She handed over the chain. He slid the key off it.

"And I'll go with Grayson," another voice added. "For good luck." Savannah's tone was perfectly pleasant on the surface—and absolutely withering underneath.

"Sav!" Gigi was delighted. "You said you weren't coming."

"I didn't, actually. You assumed."

Grayson recognized himself in the way she said those words: the set of her chin, the even pacing of the words, the absolute control.

"Do you have the ID I gave you?" Savannah asked her twin calmly.

Gigi reached down the front of her shirt, then produced the card. "Here!"

Grayson averted his gaze. "May I see it?"

"No, you may not," Savannah told him, but by the time the words were out of her mouth, Gigi had already placed Sheffield Grayson's fake ID in his hands. The first thing he noticed was the picture—and Sheffield Grayson's eyes.

His eyes.

The second thing Grayson noticed was the name that Sheffield Grayson had chosen for his false identity: DAVENPORT, TOBIAS.

My middle name. And my grandfather's—and uncle's—first.

CHAPTER 47

GRAYSON

From the beginning, Grayson's fear had been that the contents of the safe-deposit box might shed light on what his father had really been up to in the lead-up to his "disappearance." *Financial records of payments Sheffield Grayson made to have Avery watched, to have a bomb planted on her plane. Record of Sheffield's travel to Texas the days before her kidnapping. Evidence of a long-term grudge against the Hawthorne family.* The possibilities pumped through Grayson's head, rhythmically, incessantly.

The name on the ID in his hands seemed like confirmation.

Which made it all the clearer: Grayson couldn't allow Gigi or Savannah access to the box. He needed to get in himself, vet the contents, clear the box out before anyone else discovered its existence. But first, he had to switch the keys.

He strode toward the bank, Savannah beside him, and slipped the key into the pocket of his dress pants, then allowed his fingers to make their way inside the envelope in which the decoy key sat.

"I'll handle this," Savannah declared icily, her hand locking over the door handle. "Just give me the key. It doesn't belong to you."

Grayson withdrew his hand from his pocket. He gave her the decoy key. *It's done.* The switch had been smooth. Easy. He shouldn't have felt sick to his stomach.

He shouldn't have felt like he'd lost something. *Admit it*, he could hear Gigi saying cheerfully. *We're friends.*

"May I help you?" A bank employee zeroed in on them six steps into the building.

Savannah assessed the man who'd offered assistance with a small, perfunctory smile. "I may need to speak to someone more senior."

"That won't be necessary." The employee looked to be in his midtwenties. "How can I help you?"

Savannah raked her eyes over his face. "I need to access my father's safe-deposit box." She arched one delicate brow. "I have the key and his information, as well as my own."

The employee made an attempt at seeming all business, but Grayson couldn't help noticing the way his gaze lingered on Savannah. "Right this way." He led them back to a computer. "Are you an authorized user on the account?"

"Presumably." Savannah's reply was virtually arctic. "The box is under the name Tobias Davenport."

"And you have the key?" the man asked, typing in the name.

Savannah brandished it, holding it between her index finger and her thumb. The man reached for it, and she let it drop into her palm and closed her fingers over it. "I'll hold on to this until we go back, thank you."

The man visibly flushed. When he spoke again, his voice was terse. "Your identification, please."

You're not making friends here, Savannah, Grayson thought.

"Mine," Savannah said, sliding two IDs and a piece of paper across the counter. "Along with the box owner's and a signed and notarized statement granting me access."

She'd forged a notary's signature and seal? That was a felony.

"I'm afraid you're not listed on the account, Ms. Grayson." There was just the barest hint of satisfaction in the bank employee's voice. Grayson wasn't sure when, precisely, the man had tipped from wanting to prove himself to her to wanting to have power over her, but he unquestionably had.

"Hence the signed statement," Savannah replied calmly. "As I said, I may need to speak to someone more senior."

Grayson almost intervened. The tension around the man's mouth was visible now. "I assure you, even the bank's CEO would tell you the same."

"I'm afraid you misapprehend the situation." Savannah was utterly unflappable.

"I apprehend the situation just fine." The man glared at her. "The only people authorized to access this box are Mr. Davenport himself and Acacia..." The man seemed to realize what he was saying a second too late. "Grayson."

"Thank you," Savannah said, her lips tilting slightly upward on the ends. "You've been very helpful."

Grayson waited until they were back outside to speak "You were never trying to get into the box."

"Unlike my sister, I'm a realist." Savannah cut Grayson a pointed look. "And *my* last name isn't Hawthorne." Her stride was nearly as long as his own. "I'm surprised you're not fighting me on this, telling me that you can handle it."

I could, Grayson thought, but that wasn't what he said. "I'm not your enemy, Savannah." *Lies.*

"Maybe not." Savannah's cool agreement felt more like the thrust of a blade. "But you're also not my keeper—or Gigi's. We do not need you." Savannah's pale blonde hair shone in the sun. "I have everything under control."

CHAPTER 48

GRAYSON

Back at the Grayson house, Gigi went in search of her mother while Savannah kept an eye on Grayson in the foyer.

"Mom's in the library," Gigi reported when she came back, her tone morose.

Savannah reached out and squeezed her twin's shoulder. "Mom's fine, Gigi. *We're* fine."

We as in the three of them. Their family.

Gigi turned toward Grayson, her brow furrowed. "We don't interrupt Mom when she's reading. It's been a rule for pretty much forever."

"You're welcome to wait out back," Savannah told him icily.

Not an offer. An order. Grayson watched as Savannah stalked out of the room.

"Mom has her library," Gigi said quietly. "Savannah has her court."

In his mind's eyes, Grayson could see Savannah standing on the free-throw line, shooting baskets the way he swam. "And what about you?" he asked Gigi.

Getting close to them was a mistake. Feeling this way was a mistake.

Gigi shrugged. "I like eating candy on the roof."

"But not chocolate." The inference escaped Grayson's mouth before he could stop it.

"Not chocolate," Gigi confirmed, and then she grinned. "I told you I'm growing on you! Now..." Her expression grew serious again. "What do you think my dad kept in that box? It can't be good, right? I mean, as a general rule, people don't commit identity fraud to rent safe-deposit boxes under fake names for funsies."

"I don't know." Grayson lied to her, and it felt like lying to his brothers. "Why don't you go eat some candy on the roof," he suggested gently. "I'll wait here for your mom."

Grayson didn't wait in the foyer for Acacia Grayson. He went looking for the library instead. The girls' key wouldn't open the safe-deposit box, but if Sheffield Grayson's wife was an authorized user, there was a chance she could have another one issued.

Grayson had not been raised to leave anything to chance.

"It shouldn't be this hard to cancel a membership." Acacia's voice was audible through the cracked-open door. Grayson came to a standstill just outside, listening. "I know there are fees!" She paused, and Grayson could practically see the woman gathering herself. When she spoke again, it was with every ounce of poise a woman who had grown up with Engstrom wealth could summon. "The club needs an event planner. It's been more than a month since Carrie left, and I think you'll agree, based on my charity work—not to mention the events my family has hosted in your ballroom—that I am more than qualified."

This was Acacia Grayson asking for a job. Grayson pictured the expression on her face when she'd told him that she wasn't weak.

Whatever response the person on the other end of the line gave her, Acacia wasn't impressed with it. "Well, I imagine they'll say I'm bored and lost without my husband. Let them." There was another silence, longer this time, and then: "I understand."

Grayson waited until he was sure she'd hung up before gently pushing in the door. "Problems?"

Acacia looked up from the chaise longue on which she was sitting, her legs curled beneath her body, and gave Grayson a firm look. "None that you need to concern yourself with."

Grayson strode to take a seat several feet away from her. "Your husband had a safe-deposit box under a fake name." The subject change was intentional. He'd circle back to her financial problems when she was less prepared to circumvent his questions. "The girls are going to ask you to open it. You're an authorized user."

Acacia pressed her lips together. Her blonde hair was pulled back in an elegant twist, not a hair out of place. "I don't know why I would be authorized to do anything," she said quietly. "He never talked to me about financial matters—or business ones." She looked away from Grayson, then back again, like she couldn't let herself have a reprieve from this conversation or everything he represented. "I have a degree in finance, you know. That's where Sheff and I met. I was quiet and awkward, and he was..." Her voice broke slightly. "Well, it doesn't matter now, does it?"

He married you for your money. That's what you're thinking. What you're trying not to think.

"Do you ever play what-if, Grayson?" Acacia asked softly. "What if you changed one decision, one moment in your life?"

Grayson wasn't in the habit of daydreaming, but he'd relived his biggest mistakes often enough to know what those moments were, to know exactly what he would undo if he could.

"Or what if one thing had been different from the start?" There was something wistful in Acacia's expression. "I used to play all the time when I was a kid. What if I'd had an older brother? What if I'd been born with a different last name? What if I'd looked just a little less like my mother?"

What if you'd left your husband when you found out about me?

Acacia let out a long, slow breath. "But what-if is different once you have kids, because all of a sudden, everything leading up to their births, those choices, those realities are set in stone. Because if things had been even a little bit different, they might not exist, and that is the one possibility you cannot bear."

Acacia looked down at her hands, and Grayson noted that she still wore her wedding band.

"I remember about a week after Savannah and Gigi came home from the hospital, I had a dream that I was still pregnant and that my babies—the ones I'd held and fed and loved—they were just a dream. And I panicked, because I didn't want any other babies. I wanted *my* girls. And when I woke up, I stood over their cribs, and I just cried, because they were *real*." She looked back up at Grayson. "So there is no what if I'd chosen a different life or fallen in love with someone truly capable of loving me back. There is no what if I knew then what I know now. No regret. There can't be. Because as much as I want a different life right now, I want to be their mom more."

Breathing shouldn't be so difficult, Grayson thought, but it was, because he had never in his life been that for anyone, least of all Skye. And suddenly, he wanted to play what-if himself, because having that—it would have changed everything.

It would have meant everything.

Regrets are a waste of your time and mine, the old man whispered from somewhere in his memory. *Do I strike you as a person who has time to waste?*

Grayson focused, because that was what he did—who he *was*. "I know about the FBI and IRS investigations, Acacia." He softened that conversational pivot as much as he could. "I know that he was stealing from your parents. I know he drained your accounts."

Acacia Grayson breathed through the pain.

"But Savannah and Gigi don't need to know any of that," Grayson said softly.

Acacia swallowed. "You think I should just turn the safe-deposit box over to the feds?"

There was no time for Grayson to second-guess his approach here. "No," he said evenly. "I don't."

Acacia stared at him for the longest time. "I hadn't pegged you for wanting to protect my husband."

"It's not him," Grayson said, his voice low, "that I am trying to protect."

That was the truth, and really, it wasn't just Avery he was trying to protect now, either. The bombing of Avery's jet had killed two of Oren's men. Sheffield Grayson was a murderer—and none of the members of this family needed to have to live with that. Not Acacia. Not Savannah. Not Gigi.

"Give me a day." Grayson did not phrase that as a request. "You won't ever have to know what's in that box, and you won't be the one who kept the contents from the feds." Grayson could have stopped there. Maybe he should have. But he'd been taught from a very young age how to get a yes. "Your name is on the box, too, Acacia. He used fake identification for himself but your real name—and likely forged your signature. Beyond that, he's not the only one that the IRS could charge with tax evasion."

Acacia closed her eyes. When she opened them again, they were watery, but not a single tear fell. She gave Grayson an almost compassionate look. "You're just a kid."

Grayson's heart twisted in his chest. The only person who'd ever said that to him before was Nash. "My mother likes to say that Hawthornes are never really children." Grayson hadn't meant to bring up Skye—not to this woman. Not after all that talk of what-if. He course-corrected. "Did the country club take you up on your offer?"

"No." Acacia shook her head. "I don't understand why they wouldn't, but—" She cut herself off. "Like the contents of that safe-deposit box, my financial situation is not your problem."

Grayson had the Hawthorne ability to flat-out ignore assertions that weren't to his liking. "My grandfather had his faults," he told Acacia quietly, "and then some. But he taught me to put family first. I am not without means..."

"No," Acacia said firmly. "Absolutely not."

"You grew up with Kent Trowbridge." Grayson pivoted again. "His son doesn't deserve Savannah."

If he'd gone straight for discussing *her* relationship with the lawyer, Acacia might have refused to discuss it, so Grayson went for another tactic.

"Duncan and Savannah have known each other forever," Acacia said. "I've never pushed the relationship on her." She paused. "But my mother might have."

"The way she pushed you and Kent?" That was a leap, but a strategic one. "I saw him touch you the other night."

"It was nothing," Acacia said, looking away. "He's a friend of the family. He's trying to help."

Grayson leaned forward. "Is he?" No response, so Grayson made another leap. "He's the one who told you about me. Isn't he?"

"I had a right to know."

The day of your mother's funeral? Grayson thought.

"Have you told the girls anything?" Acacia asked, her voice going hoarse. "About the money?" Before Grayson could reply, she began issuing assurances. "The house is safe. Their school fees, cars, wardrobes, cost of living—all taken care of by their trusts. They'll be fine." She stood and walked toward the library door. "The rest of it, I'll just have to figure out for myself, starting with that safe-deposit box."

The door opened before Acacia reached it. *Savannah.* "He told you." She'd obviously overheard her mother's last statement. Grayson could see Acacia wondering if she'd overheard any of the rest.

"I need you to let me handle this, Savannah," Acacia said firmly.

Savannah's eyes flashed. "You don't handle anything, Mom. You just sit back and take it."

Acacia looked down. Grayson's eyes narrowed.

"I didn't mean that." Savannah looked down.

Acacia walked and put an arm around her.

"So..." Gigi popped up behind them. "Who's in an opening-a-safe-deposit-box kind of mood?"

Grayson in no way expected that to work. But after a long moment, Acacia nodded. "We'll do this together." She looked from the twins to Grayson. "All of us."

CHAPTER 49

GRAYSON

They went back to the bank. Grayson half-expected Acacia to make all three of them wait in the parking lot, but she didn't. And when she presented her identification and the key that Savannah gave her—the decoy that Grayson had swapped in—the same bank employee who had sent Savannah away called for his manager.

That manager walked them back to the vault. Inside, there were walls of safe-deposit boxes. The manager inserted the bank's key into one of the slots and waited for Acacia to insert hers. She did, but when she went to twist it, nothing happened.

She tried again.

I planned this. Grayson ignored the stab of guilt. *This is what was supposed to happen.*

"If you don't have the key, ma'am, and you're not the primary account holder, then I'm afraid you're going to have to—"

The bank manager didn't get the chance to finish that sentence.

Savannah reached beneath the high-necked shirt she was wearing and pulled out a chain, identical to Gigi's.

On the end of the chain, there was another key. "Try mine," Savannah said.

Grayson stared at her.

"Since when do you have a key?" Gigi asked.

"I found it," Savannah said quietly, "with the ID."

Grayson Hawthorne was not often taken by surprise. *This is what happens when you fail to look ten steps ahead.* Tobias Hawthorne's voice was as clear in his head as if the old man were right there. *When you let your emotions get in the way. When you allow yourself to become distracted.*

Savannah slid the key off her chain and handed it to her mother. Acacia placed it in the lock. And this time, when she turned it, the lock clicked.

The bank manager carefully removed the box from the wall and set it down on a tall glass table in the middle of the room. "I'll give you a moment," he said.

Acacia looked at her daughters in turn, then Grayson. Slowly, she opened the lid to the box.

The first thing Grayson saw was a photo of himself.

EIGHT YEARS AGO

Grayson stared at the massive ring of keys. The alternative was looking at the old man, who must have followed him all the way across the estate to the tree house.

"Yours wasn't the slowest time," Tobias Hawthorne commented, no particular emphasis in his tone. "But neither was it the fastest."

Grayson watched as his grandfather bent and laid the ring of ornate keys down on the tree house floor. There were easily a hundred keys on the ring, each with a distinct head, many of them elaborately designed and delicately made. The challenge had been to figure out which key opened the newly installed lock on Hawthorne House's grand front door.

Grayson had come in third.

"Jameson won." Grayson set his jaw, refusing to allow that to bother him. It was a simple fact, after all, and the only thing that his grandfather respected as much as winning was control.

"Do you think it was a competition?" Tobias Hawthorne queried, cocking his head slightly to one side. "I was aiming more for rite of passage."

After completion, they'd each been given a bronze pin, fashioned in the shape of a key. Grayson could feel his digging into the palm of his hand now. "Then why are you here talking about my time?"

The question came out cool, measured. *Good.*

"Jameson wanted to win." The old man's tone betrayed something else now: appreciation.

Grayson did not let himself look down. "Jameson always wants to win."

The look in his grandfather's eyes said *exactly*, but his mouth said, "And sometimes you let him."

"I didn't let him win," Grayson said, and this time, he nearly lost control, biting out the words. He reeled his frustration back in and gave his grandfather a cool, detached stare. "Is that what you wanted to hear?"

Tobias Hawthorne smiled. "Yes and no." He stared at Grayson like a man used to answering his own questions, like he could get every answer he wanted just from looking at Grayson's face. "Tell me where you went wrong."

The prompt was soft in volume, neither gentle nor harsh in tone.

Grayson felt it like a blow. He let his gaze go down to the keys, tracing back over his method of solving them. "I was looking for a code, concentrating on the wrong thing."

"Complicating something in no need of complication?" his grandfather suggested. "And in doing so, you failed to see the whole picture."

There was no word on the planet that twelve-year-old Grayson hated more than any version of the word *fail*.

"I'm sorry."

"Don't be" came the immediate response. "Don't ever be sorry, Grayson. Be *better.*"

"It was just a game." Grayson kept his voice completely steady this time.

The old man smiled. "I enjoy seeing you play. Nothing brings me more satisfaction than seeing you and your brothers enjoying yourselves, enjoying a challenge."

Then why are you here?

"I'm not upset you lost," the old man continued, as if he was perfectly capable of hearing Grayson's unspoken thoughts. "I am, however, concerned that you are beginning to seem comfortable with losing."

"I don't like to lose," Grayson replied, putting force in those words.

"Is that an unusual trait?" came the reply. "An extraordinary one?"

No one likes to lose. Grayson expelled a breath. "No."

"Are you unusual?" his grandfather pressed. "Extraordinary?"

"Yes," Grayson bit out, the words exiting his mouth with the strength of a vow.

"Then tell me, Grayson, why am I here?"

This was another test. Another challenge. And Grayson had no intention of failing again.

"Because I have to be more," he replied, his voice low, intense.

"Be more," his grandfather said, matching Grayson's tone with his own. "Do more. Faster. Stronger. Smarter. More cunning. *Why?*"

Grayson spoke the only answer that felt true. "Because I can." He had the potential. He'd always had the potential. He had to live up to it.

"Pick up the keys," his grandfather said. Grayson did as he was told. "They're beautiful, are they not? You weren't wrong to look for meaning in them. I designed each and every one myself. The story of my life is in those keys."

For the first time, this confrontation seemed less like one of his grandfather's lessons and more like the kind of conversation an ordinary boy might have with his ordinary grandfather. For a moment, Grayson let himself expect the old man to tell him that story—some part of it that he didn't already know.

But Tobias Hawthorne wasn't an ordinary grandfather. "Some people can make mistakes, Grayson. But you are not one of those people. Why?"

"Because I'm a Hawthorne."

"No." For the first time, the old man's tone grew harsh. "You're failing again. Right here. Right now. You are failing."

There was nothing—*nothing*—he could have said that would have cut more.

"Xander is a Hawthorne," the old man said intently. "Nash is a Hawthorne. Jameson is a Hawthorne. But you..." Tobias Hawthorne took Grayson's chin in his hands and tilted it up, making sure that he had his grandson's complete and undivided attention. "You're not Jameson. What is acceptable for him is not acceptable for you. *And do you know why?*"

There it was again. The question. The test. Failure was not an option.

Grayson nodded.

"Tell me why, Grayson," the old man said.

"Because," Grayson replied, his voice coming out hoarse, "someday, it's going to be me."

He'd never said the words before, but on some level, he'd known it. On some level, they all had, for as long as Grayson could remember. The old man wasn't going to live forever. He needed an heir. Someone capable of taking on the mantle, of doing what the old man did.

Growing the fortune.

Protecting the family.

"It is going to be you," Tobias Hawthorne agreed, letting go of Grayson's chin. "Be worthy—and never speak a word of this conversation to your brothers."

CHAPTER 50

JAMESON

Branford was taken into another room to be *dealt with*—the Proprietor's words—by Rohan. Jameson's secret, on the other hand, the Proprietor chose to handle himself.

"You'll write it down here." The Proprietor laid what looked like a scroll on the table, then flattened it out. He placed a quill next to the scroll. Inspecting the quill, Jameson realized it was made of metal, hair-thin but blade-sharp. That served as a reminder: What he was doing could be dangerous. It was a risk.

Jameson told himself that it was a calculated one.

On the other side of the scroll, the Proprietor set a small, shallow dish, like the ones that held the lilies in the atrium. As Jameson watched, the man poured dark purple ink into the bowl.

"By the time the ink has dried, I will have determined if your secret indeed merits entry into the Game. If so, you will be required to provide me with an assurance of some sort—proof." The Proprietor paused. "Do you," he said, his voice low and silky, "have proof?"

The muscles in his throat tightening, Jameson thought about his pocket watch, about the object he'd hidden inside. "I do, but not on me."

"If your secret passes muster, all you will have to do is tell me where and what," the Proprietor said, "and I'll send someone to fetch your proof."

Jameson recognized the signals his body was sending out: the dry mouth, the sweat he could feel beginning to make its way down his palms, the clattering of his heart in his chest.

He ignored them all. Just like he ignored the warning ringing in his mind, a female voice issuing a very pointed threat.

There are ways, Jameson Hawthorne, to take care of problems.

There was a reason he'd kept what he'd learned in Prague a secret. Even from his brothers. Even from Avery. Some secrets were dangerous.

But this was his opening, his shot. He was only going to get one. *Once you see that web of possibilities laid out in front of you, unencumbered by fear of pain or failure, by thoughts telling you what can and cannot, should and should not be done... What will you do with what you see?*

"What happens to my secret if I write it down and you do find it suitably enticing?" Jameson asked, his voice coming out calm, irreverent by design. "Does it go in the ledger?"

"Oh no," the Proprietor said with a shake of his head and a gleam in his eyes. "The ledger belongs to the Mercy. Your secret will belong to me. If you win, your scroll will be destroyed and your proof returned to you, no additional records created, my lips sealed."

"And if I lose?"

"Then I may use your secret however I wish." The Proprietor's smile was a chilling thing. "Even once control of the Devil's Mercy has passed to my heir."

Something about the Proprietor's words made Jameson think he wasn't talking about a distant future. *The man is dying,* Jameson thought. *And there is no risk if I win.*

"This must be quite a secret indeed." The Proprietor perched on the edge of his desk and reached his cane forward to tilt Jameson's chin up. "So I suppose the question, Mr. Hawthorne, is this: How badly do you want to play my Game?"

How badly do I want Vantage? Jameson Hawthorne hadn't been raised to fear risk. He reached for the quill. His hand tightening around it, Jameson took a moment to consider how best to phrase his secret: sensationally enough to gain admittance but holding back enough to minimize the chances of repercussions.

In the end, he chose four words. Passing the quill from his right hand to his left, he dipped it in the ink and began to write. Certain letters jumped out in his mind as he wrote them: a capital *H*, the word *is*, two lowercase letters at the very end: *v* and *e*.

Dropping the quill onto the desk, Jameson leaned back in his seat and waited for the dark purple ink to dry. And when the Proprietor finally reached down and smeared his finger across the page, to no effect, Jameson knew that it was done.

The scroll was rolled back up. The Proprietor closed a fist around it. "Sufficient," he declared. "And the proof?"

"There's a pocket watch back at my flat. It has a hidden compartment."

The watch was fetched. Jameson used his thumb to twirl the minute hand back and forth to the appropriate numbers. The face of the watch popped off, and underneath was a small bead, the size of a pearl.

Translucent.

Filled with liquid.

Jameson expected the Proprietor to ask what it was and how it served as proof for the words he'd written, but no question came. Instead, Jameson was handed an envelope identical to the one the Proprietor had given Zella earlier.

An invitation.

"Open it," the Proprietor told him.

Jameson did. A powdery substance exploded into his face the moment he broke the seal. Within seconds, his lungs began to seize. His muscles gave out. As his body slid from the chair to the floor and darkness closed in, he heard the Proprietor walk to stand over him.

"Welcome to the Game, Mr. Hawthorne."

CHAPTER 51

JAMESON

Jameson awoke on a cold, hard floor. He gasped and tried to sit up. The darkness around the edges of his vision threatened to become absolute. He didn't let it. Slowly, the blackness receded, and the room came into focus—starting with Avery.

She crouched beside him, her hands gently cupping his head. "You're awake."

The sound of her voice was all it took for the memory of the events that had led him here to come flooding back. *Welcome to the Game, Mr. Hawthorne.*

A realization accompanied that memory: the pockets of his tuxedo jacket were empty. No wallet, no cell phone. *Cut off from the outside world.*

"Where are we?" he asked Avery, as he climbed to his feet. "What time is it?"

"Early morning, just after dawn." Avery's answer came as his brain finally registered the scene around them: walls made of heavy gray-and-brown stone, wood paneling on the ceiling, moldings painted gold and blue. "And we're at Vantage."

If Jameson's brain had begun noting the details of this place before, it drank them in now. The room was long and thin and looked like it could have belonged in the castle that Ian had said that Vantage wasn't, *exactly*. The stone of the walls looked like the stuff of ancient fortresses; the detailing on the ceiling looked like it belonged in a palace. There was an elaborate X directly over the center of the room, with squares positioned to look like diamonds on either side. Inside each of the diamonds, there was a shield; on the shield, symbols, all in shades of gold and blue.

Aside from that detailing, the room was devoid of decoration. The stone walls were imposing, and Jameson counted only five places in the room where stone gave way to something else: two windows, one door, a fireplace cut into the stone, and, beside it, a second cut-out, equal in size and shape to the door, filled a third of the way up with firewood.

The only piece of furniture in the entire room was a long, heavy table made of dark, shining wood. The table was rectangular, plain. There were no chairs, which would explain why most of the people in the room were standing.

The other players, Jameson's brain whispered as he registered their presence. *Only three, besides Avery and me.* It was never too early to take stock of the competition.

Jameson recognized Branford and Zella, who stood on opposite sides of the table. To their left, he saw a woman gazing out one of the windows, her back to them all. The woman's hair was silvery gray. She wore a white pantsuit, and the fact that it was immaculate made Jameson wonder how *she* had managed to avoid the knock-out treatment.

Maybe she's someone even the Proprietor of the Devil's Mercy wouldn't dare knock out.

With that thought, Jameson shifted his gaze from the woman to the opposite window, where Rohan sat on the stone sill. There were no curtains on the window, no adornments of any kind, just the Factotum, lounging there, reading a book, wearing a suit the same dark purple color as the ink in which Jameson had written his secret.

An H. *The word* is. *The letters* v *and* e. Jameson pushed back against the memory, and the sense of dread pooling in the pit of his stomach.

"Are you okay?" Jameson asked Avery calmly. Focusing on her always helped. "Did they use the knockout powder on you, too?"

"I'm fine," Avery said. "And yes."

"Well, this is hardly sporting," the woman at the window commented, turning to face the room. Her silvery hair came barely to her chin, but not a strand of it fell into her eyes. "Are the two of them to be allowed to play together?"

Rohan took that as a cue to snap his book closed. He waited to be sure he had the attention of the entire room, then stood, leaving his reading material on the stone ledge. "If it's the rules of the Game you're wanting, Katharine, I would be happy to oblige."

Rohan walked to stand at the head of the table, his stride languid but his eyes electric.

"Where is Alastair?" Branford asked.

"*The Proprietor,*" Rohan replied, meeting Branford's eyes with a dark glint in his own, "has left the design and running of this year's Game to me."

"A test of sorts?" Zella said. "For the boy who would be king."

Jameson tracked each word spoken, taking measure of the

players. Zella was attempting to get under Rohan's skin, her reason for wanting to do so unclear. Branford had asked after Alastair and Rohan had come back with the Proprietor. And something about the shrewd expression on Katharine's face reminded Jameson of his grandfather.

"As you will have noticed, this year's Game has taken us to what most would agree is the Mercy's most notable win of the past decade." Rohan tossed a smirking look toward Branford. "Welcome home, Viscount." The Factotum's deep brown eyes lingered on Branford's, then his gaze shifted to Katharine's as he continued. "You are all aware of the stakes of the Game. The prizes you may choose from. *Power. Riches.*"

There was something in Rohan's tone that made Jameson wonder how long he had been waiting to run his own Game—and what he'd done to earn the right.

"Hidden somewhere on this estate," Rohan said with a flourish, "are three keys. The manor, the grounds—they're all fair play. There are also three boxes."

One, Jameson thought, *for each key.*

"The Game is simple," Rohan said. "Find the keys. Open the boxes. Two of the three contain secrets." Rohan smiled, and the expression was dark and glittering this time. "Two of yours, as a matter of fact."

Avery hadn't been required to pay her way into this game, but Jameson had—and so had Branford. Zella had been dismissed from the room before the Proprietor asked for their secrets, suggesting that she, like Avery, was in the clear. Katharine was a wild card, but she responded to Rohan's statement with the slightest, satisfied curve of her lips.

Jameson thought about what he'd written down, and it took

everything in him not to look at Avery, because suddenly, her presence here didn't seem like a boon. It was a risk.

After all, Jameson could hear the Proprietor saying, *these things are always more interesting when at least a few players have "skin in the game."*

Anyone reading those words would be bad. *Avery* reading them would open Pandora's box.

"So, two boxes with secrets. In the third, you'll find something much more valuable. Tell me what you find in the third box, and you'll win the mark." Like a magician, Rohan produced a round, flat stone out of nowhere. It was half black, half white. "The mark may be redeemed for either a page from the Mercy's ledger that has been forfeited this year or an asset the Mercy has claimed during that same time period. As for rules and limitations..."

Rohan made the mark disappear once more.

"Leave the manor and the grounds in the condition in which you found them. Dig up the yard, and you'd best fill the holes. Anything broken must be mended. Leave no stone unturned but smuggle nothing out." Rohan laid his palms flat on the dark, gleaming table, leaning forward, his arm muscles pulling at the fabric of his suit. "Likewise, you may do no damage to your fellow players. They, like the house and the grounds, will be left in the condition in which you found them. Violence of any kind will be met with immediate expulsion from the Game."

Three keys. Three boxes. No damaging the house, the grounds, or the other players. Jameson's mind reflexively catalogued the rules.

"And that's it?" Katharine asked. "There are no other limitations or rules?"

"You have twenty-four hours," Rohan said, "beginning at the top of the hour. After that, the prize will be considered forfeit."

"And let me guess," Zella said, drawing out the last word, "if we forfeit, *you* get the mark."

Rohan offered her a slow, wicked smile. "If that's your way of asking if I've made it easy for you all, I have not. No rest for the wicked, my dear. But it would hardly be sporting if I hadn't given you everything you needed to win."

Without another word, Rohan walked toward the room's only exit. He went through it, then pulled the heavy wooden door closed. A moment later, Jameson heard the sound of a bolt being thrown.

They were locked in.

"The Game starts when you hear the bells," Rohan called through the door. "Until then, I suggest you all let the wheels turn a bit and acquaint yourself with the competition."

CHAPTER 52

JAMESON

Jameson had grown up playing his grandfather's games. Every Saturday morning, a challenge had been laid out in front of them. One lesson that it had taken years for him to learn was that sometimes, the best opening move was to take a step back.

To watch.

To *see*.

"I should have known he would send you." Branford walked to stand next to Katharine. His tone was polite, his expression austere.

"Perhaps I'm here on my own behalf," Katharine replied archly. "After all, Ainsley has a secret in play, and you know I'd love to see him unseated."

"So you're saying that you're not here for Vantage?" Branford arched a brow. "That *he* has no interest in it?"

"I find it quite interesting," Katharine said evenly, "how much you want to know the answer to that question."

Jameson would have snuck a glance at Avery to see what she

was making of all of this, but Zella chose that moment to step between them.

"Checking out the competition?" she murmured.

"Who is she?" Jameson asked, well aware that Zella was *also* the competition.

"Katharine Payne." Zella had a way of pitching her voice that made him strain to hear it. "She's been an MP longer than you've been alive."

MP. Jameson's brain came at the abbreviation like a code. The answer fell immediately into place. *Member of Parliament.*

"Who's *he*?" Avery asked quietly.

"And is *he* playing for Vantage?" Jameson murmured.

"I doubt it," Zella said. "I know who she works for, and let's just say that Bowen Johnstone-Jameson isn't exactly the sentimental type."

Jameson remembered Ian claiming that the King's Gate Terrace flat didn't belong to Branford. *I have two brothers*, he'd said, days before that. *Both older, both horribly irrelevant to this story.* Except, apparently, they weren't. There were five players in the Game. One was Ian's oldest brother; another was potentially working on behalf of the second-born.

If Katharine is a powerful political figure, what does that make the man she works for?

Jameson thought about the flat, about the way the security guard had emphasized the word *he* in referring to the owner, the same way that Branford had just now, like Bowen Johnstone-Jameson wasn't a name that one just spoke.

Unless, Jameson thought, *you're Zella.*

"Are you?" Jameson asked the woman beside him. "Sentimental?"

Zella gave a little shrug. "In my own way."

"You broke into the Devil's Mercy," Jameson commented.

"And ended up with membership," Avery added.

A delicate, closed-lipped smile adorned Zella's face. "I'm *That Duchess*. There's nothing I won't do."

Or at least, that's what people say, Jameson inferred, and then he amended that thought. *Racist people.* How many Black women were there, total, in Zella's position? In the aristocracy? At the Mercy?

"What are you playing for?" Jameson asked her.

Zella tilted her head. "Wouldn't you like to know?"

"Her situation is more precarious than she lets on."

Jameson looked past Zella and Avery to see Katharine walking toward them. Her stride was neither long nor quick, her posture perfectly erect.

"Your husband," Katharine said, meeting Zella's gaze. "The Duke. I hear he's not well."

As excellent as Zella's poker face was, that got a response—just for a fraction of a second, just a slight narrowing of her eyes, but Jameson caught it. An instant later, the polished, slightly amused look was back in place. "Wherever would you hear a thing like that?"

"From my brother, I wager." Branford didn't come any closer to the four of them. He aimed a piercing glare at Katharine. "What does Bowen want with her?" Simon Johnstone-Jameson, Viscount Branford, did not mince words.

In response, Katharine gave an indelicate snort. Given her posture, mannerisms, and that immaculate suit, Jameson was fairly certain that, for Katharine, *indelicate* was a choice.

"I spanked you once when you were a child," Katharine told Branford. "Do you remember that?"

The red-haired man responded with a snort of his own. "Really, Katharine, is that your best attempt to put me in my place?"

"You know me better than that." Katharine's expression *seemed* mild, but her eyes—they were blue green and very hard. "You know your brother better than that."

It fully hit Jameson then that the Proprietor might have chosen the players of this game for reasons of his own, reasons that went far beyond who had or had not impressed him or whose secrets he was most curious to hear.

Me. Avery. One Johnstone-Jameson brother and a powerful woman working on behalf of another. If there was one thing that those Saturday morning games had taught Jameson, it was how to look for a pattern.

How to read code.

So how does the duchess fit?

"The boy is Ian's son." Branford didn't even look at Jameson as he imparted that bit of knowledge to Katharine. "Don't try to pretend that Bowen ferreted that secret out long ago. If he'd been aware of a Hawthorne connection, he would have made a play when the old man was alive."

Hearing Branford refer to his grandfather as *the old man* hit Jameson harder than it should have.

"Are you so sure he didn't?" Katharine parried. Then she spared a glance for Jameson himself—which was more than his uncle gave him. "You're playing for Vantage, then, Mr. Hawthorne, not just out of some sophomoric love of novelty."

You're playing for Ian. That was what this woman was saying. *You're just a stooge.*

Jameson turned, rather than trying to keep his face blank. "I'm playing for myself." That would have been true, back at the start, but now? Unwilling to dwell on the thought, Jameson returned his attention to the room.

The table. The fireplace. The logs. The design on the ceiling. The book on the window. It was the last of these that caught his attention and held it. *Let the rest of the players think I'm dealing with daddy issues. Hawthornes have granddaddy issues instead.*

Issues like the fact that part of Jameson's brain would always look at the world in layers, would always question the purpose behind any action that seemed, on the surface, to have none.

Actions like Rohan bringing a book into this room—and leaving it here.

Allowing himself to look angry, maybe even hurt, Jameson faced the window... and subtly picked up the book.

The Smugglers' Caves and Other Stories. It took nothing more than looking at the cover to determine that what he held in his hands was a collection of children's stories—old ones. *Now why,* Jameson thought, not bothering to mask the smile on his face now that his back was to the room, *would Rohan be reading this?*

Immediately, his brain started going back through everything the Factotum had said about the Game. *It would hardly be sporting,* he'd told Zella, *if I hadn't given you everything you needed to win.*

Jameson's adrenaline surged. The Game? It wasn't hide-and-seek. *It's Saturday morning.* Not exactly—but Rohan had left a clue. *Maybe more than one.* Jameson's brain latched on to something else that Rohan had said, when delivering the rules. *Leave no stone unturned but smuggle nothing out.*

The bastard had used the word *smuggle.* He'd left this book here. Jameson looked out the window—for real, this time, and let his eyes take in the grand scope of what he saw. Vantage wasn't just built on a hill. It was built on a cliff, overlooking a large body of water.

The kind of body of water on which smugglers sailed, Jameson thought. He looked back down at the book in his hands. *What are the chances that if we scale down the cliff, we'll find caves?*

Knowing better than to cast his lot on a single interpretation, Jameson subtly examined the book. Avery came to stand behind him. She wrapped her arms around his torso, in what likely passed for a gesture of comfort, and looked around him, to the book.

He hadn't fooled *her.*

Jameson thumbed through the pages of the book, and when something fell out, he caught it before it could fall far. *A pressed flower.* Jameson turned that over in his mind. *A poppy.*

"Keep going," Avery murmured behind him, soft words, charged ones, for only his ears.

Jameson kept going. On the back inside cover of the book, he found two words, scripted in familiar dark purple ink.

Ladies first.

CHAPTER 53

GRAYSON

Grayson stared at the photograph. He looked about sixteen in it. He was on a public street, alone. Based on the angle of the photo, it had been taking by an observer at least one story up.

A PI? Or Sheffield Grayson himself?

"This is you," Gigi said, picking up the picture. She cradled it in her hand for a minute, then turned her attention back to the box. "And you," she continued, lifting another photo out. "And you."

Each photo was another slice of the knife. Suddenly, all he could hear was Acacia asking him, *Do you ever play what-if, Grayson?*

No, he didn't. He wouldn't. *Assess the situation.* Grayson fell back on familiar thought patterns and took a step closer to the box. It was full of photographs. Dozens of them.

"And you?" Gigi asked him, picking up a picture of him at eight.

Martial arts competition. Photographer was somewhere in the crowd. Grayson continued his assessment and parted with one and only one word in response to Gigi's question. "Yes."

This made no sense.

No amount of assessing this situation could make it make sense. *Sheffield Grayson had a safe-deposit box full of pictures of me.* His throat tightened.

"I think we've seen enough." Savannah went to flip the lid to the box closed, but Gigi was faster and held it open.

"No." With her free hand, Gigi rifled through the box, down to the photos near the bottom. "You look about four in this one," she told Grayson. Her voice cracked, but she didn't stop. "Maybe two here?"

It was all Grayson could do to focus on her, not the pictures.

"That must be one of your brothers with you in this one," Gigi continued, and then she pulled out one final picture and sucked in a sharp, audible breath. "Why does my dad have a picture of you as a newborn?" She shook her head, her lip trembling. "Why does he have all these pictures?"

Grayson didn't let himself think too hard on either question, and he answered only the first, forcing his tone to stay even. "He must have bribed one of the nurses."

In the newborn photo, his infant self was asleep in a hospital bassinet. His baby arms were swaddled to his sides. A hat had been pulled down over his forehead, obscuring part of his tiny, squished face.

"I thought you worked for my dad." Gigi's words managed to break through the wall of silence in his mind. "Or maybe even that you had it out for him," she continued. "You gave me that warning and everything, but..."

Grayson had spent a lifetime practicing rigid control over his own emotions. Other people could afford to make mistakes. He couldn't. *Assess the situation and proceed accordingly.*

"Why does my dad have a safe-deposit box full of pictures of you, Grayson?" Gigi pressed. "A box that isn't even in his real name. *It doesn't make sense.*"

It wouldn't make sense to her—until it did. She would get there on her own eventually.

Grayson steeled himself. "Davenport is my middle name," he told Gigi evenly. "My grandfather's name was—"

"Tobias Hawthorne," Gigi finished. "And the box was under the name Tobias Davenport. I don't understand."

Grayson's heart twisted.

"Gigi, honey..." Acacia started to say, but Savannah didn't let her get any further.

"Dad had an affair." The older, taller, and more self-contained of the twins kept her voice as even as Grayson's. "Before we were born. Right after Colin died. With Skye Hawthorne."

Gigi went very still. Grayson had stopped noticing her tendency toward constant motion until suddenly, there was none. He saw the exact moment Gigi realized what Savannah was saying, the exact moment that every last piece fell into place for her.

"That's a pretty name," his normally bright-eyed sister said hoarsely. "Skye."

Grayson swallowed. "Gigi..."

She whirled on him, stepping back from the table, back from the safe-deposit box. "You lied to me." She shook her head, sending her curls flying. "Or maybe you didn't, maybe you just avoided the truth like avoidance is your middle name—or your second middle name, I guess? Grayson Davenport Avoidance Hawthorne. It has a ring to it."

"Breathe, Geeg," Savannah said quietly.

Gigi took another step back, gave another shake of her head. She pushed her hair roughly out of her face with the heels of her hands. "You knew," she told Savannah, and then she looked to Grayson, to Acacia. "You all knew. Everyone but me, and—oh dear lord, your name is Grayson." She was talking far too fast for anyone to make a real attempt at interrupting her now. "*Grayson* Hawthorne." She looked from him to Savannah. "And the two of you . . . No wonder you freaked out when I pretended we were hooking up! *Ewwww.* And I thought maybe you two . . ." She gestured between them. "Also *ew.*"

"I know this is a lot to take in," Acacia told her daughter quietly.

Gigi held up a hand. "I just threw up a little. Right there in my mouth. Did Dad, like, have a secret family this whole time? Like, when we thought he was on business trips was he with his *son*?" Gigi scrunched her face. "And does anyone have a mint?"

Grayson bent his head down, capturing her gaze. "No," he told her, his voice just as quiet as Acacia's had been a moment before.

"No mint?" Gigi said.

"Your father didn't have a secret family," Grayson said. *Your father, Gigi, not mine.* "He and I met exactly once. I was nineteen, and he made it very clear that I was not his son."

So. Very. Clear.

"Not clear enough, apparently," Savannah tossed out.

"Savannah," Acacia said sharply.

Gigi ignored both her mother and her twin. Her beseeching, teary eyes focused only on Grayson. "Then why did my dad have all these pictures?"

That was the question, the unavoidable black hole of a question threatening to suck him in when the answer didn't even matter. Couldn't matter.

"Why are you even here, Grayson? Why are you helping me look for him?" Gigi's breath hitched. "You must hate him. And us."

"No." Grayson spoke with the full force of the authority he'd been raised to assume in every interaction. The authority that had never worked on her. "Juliet, *no*."

I don't hate you. I could never hate you. Grayson remembered too late that Gigi had said their father was the only one who ever used her full first name.

"Why?" Gigi repeated brokenly.

"I'm here," Grayson said, "because he isn't. My grandfather had a saying: family first."

"We are not family," Savannah replied, her voice low and almost guttural. For the first time, Grayson registered that *she* hadn't looked away from the photographs. Not once.

"He's our brother," Gigi replied.

The word *brother* meant something to Grayson. It had always meant something to him, always been a foundational part of who he was.

"No." Savannah finally ripped her gaze away from the box. "He's not. Dad didn't want him to be."

He didn't want me. He despised me. Grayson should have been able to cut the thought off there. He should have had the discipline to leave it there. *But the pictures. My whole life, he...*

"I thought he was a good dad." Gigi looked up at the ceiling, then squeezed her eyes closed. "Not perfect, but..." She trailed off and pressed her lips together. "I thought he was a good husband." Her voice was gaining steam again. "That's why I've been looking for him! Because I didn't believe he would cheat on Mom and abandon us, but I guess the whole cheating and abandoning thing is just par for the course for him."

Gigi was practically vibrating with intensity now. Grayson wanted to reach for her, but something in him wouldn't let him.

"You should have told me." Gigi took a step back, then another and another. "You all should have told me." Hitting the wall, she shot each of them a final, furious look, then bolted from the room.

"Gigi!" Savannah started to go after her, but Acacia reached out a gentle hand to stop her.

"Let her go." Acacia closed her eyes for a long moment, then opened them again. "Is there anything else?" she said. "In the box?"

Grayson removed and stacked the photographs, refusing to look too closely at any of them. *My whole life, Sheffield Grayson knew about me. My whole life, he kept an eye on me.*

At the bottom of the box, near the back, Grayson found a bank envelope. It was thick. Full. He pulled it out and opened it, expecting to find a fortune in large bills, but all he saw was slips of paper. Dozens of them.

"Deposit slips?" Acacia asked, and Grayson knew what she was thinking. *The investigation. The embezzling. Her drained accounts.*

He examined the papers. "Withdrawal slips, actually," Grayson said, removing a handful of them, skimming each one with brutal efficiency. "Petty cash. This one's for two hundred and seventeen dollars. Another for five hundred and six dollars. Three hundred and twenty-one dollars." He turned one of the slips over. "There's a notation on the back. *KM*." He glanced up toward his father's wife. "Do you know anyone with those initials?"

Savannah blew out a long, controlled breath. "Probably another side piece."

"Savannah, I do not appreciate you talking about another woman that way."

"I think you mean *the* other woman." Savannah went for the jugular, like she'd utterly lost the ability to do anything else. "Or other women, plural, I guess," she continued icily. "Not that you care."

"Enough." Grayson hadn't meant to use that tone, but he didn't regret it, either. He thought about Acacia telling him that she couldn't even *think* about a life without her daughters. He thought about children's paintings displayed like fine art and handprints captured in cement.

Grayson fixed Savannah with a *look* and spoke with an emphasis capable of sending chills down spines. "Your mother doesn't deserve that from you."

"*My* mother," Savannah shot back. Her expression was a study in ice-cold fury, ruined only by the tears on her white-blonde lashes. "And as for my dad..." She titled her chin up. "I always knew he wanted a boy."

That statement affected Acacia more than Savannah's earlier barbs. She folded her daughter into her arms. To Grayson's surprise, Savannah didn't fight it. They both stood there for the longest time, their arms around each other, holding on for dear life and leaving Grayson with a feeling he barely recognized.

Hawthornes weren't supposed to long for things they could not have.

Eventually, Savannah pulled back, and Acacia turned to Grayson. "We're going to go," she told him. "Everything in this box—it's yours."

CHAPTER 54

GRAYSON

The photographs. The withdrawal slips. Grayson only allowed himself to focus on the latter. *Evidence of who knows what.*

"Sir." The bank employee's voice was stiff. "The box must be returned to the wall before the owner can leave."

The owner. Acacia. Savannah with her. Grayson was well aware of how fragmented his thoughts were, but the alternative—actually thinking in any detail about what had just happened—was even less desirable.

"I'll need a briefcase." Grayson phrased that as neither an order nor a request, but there was difference between saying *I need* and *I'll need*. The future tense implied that one expected the need to be met before it became pressing.

"A briefcase?"

Grayson stared him down. "Will that be a problem?"

Ten minutes later, he walked out of the bank holding a briefcase.

The hotel valets were very amendable to the idea of driving the Ferrari out to him. Probably a little too amendable, but when they arrived at the bank, Grayson did them the courtesy of pretending not to notice their adrenaline-soaked exuberance.

"That was *incredible*!"

Per the plan, one valet drove the other home, leaving the *incredible* car behind. Grayson wasn't sure how long he sat in the parking lot of that bank, behind the wheel of the Ferrari, the briefcase on the passenger-side floor, out of reach.

He should have left the photos in the safe-deposit box. Should have—but didn't.

What did it matter that Sheffield Grayson had kept tabs on him? *My whole life.* Those words managed to penetrate the forced silence in his brain. *He watched me my whole life.*

Grayson's hand snaked out and pressed the ignition. As he pulled out of the parking lot, he thought about the look in the valets' eyes. Clearly, both of them had taken a turn behind the wheel. Grayson wondered how fast they'd gone. How much of a thrill they'd allowed themselves.

Pulling onto the highway, Grayson pushed the pedal down farther—and farther. He looked at the positioning of the cars ahead of him, calculated the spacing between them. When Jameson needed to outrun something, he found an excuse to go way too fast or way too high. Only one of those was an option for Grayson at the moment.

It wouldn't take much to push the Ferrari up over a hundred.

You're not Jameson. What is acceptable for him is not acceptable for you. Grayson heard Tobias Hawthorne's voice as clearly as if the old man were in the seat beside him. *And do you know why?*

Grayson wasn't reckless. He didn't dance hand in hand with unnecessary risks.

Because it's going to be you. How many times had he been told that? And the whole time, his grandfather had known that it was a lie. Tobias Hawthorne had written his family out of the will before Grayson was even born.

It was never going to be me. Grayson's knuckles bulged as his grip on the steering wheel tightened. A muscle in his calf tensed, his body waiting. All he had to do was press the pedal to the floor.

Silence the old man.

Stop thinking about Sheffield Grayson.

And *go*.

Grayson switched to the left lane, and like magic, the other cars got out of the way. There was nothing stopping him now. No reason he couldn't let the car do what cars of this sort did best.

I could fly. Let go. Say to hell with safety and rules. Something like anger built inside him—because he *couldn't*.

He didn't get to hurt. He didn't get to take risks or ignore potential consequences or dwell on the fact that the father he'd been certain despised him had collected pictures of him, saving them all these years.

What does it matter? He's dead now.

Grayson switched lanes, then switched again, and the next thing he knew, he'd pulled the car onto the shoulder of the road. He managed to turn off the engine, but his other hand was still gripping the wheel.

Grayson leaned over it, breaths wracking his body like brutal, rib-breaking punches.

And then his phone rang, and somehow, he managed to drop the wheel. He answered with his eyes closed. "Hello."

"What's wrong?" *Nan.* Grayson could practically feel his great-grandmother jabbing him with her cane as she issued that question like a demand.

"Nothing is wrong." *Say it. Believe it. Make it so.*

"Young man, have you developed the notion that lying to me is a *good* idea?" Nan retorted. "Of course something is wrong! You said hello."

Grayson scowled. "I say hello!"

"And now you're yelling," Nan grunted, and Grayson could *hear* her canny eyes narrowing. "Xander was right."

Grayson's own eyes narrowed in response. "What exactly did Xander tell you?"

"*Hmmmph*," Nan replied. Grayson knew her well enough to know that *was* her response—and all the answer he was going to get.

Note to self, Grayson thought, *kill Xander*. The thought, like Nan's harrumphing, was familiar, and that familiarity let him *breathe*. Breathing let him focus. "Is everything okay?"

Nan wasn't exactly in the habit of calling up to chat.

"Did I give you permission to worry about me?" Nan harrumphed again. "I'm not the one who answered the phone sounding like *that*. What happened to you, boy?"

Grayson thought about the briefcase, the photographs, what-if, Gigi, Savannah. He thought about Acacia, about Skye, about Sheffield Grayson. "Nothing."

Nan made it very clear what she thought of that response: "Bah."

Grayson felt his eyes close again. "Did Skye ever take pictures of us when we were young?" The question came out hoarse. "Of me?"

"When it suited her." Nan's tone made it clear what she thought of that. Skye had flitted in and out of her sons' lives. Anything she did was because it suited her.

"Would she have sent any of those pictures to my biological father?" Grayson wasn't sure why he was even asking. Skye hadn't been present for most of the photos he'd seen. Why would it even matter if she'd sent Sheffield Grayson a picture or two?

"I don't believe so." Nan's tone gentled. "Come home, boy."

Home. Grayson thought about Hawthorne House. About his brothers. He tilted his head back into the headrest, his Adam's apple and trachea pulling tight against the skin of his throat. He gave himself a moment—just one—and then tilted his head back down. "Nash gave me the ring you gave him." Grayson wasn't sure why he was even saying the words. "For safe-keeping."

"Hmmmm." In Nan-talk, that was a decidedly different response than *hmmmph.* "Ask me how my day's going," she ordered abruptly.

Grayson's instincts flared. She'd definitely called for a reason. "How is your day going, Nan?"

"Abominably! I've spent far too much time with those files of your grandfather's."

The List, Grayson thought. The files that the old man had kept on the people he'd wronged. Suddenly, Xander's assertion that he had "connections" at Hawthorne House was a lot clearer. "Xander asked you to go through the List."

"He told me what you're looking for."

My father shot and killed himself when I was four years old, a girl's voice said in Grayson's memory. "You found it?" he asked Nan. "Found him?"

"What do you take me for, boy? Of course I found him."

A Hawthorne did this. "What did the old man do?" Grayson asked, his voice low.

"Bought a minority stake in this individual's only patent."

"What was the patent for?" Grayson pressed.

"File didn't say. Didn't list a number, either."

Grayson took that in. "Was there anything else?"

"A receipt. Your grandfather had flowers sent to the man's funeral. Bit sentimental for Tobias, if you ask me."

"What was the man's name?" Grayson asked. *What was her father's name?*

What's hers?

"First name Thomas, last name Thomas." Nan snorted.

"Thomas Thomas?" Grayson's eyes narrowed. That was almost certainly some kind of code. *What begins a bet?* he thought. *Not that.* "I don't suppose the file said anything about a daughter?"

CHAPTER 55

GRAYSON

Grayson made it exactly one step into the lobby before the manager locked on to his position and walked briskly to greet him. "Mr. Hawthorne, I wanted to apologize for the misunderstanding earlier, with your guest."

Gigi. The second Grayson thought the name, an image of her face came to him: bright blue eyes going round at him as she realized exactly who he was to her.

"It's fine," Grayson said, and a less ambitious hotel manager would have taken his tone as a dismissal.

This woman, however, was not so easily put off. "Would you like me to clear the pool?"

Grayson stepped out onto the pavement and became immediately aware of two facts. The first was that the pool was *not* empty. And the second was that the person treading water in the deep end was Eve.

"Does it pain you?"

"My existence?"

"Your wound." Grayson has the sudden urge to brush her hair gently back from the bruise. He dismisses it—brutally, absolutely.

"Some people would want me to say yes." There's a challenge in Eve's words. "Some people want to think that girls like me are weak."

Grayson will not *touch her—but he steps closer. "Pain doesn't make you weak."*

Eve's eyes lock on his, and for a moment, she looks nothing like Emily. "You don't really believe that, Grayson Hawthorne."

Snapping out of it, Grayson channeled an apathy capable of icing out everything else. He'd been a fool, and no one got to make a fool of Grayson Hawthorne twice.

He turned, fully intending to leave. Mattias Slater stepped out of the shadows. In daylight, the sentinel's dark-blond hair bordered on gold, but his eyes still looked almost black. With a single step, he blocked Grayson's path back inside.

Fast. Unafraid. Armed. All aspects of Grayson's earlier assessment still seemed to apply. The ink on the sentinel's biceps was more visible now—not one tattoo, but many: thick, black, curving lines, like tally marks reflected in a fun house mirror.

Or claw marks. "Get out of my way," Grayson ordered.

Mattias Slater did not get out of his way.

Grayson side-stepped. His opponent anticipated the move and blocked him again. Grayson turned and began striding toward a side gate, but before he could make it there, he heard the audible click of a gun.

You're not going to shoot me, Mattias. Grayson didn't turn around. He didn't so much as break his stride. But the next thing he heard was Eve climbing out of the pool, and *that* froze him in his spot.

It shouldn't have.

He knew better.

"Hello, Grayson." Eve's wet feet were audible against the pavement as she walked toward him.

"I have nothing to say to you." Grayson forced his body to move, but Mattias Slater was suddenly in front of him, blocking the gate.

"That's a lie." Eve passed him, then turned slowly toward him, leaving them face-to-face. "But then, we always were liars."

Grayson felt those words—and her presence—in a deep and hollow place. A singular muscle in his jaw tensed. "There is no *we*, Eve."

"At least when I lie, there's a utility to it. A purpose." Eve took a single step forward. "At least I don't lie to myself."

She'd used him. She'd made him a pawn, then discarded him. She had come after his family. Apathy was what she deserved—the *best* she deserved, and that only because Grayson wouldn't risk the complications that could come with exacting a fair price for her betrayal.

So she got *nothing*. "What are you doing here?" Grayson said, a Hawthorne question, more order or demand.

Eve responded with a question of her own. "How are things going with your sisters?"

Fury surged inside Grayson. If that was a threat...

"It's not easy," Eve continued. "Coming to a family as an outsider, seeing what might have been. What *you* might have been if things had been different."

Grayson saw how she was playing this. *We are not the same, Eve.* "You made your choice." His voice was low and full of warning.

She should have taken that warning.

She didn't. "Do you want me to say that I regret what I did to be named Vincent Blake's heir? That I wish I'd chosen to remain at your mercy? At *hers*?" That was a reference to Avery. It had to be. "Do you expect me to stand here and tell you that money and power don't matter?"

Of course they did. "I don't expect anything from you." There wasn't a hint of emotion in Grayson's tone—no way in, no weakness for her to exploit.

"You have no idea what it's like to be me right now, Gray."

She'd called him Gray. If she expected that to affect him in any way, she was going to be disappointed. "You got what you wanted," he replied with searing, emotionless precision. "You're the sole heir to a massive fortune."

"I'm alone." The words slipped from her mouth like a confession.

Vulnerability had always been Eve's weapon of choice.

"I have to prove myself every day," she continued, "knowing that if I fail, he'll take the seals from me one by one, and I'll be left with nothing." She met his eyes, waiting for a response, and when she didn't get one, she turned to her guard. "Slate, tell Grayson how many of my great-grandfather's men are loyal to me."

Mattias Slater's face remained neutral, dangerously so. "One."

You, Grayson thought.

Eve grabbed Grayson's chin, wrenching his gaze back toward hers. "Would you at least look at me?"

Why would I? "What do you want from me, Eve?"

Something like hurt flickered in her eyes. "What do I want from you?" Eve drew in a breath. Then another. "Nothing." She raised her chin. "*Yet*. When I want something from you, you'll know."

She was baiting him. And, damn it, he took the bait. "Stay away from Gigi and Savannah," Grayson bit out, brutal force in each word.

"Is that what Tobias Hawthorne would do?" Eve said. "Would he give away leverage? Would you, Gray?" Eve's stare was just as piercing as his—when she wanted it to be. "I wonder... What did you and your sisters find in that safe-deposit box?"

That was *definitely* a threat. "Move," Grayson ordered in a tone that could have been described as *arctic*. "Call off your attack dog and get out of my way."

"Or what?" Eve looked at him in a way designed to make him look at her.

"Move," Grayson repeated, enunciating the word, "or I will move you."

She didn't. "Lie all you want, Grayson. To yourself. To me. But don't forget that I know your father isn't *missing*. And the only thing keeping my lips sealed about the people responsible is the promise of an honor-bound old man who won't be around forever." She stared at and into him. "You'll want to be on my good side then."

And there it was. "If you come at Avery," Grayson said, matching her threat with one of his own, "if you even think of coming near my sisters, I'll destroy you."

Eve brought her lips to whisper directly in his ear. "Is that a promise?"

CHAPTER 56

GRAYSON

Grayson didn't so much as look at the pool after Eve left. Instead, he made his way back into the hotel, walked briskly to the elevator, hit the button for his floor, and waited for the doors to close. Once they did, a single muscle in his jaw ticked. The elevator lurched upward.

Grayson made it three floors before his hand lashed out and pulled the emergency stop button. The elevator jerked to a halt between floors. A high-pitched buzz began to sound.

Grayson's fingers curled to fists at his sides. *I am in control.* He believed that. He *was* that. Still, he found himself slipping his phone from his pocket, pulling up the photo roll. Mechanically, he scrolled back past the photos he'd taken of Kent Trowbridge's passwords and the safe-deposit box key. The next thing that greeted him was a shot of Jameson and Xander, each holding a roll of duct tape.

Nash's bachelor party. Grayson let the memory wash over him, clearing his mind of everything else like a wave crashing onto sand. *Tree house rules.* Grayson's lips ticked slightly upward, and he scrolled back farther. Most of the photographs he took were of objects, nature, or crowds—beauty in moments, captured just so: real, true, *his*.

Grayson stopped when he came to a picture of a hand on the hilt of a sword. *A longsword. Avery's hand.*

Real, true, *his*. Not the way he had imagined or longed for once, but that didn't make her matter any less, didn't make what they *did* have matter less. If Eve thought she could get in Grayson Hawthorne's head, if she thought she still had any hold over him—she was wrong.

Damn wrong.

Grayson palmed the phone and hit the emergency stop button with his free hand. The elevator jerked back into motion. *I am in control.*

The elevator made it to the top floor. The doors opened, and the second they did, Grayson was greeted by the view of Savannah sitting in the hallway outside the black-card suite, staring straight ahead. Her blonde hair was pulled into a tight braid—so tight he wondered if it hurt.

"You shouldn't be here," Grayson said quietly, closing the space between them.

"I'm getting really sick of *should*." Savannah lifted her eyes to his. "I went to Duncan's house after the bank. His father told me everything."

Grayson was the very definition of steady. "I'm afraid I don't know—"

"You do." Savannah stood, and he realized that she wasn't wearing heels. In flats, she stood like an athlete, shoulders squared, muscles ready.

"And what *everything* might that be?" Grayson prompted. Acacia hadn't wanted her daughters to know about the family's current situation. Trowbridge knew that.

"The FBI. The frozen accounts. Mom's trust." Savannah stared at him—didn't narrow her eyes, didn't glare, but he felt the power of that *look* all the same. "That was why you wanted to get into Dad's safe-deposit box, wasn't it? Evidence. At first, I thought you probably wanted him caught, charged, and convicted, but"—she arched a brow—"family first."

He'd said those words back at the bank. "Exposing your father was never my intention," Grayson said quietly.

"But you *were* looking for evidence," Savannah countered, and then she paused, the first hint of uncertainty she'd shown. "So you could destroy it?"

Grayson could feel her trying to make this make sense, make *him* make sense. "Destroying evidence would be a felony." Grayson let her read between the lines there, giving her nothing to use against him.

"It would," Savannah agreed. She looked at him a moment longer, her pale eyes clear, and then she looked past him. After a moment, she seemed to come to a decision. "Family first."

There was nothing mocking or prodding in Savannah's tone this time. She wasn't questioning his priorities. She was stating her own.

"My mom isn't strong enough to protect this family," Savannah said, still not looking at him. "Gigi's a kid."

"You're twins," Grayson pointed out.

"Your point?" Savannah asked crisply, swinging her gaze back toward him. "Because *mine* is that we need to handle this."

"We." Grayson kept his voice neutral, but the fact that she'd decided that trusting him was the lesser of two evils hit Grayson like a blade slid between ribs. Betraying Gigi, who'd worn her heart on her sleeve from the moment he'd met her, was bad enough.

But Savannah? *I should send her home to her mother.*

"*KM*—the letters on the back of the withdrawal slip, they aren't initials." Savannah looked smug. "After Duncan's father told me everything, I went home. I got on Dad's computer and pulled up his calendar, from right before he left."

Grayson wondered what exactly she'd been looking for.

"Here." Savannah held out her phone. She waited for him to take it, a silent battle of wills.

Grayson let her have this one. He took the phone. There was a photo pulled up on it, of a monthly calendar—presumably Sheffield Grayson's.

"Tuesday night," Savannah instructed. "Third Tuesday of the month."

Grayson's gaze went reflexively to the date. There were three events scheduled, but it was the last one that drew his attention: *SVNNH GM*.

"I had a game that night," Savannah told him, her voice high and clear and steady in a way that told him she was working to keep it that way. "It was the last one he ever saw."

Grayson registered the notation that Sheffield Grayson had used. He skimmed over the rest of the calendar and found a few other events written the same way.

"Savannah game." His sister spelled it out for him, in case he'd missed it.

He hadn't. "No vowels. *KM* isn't mentioned on this calendar, but *CC* is." *Not initials. A name written without the vowels.* "*CC*—Acacia. *JLT*—Juliet."

"Which seems to suggest," Savannah replied calmly, "that *KM* might be Kim or Kam. He only used that shorthand for family, but him using it for a mistress isn't out of the question."

Grayson shook his head. "It's Kim, and she wasn't his mistress." He'd assigned Zabrowski to keep an eye on the girls and their mother—and the rest of Sheffield Grayson's family. "Kimberly Wright."

There was no spark of recognition in Savannah's eyes.

"Your aunt," Grayson clarified. "Your father's sister."

Savannah saw to the core of that in an instant. "Colin's mother." She'd known about her cousin. She must have inferred there was an aunt or an uncle, but from Zabrowski's reports, it didn't appear there was much, if any, interaction between Kimberly Wright and the girls.

"Dad said she was an addict. He didn't ever talk about her. Didn't want her anywhere near us."

"She's sober now," Grayson reported. "Her other children are adults. They don't seem to visit her much."

If Savannah wondered how Grayson knew that, she didn't give any visible sign of it. "It might be nothing," she said. "The slips. *KM*. It might not matter. We *should* stop."

But she'd already told him she was tired of *should*.

"I'll look into it," Grayson told her.

Savannah's eyes narrowed. "Gigi still hadn't come home when I left. Whatever this is—the withdrawal slips, whatever laws Dad may or may not have broken—Gigi doesn't need to know." Savannah's light gray eyes locked on to his. "She doesn't, but *I* do."

The sound of the elevator opening down the hall alerted Grayson to the fact that they had company. Xander stepped out, followed by Nash.

Nash was carrying a limp Gigi.

CHAPTER 57
GRAYSON

Grayson's heart froze inside his chest. *She's so still.* Then Gigi turned her head toward them, a loopy smile on her lips. "What's black and white and black and white and black and white," she said, happily slurring the words. "And black and white and black and white and—"

"The answer is a penguin rolling down a hill," Xander stage-whispered.

Gigi wriggled in Nash's arms and made an attempt at poking Xander. "No spoilers!"

"Are you drunk?" Savannah asked her sister incredulously.

"As a skunk!" Gigi agreed amiably, then her eyes went very wide. "Hey! I've got a new one! What's black and white and black and white and—"

Grayson met Nash's gaze. "I can take it from here."

Nash set Gigi on her feet, and she wobbled slightly, then started cracking up laughing. "Whatever you say, little brother," Nash drawled.

Gigi pointed a finger at Grayson. "Is he ticklish?" she demanded.

"Grayson?" Xander replied innocently. "Very."

Gigi crept toward Grayson in what she appeared to think was a very stealthy manner, her hands held aloft, fingers wiggling midair.

"Don't even think about it," Grayson commanded.

Gigi hid her hands behind her back—for about half a second, then continued her pursuit.

"Thanks for that," Grayson told Xander darkly. He was, in fact, *very ticklish*. So much so that he was having difficulty not reacting to Gigi's slow progression.

"Tickle... tickle... tickle..." she said, creeping closer. Then she paused. "I would have made an *excellent* little sister."

Savannah stepped toward her twin. "I'll take her home."

"Nope," drunk Gigi said cheerfully.

"Yup," Savannah replied.

Gigi shot Grayson a mischievous look. "Savannah is also very ticklish."

"Must be genetic," Xander replied. He—and Nash, for that matter—were enjoying this way too much.

"I will put away the tickling fingers when you agree to negotiate with tickling terrorists!" Gigi declared. "Or terrorist, I guess. Singular. Just me. I want to see the photos from the box. I was thinking: What if they're decoys? Like, someone looks in the box and thinks, *Oh, this Sheffield Grayson guy was a tortured soul wracked with grief for the son he never knew, cursed to parent only daughters*, but really... the photos are a clue!"

"A clue to what?" Grayson had the feeling that he was going to regret that question.

"*Exactly!*" Gigi said.

A sound escaped Nash's mouth.

"Do not laugh," Grayson told him.

Nash shrugged. "It's possible that my younger siblings are also a handful."

Grayson had fought thinking of the twins that way, as being to him what he and Xander and Jameson were to Nash. But it was all out in the open now. He could almost see the way it could have been if things had been different. If it weren't for the secrets he was keeping. The ways he'd betrayed them.

And would betray them still, if that was what it took. *Protect Avery. Protect them. Family first.*

Gigi bounded to Grayson's side. "Do you have the pictures in your pockets?" she asked, patting him down and realizing belatedly that he was wearing only a swimsuit. "You don't have pockets," she said slowly. "Only abs." She frowned. "Brothers should *not* have abs."

"I agree," Xander said solemnly. "Put on some clothes, man!"

Grayson was going to kill his brothers. He'd been very clear with Nash about not needing assistance.

As if he'd heard that thought, Nash rocked back on his heels. "Tree house rules." What happened in the tree house stayed in the tree house—and none of them could kick the others out.

Grayson's eyes narrowed. "You may note that this is not, in fact, our tree house." Before Nash could reply, Grayson turned to Savannah. "You should take Gigi home."

"Don't talk about me like I'm not here." Up until now, Gigi had been—predictably—a very cheerful drunk. But she didn't sound particularly cheerful now. "And stop acting like I need other people to make decisions for me. I am an autonomous person! A dynamo of good decision-making. I am . . . an autonymo!" Gigi declared. "Show me the photos."

CHAPTER 58

GRAYSON

Drunk Gigi was remarkably determined. Grayson ended up letting her into the black-card suite. Savannah followed, and Xander and Nash made themselves at home.

Grayson opened the briefcase containing the photographs. He flipped one over without allowing himself to even register the age he'd been when it was taken. "Date written on the back," he said, his voice controlled. "Nothing else."

He checked a second photo and a third—the same. Gigi began to spread the photos out.

"What if Dad's trying to tell us something?" she said.

"What if he left," Savannah countered, "because he doesn't care?"

"Don't say that," Gigi implored. "Do you really think that I've been looking for answers, looking for Dad, for *me*?"

Savannah's expression was very hard to read. "Geeg."

"You," Gigi replied, "were everything he wanted in a daughter."

Savannah looked down. "And it still wasn't enough."

Grayson looked away from the two of them.

"On the way here, I told myself that if there was even a small chance Dad was innocent, I was going to prove it," Savannah said. She swallowed. "But maybe I just want to understand. Why he left us. Why nothing was ever enough for him."

Gigi enveloped Savannah in a hug, then her blue eyes narrowed. "Prove Dad innocent of what?"

Grayson waited for Savannah to lie to her. She was the one who'd insisted that Gigi, like their mother, needed to be protected.

"Embezzling from Grammy. Emptying Mom's trust."

Gigi took in that info. "I am starting to feel distressingly sober. I think I need another mimosa."

"You got drunk on mimosas?" Nash asked mildly.

Gigi held up a single finger.

Xander interpreted. "On *one* mimosa?"

"And four cups of coffee," Gigi admitted.

Savannah's eyes narrowed. "Oh dear lord."

Gigi looked at her twin. "I forgive you," she said, and the fact that the words came out of nowhere seemed to make them hit Savannah harder. "You were just trying to protect me." Gigi turned toward Grayson. "And I forgive you, Lord of Lies, because you need me in your life." She glanced at Xander and Nash. "He takes himself way too seriously."

"I do not," Grayson grumbled.

Gigi moved like lightning and tickled his side. "Now, about those photographs..."

Grayson swatted her hand away and jumped back when she went in to tickle him again.

"We don't need the photographs." Savannah took pity on Grayson and distracted her twin. "We already know where we're going next."

CHAPTER 59

JAMESON

The sound of church bells broke through the air. Branford made it to the door first.

It was unlocked.

Jameson let the others clear out, then turned to Avery and softly murmured directly into her ear. "We're looking for smugglers' caves. They'll be ocean-side, obviously. We'll make sense of the rest of it once we find the caves."

But first, they had to find their way out of the massive not-quite-a-castle that Ian had said was more of a home to him and his brothers growing up than any of his father's properties ever were.

His brothers, Simon and Bowen. Jameson shoved the thought out of his brain as he snaked through a corridor, Avery on his heels.

At the end of the corridor, they found a banquet hall. Wallpaper adorned the top half of all four walls; the bottom half was covered with wood paneling, the carvings on the panels geometric. The ceiling was stark white, with dozens of moldings that hung down like icicles, each ending in a sharp, triangular point.

On the far side, the hall opened to another large room, and that room—all white, bare of furniture, marked only with an elaborate wooden staircase that looked like it belonged in a cathedral—opened to a foyer, which led to a door.

The front door.

Jameson threw it open and stepped onto stone. The manor loomed behind him, but his gaze was focused ahead. An expanse of green stretched out around him. Close to the house, there were gardens. But in the distance?

Rocks. Cliffs, presumably. And down below—and out as far as the eye could see—the ocean.

"This way." Jameson didn't glance back to see if Avery had heard him. He knew she'd follow either way. Without even thinking about it, he stripped off his tuxedo jacket as he ran. She was probably wishing she could ditch the ballgown.

A paved path cut through what might have once been a manicured garden but was now overgrown. *Trees and flowers, two small koi pools—one rectangular, one circular, surrounded by a circular hedge.* Jameson clocked his surroundings but kept his eyes on the prize.

The horizon.

The ocean.

The cliffs.

They were getting closer now. Jameson paused, ignoring his screaming ribs, assessing his options, and then he pushed forward under a brick archway and into a stone garden. Tens of thousands of stones paved the uneven ground, moss and grass growing up between them.

"Don't trip," Jameson called back.

"I'm not the one who leaps without looking," Avery responded. "There's a gate up ahead. It's closed."

Jameson saw the gate, saw the wall surrounding the stone garden at that end. *What if we're locked in?* He pushed past a series of statues, a sundial, plants grown too large and wild for their planters.

He broke into a run and didn't stop until he got to the gate.

There was a large cast-iron lock. Jameson pulled on it, and the lock gave. He tried the gate. "It's stuck," he gritted out.

Avery's right hand latched around one of the bars on the gate, followed by her left. "We'll pull together," she told him.

One, two, three.

Neither one of them counted out loud. They didn't have to. And as the gate gave and the two of them stepped past the stone wall and out onto wild green grass, the rocks less than a hundred yards away, Jameson thought about the fact that the key they were racing to find might well open a box containing his secret.

Not now. That thought pounded through his brain, blocking out even the agony in his side. *Figure that part out later. For now, just play.*

Jameson ran, and Avery ran beside him. They made it to the edge, where the grass turned to rocks and the land dropped off.

Jameson looked down. He hadn't realized how high up they were. *No wonder they call this place Vantage.* The drop to the ocean below was steep—and at least three hundred feet.

"We'll need a way down," Jameson murmured. He turned and looked in either direction. The drop was just as steep all the way around. He couldn't tell exactly how much beach—if any—there was below.

But when Avery's hand made its way to the small of his back, he followed her gaze to a part of the cliffs dotted with wild poppies.

Just like the one he'd found in the book.

CHAPTER 60

JAMESON

Near the poppies, the two of them found a staircase carved into the side of the cliffs, nearly completely camouflaged from view. There was no railing, no safeguard.

No margin for error.

"You should stay here." Jameson knew better than to tell Avery that. He really did. "That dress wasn't made for climbing."

Avery contorted her arms, and the next thing Jameson heard was a zipper being undone.

"The dress won't be a problem." And just like that, Avery let it drop. She wore a small black slip underneath that covered her from hip to upper thigh and a black bra, and he deserved a medal for staying focused on anything other than the way she looked, her hair blown back from her face and all that skin on display.

"When we find the key," Jameson said, his voice coming out thick, "we'll celebrate."

"We'll celebrate," Avery Kylie Grambs told him, well aware of her effect on him, "when we find all three."

Every step down seemed a little steeper than the last. Jameson's battered body screamed its objections, but he ignored it. Luckily, balance and ignoring pain were almost as much Jameson's specialty as taking risks, and Avery was made for this.

Made for him.

He leapt over the last few steps, landing on the beach. She did the same. From where they stood now, several things were clear. The beach was narrow, more gravel than sand. The tide was currently low. A handful of caves were visible from where they stood, but there were almost certainly more—potentially dozens.

"Where to now?" Avery said, and Jameson knew she was thinking aloud more than asking, that her mind was working through this as quickly and methodically as any Hawthorne's.

This time, he happened to get to the answer first. "There." Jameson's eyes locked on to a stone statue in the distance. It stood near the edge of the beach, and he knew that in higher tide, it would be partially—but not fully—submerged.

They ran toward it, because running seemed like the only option. Wind whipped at them. Avery's hair went wild, but it didn't slow her down. Neither of them slowed at all until they made it to the base of the statue.

Jameson took one look at it and registered one thing: the statue depicted a woman. He turned to Avery. *"Ladies first."*

CHAPTER 61

JAMESON

The statue might have been of a real person or a mythological figure or an image pulled from the sculptor's imagination. Her hair was long and wavy and thick, caught in what looked like a slight wind. She wore a dress. The cut of the dress was simple at the top, almost like a shift, but near the base of the statue, the fabric became waves, like the woman was clothed in the ocean itself. Her bare feet were visible where the waves parted, her stance calling to mind a dancer. Three stone necklaces adorned her neck, the shortest a choker, the longest hanging nearly to her waist. Dozens of bracelets marked each wrist; her shoulders and forearms were partially covered by her hair. One hand hung by her side, and the other pointed out into the ocean.

Ladies first. Jameson considered the clue, then turned away from the statue to assess the rest of their surroundings. In the immediate vicinity, he counted five caves.

Smugglers' caves. But which one held the key?

Forget the caves for a second. Focus on the Lady. Jameson examined the ground beneath the statue, followed the direction she was pointing out to sea. And then, with a paranoia born of Saturday mornings and games where his brothers might swoop in at any second, Jameson looked back to the staircase carved into the cliff.

And he saw a woman in a white pantsuit descending.

"Katharine," he told Avery. If thoroughly searching the caves one by one had been an option before, it wasn't now. Moving on instinct, he waded out into the ocean, searching. *The Lady's pointing out here.*

Rohan could have weighted down a bag or anchored something to a rock beneath the water's surface.

Jameson bent to submerge his hands in the shallows and came up empty, again and again. There was no time to second-guess. No time to wait. Katharine had an inside track on this place. She might know if there was a particular cave that was suited for hiding treasure.

Ladies first.

She's pointing out here.

"But what if she wasn't?" Jameson asked. Before Avery could respond, he was running through the water back toward the statue. Avery was kneeling in the sand, examining its base. And then, just as Jameson arrived at her side, she looked up.

"I think the statue turns."

Jameson could hear it in her voice, that thing that whispered *we're the same*, that said she'd never back down from a challenge, that there was nothing her mind couldn't do.

"Together," Jameson said, and as in sync as they had been with the gate, they threw their weight into turning the Lady. The statue moved, and after a second or two, they reached a point of resistance. The statue came to a stop, as if locked into place, and a chiming sound emanated from the statue.

Bells. Rohan had set the game to start with the ringing of bells.

Jameson's mind raced. He looked up—to the Lady's finger. She was still pointing out to the water.

"Five," Avery said beside him. "There were five bells that time."

And suddenly, Jameson's knew. *Ladies first.*

"Keep pushing," he told Avery. "When we get to a position where only one bell rings, she'll be pointing us where we need to go."

First. As in, number one.

Jameson and Avery repeated the process they'd already been through, turning the statue, listening to the bells when it locked, then turning it again.

And finally, just as Katharine hit the beach a hundred yards away, the statue locked into a position where only one bell rang. Jameson looked up. The Lady pointed them onward.

Again, the two of them ran—straight into the smallest of the caves. There was a sharp turn just past the entrance, and when they followed it, the light from outside disappeared almost completely. Jameson reached for his phone to use it as a flashlight, but then he remembered: *No phone.*

"There's no time," Jameson said fiercely. "We have to keep going."

He felt along one side of the wall, and Avery felt along the other. A minute in, there was a split. *Which way do we go?*

"What do you feel?" he asked Avery.

In the darkness, he could hear her breath, and no matter the stakes, he couldn't shut down the part of his brain that imagined the rise and fall of her chest.

"Water," Avery said. "The cave on this side, it's wet."

Jameson wondered how high the tide got. Were there times of day when this cave, with its shallow ceiling and utter lack of light, was deadly?

The water made Avery's side of the cave seem that much more treacherous.

"We'll split up," Jameson said. "I'll take your side, you take mine."

"We're looking for a key." Avery didn't say that as a reminder to him—or even herself. She was steadying herself.

Like she needed it.

Like his Heiress wasn't always so damn steady.

Jameson made his way forward, aware that Katharine had to be closing in on them, that she had likely seen which way they went.

And she might have thought to bring a flashlight.

Jameson pushed himself forward, feeling his way along the damp cave wall as he went, following the twists and turns of the cave until he saw something.

Light.

The cave dead-ended into a shallow pool. And standing shin-deep in that pool was Branford.

Jameson's uncle was holding two items: a lantern and a key.

CHAPTER 62

JAMESON

The key in Branford's hand was made of shining gold, encrusted with green jewels.

Branford found the key first. A dull roar in his ears, Jameson turned back. On his way out of the cave, he didn't even bother feeling his way along the wall. He moved quickly, without a single safeguard in place to keep himself from falling.

Jameson *hated* losing.

He passed Katharine near the entrance but didn't say a word to her. Bursting back into the sunlight, Jameson wondered how long Branford had been in the cave. Minutes, definitely. But how many?

How much did he beat us here by?

Given his uncle's familiarity with the manor and the estate, Branford wouldn't have had to work to find his way out of the house, wouldn't have had to search for a way out to the edge or down the cliffs.

Had he even decoded Rohan's verbal clue? Or had he just

assumed that of course there would be a key in one of the caves? Was that particular cave known as the smugglers' cave?

Had he played there with Jameson's father as a child?

No. Jameson wasn't going to go down that rabbit hole—or any rabbit hole other than figuring out where the hell the remaining two keys were.

Katharine and Branford are here. What about Zella?

What if she had already found one?

What if the Game was already lost?

No. Jameson refused to give into that line of thinking. *If Rohan suspected how easily Branford would find the smugglers' cave key, then it won't be the one that opens the prize box.*

But it might be the one that opens my secret.

"Jameson?"

Avery's voice pulled him back to the present. Neither Katharine nor Branford had yet exited the cave. *Unless there's another way in and out.* Yet another piece of information that Branford would have had from growing up here that Jameson didn't.

"The odds are stacked." Jameson said that like a fact, not a complaint. "Branford knows this place. He got to the key first. And Katharine—I don't know who exactly she is, or how far her connection to this family goes back, but I'd guess pretty damn far."

Jameson would have bet everything he had that this wasn't her first trip to Vantage. She'd clearly known Branford since he was a child.

Since my father and uncles were children. Thinking about Ian was a distraction right now—and if there was one thing that Jameson was certain of, it was that he couldn't afford a distraction.

Couldn't afford to lose another key.

"We'll head back up." Avery's voice was steady. "There are still two more keys out there, and given that four out of the five of us ended up at the caves first, I doubt this key is *the* key."

Her mind had a habit of mirroring his own, and that meant that she knew as well as he did: The next key was *theirs*. It had to be.

They went back the way they came. And the entire time, Jameson was running through everything that Rohan had said before the start of the Game. The Factotum hadn't just intimated that he'd given them enough information to find *a* key; he'd suggested that they had what they needed to *win*.

What were his exact words? Jameson could practically hear the old man quizzing him. Hawthorne games were won and lost based on attention to detail. Fortunes were made and lost based on the same.

Jameson summoned an image of Rohan talking and played back the words he'd said—exactly. *If that's your way of asking if I've made it easy for you all*, Rohan had told Zella, *I have not. No rest for the wicked, my dear. But it would hardly be sporting if I hadn't given you everything you needed to win.*

Jameson watched where he was going, made sure that his foot never slipped. Avery was ahead of him, and he watched her climb, willing his mind to see what others might miss.

No rest for the wicked...

It would hardly be sporting...

Rohan's use of the term *smuggle* hadn't been accidental. He hadn't *accidentally* left that book. What were the chances that every other turn of phrase he'd used had been intentional, too?

Think back further. Jameson kept climbing up that cliff. Seventy feet off the ground. A hundred. No margin for error.

He went back over Rohan's every statement, starting at the top.

Hidden somewhere on this estate are three keys. The manor, the grounds—they're all fair play. There are also three boxes. The Game is simple. Find the keys. Open the boxes. Two of the three contain secrets. Two of yours, as a matter of fact.

Jameson didn't dwell on that. One foot after the other, a hundred twenty feet up.

So, two boxes with secrets. In the third, you'll find something much more valuable. Tell me what you find in the third box, and you'll win the mark.

It was called a mark. Not a chip. Not a token. A *mark*. And why was a *mark* necessary at all? It had already been established at that point that they all knew the stakes they were playing for.

Leave the manor and the grounds in the condition in which you found them. Dig up the yard, and you'd best fill the holes. Anything broken must be mended. Leave no stone unturned but smuggle nothing out.

The stone and the turning—that could have referred to the statue. But what if it didn't?

Two hundred feet up.

Likewise, you may do no damage to your fellow players. They, like the house and the grounds, will be left in the condition in which you found them. Violence of any kind will be met with immediate expulsion from the Game.

That seemed straightforward. The only words that even remotely jumped out to Jameson were *condition* and *damage*.

Were they looking for something damaged?

Something for which the condition mattered a great deal? *Art. Antiques.*

Two hundred thirty feet up.

You have twenty-four hours, beginning at the top of the hour. After that, the prize will be considered forfeit.

"The top of the hour." Jameson wondered how many clocks there were in the manor.

Two hundred seventy feet up.

If that's your way of asking if I've made it easy for you all, I have not. Jameson was retreading old ground now, and he and Avery had almost finished the climb. *No rest for the wicked, my dear. But it would hardly be sporting if I hadn't given you everything you needed to win.*

Jameson reached the top of the cliff and stepped onto solid ground. *The Game starts when you hear the bells. Until then, I suggest you all let the wheels turn a bit and acquaint yourself with the competition.*

"You're thinking," Avery commented, stepping back into her dress. "You're in deep."

Deep in his own mind, deep in the weeds of the Game.

Jameson zipped her dress for her, but this time, he didn't linger on the task. "I'm going back through everything that Rohan said. There are certain phrases that stick out."

"*Smuggle nothing out*?" Avery suggested wryly.

"That would be one," Jameson agreed, a low buzz building beneath his skin. "But not the only one."

"No rest for the wicked." That was the one Avery went for first. *"No stone unturned."* She paused. "It reminds me of the first clue in my very first Hawthorne game. The idioms in your letters, remember?"

Jameson gave her a look. Of course he remembered. He remembered everything about those early days. "Technically," he said, "that wasn't your first Hawthorne game. The keys," he reminded her. They were a Hawthorne tradition. *"No rest for the wicked. No stone unturned. Let the wheels turn a bit. Dig up the yard. Fill the holes. Anything broken must be mended. The mark."*

The possibilities and combinations twisted and turned in Jameson's mind.

The gate to the stone garden was still open. The moment Jameson stepped through, the moment he looked out upon the thousands and thousands of stones that paved the ground, he saw it.

"Leave no..." he started to say.

"...stone unturned," Avery finished. For a moment, they just stood there, staring out at this massive haystack, contemplating the possibility of one very small needle.

"There are probably a ton of stones in the manor, too," Avery commented. "The walls of the room we started in were stone."

Jameson's hand came to rest on the cast-iron lock. It had been unlocked when they'd gotten here. He turned it around, and there, on the back, he found a message.

HINT: GO BACK TO THE START.

CHAPTER 63

GRAYSON

A single call to Zabrowski was all it took to obtain Kimberly Wright's address, two towns away.

"Xan and I will wait outside," Nash told Grayson once they arrived. "I wager we can find a way of entertaining ourselves."

This was something for Grayson and *his sisters* to do alone. Now that the truth was out there, the last remains of the barriers he'd erected against thinking of them that way crumbled. The twins *were* his sisters, regardless of whether or not he was anything to them.

"It's been a while since we've heard from Jamie," Xander added amiably. "He's due for some yodeling. Take all the time you need, Gray."

Grayson exited the SUV, waited for Savannah and Gigi to do the same, and then the three of them made their way up to Kimberly Wright's front door. A three-foot-tall chain-link fence surrounded the front yard, which was all dirt and weeds, no grass. The house was painted a cheerful yellow that contrasted with the dark metal bars across the windows.

There was a No Solicitors sign on the front door.

Gigi knocked. Two seconds later, Grayson heard a dog barking, and two seconds after that, the door opened, revealing a woman in a ratty floral bathrobe. She used one foot to hold back a dachshund that looked remarkably rotund for the breed.

"That is a very fat dachshund," Gigi said, her eyes round.

"It's mostly hair," the woman in the bathrobe said. "Isn't that right, Cinnamon?" The dog growled at Grayson and attempted to get its front paws up on the foot that was holding her back.

It failed.

"I'd tell you I don't want whatever you're selling," Kimberly Wright continued, "but you've got his eyes." She was looking at Savannah when she said that, but then she shifted her gaze to Grayson. "You too."

Gigi offered up a friendly smile. "I'm Gigi. That's Savannah."

"I know who you are," Kim replied gruffly. "*Down*, Cinnamon."

Cinnamon, Grayson could not help but notice, was already down.

"And that's Grayson," Gigi continued. "Our brother."

Grayson waited for Savannah to correct her twin, but she didn't. *Our brother.*

"Well, don't just stand there," Kim said, bending down to pick up Cinnamon—no easy task. "Come in."

The house was compact: a den to the right of the front door, a kitchen straight ahead, and a short hall to the left, which presumably led to the bedrooms. Kim ushered them into the den.

"I like your recliners," Gigi said earnestly. There were four of them in a room that wasn't big enough for much else. On the back of each recliner, there was a crocheted blanket. The blankets matched; the recliners didn't.

"You're a smiley one, aren't you?" Kim asked Gigi.

"I try," Gigi replied, but the words didn't come out quite as cheerful as Grayson would have expected. It occurred to him for the first time that maybe Gigi wasn't just naturally sunny.

Maybe that was a choice.

Their aunt stared at Gigi for a moment. "You look like him, you know. My boy."

"I know," Gigi said softly.

Grayson thought about Acacia telling him that the resemblance had endeared Gigi to their father when she was very young, and for reasons he could neither pinpoint nor understand, his heart ached.

This woman was his aunt. *Their* aunt, and she'd never met a single one of them.

"Are you here to tell me why your father won't return my calls?" Kim asked bluntly.

Savannah was the first one to summon up a reply to that question. "Dad's gone."

Kim's eyes narrowed. "What do you mean?"

"He left on a business trip a year and a half ago and never came back." Savannah's voice didn't waver.

"Did you call the police?" Kim dumped her dachshund on one of the recliners. Cinnamon hopped to the floor with a thud.

"Mom did, back then. But he's not *missing*," Gigi told her aunt. "He left."

Grayson could hear how saying those words hurt her. *Now you believe he left.* That should have made Grayson happy. That had been his goal, after all. To keep her—to keep both of them—from questioning that explanation, from getting at the truth.

All I have to do is make sure it stays that way.

"It appears your brother was having some difficulties," Grayson told his aunt. "Financial and with the law."

Kim walked to the far wall. She braced her hand against it for a moment, then pulled down a framed picture. "This is him." She walked back, more slowly, then held out the frame. "Shep. He was twelve or thirteen here. That's Colin beside him."

Grayson made himself look at the photograph. A lanky young teen with silvery gray eyes held a basketball. A toddler reached up for it.

Kim let out a breath. "Shep came to live with me not long after Colin was born. Our mom died, and her husband decided he was done with kids who weren't his. It was either take Shep in or let him go to foster care, so I took him in. Colin's father was in and out of prison for years, so most of the time, it was just me, taking care of both boys."

"You call him Shep," Grayson said, because that observation felt like less of a landmine than looking at that picture and searching for any kind of resemblance between himself and the boys in the frame.

"That was his name. Not short for anything. Just Shep. He changed it the summer before he went to college. His last name, too." She snorted. "*Sheffield Grayson.* He got a basketball scholarship. Met a pretty girl." Kim settled down into one of the recliners and waited for each of them to do the same before she continued, "My brother was pretty much done with me after that. Didn't want anything to do with the rest of my kids, but he loved Colin." There was a slight pause. "Shep took care of Colin a lot growing up. Too much, probably. Used to take him with him to basketball practice when I was..." Kim looked down. "Working."

Kim was a recovered addict. Her brother hadn't just watched her son while she was *working*.

As if she could hear his thoughts, the woman looked away from

Grayson and to the girls. "After Shep married your mother, he told me that Colin was going to live with them."

"And you let your brother take your son," Grayson said softly.

"I had other mouths to feed. Shep agreed to help with that. But he wanted Colin with him."

Grayson hadn't realized, when Sheffield Grayson had said that his nephew was the closest thing he'd ever had to a son, that he'd raised the kid from the time he was a child himself.

Grayson wondered—just for a moment—if a man who'd loved his nephew like that, sacrificed for his nephew like that, could have been all bad.

He thought about the photos in the safe-deposit box, and breathing got just a little bit harder. *We didn't come here to talk about the past*, he reminded himself. "Did your brother continue to help you financially after Colin passed?" Grayson asked, steering the conversation back toward the reason they'd come.

The withdrawal slips. Petty cash, with a notation on the back.

"Not the way he could have," Kim said bitterly. "Not the way he would have if Colin was alive. Shep blamed me, you know. Said that Colin picked up my bad habits, but it's not true. Colin never touched pills until he tore his ACL. It put him out a season, but do you think the great *Sheffield Grayson* ever let up?"

Grayson didn't know much about Colin Anders Wright, other than the fact that he and a young Toby Hawthorne, Grayson's uncle, had met at a high-priced residential rehab facility more than two decades before. Colin and Toby had then reunited for a drug-and-alcohol-fueled road trip that had ended on Hawthorne Island with three dead, Colin included.

"There was just so much pressure on my Colin," Kim said. "Shep was determined he'd play college ball. I should have brought my baby back here once they started fighting, but what did I have to offer? I told myself that it would be okay, that Acacia was there, too. And Colin worshipped her. He worshipped Shep, for that matter, when they weren't fighting."

"They were a family," Savannah said softly.

Kim closed her eyes. "I always thought Shep married your mother for the money, but when he saw how she was with Colin—that's when he fell in love."

Grayson felt the way that statement hit his sisters, both of them.

"Do you still have the slips?" Savannah asked him, her voice curt, the change of subject intentional.

Grayson nodded and withdrew them from his suit jacket. "Before he left," he told his aunt, "your brother made fairly regular withdrawals of relatively small amounts of cash. Two-hundred seventeen dollars. Five hundred six dollars . . . you get the point. Your name—or what we believe to be an abbreviation of your name—was written on the back of the slips."

"He brought me money now and then," Kim admitted, her tone defensive. "Never too much. He didn't trust me with too much." She narrowed her eyes at Grayson. "Only even amounts, though. Two hundred or five hundred or what-have-you. The rest must have been for himself."

Grayson seriously doubted that Sheffield Grayson had withdrawn seventeen dollars—or six—for his own spending needs.

"He came here and brought you money," Savannah summarized. "Did he bring anything else with him when he did?"

Grayson saw the logic of her question. If Sheffield Grayson had been hiding something—like, say, records of illegal transactions—his estranged sister's house, a world away from his own, would be a good place to hide it.

"Besides the money? No." Kim shook her head—and averted her eyes.

Gigi leaned forward in her chair. "What aren't you telling us, Aunt Kim?"

Grayson instantly saw what it meant to the woman for Gigi to call her that.

"Shep would talk to me for a bit," Kim said hoarsely, "then he'd leave the money on the kitchen counter and go shut himself in Colin's room."

"What did he do in there?" Savannah asked.

"I don't know," Kim replied. "Just... sit, I guess." She paused. "One time, I tried to go in and talk to him. He yelled at me to get out. There was something on the floor. A box."

"What kind of box?" Grayson pressed.

"Wooden. Nice. Real nice. He left it here, in Colin's closet, told me that if I ever touched it, if I ever even looked at it, he'd stop coming, and I'd never see another dime from him."

Grayson exchanged a look with Savannah. *We need that box.* "Could we see Colin's room?" he asked—but it wasn't really a question.

Kim's eyes narrowed. "The room," she repeated harshly. "Or the box?"

Gigi was the one who replied. "Our dad is gone," she said simply. "He left, and he never came back. And now we're finding out that he wasn't who we thought he was." She swallowed. "Who *I* thought he was," she corrected.

Savannah met her twin's eyes, just for a moment, before turning her attention to their aunt. "I found out about Dad cheating on Mom, about the fact that he had another kid out there, when I was fourteen," Savannah said.

Grayson doubted she'd ever said those words out loud before.

"And my dad, he acted like it was nothing. But all I could think"—Savannah's words slowed—"was that he had a *son.* Basketball was always our thing, but when I hit middle school, I noticed that he stopped saying that I played basketball and started saying that I played on the *girls'* basketball team." There wasn't a hitch in Savannah's voice, but Grayson felt the effort it took her to fight it. "He started asking me why I was such a tomboy."

Kim frowned. "You don't look like a tomboy to me."

Savannah fingered the end of her long blonde hair. "Exactly." She drew in another steady breath. "Our dad loved Colin. Maybe he loved us, too, but we weren't Colin."

"Why are you telling me this?" Kim asked.

"Because I want you to understand," Savannah replied. "Our dad abandoned us, and we deserve to know why. Our mom's in trouble. Whatever Dad was keeping in that box—what if it could help her?"

Cinnamon chose that moment to squat. Spurred to action, Kim leaped to grab her. "Outside, Cinnamon! Outside!" She rushed to the door. After putting the dog down on the lawn, she came back but didn't come all the way into the den.

"Down the hall," she said gruffly, "last door on your left. That was Colin's room. Do what you want with the damn box. Not like Shep's coming back anyway."

CHAPTER 64

GRAYSON

They found the box hidden behind some loose panels in the back of the closet. Grayson examined it. *Wooden, large enough to hold a laptop or a stack of paper files.* The wood was hard and sandy in color, and there was no visible hinge or lid on the box, nothing to indicate how to open it.

Clearing a space on the bed, Grayson set the box down. His sisters came closer.

"Crowbar?" Gigi suggested. "Or a hammer of the sledge variety?"

Grayson shook his head. The top of the box—assuming that *was* the top—appeared to be made of individual strips of wood the width and length of a ruler, bound tightly together. Seams were visible, but impenetrable, so Grayson did what any Hawthorne would have done in his position. He turned the box ninety degrees and pushed at the ends of each and every one of those strips of wood.

On the seventh, he was rewarded: The piece slid out from the others. He pushed it gently until it fell off the box, then examined what lay underneath: another wood panel, solid but for a single hole, just large enough to fit a finger in.

Grayson probed both the panel and the hole before attempting to use the hole to lift the lid of the box.

No dice.

"What are you doing?" Savannah asked.

"It's a puzzle box." Grayson kept his reply brief as he turned his attention to the strip of wood he'd removed. Turning it over in his hand, he was rewarded. Carved into the back of the strip of wood, was a long, thin space—and that space held a tool. It was roughly the length of a toothbrush but very thin. One side had a point like the tip of a pen. The other was flat and heavier. *Magnetic, most likely,* Grayson thought.

"What do you mean a puzzle box?" Gigi asked earnestly.

"The puzzle is finding your way into the box," Grayson replied. "Call it an added level of security, in case your aunt decided she wanted to know what was inside."

He dipped the tool into the hole he'd uncovered, first the pen side, then the probable magnet. Nothing happened, so Grayson began running the magnet end over the rest of the box—the top, the sides, then he turned the box over and tried the bottom.

The magnet stuck, and when Grayson pulled, another small wooden panel came off the box, this one in the shape of a T. A quick examination revealed another hole—just large enough for the pen end of the tool. Grayson stuck the pen in. He heard a click, then tested the pen's movement and realized that he could slide the hole—from the top left corner of the T to the bottom center.

When he did, there was another click.

Grayson turned the box back over.

"Seriously," Gigi said. "What is happening here?"

“My grandfather was fond of puzzle boxes,” Grayson told her. “I just unlocked something. We need to figure out what.”

He attempted to remove the top of the box again, but that didn’t work.

“Why don’t we just get a saw?” Savannah asked.

“And risk destroying what’s inside?” Grayson replied mildly.

“I’m ninety-seven percent sure that I can very delicately saw that thing open,” Gigi said.

“And what if it’s tamper-proof?” Grayson asked. “For example, there could be two vials of liquid suspended inside in thin glass tubes designed to break if the box is ruptured. And if those liquids mix…” He trailed off ominously.

“Seriously,” Savannah replied. “You think our dad *booby-trapped* his *puzzle box*?”

“I think,” Grayson replied, “that he didn’t want anyone but himself accessing whatever’s inside.”

He returned his attention to the box. *Something* had been unlocked. Grayson tried coming at the top from the side again. None of the remaining strips were loose; none could be pushed out. But when he pressed on the edge of one of those strips, it depressed with a pop, the other end of the strip rising.

Grayson tried using the hole to lift the top again, no dice.

Gigi reached forward and touched another strip. It went down, the same way the one Grayson touched had. She grinned. “Let’s try all of them!”

Before Grayson could say a single word, Gigi had worked her way down the strips, like she was playing a scale on a piano. *Pop, pop, pop, pop, pop, pop, pop.* This time, she was the one who tried snaking a finger down into the hole and lifting the panel.

No go.

"It's a combination." Savannah stared at the box but didn't move to touch it. "We just have to figure out the right keys to hit."

Grayson stared at the board. *Seven keys, which can be pushed down on either side or left neutral.* "There's more than two thousand possible combinations," he said.

Gigi grinned. "Then we better get started!"

It took forty minutes of systematic attempts before they got lucky and hit on the right combination. When they did, there was another audible click, and this time, when Grayson hooked his finger through the hole in the wood panel, he was able to remove the entire top of the box.

Underneath, they were faced with more wood. Darker, smoother, polished. Grayson ran his hand lightly over its surface. It was made from a single a piece of wood. There wasn't a single seam, no parts that could be moved or removed.

There was, however, a small rectangular hole cut into its surface. *No*, Grayson realized. *Not a hole.*

"We need something to insert in that, right?" Gigi said. She leaned over him and aimed the light from her phone at the rectangle. "Something with teeny tiny pins?"

Savannah reached for the tool that Grayson had uncovered earlier, but it was much too big. The entire rectangle wasn't much bigger than...

A USB port. Grayson stilled. He thought of the object he'd found, hidden in a frame in Sheffield Grayson's office. The object that wasn't a USB.

The object that was, quite obviously now, a key.

SIX YEARS, ELEVEN MONTHS AGO

Fourth of July at Hawthorne House meant a carnival—a private one complete with Ferris wheel, bumper cars, a massive roller coaster, and dozens of challenges and games. From his perch on top of the tree house, Jameson could see it all.

And no one could see him.

"You don't have to carry me, Grayson." *Emily.* Jameson would have recognized her voice anywhere. He couldn't make out Grayson's reply, but soon, the two of them were ensconced in the tree house, and Jameson could hear every word.

"Be careful, Em."

"I'm not going to fall." Her tone was teasing. There weren't many people who made a habit of teasing Hawthornes. "Though it would serve my mother right for trying to make me stay in tonight. I mean, honestly, I think my heart could handle one little roller coaster."

The roller coaster in question wasn't little, and with Emily, there was never just *one* anything. She always wanted more.

Jameson and Emily were alike in that way.

I should have been the one to sneak her out, Jameson thought. *I should have brought her up here.*

But he hadn't. Grayson had. Perfect, never-broke-the-rules Grayson was breaking them now. At twelve, Jameson had an inkling of why that might be the case. Emily was twelve, too, Grayson thirteen.

And he brought her to our *tree house.*

"I'm going to kiss you, Grayson Hawthorne." Emily, her voice as clear as day.

"What?" Grayson, stupefied.

"Don't tell me no. I am so tired of *no*. My entire life is *no*. Just this once, can't the answer be *yes*?"

Jameson waited, unnaturally still, for his brother's reply. It never came, and Emily spoke again. "When you're scared," she told Grayson, "you look straight ahead."

"Hawthornes don't get scared," Grayson said stiffly.

"No," Emily shot back. "*I* don't get scared. You're scared all the time."

Jameson knew an opening when he saw one. He dropped from the branch he was sitting on, catching it with his hands and swinging his body in through the tree house window. He landed rough but smiled. "I'm not." *Scared*. He didn't say the word, and Emily didn't need him to.

"You're not scared of anything," she told him with a toss of her hair. "Even when you probably should be."

Jameson looked at Grayson, then back at Emily. She and her sister, Rebecca, were the only two non-Hawthorne children allowed to spend any significant amount of time on this side of the gates. *The Hawthorne brothers. The Laughlin sisters*. It was a thing.

"I'll kiss you," Jameson offered boldly.

Emily stepped toward him. "Do it."

He did. *His first kiss—and hers.* Emily smiled. And then she turned to Grayson. "Now you."

Jameson felt his brother's eyes dart to his, but they didn't stay there long. "I can't," Grayson said.

"Can't. Shouldn't. Will anyway." Emily placed a hand on the side of Grayson's face, and Jameson watched as the girl he'd kissed a moment before brought her lips very close to his brother's.

Jameson didn't let himself turn away as Grayson kissed her, too. Their kiss seemed to last longer. A *lot* longer. When it was finally over, Emily stared at Grayson. Just *stared* at him. And then she threw her head back and laughed. "It's like spin the bottle... without the bottle." For a second, she looked like she might kiss Grayson again.

"Here you are, boys." Tobias Hawthorne's voice was deep and smooth as he climbed into the tree house. "The festivities weren't to your liking?"

Jameson recovered first. "You rigged the carnival games," he accused. That was why he'd taken to the tree house to begin with.

"Then rig them back," the old man replied. His discerning gaze seemed to miss absolutely nothing as he raked it over first Jameson, then his brother, and Emily last.

"About what you just heard..." Grayson started to say.

Tobias Hawthorne held up a hand. "Emily." He cast her a mild look. "Your grandfather is down below with a golf cart. Your mother is on the verge of calling in the National Guard."

"Then I guess I should go. But don't worry, Mr. Hawthorne...." Emily looked at Jameson again, then Grayson, her gaze lingering there. "My heart and its defect are just fine."

The old man didn't say another word until Emily was long gone. The silence was uncomfortable. It was almost certainly meant to be uncomfortable, but Jameson and Grayson both knew better than to say a single word to break it.

Tobias Hawthorne reached one hand toward each of his grandsons, took them by their shoulders, and turned them toward the nearest tree house window.

"Look out there," the old man instructed. Jameson watched as purple and gold exploded in the sky, points of light streaming downward, painting the air like a weeping willow. "Magic, isn't it?" the old man whispered.

Jameson heard the words that went unspoken: *I give you boys everything, and all I ask in return is focus.*

"I didn't have brothers," Tobias Hawthorne commented, as another round of fireworks colored the sky red and white and blue. "Didn't have what the four of you have." The old man's hands were still on their shoulders. "No one else will ever understand you the way that your brothers do. No one. It's the four of you against the world, and it always will be."

"Family first." Grayson said the words, and Jameson knew, just by the way he'd said them, that he'd been told them before.

"Emily was right, you know," Tobias Hawthorne said, suddenly dropping his hold on them. "You do look straight ahead when you're scared, Grayson."

He heard it all. Jameson didn't have time to process that realization because their grandfather wasn't done yet.

"Have I ever given you reason to fear me?" he asked—no, *demanded*. "Ever raised a hand to either of you?"

"No." Jameson beat his brother to the answer.

"Would I?" the old man challenged. "Ever?"

Grayson answered this time. "No."

"Why not?" Tobias Hawthorne posed that question like it was a riddle. "If it would push you to be what I need you to be, if it would make you better—why *wouldn't* I get physical?"

Jameson felt like he had to answer first—and answer well. "Because it's beneath you."

"Because I love you." The correction felt brutal, despite the sentiment being conveyed. "And Hawthornes protect those we love. *Always*." He nodded to the window again. "Look out there. See it." He wasn't talking about the fireworks. "All of it. All we have, all we are, all I've built."

Jameson looked. Beside him, Grayson did the same.

"It was just a kiss," Grayson said stubbornly.

"Two kisses, I believe," the old man replied. "You tread dangerous ground, boys. Some kisses are just kisses. A frivolity, really."

Jameson thought of the moment he'd pressed his lips to Emily's.

"You hardly have time for such things," the old man scoffed. "A kiss is nothing. But love?" Tobias Hawthorne's voice was quiet now. "When you're old enough, when you're ready, be warned: There is *nothing* frivolous about the way a Hawthorne man loves."

Jameson thought suddenly of the grandmother he'd never even met, the woman who'd died before he was born.

"Men like us love only once," the old man said quietly. "Fully. Wholeheartedly. It's all-consuming and eternal. All these years your grandmother has been gone. . . ." Tobias Hawthorne's eyes closed. "And there hasn't been anyone else. There can't and won't be. Because when you love a woman or a man or anyone the way we love, there is no going back."

That felt like a warning more than a promise.

"Anything less, and you'll destroy her. And if she is the one . . ."

The old man looked first at Jameson, then at Grayson, then back at Jameson again. "Someday, she'll destroy you."

He didn't make that sound like a bad thing.

"What would she have thought of us?" Jameson asked the question on impulse, but he didn't regret it. "Our grandmother?"

"You're still works in progress," the old man replied. "Let's save my Alice's judgment for when you're done."

With that, Tobias Hawthorne turned away from them, away from the window, away from the fireworks. When he spoke again, it was in a tone that Jameson recognized all too well. "There are thousands of boards in this tree house. I have weakened one. Find it."

A test. A challenge. A game.

By the time they found the board, the fireworks were long over.

"Break the board," the old man ordered.

Jameson wordlessly held it up. Grayson assumed the proper stance, then threw his body into the strike. The heel of his hand hit the board just above the crack, and it split.

"Now," Tobias Hawthorne ordered, "find me a board that cannot be weakened. And when you find it," the old man continued, leaning back against the tree house wall, his eyes narrowed but burning with a familiar kind of fire, "you can tell me: Which kind of board are the two of you?"

CHAPTER 65

JAMESON

As instructed by the inscription on the lock, Jameson and Avery went back to the start, to the room where Rohan had laid out the rules of the game.

Leave no stone unturned.

Of all the phrases that the Factotum had used, that was the one that most stuck in Jameson's mind. "For the first key," he said, thinking out loud, "there was a spoken clue—*smuggle nothing out*—and a physical clue in this room."

"The book." Avery was right there with him. "If the other keys follow the same pattern, then there are clues here pointing toward wherever those keys are hidden, and those clues—"

"—will tie in to something Rohan said," Jameson finished. He turned his attention to the walls of the room. The *stone* walls.

Leave no stone unturned.

Avery laid her hand flat on one of the stones. "First person to find a stone that turns gets to choose the destination for our next trip?"

Jameson smiled. "You've got yourself a wager, Heiress."

The stones—at least the ones low enough on the wall for them to reach—were solid. Not a single one turned or was even loose.

"Think that table's too heavy to drag to the side of the room?" Jameson asked Avery, eyeing the stones out of arm's reach.

"Definitely too heavy." Avery paused. "Lift me up?"

He did exactly that, like the two of them were dancers in a ballroom, defying gravity as they made their way around the room once more, Avery stretching overhead and Jameson holding her steady as she checked stone after stone.

And still, nothing. *There are more stones, higher up.* Jameson put Avery down, then hopped onto the windowsill. He tried to find purchase against the stones, tried to climb the wall around the massive window, and all he got for his efforts was a fall to the floor.

Flat on his stomach, Jameson found himself staring directly at the fireplace. It was empty, no logs—*and made of stone.* Jameson bounded to his feet and across the room, checking the stones on the inside of the fireplace, the backing.

"Nothing," he said out loud, but he didn't stop. Instead, he turned his focus to the cutout next to the fireplace, used for storing firewood. Logs were stacked waist high. Jameson started pulling them out, tossing them to the floor, his gaze locked on the stones behind the logs.

And then he felt something carved into one of the logs. "Writing," Jameson breathed.

Avery was beside him, her body pressed against his in an instant. Jameson placed the log on the ground, flat side up. There, etched into the wood, was the letter *F.*

Jameson turned back to the remaining logs. Beside him, Avery dropped to the floor, going through the ones he'd already thrown down. "Found one," she called. "*T*."

"Both sides of this one," Jameson replied. "*O* and *A*."

In the end, there were thirteen letters, carved into eleven logs. *F, T, O, A, L, Y, C, R, E, H, S, U, W.*

"Pull out the *H*," Jameson suggested. "Unless it's at the start of a word, it probably goes with the *S*, the *C*, or the *W*." He looked for other obvious pairings. "Let's try *O* with *U* and the *L* next to the *E*."

"*E-L* or *L-E*?" Avery asked.

Jameson shook his head. "It could go either way. There aren't any duplicate consonants, and no *B* or *V*, so chances are good that the *Y* either comes after a common combination, before the *L*, or at the start of a word."

Jameson pulled five letters. *L-O-F-T-Y*. "What does that leave us with?"

"*Crush*?" Avery suggested. Jameson pulled the letters. That left three. *A*, *W*, and *E*.

"Lofty, crush, awe." Avery said the words out loud. "We could be looking for a loft. Something heavy. Awe-inspiring."

Have I taught you nothing, my boy? Jameson didn't even try to shake off the memory of his grandfather's many lessons. *The first answer isn't always the best.*

He returned the letters—all of them—to the pile. This time, he pulled the *Y* first. He'd said it himself: It probably came after a common consonant combination, before the *L*, or at the start of the word.

"*Y*," Jameson murmured. "*O, U*." He stopped there, just for a moment, then went back and pulled the *R*. *Your.*

F, T, A, L, C, E, H, S, W.

"*T-C-H*?" Avery suggested. The moment the suggestions was

out of her mouth, Jameson saw it. The answer. He pulled the *W* and the *A*, plus the combination she'd identified, making the word *watch* and leaving only four letters behind.

F, *L*, *E*, and *S*.

Or, if you reversed the order...

"Self," Jameson said out loud. Then he laid the message out—a more cohesive one this time than the mix of words they'd gotten before.

WATCH YOURSELF.

Viewed a certain way, that seemed like a warning. But viewed through the lens of the Game—through the lens of all the many games just like this that Jameson had played growing up—it read differently.

"A mirror?" he murmured. "Or a camera?"

He racked his mind for any turn of phrase that Rohan had used during his speech that might offer more specifics but came up blank.

"Watch yourself," Jameson murmured. "No stone unturned. But of course, this clue and that one might not go together. There are two keys left to find, plus the boxes."

They'd discovered *a* clue—but to which puzzle?

His mind and body buzzing, Jameson leaned his head back, his gaze cast upward, thinking, letting the chaos of his racing thoughts fall away until all that was left was a plan. "We keep searching the room," he told Avery. "Every nook, every cranny, until there's no clues left to find, and then we'll try to make sense of them. At the end of the day, we don't just want one of the remaining keys."

Avery tossed her hair over her shoulder. "We need them both."

CHAPTER 66

JAMESON

Forcing his eyes to take in every detail of the room anew, Jameson noted again that the only decorative flourish was on the ceiling: the blue and gold detailing, an elaborate X with squares positioned to look like diamonds on either side. *Inside the diamonds, shields. Inside the shields, symbols.* Jameson made out a Greek letter or two, a flower, a lion, a sword.

Jameson cycled through key phrases that Rohan had dropped, and nothing registered—until he stopped looking at the details of the ceiling above and started looking at the big picture.

The X.

"As in X marks the spot?" Jameson tossed out.

"*Marks*," Avery repeated. "That's what Rohan said we were playing for. The *mark*."

Directly beneath the X was the table. Jameson was on his back on the floor beneath it in a heartbeat. The underside of the table was smooth, plain, except in the corners. And in those corners, Jameson found round disks, each slightly smaller than a coaster.

"Not disks," Avery said beside him, lifting the word from his mind, her own racing along the exact same path. "*Wheels.* Do you remember the last thing Rohan said—the very last thing?"

Jameson thought back. *"The Game starts when you hear the bells. Until then, I suggest you all let the wheels turn a bit..."*

And acquaint yourself with the competition. Jameson didn't say that last bit out loud, because it was beside the point.

"The wheels." Jameson met Avery's eyes. "Turn them."

She took one end of the table, and he took the other. The wheels didn't *want* to turn, but if you pushed them upward and turned at the same time, the resistance fell away. The wheels turned. And once all four of them had been turned—again and again until they would no longer move—a hidden compartment on the side of the table opened.

And nestled in that compartment, there was a key.

CHAPTER 67

JAMESON

The key was old-fashioned, made of gold with bloodred jewels inlaid at the top and center. Golden vines encircled the body of the key, swirling to form a flower at the top. Small pearls dotted the vines. Jameson dragged his thumb lightly over them.

"One key down," he said. He meant the words for Avery but couldn't take his eyes off the prize in his hand. "One to go."

The chances that the key in his hand opened *the* box—the one they needed to win—were one in three, one in two if Jameson's assumption that the smugglers' cave key *wasn't* the winning key was correct. But fifty-fifty wasn't the kind of odds a Hawthorne accepted.

Not when there were better odds to be had.

"*Smuggle nothing out*, the book, the caves," Jameson rattled off. "The mark, the table, *let the wheels turn*. We've already uncovered a third clue in the room, but it's unclear which, if any, verbal clue it corresponds to."

"*Watch yourself*," Avery murmured. She had this way of speaking to herself where her voice went quiet and her lips barely moved. Jameson had always loved the feeling of eavesdropping on her thoughts, letting them weave in and out of his own. "And the remaining verbal clues," Avery continued, "the most likely ones at least—are the idioms. *Leave no stone unturned* and *no rest for the wicked*."

Unbidden, the image of the stone garden came back to Jameson. Thousands upon thousands of stones had paved the ground. Maybe what they were looking for was there, but Jameson wasn't about to risk this game on maybes.

Not when his gut was telling him there might be something else here in this room to point the way to the *correct* stone.

Not when he could almost taste the win.

"*No stone unturned*," Jameson repeated, echoing Avery's words back to her. "And *no rest for the wicked*."

It was the second phrase that held his attention now. Rohan had said it in an offhanded, charming kind of way, the words directed at Zella, but Jameson knew in his gut that the Factotum was one of those people who could make anything seem offhand.

And charming.

No rest for the wicked, my dear. Jameson let the words play in his mind over and over. *But it would hardly be sporting if I hadn't given you everything you needed to win.*

What were the chances that Rohan had given them what they needed in that exact moment, just a sentence before?

"*No rest for the wicked*." Jameson said the words again, the pace of his speech speeding up, his heart rate doing the same. "Biblical in origin. Popularly used to mean that work never stops, but in the context of the Devil's Mercy, it could imply that there are always more sins to be had... or that the wicked are given no peace."

"No peace," Avery repeated. "No reprieve. No *mercy*." She locked her fathomless gaze on his. "Biblically, that would mean what? Fire and brimstone?"

Hellfire, Jameson thought. *Damnation. The Devil's Mercy.* Those three things cycled through his mind, faster and faster, louder and louder until the words felt like they were coming from outside him.

And then Jameson's gaze locked on to the stone fireplace, and his mind went silent.

Avery followed the direction of his gaze. Without either one of them saying a word, they both began to move—back to the fireplace.

"What do you think the chances are," Jameson asked Avery, "that somewhere in this not-a-castle, we'll find something to help us start a fire?"

CHAPTER 68

JAMESON

They found matches in the kitchen in a drawer near the stove. All too aware of each minute that passed—of the fact that elsewhere on this grand cliffside estate, the competition was playing for the same prize—Jameson raced back to the start once more.

This time, Avery beat him there. She was fast when she wanted to be. Single-minded. She skidded to a stop just past the doorway, and as Jameson did the same behind her, he saw why.

Zella was in the room, sitting on top of the table. She ran her fingers along the open and empty compartment. "Your doing, I hope? Branford can't have all the fun. He'll be insufferable."

In other words: The duchess knew that Branford had found the first key. Given that Zella also seemed to have realized that a second had been found *here*, she had to be thinking that she had just one chance left for this game to go her way.

She doesn't seem bothered by that. Jameson rolled that thought over in his mind for a moment or two, which was just long enough for Zella to notice what he held in his hand.

"Matches?" The duchess studied them—then her gaze flicked to the fireplace. "*No rest for the wicked.* Of course Rohan would play it this way."

Something in her tone made Jameson wonder just how much history the duchess and the Factotum had—and what sort.

"Well, what are you waiting for?" Zella said, strolling across the room to stand beside the fireplace. "Light it up."

Jameson considered his next move carefully. *Doing this in her presence will put us on even footing—but if we don't do it, we'll have to wait until she leaves.* Who knew what Branford and Katharine would be doing in the meantime—or what they might find?

"If there's a key in there," Avery said, her chin coming up as she met Zella's eyes, "it's ours."

"There isn't a key in there, Heiress," Zella replied. On the duchess's tongue, Jameson's nickname for Avery sounded wry and pointed. "Two in one room? I hardly think so. But, yes, certainly. If you set that fire and immediately find a key, consider it yours."

Zella picked up a log from the wall, and Jameson realized that although he and Avery had left the logs on the floor, they were stacked neatly now.

She saw them. She read the words. And then she put them back, so no one else would read them.

"Can we even burn those logs?" Avery's voice broke into Jameson's thoughts. "Didn't our instructions say to leave everything in the condition in which we found it?"

Jameson saw the logic in her questions. "You can't unburn a log." He hadn't come this far to be disqualified on a technicality. "We need something else to burn."

Without missing a beat, Jameson began unbuttoning his waistcoat. Securing the key—temporarily—between his teeth, he took off the waistcoat, then the shirt underneath. Slipping the waistcoat back on, his chest now bare beneath it, Jameson tossed his shirt into the fireplace.

"Now," he told Avery and Zella, "we light it up."

It took more time than he'd anticipated for the shirt to really catch fire, but once it did, the flames seemed to multiply quickly. Jameson watched his shirt burn, watched the flames dance, watched the fire lick at the stone walls of the fireplace.

And then he watched words slowly start to appear on the stone. *Invisible ink.* Heat was a common trigger. Piece by piece and bit by bit, the writing became solid before his eyes. Four letters, three numbers, one clue.

DIAL 216.

"Thank you very much, Jameson Hawthorne," Zella murmured.

A moment later, the duchess was gone.

Jameson turned back to Avery. "Let's hope she's headed for a phone," he said, his voice a heady whisper, for her ears only.

"And we're not?" Avery gave him a look.

Jameson was aware that the smile that crossed his lips then was one that other people might have described as *wicked.* "You tell me, Heiress."

Avery stared at him, like the answer could only be found behind his emerald eyes. He saw the exact moment that she had it.

"*Leave no stone unturned,*" Avery said, her own eyes blazing with certainty and purpose. "*Dial two-one-six.* Back in the stone garden, there was a sundial."

CHAPTER 69

JAMESON

The two of them flew out of the house. As they closed in on the sundial in the stone garden, Jameson did an automatic check of their surroundings. That was a part of a game like this, always. One method of playing was beating your own path, but another was staying in the shadows, tracking the other players' progression—and only swooping in at the end.

The area was clear.

Jameson wondered where Branford had gone with his key. If he'd already found the box it went to. If the box had contained a secret—and, if so, whose.

Two keys. If we find two keys, there's a chance I can win the game and *keep my secret.*

If worse came to worst, even if Branford *did* obtain the scroll on which he'd written those fateful four words, obtaining two keys would mean that he and Avery would have Branford's secret. *Mutually assured destruction.* There were worse gambits.

And right now, all that mattered was getting that second key.

The sundial was large. The base was circular with Roman numerals carved along an inner circle and the signs of the zodiac along the outside. A bar—simple, with no carvings—jutted out at an angle, its shadow's location on the base dependent upon the location of the sun.

"Two, one, six." Jameson leaned over to touch the face of the dial, pressing and prodding at the Roman numerals in question.

"You know I'm a math person, right?" Avery said beside him.

He cut a gaze in her direction. "And?"

"And," Avery replied, a smile tugging around the edges of her lips, "two hundred sixteen is a perfect cube."

Jameson did the math. "Six times six times six." *No rest for the wicked. The Devil's Mercy. Three sixes.* Rohan really *did* think he was clever, didn't he?

"Start at the bar," Jameson murmured to himself. "The clue can't have anything to do with the shadow because the shadow moves with the sun's position. But the bar itself is stationary, an obvious starting point."

"Obviously." Avery managed to sound more amused than sarcastic.

Jameson walked around the dial, until he stood directly next to the bar. Beneath his feet, the stone paving was remarkably even, but gazing out at the thousands of other stones all around them, he saw places where the stones had cracked, places where grass and moss were growing through.

Jameson began counting stones, pacing them as he did. "Six forward, six left, another six forward." He tried the stone beneath his feet. *Not loose at all.* "Six forward, six right, another six forward." *The same.* "Six forward, six right, another six right."

Still not loose. But this time, Jameson's gaze caught on the slight smear of dirt on the stone's surface. And the grass surrounding the stone—*missing on one side.*

"Let me guess," Avery said, kneeling beside him. "We need to dig."

If you dig up the yard...

Jameson dug with his fingers, the dirt between the rocks jamming itself beneath his nails. One tore, but he didn't stop.

Pain didn't matter.

The only thing that mattered was winning.

I have to wonder, though, once you see that web of possibilities laid out in front of you, unencumbered by fear of pain or failure, by thoughts telling you what can and cannot, should and should not be done... What will you do with what you see?

The stone came loose. Jameson flipped it over. Beneath it, there was nothing but dirt. Hard dirt.

He kept digging.

My mother saw something in me, he could hear Ian saying. *She left Vantage to* me. *Win it back, and someday, I'll leave it to you.*

Jameson didn't stop.

He *never* stopped.

And finally, he was rewarded. His fingers unearthed a bit of fabric. *A brown burlap sack.* Blood smeared across the back of his fingers as he uncovered the rest of it and stood.

Inside the sack, there was a key. Like the first, it was made of gold, but that was where the resemblance ended. The design on the head of this key was harder to decipher. It called to mind a maze.

This is it. Jameson felt that all the way to his bones. He felt it in the part of him that had been forged in Tobias Hawthorne's fire. *This is the key that opens the box that will win me the Game.*

He righted the stone.

"Good." A crisp voice said, the speaker's posh accent pronounced. "You've found the final key. Hand it over, then."

Jameson stood and looked to Katharine, who cast a long shadow on the stones beneath her feet, that white suit just as pristine as it had been down on the beach.

"Why the hell would we do that?" Avery beat him to the question.

"Because," another voice called out behind them, "I want you to."

Jameson turned, his grip on the key tightening, and watched as his father stepped through the wrought-iron gate.

Ian Johnstone-Jameson met Jameson's eyes and smiled. "Well done, my boy."

CHAPTER 70

GRAYSON

I can open this box. I just have to get it back to my hotel room.

Beside Grayson, Gigi pounced. "What is it? You have *something* face."

Grayson liked to think he was a bit harder to read than that. "Pardon?" He fell back on formal speech, one extra layer safeguarding everything he thought or felt.

"What do you mean, *pardon?* I saw that light bulb go off, mister. The gears in your mind are turning. The hamster is officially on the wheel!" From her spot beside him on the threadbare twin bed, Gigi rose to her knees, putting her hands on either side of the puzzle box and leaning forward. "Six hamsters!" she amended dramatically. "Six wheels! They're all spinning."

Time to do damage control. "I think we need to go back over the box," Grayson told Gigi. "Look for something that fits this opening."

Savannah snorted. "It took six hamsters to come up with that?"

No. Grayson let the thought roll over him but kept all hint of it off his face. *We won't find what we need by examining the box. I already have it.*

He could picture Sheffield Grayson retrieving the safe-deposit box key from inside his computer, removing the faux USB drive from the picture frame, driving to the bank, withdrawing money, adding the slip to the box, and driving out here.

Clearly, their father had had a system. A routine.

"Stop." A shrill voice hit Grayson's ears like fingernails on a chalkboard. "Put the box down!" Kimberly Wright hovered in the doorway, her entire body wound tight. "You shouldn't be here."

Grayson knew somehow that she was talking to him—and *just* to him.

"In my son's room," she continued, her voice high-pitched but rough. "Sitting on his bed."

This isn't about the bed. Or the room. Grayson wasn't certain what this *was* about—or what had changed. He stood but made no move to hand over the box.

Gigi's forehead wrinkled. "Aunt Kim, we—"

"I wasn't good enough to be your aunt. Your father took my boy. My *Colin*. And once he was dead and gone, I wasn't even allowed to meet you girls. Shep didn't want me anywhere near you." Kim's eyes closed tight, and when she opened them again, they found Grayson's, like darts thrown with an unsteady hand that hit their target nonetheless. "Do you two know who he is?" Her tone turned accusatory. "I saw those other boys outside. Cinnamon got away from me, and the taller one went after her. Introduced himself."

Xander, Grayson thought. Alexander Blackwood Hawthorne had never met a stranger or baked good he didn't want to immediately introduce himself to.

"They're Hawthornes." Kim spit out the name, then whirled on

Grayson. "You're a Hawthorne," she said, the way a person might have said the words *you're a murderer.* "My brother, sometimes he'd bring bourbon with him when he came here. And the second it hit his lips, he'd start talking—about Hawthornes."

Grayson assessed his options for shutting this conversation down. Fast. "We should go," he told Gigi and Savannah.

Kim scowled. "Shep—he always said that Toby Hawthorne was the reason Colin was dead, that Toby set the fire that killed my baby. *Arson.* And Toby's father, that billionaire bastard—he covered it up."

To Grayson's surprise, Gigi stepped in front of him, shielding him from their aunt. "Even if that's true," she said, "it's not Grayson's fault."

Gigi wasn't tall enough to block Kim's desperate, angry stare.

"My brother hated you," the woman told Grayson. "All you Hawthornes. But he said—he said he was going to make sure you'd all get yours. My brother was going to—"

That was not a sentence that Grayson could allow her to finish. "Going to what?" There was no threat in Grayson's tone, just a warning. *Think carefully before you answer. I am not a person you want to cross.*

Kim clamped her mouth closed. Unlike her nieces, she wasn't immune to Grayson's ability to command a room and every person in it. "Get out," she whispered, her voice hoarse. "And leave the box."

"We can't do that." Savannah came to stand in front of Grayson, right next to her twin, and for a split second, his heart clenched.

"Did I give you a choice, girl?" Kim's voice shook. *"Get out."*

Grayson gave a slight nod toward his sisters, then calmly began reassembling the puzzle box.

"Put it down!"

"Aunt Kim—" Gigi tried.

"I said—"

"Put it down," Grayson finished calmly. He reached inside his suit jacket and removed his wallet. Opening it, he began to slip out bills. Not tens or twenties—hundreds. Staying in the black-card suite came with the expectation that one would be an excellent tipper. "Your brother isn't coming back." Grayson did not enjoy being cruel, but *bribe, threaten, buy out*—that was the Hawthorne way. "And even if he did come back, there's no money left for him to give you."

There were eight bills sticking out of the wallet now. In a single move, Grayson withdrew all of them and folded the bills in half over his thumb. His target stared at the money. *Good.* Kim brought her gaze to his. *Better.*

"I know," Grayson said softly, "that your brother hated my family. He didn't want me. We met only once, and he made that quite clear."

Sometimes, after you backed a person into a corner, the best way to ensure they took the out you offered was to show just a flash of humanity—enough to make them think that maybe the two of you didn't have to be enemies, but not enough that they forgot who was in change.

Grayson held the money out to his aunt. Kim skittered forward and snatched it from his hands. "Take the damn box," she said, her voice gravelly, "and get out."

CHAPTER 71

GRAYSON

Savannah drove in silence, and the rest of them rode the same way until Xander, who was sitting in the front passenger seat with the reassembled puzzle box on his lap, couldn't take the quiet anymore. "Knock, knock." He rapped against the box's lid.

"Who's there?" Gigi chimed from the back seat.

"Scone."

"Scone who?"

"As it turns out, it's surprisingly difficult to make up knock-knock jokes on the spot." Xander paused. "Wait! I've got it! Knock, knock!" He rapped on the box again.

"Don't break anything," Savannah ordered without ever taking her eyes off the road.

"Generally speaking," Xander responded, "I excel at dealing with things—and people—that need to be handled with care. And on that note..." He turned to glance back at Grayson. "Jamie didn't answer when I called. His phone didn't even ring. And it appears that Oren and his team *may* have lost track of our dynamic duo."

Grayson allowed his eyes to narrow. "Oren doesn't lose track of Avery."

"It's not so much that Oren doesn't know where she is," Xander admitted, "as it seems to be that he has been forbidden from following her. Curiouser and curiouser, am I right?"

Grayson recognized an attempt at distraction when he saw one.

"Who's Oren?" Gigi took the bait—but not for long. "And while I'm asking questions, Grayson, what do you think Dad meant by that whole 'Hawthornes are going to get theirs' thing?"

That question tread dangerously close to the reason that Grayson was here, the reason that he was already sorting through possible maneuvers to get that box away from Gigi and Savannah for long enough to open it and do damage control on whatever was inside. No matter how much he hated having to betray them all over again.

Whether you want to do something, Grayson, is immaterial to whether or not it needs to be done.

"I have some thoughts to share with the class," Xander volunteered, cheerfully diving on the live bomb of Gigi's question. "A lot of people hated our grandfather. It was kind of his thing—that and painstakingly creating the perfect heirs even though he always intended to disinherit us. Those were really his two things."

Grayson followed up Xander's buoyant, stream-of-consciousness reply with one of his own. "Based on the only conversation I ever had with our father, I have reason to believe that I was conceived *because* Sheffield Grayson hated my grandfather. Sleeping with his daughter, getting her pregnant, abandoning her—and me..." Grayson swallowed. "That was the Hawthornes getting theirs."

Sometimes, the easiest way to lie was to tell the truth.

“Then why did he keep all of those pictures of you?” Gigi asked.

Why even have them taken? That question crept into Grayson’s conscious mind from where it had been circling in his subconscious.

“Forget the photographs,” Savannah said curtly. “And our aunt. We need to focus on—”

“Sorry to interject, darlin’,” Nash cut in. “But we have a problem.”

Grayson turned his head toward the window on Nash’s side and took in the scene at the Grayson household. There were cars in the driveway, cars on the street. Black, unmarked.

FBI. Grayson’s initial read was confirmed the instant he saw the men in suits on the driveway.

“Savannah, put the car in park here.” The order was out of Grayson’s mouth before he’d even finalized the thought. They were still two houses away—outside the circumference of any search warrant. “Good,” Grayson said, when Savannah did as she was told. “Now climb into the back seat. Xander—”

“Driver’s seat,” Xander replied automatically. “Got it.”

Grayson looked to Nash. “Can you squeeze up front without getting out of the car?”

Nash took off his cowboy hat and eyed the space over the center console.

“Nash is remarkably flexible,” Xander called back. “I have faith.”

Savannah still hadn’t unbuckled. “Why would I—”

“Just do as I say,” Grayson told her, and it occurred to him, when she went very still, that he might have sounded like their father.

Savannah unbuckled and started scooting back over the center console.

One very cramped game of musical chairs later, Grayson continued issuing orders. “Nash, make sure the puzzle box stays out of view. Find something to throw over it.”

Nash considered his options, then stripped off his worn white T-shirt. "If anyone asks, I'll tell 'em I run hot."

Gigi blinked several times, as if the sight of Nash Hawthorne shirtless had broken her brain.

"Get out of the car," Grayson told her with a gentle nudge. "Savannah and I will follow. Xander will wave and drive off. Savannah, do not under any circumstances volunteer the information that this is your car. And if you are specifically asked—about the car, about anything else—feign outrage. No answers. Gigi—"

"Trust me, my sister isn't going to be *feigning* outrage," Gigi said cheerfully. "We all have to play to our strengths, am I right? Luckily, I am still highly caffeinated, and I can get drunk just thinking about mimosas." She closed her eyes. "*Mimosas*," she whispered, and then she opened them. "The guys in suits won't know what hit them."

CHAPTER 72

GRAYSON

"Savannah and Juliet Grayson?" An FBI agent intercepted the three of them at the end of the driveway.

"She goes by Gigi," Savannah replied. "Not Juliet."

Cool tone, nonanswer, Grayson thought. *Well done, Savannah.*

"We'll need you two to stay out here while we finish our search." Mr. FBI didn't so much as try to soften that statement with a smile. "May I ask who just dropped you off?"

"You may not," Grayson said, looking past the agent. That was another of Tobias Hawthorne's many tricks for seizing control. Sometimes, staring a person down did nothing but give them power. And why would a Hawthorne ever do that? "I assume," Grayson continued, "that the lady of the house has a copy of the warrant?"

That wasn't really a question. It was a signal to the agent: Grayson was the type of person capable of reading the fine print—and enforcing it.

"And who are you?" the FBI agent asked, his eyes narrowing.

Grayson looked past him again, as if this entire encounter were quite boring. "A person under no legal obligation to answer your questions at this time." Grayson's visual search finally hit on the person he'd been looking for: Acacia. She was standing in between the fountain and the portico, flanked by agents herself.

"Mom!" Gigi practically leapt forward. The agent who had been questioning Grayson stepped in front of her. When Gigi attempted to dodge around him, he grabbed her arm.

"Remove your hand from my sister's body," Savannah said. "*Now.*" That *now* was impressive. It should have been effective. Coming from Grayson, it would have been.

But in response to his sister's demand, the agent just held up his free hand. "Let's all just calm down here," he said, like Savannah was hysterical

Grayson let his gaze travel to the man's face. "She sounded perfectly calm to me."

"Look, kid—"

Grayson arched a brow. "Do I look like a kid to you?" There was a reason he'd started wearing suits as a teenager.

If you're not wondering who the hell you're talking to by now—you really should be.

Out loud, Grayson opted for a different statement. "If you'll excuse me, I'm going to go acquaint myself with the limitations of your warrant."

Hawthornes didn't wait to be excused. Grayson started walking. Savannah followed suit. Gigi, on the other hand, stayed at the end of the drive, staring owlishly at the FBI agent.

"Are you all right, Miss Grayson?"

Grayson glanced back. Gigi continued staring at the agent,

unblinking, intense. Then she shrugged. "Still not telekinetic," she announced, before flitting past the agent. She hooked her arms through Savannah's. "You never know until you try."

"You shouldn't agitate the agents," Acacia told the three of them quietly. She stood with her hands by her sides, her posture straight, looking paler than Grayson had seen her. "There's no need for it. They'll be done shortly."

You almost but didn't quite sell your confidence in that statement, Grayson thought. Acacia was shaken—badly—and only showing it a little.

"They're tearing our home apart," Savannah said, her voice low, as two agents walked by carrying parts of a computer. Acacia drew in a jagged breath.

"Everything is going to be fine," Grayson said. He laid a steadying hand on Acacia's shoulder. To his surprise, Acacia brought her hand up to his and squeezed it. Grayson had the oddest sense that she was trying to comfort *him.*

Grayson knew suddenly and with stunning clarity that if his father *had* acknowledged him, if he had spent any time at all here growing up, she would have been the one to bandage his knees.

Grayson and his brothers had bandaged one another's.

I'm supposed to be steadying you, he thought in Acacia's direction, and then he looked to the girls. *All of you.*

"You have a copy of the warrant?" Grayson asked, his tone brisk, his volume low.

Acacia reached into her purse. Two minutes later, Grayson had skimmed the whole thing. The warrant was for the Grayson residence, the grounds, and three vehicles registered in Sheffield Grayson's name.

The girls' cars weren't among them.

"Where is your lawyer?" Grayson asked Acacia. The details of this search made no sense. The number of agents. The breadth of the warrant. The timing. Given how long ago Sheffield Grayson had disappeared, the case should have been cold by now.

Unless someone is deliberately heating it up. In his mind's eye, Grayson saw Eve treading water in the pool. He thought of her asking him what Tobias Hawthorne would have done in her position.

"Kent offered to come," Acacia replied. "As a friend. But I can't afford a lawyer right now."

Grayson's instincts said that Trowbridge had very little desire to be Acacia's *friend*.

"Savannah and I will pay for a lawyer," Gigi volunteered. "From our trusts."

Savannah looked down. "We can't. Unless..."

Acacia took a step forward and searched her daughter's face—for what, Grayson wasn't sure. "I wouldn't let you," Acacia told Savannah, her voice quiet but fierce. "Either of you. I'm fine. *Everything is fine.*"

"Of course," Grayson agreed. "But as it happens, I know a lawyer who would relish taking care of this situation, and it won't cost you a thing."

"I can handle this," Acacia insisted.

"There's nothing to handle." A woman wearing a navy suit approached the four of them. Another person might have misread the situation, thought that the other agents had sent someone with a softer, more feminine touch to question them, but the part of Grayson's brain that instantly calculated dominance and hierarchies ruled out that possibility immediately.

This was the woman in charge.

"We're looking for evidence of your husband's crimes and whereabouts," the FBI agent continued. "If, as you maintain, you truly have not heard from him and truly are not withholding material evidence of his crimes, then you have very little to worry about."

If, on the other hand, you're holding something back...

Grayson, as a rule, did not respond to silent threats. He held the warrant back out to Acacia. "I'd have your new lawyer look into the judge who signed it and the agent who filed the request," he advised her. "I'm hardly an expert, but it seems odd to execute a search when the suspect hasn't been seen at the location in question for a year and a half, particularly when the individuals still living in the domicile are, in fact, the victims of the alleged crime."

Grayson let his gaze slide to the agent in charge. "After all," he continued, "if there was any embezzlement, the suspect was essentially embezzling from them." Grayson wasn't angling for a response, and he didn't wait for one. "Why now?" There was an art to pausing in a way that didn't let the other party interject. "A tip from an anonymous source? A powerful person pulling just the right strings?"

The FBI agent had no visible reaction to that possibility, but that didn't stop Grayson from responding as if she'd tipped her hand. "I see."

"Grayson." Acacia's tone was firmer now, like she'd remembered that she was an adult, and he was, in her words, a *kid*.

Grayson reached into his suit pocket, withdrew his wallet, and offered her a card. After a long moment, Acacia took it, and then she looked at the FBI agent. "If you have any more questions for me," she said, her voice steely, "you'll have to address them to my lawyer."

Grayson excused himself make a call. "Alisa? I'm going to need a favor."

Two minutes later, he made another phone call from the end of the driveway. As much as part of him wanted to stay here, to protect this family, the longer he stayed, the greater the chances became that someone would realize that there was nothing to be found here because what they were looking for had *already* been found.

"The Haywood-Astyria." The private concierge answered on the second ring.

"Yes," Grayson said, not bothering to identify himself. "I'm going to need someone to drive my car out to me again."

CHAPTER 73

GRAYSON

Nash and Xander were waiting in the black-card suite. The puzzle box was on the floor. One glance told Grayson that his brothers had gotten as far on it as he, Gigi, and Savannah had.

"It's obvious what we need." Xander eyed the opening in the box's surface.

"Just haven't found it yet," Nash put in.

Grayson got the distinct feeling his brothers were avoiding asking about the FBI situation on purpose. *Their version of giving me space.*

"And you won't find it," Grayson replied. He walked over to the hotel desk and retrieved the small not-a-USB-drive from the drawer. "What you're looking for wasn't built into the box. He brought it with him each time he visited his sister."

"*He*, as in...your father." Xander was treading carefully now. Given that he was the second-least-cautious Hawthorne, that really said something.

"Isaiah is a father, Xan." Grayson fought every ounce of emotion that wanted to creep its way into those words. "Sheffield Grayson was something else."

Nash looked at Grayson for a long moment. "Things okay back at the house?"

Grayson studied the exact expression on his oldest brother's face. "Alisa called you," he surmised.

"She did," Nash confirmed. "She'll do whatever you need." His lips twitched up on the ends. "And knowing Lee-Lee, she'll enjoy it."

"Only if it gets nasty," Xander interjected.

"It's already nasty." Grayson kept his explanation brief and to the point: "Sheffield Grayson was allegedly siphoning money from his company, thereby cheating the majority owner out of significant profits. That owner was his mother-in-law. She's dead now, and her stake in the company passed to Acacia and the twins. The company was sold. My so-called father emptied Acacia's trust shortly thereafter but wasn't able to touch the trusts belonging to the girls."

"And as a bonus, the guy's gone missing." Nash let out a long, low whistle.

Nash knew that Sheffield Grayson wasn't *missing*. Grayson knew that he knew. "Now Eve's sniffing around," Grayson continued, the muscles in his jaw going stone hard. "She knows what happened. Today's search? Probably courtesy of her."

Someone had been pulling strings, and Eve had made it clear she wasn't above playing power games.

"Eve?" Nash repeated. "Your head on straight, Gray?" There wasn't an ounce of judgment in that question.

There didn't need to be for Grayson to judge himself. "Isn't it always?" he replied, his tone a match for his expression—like it had been carved from ice.

"*Betrayed by the Girl with the Face of Your Dead Girlfriend: The Grayson Hawthorne Story.*" Xander jumped down off the desk.

Grayson felt his eyes turn to slits. "Not now, Alexander."

"Too fresh?" Xander asked. "Sorry, double sorry, triple, up to and including octuple sorry. You needed someone to get you out of your own head, and Nash keeps telling me that there are times when tackling people is inappropriate."

"Most times," Nash said.

Xander was not so convinced. "Personally, I think tackling is a valid love language, but let's not debate semantics here." He brought his eyes to rest on Grayson's. "What do you need?"

Being a Hawthorne meant many things, and the best of those was this. *Them. Us.* "Got any cookies?" Grayson asked quietly.

"I always have cookies!" Xander disappeared into the suite's kitchen and came back with a half-empty package of double-stuffed Oreos and the single tallest Oreo that Grayson had ever seen. "Octuple-stuffed Oreo?" Xander offered.

Grayson took it.

"It was made with love," Xander told him. "Just like I tackle with love."

"No tackling," Nash said.

Grayson ate the cookie in silence, and then—and only then—did he speak. "I'm slipping." His brothers were the only people in the world he could have admitted that to. "Getting too emotionally involved."

"With Eve?" Xander asked.

Grayson set his jaw. "With Gigi and Savannah—and even with their mother."

"That's not slipping, Gray." Nash had a way of going quiet just when the things he was saying mattered most. "That's living."

Inexplicably, Grayson thought—again—about that damn ring. "I need to focus."

"On opening the puzzle box?" Xander guessed.

"Opening it. Going through its contents." Grayson came to stand directly over the puzzle box. "Removing anything that could tie Sheffield Grayson to the attacks on Avery and anything that suggests he didn't just disappear. Then I'll reassemble a harmless version of the box and its contents to give back to the girls."

"Are you okay with that?" Xander asked.

Grayson thought of the way his sisters had come to stand between him and their aunt. Protecting him. He thought about Acacia, squeezing his hand.

Are you okay with that?

Grayson knelt and fit the not-a-USB into the box. "I have to be."

CHAPTER 74

GRAYSON

Grayson turned the lock. There was an audible click. *A release.* He kept his grip on the faux USB and pulled. The entire panel came off the box, revealing a compartment underneath. With steady hands, Grayson turned the panel over. He wasn't surprised to see a collection of glass vials affixed to the underside. *Break the box, break the vials. Break the vials, mix the liquids. Mix the liquids, destroy the contents of the box. Specifically...*

Grayson turned his attention to the compartment he'd revealed. There were two and only two things inside: a Montblanc pen and a leather-bound journal.

"He kept records." To Grayson, that was obvious.

"Records of what?" Nash zeroed in on the key question—the only one that mattered right now.

If there was record of Sheffield Grayson's last acts before he "disappeared," if this journal could tie the man to Avery or the Hawthorne family... it had to be destroyed.

There was a comfort in certainty.

"Can I see the pen?" Xander asked. Grayson handed it to him, and the youngest Hawthorne brother immediately began his inspection, dismantling the pen.

Some parts of a riddle hold meaning, Grayson could hear the old man saying, *and others are nothing but distraction.* In a Hawthorne game, the pen would have been the clue, not the journal. But Sheffield Grayson was not Tobias Hawthorne, and this wasn't a game. There were no *clues*, just the extreme steps a paranoid dead man had taken to secure his secrets.

Grayson opened the leather journal. *This is what my father's handwriting looked like.* That thought had no place in his mind, so Grayson shoved it to the side and focused not on the writing but on what had been written.

Numbers.

Grayson flipped through the pages—nothing but numbers, and the only ones with recognizable meanings appeared at the beginning of the various entries: *dates.*

Sheffield Grayson had dated his journal entries. Grayson pictured him doing it. He *saw* his father sitting on the edge of that cheap twin bed in Colin's room and putting pen to the page. Grayson imagined "Shep" dating a journal entry, and then beginning to write.

Grayson turned all the way to the last entry, just a few pages from the end of the book. *Still nothing but numbers.* Seemingly endless strings of them.

"A code." Grayson reached the obvious conclusion.

Xander edged in beside him to get a peek at the pages. "Substitution cipher?"

"Most likely," Grayson confirmed.

"Monoalphabetic, polyalphabetic, or polygraphic?" Xander rattled off.

Nash leaned back against the wall. "That, little brother, is the question."

None of the simple ciphers worked. Grayson had tried all twenty-six of them. First *A* as 1, *B* as 2, *C* as 3 on to *Z* as 26. Then *A* as 2, *B* as 3, and so on, looping Z back to 1. No matter what base Grayson used, the journal's translation was gibberish.

Evening turned to late night. Gigi texted when the FBI left. Grayson didn't text back. His eyes bleary, he refused to back down from the task at hand.

You didn't use a basic cipher. Grayson didn't want to be mentally addressing his father, but to solve a puzzle, sometimes you had to think about its maker.

"Let me take a stab," Xander said, wriggling between Grayson and the journal. "I'll try to spot common two- and three-item combinations and go from there."

Grayson didn't object. Instead, he stopped fighting the mental image that wanted to come: Sheffield Grayson sitting on that twin bed, a pen in his right hand, the journal on a nearby nightstand. *Or on the bed? On his lap?* The image in Grayson's mind wavered, changed, and then Grayson asked himself a simple question: *Where was his cheat sheet?*

Unless his father had memorized the code—whatever it was—he would have needed a reference as he was writing.

Grayson closed his eyes, picturing the entire scene: the man, the pen, the journal, a reference of some kind... *The box.* Grayson's eyes flew open. He knelt, running his hand over the now-empty compartment. And then he felt a seam.

And another.

Another.

The workmanship was flawless. None of the seams were visible. But they were there, in the shape of a square roughly the size of Grayson's palm. That was the thing about puzzle boxes. You never really knew when the box's last secret has been uncovered.

Grayson reached for the double-sided tool—there was no saying a puzzle couldn't use the same trick twice. He ran the magnet end along the inside of the compartment, directly over the square he'd felt.

It caught.

Grayson pulled, and the square popped out. Turning it over in his hands, he saw two wooden disks, concentric, with a metal brad through the middle.

"A cipher wheel," Grayson he told his brothers.

Nash and Xander were on him in an instant. This wasn't the Hawthorne brothers' first time encountering a cipher wheel—or even their twentieth—so all three of them knew what to look for. The larger of the two wheels had letters carved around the edge, *A* through Z, plus a handful of common digraphs—*Sh*, *Ch*, *Th*, *Wh*, *Ck*, *Kn*. The inner wheel contained numbers, 1 through 32, but not in order, which explained, along with the inclusion of digraphs, why Grayson's initial rudimentary attempts hadn't broken the code.

"All we need to know now," Xander said buoyantly, "is where to set the inner wheel."

Going through the options manually was a possibility, but the part of Grayson that had grown up *racing* to complete those Saturday morning games wouldn't let him.

Sheffield Grayson had a system. A routine. He retrieved the safe-deposit key and faux USB from his office, then retrieved his fake ID.

He went to the bank. He withdrew money and left the slips in the safe-deposit box. He went to his sister's house.

Grayson skirted thinking about what, besides the slips, had been in that box. Instead, he asked a simple question out loud. "Why save the slips?"

The answer came to him like a lightning strike. He went back to the pile. On each slip, there was a date. *The same dates in the journal?* That would be easily enough to verify. What he was more interested in right now was the withdrawal amounts.

Two hundred seventeen dollars. Five hundred six dollars. Three hundred twenty-one dollars.

But according to Sheffield Grayson's sister, he'd only given her even amounts.

"He set the wheel to a different position for each entry." Grayson didn't phrase that as a possibility or a question. "And kept the slips as a record to help him decode his own writing."

17. 6. 21. Most likely, those were the numbers set to the *A*. All he had to do was match the dates on the slip to the date on the journal entries, turn the wheel to the appropriate spot, and...

Grayson put the pen that Xander had dismantled back together and retrieved his own leather notebook. Ignoring how similar it looked to his father's, he turned to the first entry that Sheffield Grayson had written and began to decode.

At first, all he got was nonsense. *Again.* But this time, Grayson didn't stop. He kept going, and eventually, the numbers on the page turned to words. *Fifty thousand dollars to shell five, Cayman Islands, via shell two, Switzerland...*

Eventually, the code settled back into gibberish. Noise. On the next page, Grayson found the same thing: meaningful content embedded in noise. The real message was in a different location on this page.

How was that determined? Grayson didn't *need* to know the answer to that question. He had no actual need to understand exactly how his father's mind had worked. But on some level, he wanted to, so when he noticed two subtle tears at the top of the current page, when he turned to the next and saw two more tiny tears in the paper—in a different position—he brought his finger to lightly touch them.

Not tears, Grayson thought, his gaze darting to the hotel desk, where the white index card he'd removed from Sheffield Grayson's office still sat. *Notches*.

CHAPTER 75

JAMESON

Well done, my boy. Jameson didn't just hear Ian say that; he *felt* the words. Physically. Like he'd been holding a breath too long, finally gasped in air, and discovered that breathing hurt.

He just asked me to hand over the keys. To hand over the entire damn game.

Avery shifted closer to Jameson, the back of her hip brushing his leg. Without a word, Jameson pressed the key he'd just discovered—with its shining, maze-like head—into her hand.

Almost like he didn't trust himself with it.

"What are you doing here, Ian?" Jameson asked. He'd meant for the question to sound sharper.

Ian Johnstone-Jameson strolled casually forward, like his appearance in the middle of the Game was only natural, like Jameson shouldn't have been surprised to see him in the least.

"Is that your way of asking if the Factotum knows I'm treading on these hallowed grounds, interfering in his little game?" Ian asked with an expression that danced the line between a smile and a smirk. "If so, the answer, I'm afraid, is no."

He's not supposed to be here. Jameson managed to pry his gaze away from Ian and glance at Katharine. *She must have tipped him off about the location of the Game.* Did she have a phone hidden somewhere? *Does it matter?*

"You have two keys," Ian murmured, his gaze lingering on the key in Avery's hands. "Two out of three—and only one for my holier-than-thou brother. I'm liking our odds."

Our as in yours and mine? Jameson thought bitterly. *Or yours and Katharine's?* "What's she doing here?" he demanded.

Katharine looked slightly amused at the question, like nothing Jameson could say or do would amount to more than childish antics in her mind.

"The formidable Katharine and I have come to an agreement of sorts." Ian's lips curled again, more smile than smirk this time and wholly self-satisfied. "You'll give her those keys," Ian continued grandly, "and everyone will leave here happy—except my oldest brother, of course, which I have to admit has its appeal."

"What about Vantage?" Jameson asked. He had enough self-awareness to know that what he was really asking was *what about me?*

Ian gave a little shrug. "I really don't see how that's any concern of yours."

And that was the thing, Jameson realized. Ian really *didn't*. The offer to leave Jameson Vantage had been impulsive, spur-of-the-moment. *Forgotten.*

"You sold me out." Jameson's could feel the intensity in his voice.

"You asked me to play this game. You aimed me like an arrow at an almost impossible target."

And now, when Jameson was on the verge of hitting the bull's-eye—after working his way into the Devil's Mercy, after everything he'd done to win entrance to the Game, after putting *that* secret on the line, coming here and solving puzzle after puzzle—Ian expected him to *pull back*?

"What did Katharine offer you?" Avery's tone was flat as she assessed Ian like a speck beneath a microscope. "She's working for your other brother, right? What did *he* offer you?"

"I'm afraid the terms of our deal are confidential." Katharine wasn't the smiling type, but there was a certain amount of satisfaction in her tone. "The keys, if you please, children?"

"No." Jameson didn't think, didn't consider his options—because there weren't any. He hadn't come here, hadn't put everything on the line, to back down now.

"No?" Katharine arched a brow, then turned her head toward Ian, a silent *fix this*.

"No," Jameson repeated. "As in the opposite of yes, to decline, deny, or negate. *No*."

"Jameson." Ian walked to stand directly in front of him and laid a hand on his shoulder. "You did what I needed you to do, son."

I have his eyes. Jameson let himself think that, just this once. *Grayson has his father's eyes, and I have mine. I have his laugh.*

"You said you needed a player," Jameson replied, ignoring the hand on his shoulder. Nothing could hurt you unless you let it. "Someone smart and cunning, merciless—"

"But never dull," Ian cut in. "Yes, yes, I know. And you played. Well done, you. But now, the plan has changed."

Your plan, Jameson thought, emotions twisting in his gut like brambles full of thorns. He'd known from the beginning that Ian was using him. He'd *known* that. But at least he'd been indispensable to the plan before. But now?

I'm disposable. "You wanted a player who could calculate odds," Jameson said, and he could hear the wild fury building in his own voice. "Someone who could defy those odds."

And I did that.

"I needed a player, and you played," Ian said, sounding annoyed now. "It's over. Now give me the keys."

You love a challenge, Jameson could hear the man in front of him saying. *You love to play. You love to win. And no matter what you win, you always need more.*

For a brief time, Jameson had almost felt seen. "I'm not giving you anything," he said fiercely. "Would the deal you've struck even give you Vantage back?" Jameson let the question hang in the air, but he knew the answer, had known it the first time he'd uttered the words *What about Vantage?*

Katharine—and his other uncle—weren't playing for Vantage. They were playing for the damning secret of a powerful man, which meant that Katharine must have offered Ian something else, something he wanted more than the estate his mother had left him. The place where he grew up. A property that had been in his mother's family for generations.

He doesn't care. Not about family. Not about this place. Jameson breathed in. *Not about me.*

"Time is wasting," Katharine declared, her tone brisk. "And I'll still need to locate the boxes that those keys unlock."

Ian's eyes narrowed at Jameson. "I know that you aren't wired to lose, Jameson," he said, his voice silky. "But you need to do what I say, because neither am I."

That was a warning. A threat.

"Do I look like a person who's easy to threaten?" Jameson smiled, even though it hurt his bruised and battered face.

"Not particularly." Rohan appeared as if by magic, stepping out from behind a statue. "Some people," the Factotum continued, "just don't know when to stay down."

Jameson wasn't sure if that was a reference to Ian or himself. Either way, it didn't matter. Jameson was done talking. *What happens to Ian now—what Rohan does to him for interfering—is none of my concern.*

"Let's go," he told Avery, a lump rising in his throat. He'd gone a lifetime without a father. He didn't need one now.

All Jameson Winchester Hawthorne needed was to win.

CHAPTER 76

JAMESON

Two of the three keys had been found on the grounds. Jameson's gut said that the boxes those keys opened would be back inside the manor. He listened to his gut and paid no attention to the storm of emotions churning inside him—and even less to the sound of Ian shouting after them.

"Jameson." That was all Avery said, once they were out of earshot of the others.

"I'm fine," he told her. That was a lie. They both knew it was a lie.

"You're better than fine," Avery told him fiercely. "You're Jameson Winchester Hawthorne. And we're going to win this game."

Jameson came to a stop and turned to face her, so he could quiet the storm inside in the only way he knew how. He pushed Avery's wild, wind-blown hair back from her face. She tilted her head back, and he brought his lips down on hers—not hard this time but soft and slow. His mouth hurt. His face and body hurt. Everything hurt. But kissing Avery?

That hurt in the best possible way.

"*Watch yourself,*" he murmured, his lips just barely pulling back from hers. This was what it meant to focus. To *play.*

"The last clue," she murmured back. "One last chance to win this game."

Screw Ian. Jameson didn't need *Ian.* It was—now and always—Jameson and Avery against the world.

Back inside the manor, they started looking for mirrors. In a house of this size—of this type—there were dozens, many of them too large and heavy for even two people to lift. So instead of lifting them, Jameson and Avery probed the frames, running their fingers along the sides, looking for hinges, a button, a hidden compartment.

Eventually, they hit paydirt.

In a long hall on the fourth floor, they found an enormous mirror with a bronze frame. When Jameson pulled on the side of the frame, there was no resistance. It swung open like a door.

Watch yourself. Jameson stepped into a long, nearly empty room, Avery on his heels. The room was dark, lit only by candles on a single chandelier in the center. Although the ceiling was at least twenty feet tall, the chandelier hung low, almost to the floor. Looking at it called to Jameson's mind a pendulum.

As the mirror swung closed behind Avery, Jameson realized just how little light the candles provided. The dark green walls looked almost black. Portraits hung every ten feet, all the way down the length of the room.

Jameson didn't see a treasure box, let alone three. *There's nothing in this room except for the chandelier and the portraits.* He strode to examine the closest one. Ian smirked back at him from the frame.

Jameson set his mouth in a firm line. It made sense. Ian Johnstone-Jameson was the most recent owner of this place. Jameson looked to the next portrait and saw a woman. The resemblance between her and Ian was uncanny.

"I guess I don't just have his eyes," Jameson said quietly. "They're yours, too."

He'd grown up with a grandfather, singular, and no grandmother. This woman, the one in this portrait, was every bit as related to him as Alice Hawthorne—and just as much of a stranger.

You had three sons. Jameson addressed those words silently to the portrait. *You raised them here, when you could.* Vantage was her ancestral home—*and that makes it mine.* Jameson ran his fingers along the edge of first one frame and then the other. Once he was satisfied that these two were clean, he began to move to the next one.

"Jameson." Avery's voice cut through the air. "This one's you."

He whirled to face her. "Me?" Jameson had no intention of letting that matter, so why did each breath he took suddenly feel like sandpaper in his throat? Why, as he crossed the room and stared at the portrait that someone had commissioned of *him*, did some part of him want to be on those walls?

To belong here.

Jameson locked his fingers around the frame, then pulled—first one side, then the other. Nothing happened until Avery ran her fingertips around the edges of the wood. Jameson knew the exact second she found the release. Once it was triggered, the portrait swung away from the wall, revealing a hidden compartment. Nestled there was a jeweled chest, its dominant colors emerald green and shining gold.

The Game is almost over now. Adrenaline coursing through his veins, Jameson absorbed every detail of this moment and knew three things immediately, courtesy of instincts hard-won over years and years of playing games just like this. First, the chest was green, and that made it a match for the key that Branford had found in the caves. Second, the chest had been hidden behind Jameson's portrait, which he was willing to bet meant that it held *his* secret. And finally, this portrait hadn't been painted in quite the same style as the portraits of Ian and his mother. That, combined with the fact that his uncles really *hadn't* seemed to know about Jameson's existence, suggested that this painting was likely a recent commission.

Very recent.

Rohan did this. How did he even know the Proprietor would choose me for the Game?

Right now, that wasn't the question that mattered most. "We need to find the other two boxes," Jameson told Avery. He started running from portrait to portrait, even more adrenaline flooding his veins, an old friend, a needed rush. He stopped when he reached a portrait of Branford.

Jameson's fingers found the release almost instantly, and the portrait swung away from the wall to reveal another jeweled chest—gold again, with pearls inlaid. *A match for the second key.*

Jameson inserted the pearl key in the lock. It turned. The lid to the box opened. Inside, there was a scroll. He undid the ribbon, unwound the scroll, and was greeted with words scrawled in sharp and angular script.

I have a son.

Jameson knew almost nothing about Simon Johnstone-Jameson, Viscount Branford. He didn't know if his uncle was married, or if he had any other children, but the Proprietor had been very specific about the kind of secrets he was interested in.

The kind men would kill and die for. The kind that shakes the ground beneath our feet.

Jameson tucked the scroll into his waistband, then gave the jeweled chest a once-over, just in case.

"Jameson!" Avery's voice cut through the air like a knife. Immediately, he looked toward the door. *Branford—and he's not alone.* Zella strolled in behind the viscount, and Jameson thought to wonder if Katharine wasn't the only one who'd struck a deal.

"Avery!" Jameson called. "The chest!"

If Avery had the green box, Branford couldn't use his key to unlock it. Jameson expelled a breath when Avery got to the portrait first, when she held the chest in her hands.

Held his secret in her hands.

And that was when Jameson realized: Zella and Branford hadn't moved from the doorway. Neither one of them had so much as glanced at Avery or the green box.

Branford reached into his suit jacket.

Jameson knew then, before Branford even pulled out the scroll. *He's already been here. He already found the green box. He already unlocked it with his green key.*

He already has my secret.

"I understand you found the other two keys." Branford's path was straight, his stride long as he made his way toward Jameson like a missile zeroing in on its target. "I believe I have something of yours. I haven't read it yet. This secret—whatever it is—will stay secret if you're willing to make a trade."

Jameson plucked Branford's scroll—*his* secret—from his waistband. "I'm open to the idea."

Branford's shrewd eyes missed nothing. "You've already read it."

Jameson wished he hadn't. "I'll give it to you and never breathe a word of it to anyone else." *Your secret son can stay a secret. What's it to me?*

"It's not a bad offer, Branford," Zella said. "Maybe you should take it." There was something in the way she delivered that statement, a twist to her tone that made Jameson think her real goal was to push the viscount into doing the opposite.

What are you up to, Duchess?

"The trade you've proposed," Branford told Jameson evenly, "would only be an even trade if I read your secret before returning it to you."

The room suddenly seemed small. Jameson could hear his heart beating in his ears, could feel it in the pit of his stomach. *There are ways, Jameson Hawthorne*, he'd been warned, *to take care of problems.* He thought about the bead he'd offered up to the Proprietor as proof of his secret. *Poison*, he'd been told in Prague, *undetectable and quite deadly.*

That had been a warning.

He'd known that he was taking a risk, but he'd told himself it was a calculated one. *A miscalculation.* Sweat trickling down his jaw, his neck, Jameson took a step toward Branford. "You don't want to know my secret," he told his uncle. "People who know that secret tend to meet unfortunate ends."

"This is about Prague, isn't it?" Avery said, making her way slowly toward him, the green box still in her hands.

"Don't," Jameson told her, the word coming out with almost violent force. "Just leave it, Heiress. Stay back."

Away from Branford. Away from that scroll. Away from me.

"There is another trade I would accept." Branford didn't have Jameson's height, but he somehow managed to look down at him nonetheless. "Your secret for the remaining key."

The key. The one that opened the final box, the box they hadn't even located yet.

We're so close. Jameson looked up, the way he always did when he was thinking through something, playing it out as a web of possibility laid out across a ceiling or a sky. And when he looked up, he saw the long chain connecting the low-hanging chandelier to the ceiling.

At the top of that chain, he saw a box. Unlike the other two, this one wasn't shining or gleaming. It bore no jewels. From a distance, it looked silver, possibly tarnished.

Jameson brought his gaze back down—to Avery. *She* had the last key. As she finished closing the space between them, he traced an arrow onto her palm. *Up.*

He saw the spark of realization in Avery's eyes. She didn't look up, not immediately, not in a way that Branford or Zella would notice. *But she knows.*

Jameson stepped away from Avery and made a move to draw his opponents' attention back to himself. "Counter proposal," he said, walking toward Branford and Zella—and away from Avery. "You set my secret on fire, Branford, and I do the same for yours. You leave this room. I win the Game, and once I've won the prize that we're both after, I'll give you Vantage."

Jameson had Branford's full attention now—and Zella's. *Good.* He kept walking.

"What's the difference," Branford said tersely, "between giving me Vantage and giving me the key right now? If you're hoping to double-cross me—"

"I'm not," Jameson said. To his own ears, his voice sounded raw, like he'd been in this room screaming into the void for hours.

"Vantage belonged to your mother. It means something to you—more than it means to either of your brothers, apparently."

Jameson didn't let himself think about Ian.

He tried not to think about Ian.

He failed.

"You asked what the difference is between the deal you proposed and the one I did." Jameson didn't allow his voice to shake. "The difference is that under my deal, I win."

All Jameson needed was to finish this. To prove that he could.

"You'd risk whatever *this* is," Branford said, holding up Jameson's scroll. "A secret you claim is deadly, a price you never should have paid to be here, to win a prize that you don't even want?"

To Jameson's left, Avery looked up.

In the span of less than a second, Jameson considered his next move. If he ran, would Branford follow him? Would Avery be able to climb that chain, retrieve that box, unlock it?

One of them winning was both of them winning. Jameson knew that, almost believed it.

"You really are my nephew," Branford said intently. "Far too much like my brother."

That hurt. It hurt, but it didn't matter that it hurt, because Branford was wrong. *I'm nothing like Ian.*

"I can't take your deal, young man." In one fell swoop, Branford returned Jameson's secret to the inside pocket of his suit. "My father is not well. I'm the head of this family in every way that matters, and like it or not, you are our blood. If you've got yourself in too deep, if *you* are in danger, I'm afraid I need to know." The expression on the viscount's face was implacable. "I can't give you your secret—not even for the final key."

Family. That one word was seared into Jameson's mind like a brand. He had the sense that it wasn't one that Simon Johnstone-Jameson, Viscount Branford, used lightly. *The bastard feels honor bound to protect me. And he's willing to sacrifice Vantage to do it.*

To Ian, Jameson had been disposable. To Branford, apparently, he was not.

That doesn't change anything. It didn't even matter if Jameson believed that, because the truth was that even if Branford's words *did* mean something to him, even if something *had* changed something—Jameson's need to win hadn't.

He *was* extraordinary. He had to be. There was no other choice.

Drawing in a breath that felt like needles in his lungs, Jameson made his way back to the chandelier and removed the five burning candles one by one, placing them on the floor. Then, without a word to anyone else—even Avery—he eyed the positioning of the chandelier's chain, jumped, and caught it in his hands.

And then, he began to climb.

CHAPTER 77

JAMESON

The chain didn't feel very sturdy, but it held his weight. The muscles in Jameson's arms tightened and rippled as he climbed. Pain meant nothing. His bruises and battered ribs meant nothing. *Just a few more feet.*

Down below, Simon Johnstone-Jameson, Viscount Branford, still held his secret. *Four words. An* H. *The word* is. *The letters* v *and* e.

Jameson made it to the top. The final box—silver, antique, elaborately made—was attached to the chain with wire. Shifting his weight to his left hand, Jameson began pulling at the wires with his right. Eventually, the muscles in his arm began to burn. The wire bit into his fingertips, but Jameson pulled harder.

Even when his grip on the chain started to slip, even when the wire cut at his fingers and his right hand became slick with blood, he still kept at it. And finally, he ripped the box loose. "Heiress." He looked back down over his shoulder, at the ground below. "Catch."

He dropped the silver chest, and she caught it.

With slick hands and aching muscles, Jameson began to climb back down. He made it halfway—maybe a little more than that—and then just dropped. He landed in a crouch, his legs absorbing the shock, his entire body screaming.

And then, he turned to Avery and reclaimed the chest. She held out the key, but before he could take it, Zella spoke.

"I'm going to need that," the duchess said, not specifying whether she was talking about the box or the key. *Both.* That was what Jameson's gut said as Zella strolled across the room to stand toe-to-toe with Avery.

"The viscount here might not have been able to, in good conscience, make a deal for the final key," Zella said. "But I am not so burdened." There wasn't any audible triumph in her tone—but there was something else, something deeper. "Branford doesn't have your secret, Jameson. I do." She tugged a flattened, folded piece of parchment out of the top of her dress. "My apologies," she told Branford. "I made a little switch on our way here."

Branford stared at her. Hard. "That's not possible."

The duchess gave a little shrug. "I happen to specialize in impossible."

She was the only person who'd ever successfully broken into the Devil's Mercy, and she'd talked her way into membership thereafter. Jameson had known from their second meeting: The duchess was a woman who *saw* things, one who played the long game.

She chose her competition. Jameson looked at Zella, really looked at her. "Have you read my secret?"

"I'm about to," she replied. "Out loud. If you want to spare your heiress from hearing it, you'll tell her to give me the last key. Otherwise, any danger that comes from this little bit of forbidden knowledge... well, I can only assume you'd like to protect Avery here from that."

Jameson looked to Avery. He saw nothing in the room *but* Avery. "Give the key to Zella," he said softly.

There were some things he wouldn't risk, not even to win.

"You have three seconds," Zella warned. She began unfolding the parchment. "Three..."

"Do it," Jameson commanded. "The Game—it doesn't even matter anymore." *Lie.*

"Two..."

"Just do it, Heiress."

Avery mouthed two words: *I can't.* And the next thing Jameson knew, she'd leapt toward Zella, her hand latching around the parchment. Zella fought. Jameson watched as his Heiress took the duchess to the ground.

"Enough!" Rohan's voice boomed through the air.

Zella froze, but Avery didn't. She pulled herself to her feet, the parchment in her hand, and held it to the flame of the closest candle.

"I said *enough*!" The Factotum told her.

Avery didn't back down. She never backed down. And by the time Rohan had made it to her, the parchment was ashes. Jameson's secret was ashes. *You didn't look at it, Heiress. You didn't read it. You could have, but you didn't.*

Zella stood, grace incarnate, and smiled. "Correct me if I'm wrong," she told Rohan, "but wasn't there a rule about violence of any kind leading to immediate expulsion from the Game?" Her eyes lit on the key still in Avery's possession. "And wouldn't expulsion from the Game mean that any key held by that player is surrendered?"

There was a flash of something in Rohan's eyes—not anger, not exactly—but a moment later, it was gone. He turned toward Avery with the rogue's smile firmly in place. "Indeed," he said in reply to Zella's question, "it would."

CHAPTER 78

GRAYSON

Decoding Sheffield Grayson's journal took all night. The longer Grayson worked, the faster he went, transcribing the translation in his own notebook—leather, just like his father's. Grayson ignored the similarity. He ignored everything but the shifting code and the words it gave him.

In the beginning, Sheffield Grayson appeared to have used this journal as an off-the-books ledger, recording where the money he embezzled from his company went. There were no account numbers, but with the dates and the locations of the accounts, there was a trail to follow.

The kind the FBI would definitely be capable of following.

But as Grayson got further and further through his translation and the dates at the top of the entries showed months and years passing, the tone and content of Sheffield Grayson's writing changed. The journal entries went from focusing almost entirely on documenting illegal transactions to something more . . . *confessional.*

That was the word that Grayson kept coming back to as he decoded and transcribed what his father had written—except that wasn't quite right. The word *confession* implied something like guilt or the need to unburden oneself. Sheffield Grayson hadn't been burdened.

He'd been angry.

Cora's funeral was today. It should have been a time of mourning. I should have been Acacia's rock. Without her mother there to interfere, to hold her threats over my head, it should have been the two of us, husband and wife, against the world. Not so. Trowbridge made sure of that. He got Acacia alone at the wake. He told my wife things he had no business knowing, let alone saying.

She had so many questions.

Grayson didn't let himself pause in decoding, didn't linger on any one entry, no matter what it said. But even as he kept his focus on turning numbers to letters and letters to words, on finding the exact location on each page in which meaningful content was embedded, his brain still processed every word he wrote.

The overall picture was becoming clearer and clearer in his mind.

Cora left everything to Acacia and the girls. No surprise there. It's all tied up in trusts. No surprise there, either. Acacia is her own trustee, thank God, but Cora named Trowbridge trustee for the girls. The bastard is already asking to see financial records. I'll force a sale of the company before I let that pathetic excuse for a man question me.

The next few pages detailed the sale of the company and Sheffield Grayson's efforts to ensure the buyer took the financial records they were given at face value. But after that, the tenor of his words shifted again.

Acacia keeps asking about "my son." As if he's any business of hers—or mine, for that matter. As if the Hawthorne family hasn't already taken enough from me. Acacia is too soft-hearted to understand. She won't listen to reason—not about the boy and not about her trust.

And then, two pages later, there was another entry, a brief one: *Tobias Hawthorne is dead at last.*

It took another few weeks, but then, right after Avery had been named heir, the entries started up again.

That conniving bastard left his money to a girl not that much older than the twins. A stranger, they say, but there are whispers that she's Hawthorne's child.

Grayson could feel the seething anger building in these pages. The entries became more frequent. Some were about Colin, the fire, the evidence that Sheffield Grayson had put together that it was the result of arson—evidence that the police ignored. Other entries focused on Avery and Sheffield Grayson's obsessive theories about who she was to the old man, to the Hawthorne family.

Theories about Grayson's supposedly dead uncle, Toby Hawthorne.

Grayson was able to pinpoint the exact moment that Sheffield Grayson had decided to have Avery tracked, to spy on her. The man was convinced she'd lead him to Toby.

And since he's already a dead man, well... they can hardly charge me with his murder, now can they?

Grayson didn't let himself pause, even for a second, when he transcribed the word *murder*. He just let this almost Shakespearean drama play out: the unseated king stripped of power by the machinations of his dead mother-in-law; a rising heir entangled with the king's archenemy. A family with blood on their hands. A debt that *would* be paid.

Grayson was getting closer and closer to the end of the journal. And then he wrote down a date that made him look up from the page, made him close his eyes.

The interview. Mine and Avery's. Grayson could recall each question that he and Avery had been asked. He remembered the way Avery's body had turned toward his, the way he'd let himself look at her, *really* look at her, in service of letting the world see that the Hawthorne family had accepted Tobias Hawthorne's chosen heir.

But mostly, Grayson remembered the moment they'd lost control of the narrative—and the way he'd taken that control back.

Pulling her body to his.

Bringing his lips to hers.

For one damn moment, he'd stopped fighting himself. He'd kissed her like kissing her was what he had been born to do, like it was inevitable, like *they* were. And not long after, everything had exploded.

The way it always did. The way it had with Emily. With Avery. With Eve.

Why not you? Grayson forced his eyes open. He let himself stare at the date he'd written down, then he took Sheffield Grayson's index card, matched its notches up to the notches on the page he was decoding, set the cipher wheel to the appropriate number, based on the withdrawal slip with that date. And then, he decoded, read, and wrote.

Sheffield Grayson had watched the interview. He was the one who had set them up to be broadsided with the bombshell accusation that Grayson's uncle Toby was still alive. Sheffield Grayson had believed that Avery was Toby's daughter. He'd wanted confirmation, but that confirmation had never come, because Grayson had taken matters into his own hands.

That kiss.

Grayson's father's resulting rage was palpable, even now. *Toby Hawthorne's daughter*, he'd written, *doesn't get to kiss my son.*

Grayson leaned his head back until swallowing hurt. *He called me his son.* No quotation marks. No dismissal. Nothing but possession and fury—and with that fury, purpose.

"Gray?" Xander said quietly beside him.

Grayson shook his head. He wasn't talking about this. There was nothing to talk about. He focused instead on finishing what he'd set out to do. There were exactly three more entries in the journal. Grayson made his way through them with military precision and merciless speed. After the night of the interview, Sheffield Grayson had returned to the detached record-keeping style of his earlier entries.

The first of the three entries documented a cryptocurrency payment to a "specialist." The second included payment information for a Texas storage unit. The third simply had a list of supplies that Sheffield Grayson anticipated needing. *Chloroform. Zip ties. Accelerant. A gun.*

And that was it, the end of his records.

Grayson stopped writing. He dropped the pen, allowed the journal in which he'd written the translation to close.

"Reckon I know better than to ask if you're okay," Nash said quietly.

"I ate the rest of the Oreos," Xander announced gravely. "Here, Gray. Have some pie!"

Grayson seized on the distraction his younger brother had offered. "When did you stop for pie?"

"When *didn't* I stop for pie?" Xander replied philosophically.

The vise in Grayson's chest loosened. Not much. Not enough. But at least he could breathe—and *think*. Not about the fact that Sheffield Grayson had finally referred to him as his son. Not about the role *that* kiss had played in setting off everything that followed: the bomb, Avery's kidnapping, Sheffield Grayson's death.

No, Grayson thought, as he always did, about what to do next. Some people could make mistakes. He wasn't one of them.

Eventually—most likely within hours—Gigi and Savannah were going to come looking for the puzzle box. Without the faux USB key, they might never get it open, but Grayson knew better than to underestimate his sisters. If they opened the box to find it empty, they would be rightly suspicious.

His course of action decided, Grayson stole Xander's fork, took a bite of pie, then placed a call to the concierge. "I need a plain leather journal," he said. "Expensive, brown leather, lined paper, no brand name or other identifying marks on the leather or pages."

CHAPTER 79

GRAYSON

While Grayson waited for his request to be fulfilled, he picked up his father's fountain pen and a hotel notepad. Returning to the first page of Sheffield Grayson's journal, Grayson studied the minute details of the man's handwriting. His *1*s were straight lines; the slight thickening of that line near the top suggested he made them from the bottom up. The 3s were curvy, the ends angled slightly inward. His 6 had a smaller loop than his 9; 4s and 5s had sharp corners, harsh angles.

I can do this. Pen in hand, Grayson replicated a single line of numbered text. *Close, but not quite.* He tried again. Again. By the time the hotel delivered the new journal, Grayson was ready. Slowly, painstakingly, he transcribed the numbered entries, creating a duplicate journal that stopped just after the girls' grandmother's funeral. Grayson placed the duplicate journal in the central compartment of the puzzle box, then began reassembling it. This time, he tucked the faux USB beneath a strip of wood on the outermost layer.

His sisters deserved that much, at least. A chance to open the box. A chance to decode the journal. A chance to know who their father had been—even if Grayson couldn't allow them to learn it all.

Standing, he turned and gave the original journal to Nash. "Take this back to Hawthorne House," he said. "Hide it in the Davenport at the bottom of the stairs hidden behind the bookshelves in the loft library." Grayson looked down at his notebook, the one in which he'd decoded the original, and, after a moment, he handed it to Xander. "This, too."

With both the original and the decoded transcription hidden away at Hawthorne House, the situation would be defused. The truth of Sheffield Grayson's demise would remain hidden. Avery would be protected.

"Burn this," he told his brothers finally, handing them the notepad on which he'd practiced Sheffield Grayson's writing. *One last string to tie up.*

"You expect us to just leave you here?" Nash leaned against the doorframe, crossing his right foot lazily over his left ankle in a way that said *I have all day, little brother.*

"I'm fine," Grayson told him. "Or at least, as fine as I ever am."

For now, at least, he had purpose. The twins needed him still, in a way that his brothers didn't, in a way they hadn't for a very long time. The FBI needed to be dealt with. Then there was Acacia's financial situation. Finding the offshore accounts referenced in the journal. Acquainting himself with the fine details of the twins' trusts. Keeping an eye on Trowbridge.

"I want to stay," Grayson told Nash. "For a few weeks at least. Someone has to keep Gigi out of trouble, and Savannah is carrying far too much."

"She's you," Xander said emphatically. "But female!"

Nash pushed off the doorway. "Sounds like you'll have your hands full . . . big brother."

Within the hour, Nash and Xander were gone. Grayson looked down at the puzzle box, then he picked up his phone. He texted Gigi and got three texts back in rapid succession—and also, three pictures of cats.

Mom didn't sleep at all last night. House is in shambles. The FBI is on MY LIST. That text was accompanied by a cat with narrowed, grumpy eyes. Next, there was a picture of a cat rolled up in brown paper like a submarine sandwich. *Savannah has locked herself in her room.* The final picture was a cat on its hind legs, with tongue stuck out and its eyes opened wide. *PS: I'm outside your hotel right now. You are very popular with the valets.*

Grayson almost grinned. In the elevator, on the way down to fetch her, he received a fourth text—no cat picture this time. *PPS: I like your friend!*

CHAPTER 80

GRAYSON

Grayson Hawthorne did not have friends. He definitely didn't have friends in Phoenix. The muscles between his shoulder blades tightened as he stepped off the elevator and cut through the lobby.

Someone had approached Gigi, claiming to be his friend.

Grayson's hand hit the door, throwing it open. He heard Gigi's voice almost immediately. "Take that! I made you smile."

Grayson turned to see his little sister standing within two feet of Mattias Slater. *Eve's spy.*

"I don't smile." Slate—as Eve had called him—stared Grayson's sister down.

"Of course not," Gigi said solemnly. "The upturning of your lips that I saw a few moments ago was nothing more than a twitch. A dark and broody twitch."

Grayson was beside them—between them—in an instant. He

locked eyes with the threat. Slate's blond hair hung in his face, but behind it, his dark stare was piercing.

"The two of you must have so much fun," Gigi deadpanned.

Grayson turned his back on his opponent—an insult, and Mattias Slater knew it. Grayson caught Gigi's gaze and held it. "Go inside."

Gigi did not go inside. "I can't! Your friend promised me mimosas and grilled cheese."

"I did not."

Grayson could practically hear Slate's scowl.

"You did," Gigi replied, leaning around Grayson to shoot an impish look at Eve's lackey. "With your eyes!"

Grayson shifted, shielding Gigi once more. He turned his head slowly toward Mattias Slater's. *"Step. Back."*

A valet hurried over. "Is there a problem here, Mr. Hawthorne?"

Grayson kept himself under control, even though the idea that this guy had gotten close enough to Gigi to hurt her made him want to take care of the problem permanently. "Have him removed."

The valet rushed to call security.

Mattias Slater still hadn't stepped back. "Vincent Blake had a heart attack this morning. A bad one." His voice held no emotion whatsoever; the absence of it—and any hint of his humanity—was chilling. "He's in surgery. Eve has called me back to Texas. She could be in danger, given the circumstances."

The circumstances being that she was Vincent Blake's sole heir—but hadn't been for all that long.

"And that matters to me why?" Grayson asked.

"Maybe it doesn't," Slate replied. Then, with speed and grace that was nothing short of lethal, Mattias Slater somehow made his way past Grayson to Gigi.

“Careful with this one, sunshine,” the light-haired, dark-eyed spy murmured to her, nodding to Grayson. “He’s playing his own game. I’d hate for you to get burned.”

Grayson didn’t hold back this time. He went for Slate, but the slippery bastard wasn’t standing where he’d been a moment before. Aware of Gigi’s dismay and the security guards incoming, Grayson managed to reel himself in. *Barely.* “Tell Eve that I know that she tipped off the FBI. If she wants my attention, she’s got it.”

And she’s going to wish she didn’t.

“I’ll tell her.” Slate cast one last look at Gigi. “Take care, sunshine.”

Grayson didn’t look away from Mattias Slater until he’d disappeared around the corner. Then he turned his attention to his sister.

“On the one hand,” Gigi said earnestly, “my powers of inference suggest that he’s probably bad news? But on the other hand...” Grayson absolutely did not trust the spark of glee in her eyes. “He’s probably *very* bad news.” Gigi said that like it was a good thing.

It was *not* a good thing. “Don’t even think about it,” Grayson told her.

His sister grinned. “Who’s Eve?”

Grayson took advantage of the fact that they had an obvious audience to delay answering that question. He gave Gigi a look. “Upstairs.”

CHAPTER 81

GRAYSON

Gigi restrained herself while they were in the elevator, but Grayson could see her practically bursting with questions. In less than a minute, he'd have to supply her with answers of some kind.

Consider your options. Project the likely outcomes. Calculate risks.

The moment the two of them were alone in the black-card suite, Gigi burst. "So . . . who's Eve?"

"It's complicated."

Gigi grinned. "I love complicated!"

"She's Toby Hawthorne's—now Toby *Blake*'s—recently discovered biological daughter." Grayson committed to a course of action. He'd lied to Gigi enough. In the future, he'd probably have to lie to her more. This wasn't a secret he had to keep.

"Family drama." Gigi clapped her hands in front of her body. "I dig it! And Toby is . . ."

"My uncle."

"So Eve's your cousin?"

Grayson's entire body clenched at that question. "Legally, no. Biologically, also no." Toby was adopted. Eve had another man's name on her birth certificate. She'd only met the Hawthornes—Grayson and Toby included—in adulthood. "Like I said, it's complicated. What's not complicated is that she's dangerous—and so is that guy you were talking to outside."

"Just out of curiosity," Gigi said, her tone wheedling, "does *he* have a name?"

Mattias Slater. "Not one that you need to know," Grayson told Gigi. "I need you to promise me that if you ever see him again, you'll run."

"Well...," Gigi hedged. "What if..."

"No," Grayson told her. "Just no, Juliet. If you see him, you get the hell out of there, and you call me. I'm fairly certain that Eve is responsible for setting the FBI on your mother yesterday, and I can't swear that she won't do worse."

Eve had been a mistake, and if there was one thing that Grayson Hawthorne knew with every fiber of his being, it was that his mistakes always came back to haunt him.

"Why would she do that?" Gigi asked, crinkling her nose. When Grayson wasn't forthcoming with an answer, she sighed. "Fine. If I see Mr. Tall, Dark-Eyed, and Broody again, I'll call you. Code name: *Mimosas*. And if you're wondering if it's because I could get drunk just looking at the eyes, the cheekbones, the tattoos, honey-golden hair and sun-kissed skin, that little scar through his eyebrow..."

Grayson gave Gigi his most quelling look, and she plopped down on the floor next to the reassembled puzzle box.

"Any progress?" she asked.

Grayson didn't say no. He didn't lie to her *per se.* Instead, he sat down on the floor next to her and met her eyes. "I thought it might help to start again from the beginning."

And that was what they did. They removed the loose strip of wood from the top of the box, sliding it out, then flipping it over to remove the tool. Gigi turned the box upside down, and Grayson used the magnet end of the tool to remove the panel on the bottom of the box, revealing a hole in which the other side of the tool could be inserted. That loosened the strips of wood on the top, allowing them to be pressed down on the ends to enter the combination that triggered another release. Off came another panel on the box, revealing a small opening, barely larger than a USB.

"Have we tried shaking it?" Gigi said thoughtfully. She didn't wait for an answer. She shook the box—and out fell the USB key.

Grayson wondered then if he'd made a mistake by making it easier for the girls to open the box, but he didn't let himself linger on the question for long. *Regret never pays dividends, boys. Remember that. Once you start second-guessing yourself, you've failed.*

"Was this here before?" Gigi asked, scrunching up her forehead. "Because I kind of feel like this wasn't here before."

"We didn't check," Grayson told her, willing her to drop it.

With a grin, Gigi did. She stuck the faux USB into the opening and twisted it, then hesitated. "We should wait for Savannah," she declared, fishing her phone out of her pocket and firing off a text. "She'll want to be here for this."

There was something about the way that Gigi said her twin's name that put Grayson on high alert. "Is Savannah okay?"

Gigi nodded, but she also didn't quite meet his eyes. "She and Mom had a fight last night after you left. About our trusts."

The trusts that Zabrowski *still* hadn't gotten him the paperwork on. "Everything is going to be okay, Gigi." Grayson came this close to calling her *little sister*, the way Nash liked to use *little brother*. "I promise."

Grayson didn't realize that he was going to pull her into a hug until he did it. Gigi hugged back. She fit under his chin, and for a single moment in time, Grayson felt like he was exactly where he belonged.

"Give me your phone," Gigi told him. Clearly, that was an order.

Grayson gave her his phone. She turned it toward his face, unlocked it, and then leaned in next to him again. "Now smile and say *I like my sister!*"

Three days ago, Grayson would have resisted every part of that request. "I like my sister."

"I'm not sure that counts as a smile," Gigi informed him after she'd snapped a picture. "But kudos for the effort. Now let's take one posed next to the box. Say *we did it!*"

"We did it," Grayson said.

"We are the best!" Gigi was snapping pictures like mad.

"We are the best," Grayson repeated.

"Code Name Mimosa's real name is..."

Grayson narrowed his eyes. "Gigi," he said, putting more than a little warning in his tone.

Gigi was absolutely unabashed. "What a coincidence," she said seriously. "My name is also Gigi." She scrolled through the photos she'd taken. "I like this one," she told him. "You're actually smiling. I'll make it your wallpaper."

Grayson grabbed for his phone, but she dodged.

"Now, I'm sending it to myself...and also to Xander....And... done." Gigi stared at Grayson's phone for a second or two longer, then flicked her gaze back to the puzzle box. "I changed my mind. Let's not wait for Savannah." Gigi squatted, locked her fingers around the faux USB, and pulled out the board, the last remaining barrier to the compartment that held the journal.

Not the real one. Grayson buried the guilt, buried it so deep that no amount of discussion or bonding with Gigi now could unearth it.

His sister flipped through the pages of the duplicate journal. "It's full of numbers," she said, frowning. "Just strings and strings of numbers."

"Let me see it," Grayson said, the way he would have if this was his first time in a room with that book. Gigi handed it to him, and Grayson made his own inspection of it, page by page. "It's a code, obviously," he said. "Some kind of substitution cipher, perhaps."

Not perhaps. Not just any cipher.

"I'm going to need some coffee," Gigi declared. "Oooh! Look! There's a coffee maker!"

Grayson held out an arm to stop her. "You do not need any coffee."

"You like me," Gigi reminded him, poking him in the chest. "You find me charming."

The muscles in Grayson's throat tightened. "I like you," he said quietly. "And I am still not giving you coffee."

"Decaf," Gigi countered. "Final offer!"

Grayson gave a roll of his eyes. "Fine."

He walked into the kitchen to make her decaf. When he came back, she wasn't sitting near the puzzle box. She was standing—and staring at his phone.

"This isn't the picture you sent me." Gigi's voice was very quiet. "The passwords. The ones from Mr. Trowbridge's office. You sent me a picture, but this..." She held up his phone, his photo roll. "These aren't the passwords you sent me, Grayson."

He saw, all at once, the mistakes he'd made. Letting his guard down. Letting her in. Giving her his phone. Letting her pull up his photos to scroll through the ones she'd taken of the two of them. Failing to take the phone back before he'd left the room. *Was it still unlocked, or did she figure out the passcode?*

Did it matter?

"And my key..." Gigi was staring at the photo roll, just staring and staring at it like she expected it to stop being what it was. "You took a picture of my key. I knew that. I didn't think anything of it. I *gave you* my key, and then you gave it to Savannah. But my key didn't work." She looked up from the phone, stricken. "Why didn't it work, Grayson?"

Grayson Hawthorne had been raised to take control of every situation, but he didn't know how to make this stop. He didn't know how to lie to her—even though he'd done nothing but lie to her so far.

"Where did you get this?" Gigi held up the not-USB. "It wasn't in the box before, was it? Have you already opened it?" Gigi dropped the USB, and the next thing Grayson knew, she was holding the journal—holding on to it for dear life. "Is this even real?"

It was real, Gigi. In his own mind, Grayson wasn't focused on the journal.

"This is the part where you tell me that you can explain," Gigi said, her voice catching. "Go ahead. Explain, Grayson."

Grayson's brain formulated a response. He looked her straight in the eyes. "I was trying to protect you."

"Okay." Gigi nodded, and it was like once she started nodding, she couldn't stop. "I believe you. Okay? Because I'm the type of person who believes in people." She smiled, but it didn't look like a Gigi smile. "Because what fun is it going through life any other way?"

Grayson felt like she was ripping his heart out. He didn't have any choice but to keep lying to her. And she would keep believing it, believing in him, because that was who she was.

"Only..." Gigi's voice shook. "What exactly were you protecting me from?" She held up the journal again. "What's in here?" She paused. *"What's not?"*

Grayson couldn't answer. Even if he had wanted to, his body

wouldn't let him. *Some people can make mistakes*, he could hear the old man saying. *But you are not one of those people.*

He'd known that he was emotionally compromised. He'd known that.

"I trusted you," Gigi said, like the words had been ripped out of her. "Even after you lied to me. You're my brother, and you lied to me, and *I trusted you anyway.* Because that's what I do."

"I can explain," Grayson said, but that was just another lie, because he couldn't. He wouldn't ever be able to explain this to her because the secrets he was keeping—they had to stay hidden.

No matter the cost.

"Go ahead," Gigi told him, tears streaming down her face. "Tell me you haven't been sabotaging me—sabotaging *us*—from the beginning."

Grayson couldn't tell her that. He couldn't tell her a damn thing.

"That guy outside, the one you claim is so dangerous, he said that you were playing your own game. He warned me. *Careful with this one, sunshine.*"

Grayson would never forgive himself if she ended up putting herself in danger because of him. "Gigi—" Grayson was not a person who pleaded, but he was pleading now.

"Don't," Gigi said, her voice low and guttural. "Just shut your mouth and give me what you really found in this box, because I don't believe for a damn second that you haven't already opened it."

Grayson's chest hurt. Every single breath he took hurt. It all hurt. "I can't."

Gigi swallowed. "Then stay the hell away from me—and my sister."

She opened the door. Savannah was coming down the hall, but she took one look at her twin and brought her diamond-hard gaze to Grayson's, and he knew.

He'd lost them both.

TWO YEARS AND EIGHT MONTHS AGO

Grayson sat hunched on the floor of the tree house, his knees pulled to his chest. *Posture unbefitting of a Hawthorne*, he thought dully. The words didn't hurt the way they should have.

He ran his thumb over the bit of metal in his hand. Grayson remembered being eight years old and writing haiku after haiku, crossing out the words, calmly tearing sheet after sheet out of his notebook. Because when you only got three lines, they had to be perfect.

He had wanted—*so badly*—for them to be perfect. He'd agonized over focus and content, metaphors and wording. *A drop of water. The rain. The wind. A petal. A leaf. Love. Anger. Sorrow.* But reading over the final product now, all he could think was that what he'd written hadn't been perfect.

He hadn't been—and this was the cost.

Everywhere Grayson looked, he saw Emily. *Emily's amber hair blowing in the wind. Emily's wild, larger-than-life smile. Emily lying on the shore.*

"Dead." Grayson made himself say it out loud. It didn't hurt the way it should have. Nothing hurt enough.

He read the damn haiku again, his grip on it viselike, the metal biting into his fingers. *When words are real enough*, he remembered telling Jameson, *when they're the exact right words, when what you're saying matters, when it's beautiful and perfect and true—it hurts.*

Grayson had wanted Emily to love *him*. He'd wanted her to choose *him*. Being with her had made him feel like perfect didn't matter. Like he could afford, every once in a while, to lose control.

This was his fault. He'd taken her to the cliffs, when Jameson wouldn't. *Some people can make mistakes, Grayson. But you are not one of those people.*

A sound like a fist beating flesh broke the silence in the tree house. Brutal. Repetitive. Merciless. And the more Grayson listened to it—without moving, without blinking, barely even breathing—the more he realized that the vicious, ruthless *thwack, thwack, thwack* he was hearing wasn't the work of a fist.

Splintering wood. A crash. Another. More.

Grayson managed to stand. He walked over to the tree house window and looked down. Jameson was on one of the bridges below. There was an ax in his hand and other blades at his feet. *A longsword. A hatchet. A machete.*

The bridge was barely holding on, but Jameson didn't stop. He never stopped. He attacked the only thing holding him up like he couldn't wait to fall.

Down below, Nash ran toward the tree house. "What the hell are you doing, Jamie?" In a flash, he was climbing to Jameson, who swung the ax harder, faster.

"I would think the answer's apparent," Jamie replied, in a tone that made Grayson think that he was enjoying this, destroying a thing they both had loved.

He blames me. He should blame me. It's my fault she's gone.

"Damn it, Jameson!" Nash tried to lunge forward, but the ax came down right next to his foot. "You're going to hurt yourself."

He wants to hurt me. Grayson thought about Emily's body, her hair wet, her eyes vacant. "Let him." Grayson was surprised at the sound of his own voice. The words felt guttural, but they sounded almost robotic.

Jameson flung the ax down and picked up the machete.

Nash eased forward. "Em's gone," he said. "It's not right. It's not fair. You want to set something on fire—either of you—I'll help. But not this. Not like this, Jamie."

The bridge was decimated now, hanging by threads. Jameson stepped back onto a large platform, then swung. Nash barely had time to jump to the other side.

"Exactly like this," Jameson said, as the bridge came crashing down. The remaining blades fell roughly to the dirt.

"You're hurting." Nash made his way down the tree and over to the other side—to Jameson.

All Grayson could do was watch.

"Hurting? Me?" Jameson replied, going at the tree house walls with the machete. *Thwack. Thwack. Thwack.* "Nothing hurts unless you let it. Nothing matters unless you let it."

Grayson didn't realize he'd moved, but suddenly, he was on the ground, right next to the longsword.

"Don't come any closer, Gray," Nash warned him.

Grayson swallowed. "Don't tell me what to do." His throat felt swollen and rough.

Jameson looked directly at him. "So says the heir apparent."

If you're so perfect, Grayson imagined his brother saying, *why is she dead?*

"It's my fault." The words felt like they stuck in Grayson's throat, but Jameson heard them all the same.

"Nothing's ever *your* fault, Grayson."

Nash moved in, and when Jameson went to raise the machete again, Nash caught his wrist. "Jamie. *Enough*."

Grayson heard the machete clatter to the floor of the platform on which his brothers stood. *My fault*, he thought. *I killed Emily.*

That sentence rang in his mind: five syllables, so real and true they hurt. Grayson dropped his long-ago haiku to the ground. And then he bent, picked up the longsword, turned back to the tree house, and started swinging.

CHAPTER 82

JAMESON

"Now that Ms. Grambs has been removed from both the premises and the Game, there is the matter of her key." The Factotum said the word *removed* in a way that made Jameson want to go for his throat. Rohan hadn't laid a hand on Avery—not in Jameson's sight, at least—but now she was gone, and the rest of them were back in the room where this had all started.

"I'm the one who was attacked," Zella said with an aristocratic tilt of her chin. "That makes the attacker's key mine, does it not?"

"Where's Avery?" Jameson demanded. "What did you do with her?"

Branford placed a hand on his shoulder. "Easy, nephew."

"Soft touch," Katharine scoffed. "You always have been, Simon."

"Enough." Rohan held up a hand, silencing all four remaining players. Then he turned to Zella. "Do you really expect me to just hand this over to you?" He brandished the final key.

"No." Zella's smile looked almost serene, but to Jameson, it didn't *feel* like a smile. "Truthfully, Rohan, I make it a rule to have no expectations at all where you are concerned."

Rohan openly studied the duchess for a moment, like she was a puzzle he hadn't quite solved—and didn't particularly enjoy solving. "As to your question, Mr. Hawthorne," the Factotum said, his gaze still locked on Zella, "Avery Grambs has been returned to her rather overzealous bodyguard—a touching reunion, I assure you." With a flourish, Rohan held the key up once more. He hopped onto the stone windowsill "The Game will begin anew," he announced, "with the striking of the bell."

The Factotum smiled. Jameson did not trust that smile.

"I sincerely hope," Rohan continued, jumping down and making his way to the door, "that none of you are afraid of heights."

Time slowed to a crawl. Jameson turned his attention first to what Rohan had said, then to searching the room from top to bottom again, and finally to the silver chest in his hands. Elaborate, raised swirls marked the top and sides of the box, fine metal fashioned to look like twisting, twirling ropes.

"You may as well set that down, young man," Katharine told Jameson. She walked toward him and stopped at the table, placing her palms flat on its surface. "You have no use for it as of yet."

Nice try, Katharine. Jameson gave the older woman a look. "You didn't know my grandfather, did you?"

Brilliant, mercenary Tobias Hawthorne had raised no fools. Jameson might have lost the key, he might have lost his partner in the Game, but he had the chest, and as long as he held on to it, no one was winning but him.

"This," Jameson said, his voice low and intense, "is mine."

"You earned it." Katharine let her hands fall away from the

table. "That's what you're telling yourself, is it not?" She let the question hang in the air.

I did earn it, Jameson thought.

"But really..." Katharine's shrewd eyes locked on to his face. Jameson almost felt like he was back in the old man's office, his every effort judged. "When have you, Jameson Hawthorne, ever earned anything? Even now, you defend yourself by throwing around your grandfather's name. What are you without him?" Katharine made a noise like a hmmm, but sharper somehow, more pointed. "Without your heiress?"

Compared to your brothers—Jameson couldn't shake the memory—*your mind is ordinary.*

"In my experience," Katharine continued, "third-born sons are...disappointing. Always have something to prove, never truly manage to prove it."

"That's enough, Katharine," Branford told her sharply.

The silver-haired woman paid him no heed. "What are you without the Hawthorne name?" she asked Jameson, each word a slice of the knife. "Without the money. Without borrowing against someone else's power. Without Avery Grambs by your side."

Ordinary. Jameson pushed back against that word and all it entailed. He knew Katharine was trying to manipulate him, get under his skin, bait him into making a mistake.

"I said *enough*, Katharine." Branford crossed the room to stand right in front of her.

Whatever else the viscount said to her, Jameson couldn't hear it as he held tight to the chest he'd retrieved, his one advantage in the Game going forward. Jameson Winchester Hawthorne wasn't giving that up. He wasn't giving up, period.

What are you without the Hawthorne name?

He wasn't Grayson, who could command respect as easily as he could breathe, who was Avery's right hand at her new foundation, who had pretty much been born with purpose. He wasn't Xander, who turned napkin doodles into patents and thought so far outside the box that sometimes he couldn't even *see* the box. Jameson wasn't even Nash, who'd spent most of his adult life pretending his last name wasn't Hawthorne and gotten by just fine.

The truth, Jameson, is that you are indeed intelligent. But what had he done with his gap year? What had he ever really done, period, that was his? Not Avery's. Not his grandfather's. *His.*

Do great things. Jameson had spent his entire life knowing that if he wanted to be extraordinary, he had to want it more. He had to be willing to risk more.

Third-born sons are... disappointing.

Jameson banished that thought, banished every memory of coming in second—or third or fourth. He breathed in a ragged breath, then a steady one. He kept right on breathing.

And then the bell rang.

CHAPTER 83

JAMESON

Jameson was the first one out of the room, the first one through the halls, the first one to burst out the front door and look up. Rohan hadn't been as wordy this time, so there wasn't as much to parse for verbal clues, but what he had said indicated that the key would be hidden high.

I sincerely hope that none of you are afraid of heights.

Jameson couldn't see all of Vantage this close up, so he turned and ran farther away for a better view. Dusk was approaching. Lights from the ground shone on the house.

The castle. From this view, he couldn't think of it as anything else. He counted five turrets, but the highest point was around the back—a large, square tower that soared over the rest.

Jameson started running again—around the castle, to the back—and that was when he realized that Vantage hadn't just gotten its name because it sat high above the sea. There were cliffs on this side, too.

The entire estate sat on top of a massive, steep, flat-topped hill nearly completely surrounded by ocean, a world unto itself. A single winding road had been cut into the cliffs on this side, but that was the only thing that connected Vantage to the isthmus back to the mainland.

Jameson walked to the cliff's edge, Rohan's words ringing in his mind. *I sincerely hope that none of you are afraid of heights.*

A sudden wind whipped Jameson back, strong and wild, seeming to come at him from three sides. He turned to look up at the castle, at the tower he'd seen from the other side. It sat nearer the cliff's edge than the rest of the house and soared a story or two above it.

Ninety feet off the ground? More? Near the top of the tower, Jameson saw a large, white-faced clock.

"Clock tower," he said out loud. Beneath the clock, a platform wrapped the building, its railing dark and ornate. And maybe five feet below that platform, Jameson could make out an opening cut into stone.

And through that opening, he could just almost see . . . *something.*

"Not something," Jameson realized, his voice nearly lost to the brutal wind. "A bell."

The clock tower was also a bell tower, and right before Rohan had made his comment about fear of heights, he'd informed them that the Game would begin anew *with the striking of the bell.*

Jameson didn't just run this time. He flew. The door at the base of the tower was made of metal lattice, the kind one could easily imagine a knight shooting an arrow through. There didn't seem to be a way of opening it from the outside, but before Jameson could formulate a plan to circle back and find an interior entrance to the tower, there was a sound halfway between thunder and the turning of gears, and the metal door began to rise.

Simon Johnstone-Jameson, Viscount Branford, stood on the other side. His gaze locked on to Jameson's.

Jameson wasn't sure what to read into that gaze. "Why would you help me?"

In response, his uncle didn't smile, didn't even blink. "I told you before," the red-haired man said. "I'm the head of this family in every way that matters. Ian might shirk his responsibilities, but I do not."

That hadn't mattered to Branford back at the Devil's Mercy. It hadn't mattered at the beginning of this Game. So why did it matter now?

"Does this have something to do with your secret?" Jameson asked. *Your son.*

Branford provided no response, and Jameson didn't waste any more time waiting for answers that didn't matter—at least, not now.

What are you without the Hawthorne name? Without the money. Without borrowing against someone else's power. Without Avery Grambs by your side.

Jameson pushed past Branford. A twisting staircase was built into the side of the tower—no railing. Without a moment's hesitation, Jameson tightened his hold on the chest and began to climb. Behind him, Branford did the same. The staircase took a ninety-degree turn each time they hit one of the tower's four walls. Up and up it went.

Up and up they went.

Finally, when they made it high enough to see the massive bell—ten feet tall, five across at its widest point—Jameson's eyes caught on something else: a delicate bit of metal, gleaming in what little light came in from the outside.

The key.

Jameson climbed higher, faster, and when Branford took out his flashlight, Jameson realized that he'd been wrong. What he'd seen, it wasn't *the* key. It was *a* key, one of dozens suspending midair, hanging from long and nearly invisible strings. There were at least sixty or seventy keys total, scattered all around the bell, none of them touching, only a handful of them positioned so that Jameson could reach them from the stairs.

He knew that none of those keys was the one he was looking for. *Rohan wouldn't make it that easy.* Jameson gauged the distance between the edge of the stone steps and the bell. *Three and a half feet.*

Branford placed a hand on Jameson's shoulder, the way he had in the midst of Katharine's taunting manipulation. But this time, the man's hand wasn't meant to be comforting.

It was meant to hold him back.

"Don't," his uncle warned, in a tone that reminded Jameson of Grayson—and also Nash, when Nash thought one of them was on the verge of doing something unwise.

Jameson turned his head and met the man's eyes. "I appreciate the advice."

"That wasn't *advice*," Branford told him.

The sound of creaking wood was the only warning the two of them got before a trap door swung down from the ceiling above the bell. There was a flash of blue, and an instant later, Zella landed on top of the bell.

Jameson eyed the space between the staircase and the bell again. *I can make it.* The seventy-foot drop barely registered, but even he wasn't reckless enough to attempt the jump holding a solid silver chest.

"Jameson." Branford practically growled his name. In response, Jameson took a calculated risk.

"Hold this for me." He thrust the chest at Branford, and the second the man had a hold on it, Jameson leapt.

CHAPTER 84

JAMESON

He hit the bell and held on with his entire body as it swung.

"Thanks for that," Zella called down.

As the bell steadied, Jameson edged around its side. Then he began scanning the closest keys. He knew what he was looking for. *A key made of shining gold. A head like a maze.*

"You asked me earlier if I read your secret," Zella said, her tone conversational, as she made her own search above. "Why don't you ask me again?"

She was trying to distract him, trying to get to him. Jameson didn't let himself think about his secret—or anything else. He stayed focused on his task, but that didn't keep him from turning the tables on his opponent.

"I'd rather ask about you," he said, moving farther around the bell, checking another key and another. *Two up there. One up farther. One hanging down low.* "And Rohan." Jameson didn't hesitate, didn't question whether he'd chosen the correct method of getting under the duchess's skin. "There's history there. You learned not to expect anything from him at some point. But what kind of history, I wonder? You're, what, seven or eight years older? And married..."

Jameson was guessing the history between them wasn't *that* kind of history. But he was also pretty sure the duchess didn't want anyone to realize there was history there at all.

That's seven more keys—and none of them the *key.*

Up above, Zella shifted, and the movement sent the bell swaying again.

"Appreciate that," Jameson told her.

"You so desperately wanted to prove yourself." There was nothing cruel in Zella's tone, but clearly, the gloves were off. "To Ian. To the old man."

The old man. That was the way Jameson and his brothers had always referred to their grandfather. How had she known that? Had he used the phrase around her?

He wasn't certain he had.

Zella slid down the side of the bell. She moved with incredible, gravity-defying grace, like there wasn't a single muscle in her body over which she had anything less than perfect control.

"I told you before," she murmured. "The benefit to choosing one's competition is knowing one's competition."

Jameson forced himself to move faster. He'd ruled out maybe twenty keys, twenty-five at most. There were another two dozen up where Zella had been before. That left, what? Around twenty keys that neither of them had inspected yet?

"You're playing to win, Duchess." Jameson kept the conversation going because he'd scored at least one point off her already. Because he *would* find a way to score more.

"The world is kinder to winners." Zella brought the bottoms of her feet up to rest on the bell. Jameson wasn't sure why, until she pushed off, somehow managing to hold on, even as she sent the bell swinging.

Every muscle in Jameson's body went tight. But he didn't stop looking. He couldn't.

Do great things.

What are you without the Hawthorne name?

"The world is kindest, of course," Zella continued, her voice steely now, "to rich white boys, regardless of whether or not they deserve to win."

Jameson shouldn't have been able to hear her over the ringing of the bell, but he did—and that wasn't the only thing he heard. The jarring, rumbling clang of the bell that threatened to shake off his grip—that wasn't the only sound the bell was making.

There was also a lighter, softer, unmistakable *ting.*

The sound of a key, Jameson thought, *suspended* inside *the bell.* He wondered if Rohan had lost his mind, wondered if the Devil's Mercy's infamous Game had cost any players their lives before—and, if so, how many.

But mostly, Jameson wondered how he was going to get to the key without Zella realizing what he was doing. They were on opposite sides of the bell now, and as it steadied, he slid his body down, letting his feet lodge at the bell's rim. He bent sideways, latching his left hand around the rim as well.

Down below, on the ground, a white-clad form entered the bell tower. *Katharine.* Jameson wondered idly if Rohan was somewhere, watching. He moved his right hand down. He was crouching at the bottom of the bell now, holding on with gravity-defying force.

It really was a good thing he wasn't afraid of heights.

What next? Jameson's heart raced, beating faster and faster with familiar urgency and speed, the kind that made it impossible to forget that you were alive. The kind he *lived* for. Unencumbered by fear of pain or failure, Jameson saw the world as it really was.

Rohan wasn't gone that long when he rigged all of this. He must have had a backup plan from the beginning. He must have had a way to get the key inside the bell. Crouching farther, Jameson slid one hand carefully from the outside of the bell to the inside.

He felt handles. More than one. And the next thing he knew, the bell was swinging again, and Zella had latched her hands on to two of them.

Two years earlier, Jameson wouldn't have hesitated to do the same. He would have welcomed the danger, the thrill, used it to wash away everything else. But now? He could see Avery in his mind's eye.

No matter what you win, he could hear Ian saying, *you always need more.*

Expelling a breath, Jameson locked one hand around a handle. He could hear Branford yelling at him, as if from a distance. His other hand locked around another handle. He lowered his body until it was dangling, then let go of one of the handles, just long enough to turn his hand around. Then the other hand.

He swung himself up and into the bell. *This was a very bad idea*, Jameson thought, and then he realized: The entire inside of the bell, except for the spots that the metal ball was meant to strike, was covered with handles and footholds.

Maybe Rohan wasn't trying to kill them after all.

Jameson looked for the key. He saw it—closer to him than Zella. His position was better. Despite his moment of hesitation, he was going to get there first.

Going to *win*.

His body knew exactly what to do. Jameson moved quickly, confidently. He got there first. He latched one hand around the key, his other holding himself aloft, and began working at the string that held the key.

And that was when Zella jumped. Or maybe *leapt* was the better word. Flew. She landed with one hand gripping the bell's rim and the other over his on the key.

"Are you *unhinged*?" Jameson hissed. Her feet were dangling now—and the string that held the key was thin.

It's going to snap.

"I'm going to fall." Zella spoke in the calmest voice he'd ever heard. "If you don't let go of the key, if you don't let me have it, if you don't grab my arm in the next three seconds, I'm going to fall."

She was.

Jameson stared at her. *That Duchess.* The person who'd just told him that the world was kinder to winners—and kindest to boys like him.

She'd taken a risk, an insane but calculated risk. And she'd calculated correctly.

In less time than it took to blink, Jameson let go of the key, her hand latched around it, and his latched around her.

CHAPTER 85

JAMESON

They both survived. They both made it back to solid ground, and when they did, Zella met Jameson's eyes. "I owe you one," she said. "And I intend to be in a very good position to repay my debts."

Then, to Jameson's absolute shock, the duchess tossed the key she'd risked her life for over the edge of the stone staircase, and it fell all the way to the ground.

To Katharine.

Jameson turned to Branford, whose face had gone as red as his hair, absolute fury etched into every line on his forehead. "The chest?" Jameson said. "You can yell at me later."

"If I'd had any hand in raising you," Branford said, the intensity in his eyes an exact match for *that* tone, "I would be doing a hell of a lot more than yelling."

"Simon." Katharine's voice rang through the bell tower. She began to climb the stairs and spoke again, three words said with almost startling clarity. *"Ontario. Versace. Selenium."*

"The chest," Jameson requested again.

His uncle looked down. *"Damn you, Bowen."*

Bowen, Jameson's other uncle. The uncle that Katharine worked for—Katharine, who'd just said three seemingly random words that had caused Branford to curse his brother.

Branford, Jameson thought, *who still has the chest.*

"No," Jameson swore.

"I'm sorry," Branford replied stiffly. "My brother holds one card over me—just one, and he apparently gave it to her to play here today. Those words, they're a code, my debt called in."

"*No*," Jameson said again.

Katharine already had the key. Once she finished her ascent, Branford gave her the chest.

Before Katharine opened it, she deigned to look at Jameson one more time. "You don't have to be a player to win the game," she said, and he was reminded again of his grandfather, of the old man's many lessons. "All one really has to do to win is control the players."

That bit of wisdom imparted, the older woman fit the key inside the lock and turned it. The lock gave. The lid popped open. Inside, there was a small silver ballerina standing on one toe, the other leg extended. The figurine began to turn in a silent, steady dance.

Katharine made a quick and frighteningly efficient search of the box. Finding nothing else, she took the ballerina in her hand and viciously tore it out. Her goal met, she shoved the now-empty box back at Jameson and began to descend the stone staircase.

Jameson watched her go, then frantically began his own search of the box. This wasn't over. It didn't have to be over.

"Leave it," Zella told him gently.

Jameson didn't. He pulled up the velvet fabric that lined the chest's interior. *Nothing.* In the back of his mind, he heard voice after voice.

Compared to your brothers, your mind is ordinary.

You love a challenge. You love to play. You love to win. And no matter what you win, you always need more.

What are you without the Hawthorne name?

"It's over," Branford told him.

Jameson paid no attention to those words, because in his memory, the old man spoke again. *A person can train their mind to see the world, to really* see *it.*

Jameson stared at the box. He thought about the silver ballerina—and then about one of his grandfather's Saturday morning games and another ballerina, made of glass. Jameson thought about misdirection, double meanings, and what it meant to see your way to the answer.

Once you see that web of possibilities laid out in front of you, unencumbered by fear of pain or failure, by thoughts telling you what can and cannot, should and should not be done... What will you do with what you see?

Jameson closed his eyes. He thought back to the very beginning of the game. He remembered the instructions that Rohan had given them. And then he smiled.

CHAPTER 86

GRAYSON

Gigi was gone. Savannah was gone. And Grayson was alone. That wasn't a problem. It shouldn't have been a problem.

Being alone had never been a problem.

"It's done." Grayson's voice sounded steady to his own ears. *Good.* He bolted his hotel room door and began packing his bag.

He'd come to Phoenix to get Gigi out of jail, and she was out. He'd stayed to defuse the situation with the safe-deposit box, and it was well and truly defused. His sisters would never read their father's actual journal. They had no idea why Grayson had betrayed them.

And they never would.

Avery was safe. The secret of Sheffield Grayson's demise was safe.

And I'm alone. Picking up his phone, Grayson opened his work email and began assembling a mental to-do list.

It was better this way.

He managed to believe that, until, for some unknowable reason, his index finger navigated away from his email and to the photo roll on his phone. He'd made a critical error in leaving the original photograph of Trowbridge's password accessible. Just like he'd made an error in giving Gigi his phone in the first place. He'd made far too many mistakes, and now he was paying the cost. Because when Grayson Davenport Hawthorne made mistakes, there was always a cost.

He'd taken Emily cliff-jumping, and she'd died.

He'd failed to go to Avery when his father's bomb had nearly killed her, and he'd lost her to his brother.

He'd trusted Eve, and she'd betrayed him.

Some people can make mistakes, Grayson. But you are not one of those people. He knew that. He'd known it since he was a child, but he just kept making them anyway, and every time he fell short, every time he made an error in judgment, every little mistake cost him someone he cared about.

Every time he let himself care about someone, he lost them.

Grayson scrolled across the photo roll and saw himself with Gigi. Every picture she'd taken of the two of them was a little off-center or too close-up. She was beaming in every single one.

Minimizing the photos, Grayson focused on what had to be done. He arranged a flight back to Texas. Robotically, he finished packing his suitcase. That only left the puzzle box, the photographs, and the withdrawal slips.

I can't leave them here. There was still the FBI to consider. If they ever obtained the box, if they realized the journal was a fake, if they found his fingerprints all over it...

Grayson was done making mistakes.

He put the withdrawal slips in the box, alongside the fake journal, then reassembled it. He called down to the concierge, requested that an additional piece of luggage be acquired on his behalf, and sent her the specifications he needed.

Then Grayson turned his attention to the photographs. He began stacking them facedown, avoiding looking at any of the pictures.

He didn't think about his father.

He didn't think about the boy in these photographs, the boy he'd been.

He didn't think about anything except what needed to be done now.

That worked until it didn't. The photograph that pierced his protective shields had been taken during his gap year, halfway around the world. *My whole life, my father watched me. Even when I was grown. Even when I was traveling.*

How much money did he spend having these pictures taken?

How much time did he spend looking at them?

Clamping his jaw, Grayson flipped the photo in his hand over and stacked it with the others. His gaze caught on the date on the back of the photograph. *He got the date wrong.* Grayson wasn't certain about the day, and the year was correct, but the month was off.

What did it matter? What did any of this matter?

Grayson finished stacking the photographs and returned them to the briefcase the bank had provided. "Done." As the word left his mouth, his phone rang—an unknown number. He answered. "Grayson Hawthorne."

"Most people just go with *hello*." The sound of the girl's voice washed over him, a balm on open wounds, and the second Grayson recognized the effect it had on him, the muscles in his face tightened.

"What is it?" he asked, clipping the words.

"I guess you don't have any answers for me." Her tone was thorns now, not roses, rough and sharp.

Grayson swallowed. "I don't have answers for anyone," he said. "Stop calling."

After another second or two, the line went dead. It didn't matter. *None* of this mattered. He had a life to get back to, work to do.

On his way to the airport, his phone rang again. *Eve.* Grayson didn't bother with hello this time, either. "I am done with this," he said instead, the only greeting she deserved. "Done with you."

She'd threatened him, threatened his sisters. The FBI's sudden raid on the Grayson household was proof enough that Eve had already started making good on those threats.

"You don't get to be done with me," Eve said.

Grayson went to end the call, but she spoke again before he could.

"Blake's still in surgery." Her voice grew hoarse. "It's taking too long. The doctors won't tell me anything. I don't think he's going to make it."

The death of Vincent Blake would be no great tragedy. He was a bad man, a dangerous man. Grayson steeled himself against Eve's tone and focused on the *only* thing he had to say to her. "I warned you to stay away from my sisters."

"I haven't done a damn thing to your sisters." Eve was an easy person to believe. True liars always were.

"You sicced the FBI on their mother." Grayson's fingers tightened around the steering wheel. "You said it yourself: If Vincent Blake dies tonight, there won't be anything holding you back."

"I say a lot of things, Grayson."

His chest tightened, but he didn't give her the courtesy of a reply.

"Forget it," Eve bit out. "Forget I called. Forget *me.* I'm used to it."

"Don't, Eve."

"Don't what?"

"Don't bleed for me. Don't show me your wounds and expect me to tend to them. I'm not playing that game with you again."

"Is it so hard to believe that I'm not playing?" Eve asked. "Vincent Blake is my family, Grayson. And maybe you think I don't deserve one. Maybe I never did. But can you at least believe me when I say that I don't want to be alone right now?"

Grayson remembered calling her Evie. He remembered the girl he'd thought she was. "You have Toby. He's your father."

For the longest time, there was silence on the other end of the line. "He wishes I was her."

For Eve, there was only one *her.* Eve was Toby's daughter biologically, but Avery was the one that Toby had watched out for longer, the one whose mother he'd loved with that once-in-a-lifetime, undying, ruinous, Hawthorne kind of love.

"I'm not your person, Eve. You don't get to call me. You don't get to ask me for anything."

"Message received. I don't matter. Not to you." Eve's voice went dangerously low. "But believe me, Grayson, I will."

She ended the call—or maybe he did. Either way, Grayson drove the rest of the way to the airport unable to shake the feeling that he'd just made another mistake.

Who would he lose this time?

Trying to banish that question, Grayson parked the Ferrari in long-term parking, left the key under the mat, and sent a text to the contact who'd provided him with it documenting its return. And then, staring down at his phone, he thought about everything that had happened, all of it, since he'd come to Phoenix. He thought about everything that had happened before that.

Look where repressing my emotions got me before. Grayson knew better now—or at least, he was supposed to. If he couldn't stop making mistakes, he could at least stop making the same ones, again and again.

He could admit this time that, like Eve, he didn't want to be alone.

Letting out a long, slow, painful breath, Grayson sent a text message to his brothers. No words, three numbers.

911.

CHAPTER 87

JAMESON

Jameson found Katharine and Rohan outside, near the cliffs. The older woman's hand was extended, the silver ballerina lying flat on her palm.

"Give me the mark." Katharine's words were nearly lost in the wind, but a moment later, the wind stopped suddenly and completely.

"I'm afraid that's not how this works." Rohan's white dress shirt was untucked and unbuttoned nearly halfway down. Something about the way he was standing reminded Jameson of the chameleon he'd met outside the club—and the fighter he'd met in the ring.

"You said that whoever brought you what was in the final box would win the game and receive the mark." Katharine straightened.

"Technically," Jameson put in, strolling toward the two of them, a rakish smile on his face, "that isn't what he said. I believe the exact words were: *Two boxes with secrets. In the third, you'll find something much more valuable. Tell me what you find in the third box, and you'll win the mark.*"

Rohan hadn't said that the winner would be the one who brought him the object in the box. He'd said that it would be the person who *told him* what was in the box—and whatever that thing was, it had to be more valuable than even the most dangerous secrets.

"Fine, then," Katharine said briskly. "A ballerina. A figurine. A piece of silver. That's what was in the box."

"Wrong answer," Rohan told her. Slowly, he turned toward Jameson. The last time they'd faced each other this directly, Rohan had just told him to *stay down*.

Jameson thought the Factotum knew him a little better now.

"Have a different answer for me, Hawthorne?" Rohan asked.

"As a matter of fact," Jameson replied. "I do." He held Rohan's gaze, his own blazing, adrenaline coursing through his veins. "*Silence.*"

Jameson let the answer hang in the air, just for a moment.

"More valuable than secrets," he continued. *The ability to say nothing, to keep those secrets. Silence.* "And this"—Jameson nodded toward the silver chest—"isn't just a box. It's a *music* box. The music plays, the ballerina turns. Except this time, no music. *Silence.*"

Rohan's lips slowly curled into a closed-mouthed smile. "It looks like we have a winner."

Euphoria exploded in Jameson like a speeding train crashing through wall after wall after wall. The world grew brighter, his hearing more acute, and he felt *everything*—every bruise, every wound, the rush of adrenaline, the taste of the seaside air, the breath in his lungs, the blood in his veins—*all of it*.

This was *more*.

"And so," the Factotum continued, "this year's Game is concluded." With a flourish, Rohan produced the stone mark: half black, half white, entirely smooth. He held it out to Jameson, who took it. The stone felt cool in his palm, like a disk made entirely of ice.

I did it.

"You may have a day," Rohan told him, "to decide what you wish to trade that in for."

All Jameson could think was that *this* was what he was—without the Hawthorne name, without the old man, without Avery, even. Jameson had played this *his* way, and he'd won.

He could feel Katharine's eyes on his face, assessing him, determining her next move. *You don't have be to a player to win the game. All one really has to do to win is control the players.* She was going to offer him something—or threaten him. Maybe both. She'd already tried to use Ian against him, and who knew where Ian was—or what he was doing—now.

Jameson wasn't about to give Katharine another twenty-four hours to determine her—and his mysterious uncle Bowen's—next move. "I don't need a day," he told Rohan.

The Proprietor of the Devil's Mercy kept control of its membership through use of a ledger that held their secrets. Powerful secrets of powerful men—and some women, though not many.

Jameson looked to Zella. Her lips ticked very slightly upward on the ends. Whatever she'd wanted from Katharine—or Bowen Johnstone-Jameson—she'd presumably secured it. She'd fulfilled her end of whatever deal she'd struck with them by handing over the last key. And now, the duchess owed Jameson a debt, one she seemed to think she'd soon be in excellent position to repay.

Jameson looked to Branford next: uncle, head of a family that wasn't Jameson's in any way but blood. And yet... Jameson had to put real effort into looking away from the man, and when he did, it was to look up at Vantage. He thought of the portrait of his paternal grandmother. This was her ancestral home, and through her blood, his.

Jameson held the mark back out to Rohan. “I like this place,” he told him. “Though I might get rid of that damn bell.”

CHAPTER 88

JAMESON

Walking through the front door of Vantage felt different this time. It felt *right*. Jameson moved slowly to the bottom of the grand staircase. He looked up. *Mine.* He'd grown up being handed every opportunity, every luxury, in a mansion easily larger than this place, but Jameson's entire life, nothing had ever been just his.

"It suits you," Zella called from somewhere behind him.

Jameson didn't turn. He barely heard her.

"You would think so." That was Rohan, also behind him. Katharine had made her exit.

Branford strode past the others, making his way to Jameson and fixing him with a stare so pointed that it drew to mind a threat: *If I'd had any hand in raising you, I would be doing a hell of a lot more than yelling.*

"We need to talk." Branford didn't wait for Jameson to reply before nodding sharply toward the stairs. As Jameson took the first step, the viscount turned to shoot a warning look at anyone who might be tempted to follow. "I need a moment with my nephew. *Alone*."

At the top of the grand staircase, Jameson found a window, one that faced out over the stone garden, the view stretching all the way past the cliffs to the ocean and the hint of a storm brewing on the horizon.

"Do you have a death wish, nephew?" Branford's tone walked the line between an accusation, an order, and a threat. "Answer me."

Jameson recalled telling his uncle to yell at him *later*—which was, apparently, *now*.

"No." Jameson tore his gaze away from the window and looked back toward the red-haired, sharp-featured, scowling viscount. "I don't have a death wish."

"But it doesn't bother you," Branford countered. "The idea of dying." The viscount's tone was almost too controlled now, a danger sign Jameson recognized all too well.

"I didn't say that." Jameson thought back to the moment before he'd leapt onto the bell. He'd hesitated, one thing—one person—on his mind. *Avery*. Jameson was fast cars and tantalizing risks, laughing in the face of danger and stepping right up to the edge of magnificent drops.

But he was also *hers*.

"I definitely wouldn't say that I'm unbothered by the idea of dying," Jameson continued. "It's not true." *Anymore*. He didn't go out of his way to risk his life *anymore*.

Branford's brows pulled together, his expression severe. "Then I can only conclude that you are completely without sense? That there was perhaps some sort of traumatic head injury when you were a child? Perhaps several? Because I can think of no other explanation for the reckless, ill-considered, impulsive display I witnessed back there."

It was an odd feeling, being scolded like a child. Like he was *someone's* child. Jameson took half a step forward, hands dangling loose by his side. "I don't need a father," he told the viscount.

Branford took his own step forward—no half measures. "You don't have one." His uncle didn't pull that punch. "I bear some responsibility for your lack, for the kind of man that Ian is. This family has let him get away with far too much for far too long." Branford's mouth settled into a grim line. "That ends. Now." The full weight of his focus settled on Jameson's eyes. "With you."

Jameson thought about the deal he'd struck with his father and the way Ian had tossed it away, tossed him away. "I don't want anything from your brother," he said, and he meant it.

He never needed to see or talk to or hear about Ian Johnstone-Jameson again.

"My brother," Branford replied, "will want plenty from you."

His meaning sank in like a rock in quicksand. If Ian expected Jameson to hand over Vantage after what he'd pulled, the youngest son of the Earl of Wycliffe was going to be sorely disappointed. But Branford?

Jameson couldn't help looking at his uncle, studying him, thinking about the way the man had torn into him about unacceptable risks. There was care there—genuine care. "The offer I made you," Jameson said abruptly. "Back before the game was done. Vantage—"

"*—is yours.*" Branford glared at Jameson. "I'll brook no argument on that. Not from you, not from my brothers. You won it. Honestly. Fairly."

Jameson cocked a brow. "Weren't you just British-yelling at me about *how* I won it?"

"We all felt invincible once." Branford's voice grew quieter. "We all had something to prove."

"I don't have anything to prove," Jameson said. "I *won*."

"You," Branford countered, "gave up the game." Those words hung in the air. "I could hear everything that you said, Jameson, everything that Zella said. When she was barely holding on, when you had to choose between winning and saving her—you didn't call her bluff."

Jameson could feel himself, right back in that moment. "I wasn't sure that she was bluffing."

"Ian would have taken that risk." Branford's tone was measured, no frills, no illusions. "He would have let her fall. Bowen, too, though he would have had a plan for deflecting blame. But you?" The viscount took another step forward, until he and Jameson were practically eye to eye. "You thought you were handing over the game, Jameson, and you chose to put the life of another person over winning. You can call that whatever you like. I call it honor."

Jameson swallowed, unsure why he suddenly needed to. "I won anyway."

"And I'll see to it," Branford replied, "that no one takes that away from you, takes *this* away from you." The next thing Jameson knew, his uncle's hands were on his shoulders, turning him back toward the window, toward that view. "Vantage is yours now. There's a trust to see to its upkeep, which I administered for Ian and will continue to administer for you." The viscount's voice softened. "Come and go as you will. She's yours now."

She as in this place, this slice of history, a family legacy that Jameson had been willing to fight for when he wasn't even considered family.

"Why would you do that for me?" The question caught in Jameson's throat. "Why would you do anything for me?"

"Had I known about you when you were born," came the response, quiet and deep, like a river gone suddenly still, "I would have done something then."

Jameson thought about Xander and Isaiah, about what it must have been like the moment his brother had realized that he had a father who *wanted* him.

My uncle would have come for me. Jameson swallowed again. "My grandfather wouldn't have let you." What had happened with Xander's father was a testament to that.

"Bold of you," his uncle replied, "to think I would have left him the choice."

Jameson snorted. "You don't know what my grandfather was like."

"And Tobias Hawthorne," the viscount said, "did not know me."

For a second, Jameson could almost believe that Branford could have faced the old man down. But believing that he *would* have? Jameson shook his head. "You don't owe me anything," he said.

"And if you'd chosen to let the duchess fall, perhaps I could believe that. But like recognizes like, Jameson. You are not your father. I fear you're far more like me."

That statement should have sounded ridiculous. It should have *felt* ridiculous. It shouldn't have meant anything—but it did.

"I'm not your responsibility," Jameson tried again, his heart clenching in his chest.

"Everything is my responsibility." Branford raised a brow at him. "As for your secret..."

It's ashes now, Jameson thought. *And safe. The proof will be returned to me. The Proprietor will say nothing.*

"You will tell me what I need to know to protect you," Branford ordered.

Luckily, thanks to Grayson, Jameson had plenty of practice at ignoring orders. "As long as the Proprietor keeps to his word, my secret will remain a secret, and I should be fine." He paused. "Unless the duchess is a problem."

"She won't be." Branford sounded far too certain of that. "But you're still going to need to tell me—"

"Absolutely nothing?" Jameson suggested, offering the viscount a charming smile.

"I do not trust that smile," his uncle said.

Jameson shrugged. "That's only because you definitely shouldn't." He paused. "And about *your* secret..."

A change came over Branford. "It needs to stay a secret." There was a single moment's silence. "*He* does."

Jameson was hit with the sense that Branford had rarely, if ever, referred to his own son. A million questions burned in his mind. "I'm supposed to believe that if you'd known about me, you would have been a part of my life, but I'm only your nephew. If you have a son—"

"He has a father." The tightness in Branford's tone when he said those words was palpable. "A good one. And a title."

"A good one?" Jameson suggested.

Branford's voice grew quiet as he looked out at the view, out at the ocean and the storm on the horizon. "If his true paternity became known, lives would be ruined, his and his mother's among them. I cannot allow that to happen." He turned from the window and brought the full force of his gaze back to Jameson. "Do you understand?"

"I do. Some secrets are best forgotten." Jameson thought about the words he'd written on his scroll, about the way that night in Prague had gnawed at him for weeks, the way he'd fought and fought with himself, resisting the urge to tell—not because he didn't trust Avery, but because he didn't trust himself.

Jameson Hawthorne had been raised to solve puzzles and take unfathomable risks, to push boundaries and cross lines if that was what it took to win. But for once, the voice that Jameson heard in the back of his head wasn't the old man's.

It was Branford's. *I call it honor.*

"I believe Vantage is in good hands," Branford said beside him. "My mother . . . she would approve."

"I'm not looking for anyone's approval," Jameson said, and somehow, for the first time ever, that felt true.

CHAPTER 89

JAMESON

Back downstairs, Jameson found Rohan and Zella on opposite sides of the foyer, waiting for them.

"Family business all sorted?" Zella asked. She slid her gaze from Branford to Jameson. "I didn't read your secret, by the way."

Jameson's gut said that wasn't a bluff. Probably. "You still owe me," he told her. "Your Grace."

"I always pay my debts," she replied. "Boy."

"That *boy* beat both of you." Rohan pushed off the wall and strolled forward. "The Proprietor will be disappointed. He tries to hide it, but you were clearly his favorite this year, Duchess."

Zella smiled at Rohan. "I won what I set out to win, and I doubt the Proprietor will be *that* disappointed. Honestly, I think he made me a player this year just to prepare me for next year."

Rohan's expression didn't darken or shift, but Jameson *felt* a change come over him. "Next year?" the Factotum said lightly. "Counting on another invitation to the Game?"

Zella walked toward Rohan, never taking her eyes from his. "Next year," she said. "I'll be planning and running it. The Proprietor has already promised as much." She didn't stop walking until her body was even with his, and then she turned her head to the side. "Surely you didn't think you were his only possible heir, Rohan. If there's one thing the man loves, it's competition."

"You won." Those were the first words out of Avery's mouth the second she saw him—a statement, not a question. "Tell me everything."

Jameson's lips curved into a lopsided smile. "Where do you want me to start, Heiress? The seventy keys, the bell tower, the moment I altruistically chose to save a life and lose, or the instant I knew how to win?"

Avery lifted her head, angling her lips up toward his. "I said *everything*."

He kissed her the way he would have if she'd been there the moment he'd won—all the adrenaline, the wild beating of his heart, the need to keep that feeling going, the need to make her feel it, too.

Her body fit perfectly against his, hard in places, soft in others. He wanted her the way he'd always wanted her, the way that fire wants to burn. This time, the kiss came laden with memories—the way their bodies knew each other, the way *they* knew each other, the many, many times when the only thing in his life that felt right was *this*.

Jameson forced his lips away from hers—but barely. "You got yourself disqualified for me, Heiress."

"This was your game, Jameson. Not mine."

"You burned my secret." He looked at her eyes. There were rings of colors there, more shades of brown and gold and green than plain "hazel" eyes had a right to. "You didn't read what I wrote. You could have, but you didn't."

"It was your secret," she said simply. "Not mine."

Jameson closed his eyes. Before, he hadn't trusted himself to tell her. But now? "Say the word, Heiress." *Tahiti.* "Say it and—"

"I don't need to know." Avery's voice was steady. "If what you need is for me not to know, then I don't need to."

Jameson brought his lips to hers again and murmured a single word. "Liar."

Beside them, Oren cleared his throat. Loudly. "Cell signal's back," he announced. "I have your phone, Jameson, courtesy of Rohan."

"He was blocking calls before," Avery clarified. Jameson heard what she didn't say: *I'm not lying about not needing to know. I'm pretending. There's a difference. And if what you need is for me to keep pretending, Hawthorne—I will.*

Jameson felt a lump rising in his throat, a single sentence burned in his mind still. An *H*, the word *is*, the letters *v* and *e*.

Not today, Jameson told himself. Today, he was going to savor his win, savor her. *But soon.*

"I know you've transferred most of the foreign properties over to the foundation," he murmured, "but what are your thoughts on Scottish castles?"

Vantage was *his*—and based on Avery's expression, he had a feeling he was going to like her thoughts on Scottish castles very much.

But before she could make good on the promise in her eyes, Jameson's phone buzzed, as voicemails, texts, and missed calls came through on a delay. He stared at the most recent, a text. *From Grayson*, he realized.

911.

CHAPTER 90

GRAYSON

When Grayson arrived at the gates of Hawthorne House, he got out of his hired car and sent the driver on his way. It was a long walk to the House—and an even longer one to the tree house.

Or what was left of it, anyway.

Grayson stared up at the havoc he and Jameson had wreaked after Emily died. Slipping off his suit jacket and laying it over a low-hanging branch, he began to climb. Most of the walkways between the trees had been destroyed. Only one of the soaring towers remained intact. The main body of the house had angry, gaping holes.

Grayson made his way from a series of branches to one of the slides and climbed in through a window.

"Peek-a-boo!" Xander jumped down from the rafters. "And welcome home. Your nine-one-one was bare on details, so I took the liberty of extrapolating a bit."

Grayson eyed his brother, then scanned the tree house. Xander "extrapolating" was rarely a good thing. "I don't want to talk about it," Grayson said. *The reason for that nine-one-one. What happened after you and Nash left Phoenix.*

"So don't talk," Nash called from down below. Without another word to Grayson, he hauled a series of brown paper grocery bags up into the tree house, handing them off to Xander.

"You heard from Jamie yet?" Nash asked.

Xander raised a hand. "I have. He and Avery are on their way back. ETA tomorrow morning."

Nash swiveled his gaze back to Grayson. "Guess that means we're having ourselves a little slumber party out here first."

Jameson made it back just as they were waking up the next morning. Like Nash, he, too, had come prepared. Unlike Nash, Jameson didn't make the rest of them wait to find out what was in his bag.

The first thing he took out was a massive water bottle. A massive, *empty* water bottle. The next three things out of the bag were ketchup, a gallon of milk, and a liter of root beer.

Grayson saw where this was going almost immediately—and so did Xander, who gleefully adopted an announcer's voice. "It's time," he boomed, "for that standby Hawthorne classic . . . Drink or Dare!"

Ten minutes later, the empty water bottle was very full—and a disturbing shade of milky brown.

"I'll go first," Xander volunteered. "Jamie, I dare you to tell us the absolute most banana pants thing that happened while you were in England."

"Met my father. Won a castle. Saved a duchess from certain death. Not in that order." Jameson leaned back against the wall of the tree house, pretending—as the rest of them had all night—that it was still fully intact.

"Which one of those explains your face?" Nash asked Jameson. The bruises and swelling clearly suggested that their brother had been in one hell of a fight.

"Some faces need no explanation," Jameson replied. He gestured to his own. "Work of art. And now it's my turn. Nash." The gleam in Jamie's eyes was downright wicked. "I dare you to eat your hat."

Grayson very nearly laughed but covered it with a cough.

"Excuse me?" Nash drawled.

Jameson leaned forward. "Literally. Eat. Your. Hat."

For the first time since Gigi had found that picture of the passwords on his phone, Grayson almost smiled.

"A bite will do," Jameson continued.

Nash ran his hand along the brim of his cowboy hat. "And how am I supposed to..."

"I brought utensils!" Xander volunteered, because of course he had. "And kitchen shears. You never know when you're going to need kitchen shears."

Nash looked to the murky liquid in the water bottle. Per the rules of the game, any player who failed to fulfill a dare had to take a nice, long swig, at least three seconds in duration. "Remind me what's in there?"

"Milk, root beer, ketchup, pickle juice, oregano, chili powder, beef broth, and chocolate syrup," Xander announced happily.

Nash removed his cowboy hat and narrowed his eyes at Jameson. "How big a bite are we talkin' about here?"

Three hours later, Grayson had no shirt, and there was a giant face drawn on his stomach in permanent marker. Jameson's eyebrows were neon purple. Nash *still* smelled like dog breath and peanut butter. And Xander had successfully built a Rube Goldberg machine the purpose of which was smacking his own ass.

The tightness in Grayson's chest and the heaviness in the pit of his stomach were gone.

So, of course, Jameson took that as his cue to push things. "Grayson." Green eyes met Grayson's ice-blue ones. "I dare you to admit that you're not okay."

He wasn't. Of course he wasn't. But a Hawthorne didn't just admit such things—especially *this* Hawthorne. Grayson reached for the now half-empty bottle, but Nash swiped it before he could.

"This is a safe place," Xander told him encouragingly. "Unless you're my ass."

Grayson snorted, then the snort turned to a laugh, and then the laugh turned to something else, this horrible, strangled sound in his throat. He'd known, when he sent that nine-one-one, that the end result wouldn't be all fun and games.

"Well?" Jameson asked him. "What's it going to be, Gray?"

I dare you to admit that you're not okay.

"I'm not okay," Grayson said. "My sisters will probably never speak to me again, and I'm not good at losing people." Grayson paused. "Either that," he continued hoarsely, "or I am exceptionally good at losing people."

Every time he let someone in...

Every time he let his guard down...

Every time he was anything less than perfect...

"You haven't lost us, little brother," Nash said fiercely.

"Do you want to make fun of him for that?" Jameson asked Xander. "Or should I?"

Nash reached into one of the bags he'd brought and withdrew

a stack of metal cups and some whiskey. "Just for that," he told Jameson, "I'm not sharing—at least, not with you."

Nash took one of the cups and poured himself a bit of whiskey, then did the same with a second cup and handed it to Grayson. Nash took a sip of his own, then looked out the tree house window. "A few years ago," he said, his voice somehow a match for the whiskey, "when I realized that Alisa and I weren't going to make it, I knew in my bones that it was because there was something wrong with me. *Just look at me*, I thought. No father. Skye's never been the maternal type. Even the old man—he wasn't for me what he was for you three. What did I know about trusting someone, relying on someone, being there? What did I know about staying put? How could someone like me even think the word *forever*?"

Grayson had never heard his brother talk like this. "And now you have Libby," he told Nash. Grayson thought back to the heirloom ring that Nash had given him. His throat tightened. "I'm not ever going to have a Libby."

"Bullshit." Nash stared him down. "You know how to love people just fine, Gray. We all do. The proof of that is right here."

Grayson's father hadn't wanted him. His mother had never really been there. The old man had been more concerned with forging them into what they needed to be than what *they* needed. But Grayson had always—*always*—had his brothers.

"I don't want to break again." Grayson could admit that to them now.

"Pretend your heart is a bone," Xander advised. "When has a broken bone ever slowed a Hawthorne down? Give it time, and a fracture just heals stronger."

Grayson could see the Xander-logic there. Still, he turned to

Jameson. "Do you remember what the old man said to us that Fourth of July when he caught us up here with Emily?"

"All-consuming," Jameson murmured. "Eternal. And only once."

"You know what I think, Gray?" Nash finished his whiskey and stood. "I think the old man was full of shit."

"Breaking news," Xander intoned. "Full report at eleven."

Nash ignored him. "And your broken heart—right here, right now," he continued, his gaze locked on Grayson's. "That's not about romance. It's about family. It's about you being scared that if you let someone in—anyone, in any capacity—they're going to leave you. And you can't let that happen, so you leave first."

Grayson's grip on his own glass tightened. "That's not true."

Except it was. Wasn't that what he'd done with Avery?

"You left Phoenix," Xander pointed out in his most helpful tone.

Grayson shook his head. "Gigi made it very clear that she wanted nothing to do with me. Savannah will feel the same, once she knows what I did."

"So you left," Nash said, cocking a brow.

Grayson slammed his glass down. "I can't make this better! I can't explain myself to them. I can't apologize. I can't do a damn thing, not without putting Avery at risk."

Jameson leaned forward, snagged Grayson's glass, and took a drink. "Then maybe you and *Monsieur Belly*"—Jameson nodded to the drawing on Grayson's stomach—"should have a chat with her."

CHAPTER 91

GRAYSON

That night, Grayson went swimming—not to forget this time, but to stall. It didn't work. He felt Avery's presence the moment she stepped onto the patio. He took one more lap, then pulled himself out of the pool.

Avery eyed the drawing on his torso. "I'm not going to ask."

Grayson bared his teeth. "Please don't."

"Jameson told me about your sisters." Avery gave him a look, one of those very Avery expressions that was worth a thousand words. In this case, her eyes said, *I'm sorry you're in pain.* The set of her mouth said, *You should have called me.* The delicate line of her jaw said, *You continue to be one of the most infuriating men on the planet.*

Grayson couldn't argue any of those points, so he rebutted her verbal statement instead. "I didn't tell Jameson that much."

"You told him enough," Avery shot back. "If I could go back in time to when your father kidnapped me, when Mellie shot him—I'd call the police."

Regret. Grayson recognized the depth of emotion in her tone all too well.

"Toby and Oren took care of it," Avery said. "But I shouldn't have let them. Calling the police would have led to a media circus, but we would have survived."

Grayson brought his eyes to hers and didn't speak until he was certain that she wouldn't look away again. "We do that," he told her quietly. "Survive."

Avery smiled, a barely there hint of a smile, and Grayson realized suddenly that for the first time since he'd met Avery Grambs, there was nothing tense or painful about standing this close to her.

She'd told him once that they were family. Maybe a part of him had been running from that, too.

"What do your sisters think happened to their father?" Avery always had a way of cutting straight to the questions that mattered most.

"I don't know for sure what they believe," Grayson told her. "Popular consensus is that he skipped town. I think they think that he's capable of that now. They know he's under FBI investigation."

"So maybe he did skip town," Avery told Grayson. "But maybe he hired someone to go after me on his way. You don't have to tell your sisters everything, but you could tell them he was behind the bombing, tell them that you were protecting them from the truth and protecting me from having to relive the worst time of my life."

This is Avery, protecting me. "As a general rule," Grayson told her, "voluntarily opening a can of worms rarely goes well."

"As a general rule, Gray, when people get close to you, you bolt."

No one except his brothers was allowed to talk to him like that. No one except her.

"Toby called me," Avery continued after a moment. "He was under the impression that Eve called you."

What seemed on the surface like a subject change probably wasn't, coming from her.

"You don't need to worry about Eve calling me." Grayson clipped his words. "You don't need to worry about Eve and me, period."

"Toby said that Vincent Blake survived his double bypass." Avery's own tone was measured. "He's expected to make a full recovery." She took a step toward him, just as measured as her words. "Toby asked me to tell you that Eve has been surveilling your sisters."

"I am aware." Grayson gave her a quelling look meant to end this conversation, but she was Avery Grambs, and he was Grayson Hawthorne, and she'd never once been quelled by anything he'd thrown at her.

"Eve sent someone to *watch* your sisters," Avery reiterated, "but that's all she did, Grayson—surveillance, nothing else. Eve hasn't made a move against your family. Toby's sure of it."

Grayson had been raised a skeptic, but Avery, he bone-deep believed. "Toby's sure of it," he echoed. "And you're sure of him."

"He called me *horrible girl*." Avery smiled wistfully. "He's telling the truth."

"You are pretty horrible," Grayson agreed, his tone deadpan, a ghost of a smile pulling at his lips. His mind began sifting through the implications of Toby's claim, disassembling a puzzle Grayson had thought was solved, piecing the elements back together a different way.

"What are you thinking?" Avery prodded.

Grayson removed his phone from his pocket to call his brothers. "I'm thinking that if Toby's right, if the FBI's sudden burst of interest in the Sheffield Grayson case really wasn't Eve's doing—I need to get back to Phoenix."

CHAPTER 92

JAMESON

The game is afoot. Jameson relished the thought, knowing perfectly well that the meaning of the phrase had nothing to do with the kind of game you played, but rather, the kind of game you hunted.

None of them were about to let Grayson go hunting alone.

This *nine-one-one* had just gotten a lot more interesting.

"Details," Xander said encouragingly, as the whole lot of them piled into a bulletproof SUV. "Don't be shy, Gray. We're all family here, and most of us can look you in the eye without thinking about the face drawn on your stomach."

Grayson was clad once again in a suit. Jameson had made the symbolic decision to don one of his own—and he wasn't the only one who'd done so. Four Hawthornes, four suits. Avery wore black.

Jameson didn't know who had landed in his brother's crosshairs, or why, but finding out would be half the fun.

"Right before I left Phoenix," Grayson said, as Oren began the drive to the airstrip where Avery's jet awaited, "the FBI raided the Grayson family home. It's been more than eighteen months since Sheffield Grayson was last seen. Even if the investigation into his questionable business practices is ongoing, a warrant like that doesn't just suddenly happen, eighteen months out, without someone stirring the pot."

Someone, Jameson thought, *who is going to regret it.*

Nash was the first to reply to Grayson's statement out loud. "You thought that someone was Eve."

Xander twisted in his seat. "It's not?"

"Kent Trowbridge," Grayson bit out. The name meant nothing to Jameson—yet. "He's a lawyer," Grayson continued. "Worked for Acacia Grayson's mother. There's history there."

"Lawyerly history?" Xander queried.

"If I were a betting man," Grayson stated calmly, "I would guess the history between Acacia and Trowbridge is more of the 'you married a penniless Sheffield Grayson instead of me' variety."

Jameson cocked his head to the side, the first hints of adrenaline making their way into his bloodstream. "I *am* a betting man."

Grayson smiled darkly. "I know."

It had been a long time since all four of them had been presented with a challenge like this one—all *five* of them, counting Avery.

Jameson leaned back in his seat. "Tell us more."

Grayson obliged. "Sheffield Grayson came from poverty. He married money, and his wife's parents funded his business endeavors. He siphoned funds away from those endeavors for his personal use, stockpiling them in foreign accounts. When his wife's mother died, she left everything to her daughter and granddaughters, tied up in trusts. Acacia is her own trustee, but the trustee for the twins' trusts is..."

"Kent Trowbridge?" Jameson guessed.

Grayson nodded curtly. "My father kept a journal detailing his own illegal transactions. He supposedly emptied Acacia's trust, but there was no record of that in the journal. Records of embezzling from his own company? Yes. Records of his plot against Avery? Yes. But there was *nothing* about emptying Acacia's trust."

Now, Jameson's mind was whirring. "Would Trowbridge have had access to it?"

"He comes from a prominent family of lawyers with close ties to Acacia's mother's family," Grayson replied. "If Trowbridge didn't set up the trust, someone in his family probably did. Assuming Acacia's trust used the same financial institutions as the girls' trusts, I'd say it's likely Trowbridge could figure out a way to access it. And if it appeared to him that Sheffield Grayson had been engaged in illegal activities and skipped town..."

"Trowbridge could fairly easily assure that Acacia would blame her husband for the empty accounts," Jameson finished. "Everyone would. How much money are we talking about here?"

Grayson did some mental calculations. "If I were guessing, I'd say between ten and twelve million in Acacia's trust and an equal amount for each of the girls. It's possible that Trowbridge was in some kind of financial trouble..."

Jameson knew his brother well enough to read into his tone. "But you don't think so."

"No." Grayson's eyes hardened. "I think this is about Acacia."

"He wants to control her?" Nash said. There was nothing that got under Nash's skin like a man mistreating a woman.

"He's boxing her in," Grayson replied, a dark undertone in his voice. "Turning up the heat. I overheard him telling her that he was there for her, she just had to *let* him be there for her. I heard him reminding her that her parents were gone, that her husband was gone, that she had no one. And wouldn't you know it, when the FBI came to the house, he was nowhere to be seen, because she couldn't afford a lawyer, and his only offer was to come as a *friend*."

Grayson stopped there, but Jameson knew instinctively that his brother wasn't done. He was still thinking, still piecing together the big picture.

All they had to do was let him.

"Trowbridge told Savannah about the accusations against her father," Grayson stated with blade-like precision. "And about her mother's emptied trust. Plus, right before Gigi and I fought, she said that Savannah and their mother had an argument about the girls' trusts. They wanted to use them to help pay for a lawyer, but Savannah said the trust terms wouldn't allow that unless..."

"Unless Trowbridge signed off on it?" Nash drawled.

"Maybe," Jameson replied. "But Grayson thinks there might be more to it than that. Don't you, Gray?"

"I think," Grayson said, his voice low, "that if my private investigator hasn't managed to get a copy of the trust paperwork by now, he's fired."

CHAPTER 93

JAMESON

They went from SUV to private jet and by the time they had, Grayson had gotten ahold of that paperwork. He set his tablet down with an audible click for the rest of them to see. Avery beat Jameson, Xander, and Nash to picking it up.

"The money is under the control of the trustee until the beneficiary is thirty years old..." Avery's eyes widened, and she looked up from what she'd just read. "Or married."

Grayson's expression was grim. "Savannah is seventeen, eighteen in seven months. She has a boyfriend, and that boyfriend is Kent Trowbridge's son."

Jameson didn't know these people as anything other than names in a story, but he thought about what Grayson had already said. The elder Trowbridge was boxing Acacia Grayson in, draining her finances, using the FBI to rattle her, ensuring that her only options were him... or his son.

"I take it we do not like this boyfriend?" Xander queried.

Grayson's expression became, in a word, *murderous*. "He touches her when she doesn't want to be touched. I saw the father do the same thing to Acacia—a hand on her shoulder, inching toward her neck." There were slabs of granite softer than Grayson's jaw at that moment. "The son is whiny," he told them. "The father is dangerous."

"So we take him out." Nash took off his second-favorite cowboy hat.

Jameson smiled. Kent Trowbridge didn't know what he'd gotten himself into. No one stood a chance against any two of the Hawthorne brothers, let alone all four. "What do we have to work with, Gray?"

Grayson's reply was immediate. "Illegal activity to hold over his head if we can find proof that he's the one who emptied Acacia's trust." Grayson's smile was measured and slow. "There's a safe in his home office. I didn't have time to crack it the last time I was there, but this may call for a return trip."

Jameson leaned forward, ready to play. "What else?"

Grayson leaned back. "I have all of his passwords. Guy kept them taped to the inside of his desk."

Unfortunate for him, Jameson thought. *And very fortunate for us.*

Across the aisle of the plane, Nash looked from Xander to Avery. "You two thinking what I'm thinking?"

Xander grinned. "This should be fun."

CHAPTER 94

GRAYSON

Every problem had solutions, plural. Complex problems were fluid, dynamic. But as it turned out, Kent Trowbridge wasn't all that complex, and Grayson was certain that he wouldn't be a problem for long.

Two days. That was how long it took for Grayson and his brothers to get what they needed, which gave Grayson plenty of time to consider the where and when of this confrontation.

Racquetball wasn't one of Grayson's sports of choice, but the racquetball court that Trowbridge had reserved for his weekly game against a family friend suited Grayson's purposes nicely—particularly given that the friend in question was a federal judge.

The same judge who'd signed the FBI warrant.

The clear glass wall separating the hall from court number seven allowed Grayson the perfect view of his quarry. Even better, it allowed his quarry to eventually realize that he was being watched.

Grayson had dressed for the occasion: expensive suit, expensive shoes, a black-and-gold Rolex on his wrist. He didn't look like he belonged in an athletic facility. There was an advantage to making sure your opponent felt underdressed.

The judge noticed him first. Grayson didn't bat an eye. He just kept watching the two of them, the way a man on the floor of the stock exchange might watch the boards.

It took all of a minute for the game to come to a pause. The judge pushed open the glass door, annoyed. "Can we help you?"

"I can wait." Grayson put very little inflection in those words. "I'd hate to interrupt your match."

Trowbridge made his way out into the hall, his racket dangling from one hand. He scowled. "Mr. Hawthorne."

Grayson had the general sense that Trowbridge was using *mister* the way a high school principal might. It wasn't a sign of respect, that was for sure—but either way, the form of address he'd chosen backfired.

"Hawthorne?" the judge asked.

Grayson offered the man the most perfunctory of smiles. "Guilty as charged." He turned the full force of his gaze and attention to the judge. "You recently signed a federal warrant for my younger sisters' home." Grayson's tone was conversational, because he'd learned from the master that the most powerful people in the world never needed to do more than converse. "What a coincidence that the two of you know each other."

Trowbridge, Grayson saw with no small amount of satisfaction, was getting irritated. "Whatever you think you're doing here, young man, Acacia won't thank you for it."

That was doubtlessly true. "She probably won't thank the forensic accountants I hired, either."

A vein pulsed near Trowbridge's temple, but he made a valiant attempt at holding on to his calm. He turned to his racquetball partner. "Same time next week?"

The judge looked long and hard at Grayson, then glanced back at Trowbridge. "I'll let you know."

Soon enough, Grayson and his prey were alone. Right on cue, Trowbridge's phone buzzed.

Grayson smiled. "I'm sure that's not anything too critical."

Trowbridge visibly resisted the urge to answer his phone. "What can I do for you, Grayson?"

First name now. Interesting choice. "Once you've been disbarred," Grayson replied, gloves off, "not much."

"I've had enough of this," Trowbridge told him. "They never even should have let you past the front desk."

Grayson stared at the man for a moment, watching that vein throb, and then he said a string of numbers, one after another, evenly paced, no particular emphasis on any one digit. "That's the account that the money from Acacia's trust was transferred into. The records of the receiving bank in Singapore are, of course, nearly impossible to access." Grayson gave the slightest of shrugs. "Nearly."

Trowbridge was really sweating now, but when men like Trowbridge felt threatened, they blustered. "Are you suggesting you know where your father is?"

In response, Grayson recited another number. "That's the combination to your safe," he clarified helpfully.

"How *dare you—*"

"My brothers and I are fond of dares," Grayson replied. "And foreign banks like the one you used—they're awfully fond of billionaires."

"You aren't a billionaire," Trowbridge spat. "You have nothing."

"A Hawthorne," Grayson replied coolly, "never has nothing." He paused, the silence a knife to be wielded just so. "You're thinking about everything you keep in that safe."

"I'll have you *arrested*."

"Oh, don't worry," Grayson told the man. "I'm sure that once the FBI realizes—if they haven't already—that the entirety of Acacia Grayson's inheritance has been restored to her trust, they won't stop until they track down the party responsible." Grayson held Trowbridge's gaze in a way designed to hold him in place. "They'll think it's her husband at first, I'm sure..."

Trowbridge narrowed his eyes. "Don't you mean your father?"

It was almost amusing, the way this man thought there were points to be won in this little back and forth. The way he didn't realize—refused to realize—that he was *done*.

"My father," Grayson agreed amiably. "I can't say I have any affection for the man. But at least he—or whoever took Acacia's money—had a sudden burst of conscience." Grayson leaned forward, just slightly. "I hope for that person's sake," he said softly, "that they weren't sloppy."

There was an art to saying things without saying them. Things like *I know you took the money*. And *the FBI will know that soon, too.*

"You're done," Trowbridge blustered. "If you think your name will protect you..."

"I don't need protection," Grayson said simply. "It wasn't my safe. Those weren't my accounts."

Trowbridge's phone buzzed again.

Grayson continued blithely, "I certainly didn't send those emails."

There it was—the bob of his opponent's Adam's apple. "What emails?" Trowbridge demanded.

Grayson didn't reply. He glanced pointedly at court number seven. "You'll have to let me know if the judge still wants to play next week."

Within the week, said the promise beneath that seemingly innocuous sentence, *no one will be willing to risk a connection with you.*

Grayson turned to leave.

"He didn't deserve her!" Trowbridge wasn't yelling so much as vibrating with fury. "She should have listened to me."

"On the day of her mother's funeral?" Grayson didn't even bother turning back to face the man. "Or years earlier when she said that the two of you would be better as friends? Or maybe more recently, when you set Savannah up to think that in seven short months, she would be in a position to solve her family's problems?"

Protect them.

"Acacia was never going to let Savannah do that," Trowbridge snapped.

Grayson still refused to turn around. "Acacia would say yes to you first," he said quietly. "That was the plan, was it not?"

Trowbridge was incensed now, bordering on apoplectic. "You arrogant, spoiled, cocksure—"

"Brother," Grayson finished. "The word you're looking for is *brother*." Now, he looked back. "No one hurts my family."

Whatever Gigi and Savannah thought of him now, he *would* protect them.

Trowbridge's phone buzzed again. He looked down at it this time and paled at the number that flashed across his screen.

"I'll let you get that," Grayson said with one last, well-targeted smile. "Something tells me that it just might be critical after all."

CHAPTER 95

GRAYSON

That night, after they'd made it back to Hawthorne House, Grayson lay in his bed staring up at the ceiling. Tonight was clearly going to be a night when sleep didn't come easily, if at all. His mind wasn't racing. He wasn't tossing or turning. He was just . . . awake.

Trowbridge was taken care of, in a way that would divert the FBI's investigation for the foreseeable future. Acacia's financial woes had been remedied. She now had a very good lawyer. Grayson had checked every item off his Phoenix to-do list.

His Grayson family to-do list.

Do you ever play what-if, Grayson? The question Acacia had asked him came back to Grayson, and for just a moment, he let the answer be yes. If he'd had a more normal childhood, if he'd spent even a few weeks a year with his father, with Acacia and the girls, would it have changed anything?

Changed him?

Bullshit, he could hear Nash saying. *You know how to love people just fine.* Grayson thought about the ring tucked inside his suitcase. In his mind, he could see the magnificent stone as if he were looking straight at it.

Grappling for a distraction, for something—anything—else to hold on to, Grayson considered a riddle, one he could still hear said by a girl with a honey-rich voice.

What begins a bet? Not that.

As if summoned by some unholy magic, his phone rang on the nightstand where it was charging. Grayson sat up, the sheet falling away from his chest. In his gut and in his mind and in his aching body, he somehow expected the caller to be that girl.

But it wasn't.

It wasn't Eve this time, either.

It was Gigi. Grayson stared at her name on the screen, unable to quite bring himself to pick up. Less than a minute later, he received a text. No cat picture this time, just words.

I'm at the gate.

Grayson had no idea what Gigi was doing at Hawthorne House—or how she'd even gotten there. But his sister didn't give him a chance to ask a single question.

"Inside," she told him. "We'll talk inside. You look creepy in the dark."

Grayson tried his best not to take that personally. Whatever she threw at him, whatever she'd come here to say or do—he wouldn't take it personally.

The two of them rode from the gates to Hawthorne House in silence. Grayson was well aware of the fact that their progression was being tracked by security, but none of Oren's men tried to stop them.

In the grand foyer, Gigi didn't mince words. "Mom says her money's back." Bright blue eyes pinned his. "You did that, didn't you?" She paused. "Or you convinced Dad to?"

Grayson's heart twisted in his chest. After everything, she was still holding out hope. Because that was what Gigi did. She *hoped*. "Gigi…"

She stabbed her index finger in his general direction. "How dare you do something wonderful when I'm mad at you?" Mad at him? He'd thought she was *done* with him. "Do you know how hard it is for me to stay mad at people?" she continued, scowling. "How very dare you!"

Grayson couldn't let himself smile, not even a little. He couldn't risk it. "Your father didn't return the money," he told Gigi, "because he wasn't the one who took it from your mother's trust. Trowbridge did."

Gigi glared at him. "Kent or Duncan?"

"Kent."

Gigi blew out a long breath. "Can I hate Duncan anyway?"

This time, Grayson couldn't help the slight twitch of his lips. "Please do."

"Good," Gigi said. "Because as bad as I am staying mad at people, I truly excel at holding permanent and unholy grudges against anyone who hurts my sister. May his crotch forever itch in places that are very difficult to scratch and his fingers turn to sausages on his hands."

It was probably a good thing that Gigi had been as yet unsuccessful at her attempts to develop magical powers.

"You were wrong earlier," Gigi told Grayson, her change of subject swift and firm. "You said *your father*—but he isn't just my father, Grayson, or Savannah's. He's yours, too. You must have had a reason for what you did—not the good stuff, not the money stuff, but the rest of it."

Sabotaging their efforts. Betraying her.

"I warned you from the beginning not to trust me," Grayson told her. He waited for anger that never came.

"Why?" Gigi said. "Even after everything, you helped us, Grayson. You got Mom a lawyer. You found the money somehow. You beat the bad guy." She paused. "You did beat the bad guy, right?"

Grayson nodded. "Yeah," he told Gigi. "I did."

"Why?" his little sister demanded again. "Because it looks an awful lot to me like you care." She stared at him. "You do. I know you do. So why would you—"

"I had to." Grayson hadn't meant to say that, and he hadn't meant for the words to come out tortured and low. "I *had to,* Gigi." Maybe he should have left it there. A week ago, he would have. "I know something about your father that you don't know, something that you shouldn't know."

"Our father" came the stubborn correction.

"He wasn't a good guy, Gigi."

"Because of the whole embezzlement-and-tax-evasion thing?"

I could say yes. I could leave it there. And I could lose her. Grayson thought back to his conversation with Avery—Avery, whom he wanted to protect more than just about anyone else in the world.

Just about.

"Before he disappeared, your father—" At his sister's glare, Grayson corrected himself. "Our father... he tried to kill someone who matters to me. You might not have seen it in the news back then—"

Gigi stared at him. "There was a bomb, right? On a plane? Someone tried to kill the Hawthorne heiress." Gigi frowned. "Wasn't your mother arrested for that?"

Grayson swallowed. "They arrested the wrong parent."

Gigi's eyes were very round. "Dad?" she whispered. "That whole thing with Aunt Kim and the Hawthornes getting theirs..."

Grayson was walking a dangerous line now. He knew it, just like he knew that no matter what he said, Gigi might still choose to walk away. But he had to try. "He wanted revenge." Grayson gave her as much of the truth as he could. "For Colin."

Gigi drew in a long breath and looked up at the ceiling that soared overhead, doing everything she could not to blink. *Not to cry.*

"It's always Colin." Gigi kept right on staring at the ceiling. "I remember being three years old and knowing that my dad loved me...and that he especially loved the way I looked." Gigi swallowed. "Because I looked like Colin. And as long as I was happy and bubbly and just a silly little girl who didn't try to matter too much, that was a good thing."

Grayson pulled her in, and the next thing he knew, his sister's head was resting on his chest, his arms enveloping her.

"Grayson?" Gigi said softly. "You said *wanted*. Past tense. You said that Dad *wanted* revenge. But once he wants something...he doesn't stop. Ever."

He didn't stop with the bomb. He had no intentions of stopping until Toby Hawthorne paid—with Avery's life and with his own.

Gigi angled her head up toward Grayson. "I guess I'm a lot like Dad that way, with the not stopping."

Grayson wondered if that was Gigi's way of telling him that she was going to keep asking questions, keep pushing. He wondered if he'd made a mistake telling her as much as he had.

But all he said in reply was "You are nothing like our father."

There was a long, painful silence. "He's not coming back, is he, Grayson?"

No answer would have been an answer, so he gave her what he could. "No."

"He *can't* come back, can he?"

No answer was an answer, the only one he could give her this time.

For more than a minute, Gigi didn't move. Grayson held her, bracing himself for the moment when she would pull back.

Finally, she did. "You're going to have to give me the puzzle box back," she told him. "For Savannah. We're going to have to make sure there's something in it, something that gives her an answer she can believe. One that doesn't involve our dad being an evil mastermind of the non-white-collar variety."

Grayson stared at her. "What are you saying?"

Gigi stepped back. "My whole life, Savannah has tried to protect me. I mean, she knew about you for years, about Dad's affair, and she did everything she could to make sure I didn't have to know. And all of this? With Dad? *She doesn't have to know.*" Gigi said those words like an oath. "Savannah loves Dad. She was always closer to him than Mom. She pushed herself so hard *for him.* So we're going to protect her this time. You and me. Because I remember something else about the Hawthorne heiress plane bombing. People died. Our father *killed* people, Grayson. And now he's..." Gigi didn't say the word *dead.* "In Tunisia," she finished, her tone steely. "And that's where he needs to stay."

Grayson could feel her pushing down her pain, and the idea of it almost destroyed him. "I can't ask you..." he started to say.

"You're not asking me to do anything," Gigi told him. "I'm telling you how it's going to be. And in case you haven't noticed, I'm very good at getting what I want. And I want a happy sister and a big brother who keeps a very open mind about any mysterious, nefarious types I might choose to pursue for brief romantic liaisons."

Grayson narrowed his eyes at her. "Not funny."

Gigi smiled, and something about the set of her lips felt like pins through his heart.

"I never meant to hurt you," Grayson told her.

"I know," Gigi said simply.

She's not leaving. I haven't lost her. Grayson didn't ignore the emotions twisting in his gut and rising up inside him. For once in his life, he just let them come. "I like my little sister," he told her.

This time, there was nothing pained about Gigi's smile. "I know."

CHAPTER 96

GRAYSON

The next morning, after reassembling the box with the fake journal inside and sending it back with Gigi, Grayson found himself picking up the briefcase of photographs from the safe-deposit box. He made his way through the wing where he and his brothers had spent hours upon hours playing as children, up to their childhood library—the loft library. Behind one of the bookshelves, there was a hidden staircase. At the bottom of the stairs, there was a Davenport desk.

Grayson opened it and found two journals inside: Sheffield Grayson's original and his translation. Grayson opened the suitcase and methodically began to pull out photographs of himself—nineteen years of photographs, starting the day he was born—and place them in the desk.

Faceup this time.

When he came to the photograph he'd paused on before, he

turned it over in his hands, and looked at the date on the back. The wrong date. And then he paused.

Grayson searched through the photos, for another one he could precisely date. The year was right. The day was, too.

But the month was wrong.

Grayson grabbed another picture, then another. *The month is always wrong.*

He hadn't let himself spend much time thinking about these pictures, about what might have led a father who had made it very clear that he was not wanted to take and keep them. Maybe part of it was a sense of possession. A desire for a *son.* But these pictures had been in a box with the withdrawal slips that served as a key for decoding the journal. And in that journal, Sheffield Grayson had documented illegal transactions by identifying the countries in which he kept accounts. Just the countries.

There hadn't been a single account number, no routing numbers, no numbers at all.

It took Grayson three days to piece together all of the account information, using the numbers on the back of the pictures—the wrong months, in chronological order based on the photos they corresponded to. There were seven accounts total, millions of dollars.

All of it untraceable.

When he was sure he had it all, Grayson called Alisa. "Hypothetically, if information about all of Sheffield Grayson's offshore accounts somehow made its way to the FBI, how likely do you think it is they'd keep looking for the man himself?"

Alisa considered the question. "Hypothetically," she said, "if the right strings were pulled? Very unlikely."

Grayson hung up the phone. It was as good as done, another thread tied off, another secret buried—for good, he hoped.

Gigi knows the truth, and I didn't lose her. She knows, and she didn't leave.

Later that night, Grayson unpacked the bag he'd taken with him to London and Phoenix. He unpacked the velvet ring box that Nash had entrusted to his keeping. And for the first time since Nash had given him the damn thing, when that question echoed in his mind, Grayson didn't run from it.

Why not you, Gray? Someday, with someone—why not you?

He thought about the made-up story he'd spun for Gigi about his "girlfriend," about meeting someone at the damn grocery store buying limes.

He thought about phone calls and riddles, about burying himself in his work, about Nash breaking things off with Alisa, certain that there was something wrong with him.

About the way Nash *fit* with Libby.

Moving with purpose—the way he always did—Grayson took the black opal ring out of the box and turned it over in his hand. He stared at it, at the flecks of color in the jewel, at the diamond leaves that surrounded it, and he swallowed.

"Why not me?"

CHAPTER 97

JAMESON

It was Jameson's idea to rebuild the tree house. Every now and then, as they worked, he dropped tantalizing bits of information about the father he'd met, the castle he'd won, the duchess he'd saved—not in that order.

He didn't tell his brothers about the Devil's Mercy, but he did tell them about the Game—not about the prizes at stake or the powerful figures behind it, but about the riddles, the cliffs, the stone garden, the chandelier, the bell tower.

The silver ballerina.

It took his brothers the better part of a day to figure out the final answer, though Jameson knew they would have been much quicker if they'd seen the silent silver music box themselves.

After that riddle had been solved, Grayson offered up a challenge of his own. "Another riddle," he told them. *"What begins a bet? Not that."*

No matter how much Jameson prodded, Grayson wouldn't tell

them where he'd heard the riddle, but one night, Jameson caught him looking at a file, one of their grandfather's, which he quickly hid away.

A bet began with a challenge, a wager, an agreement, a risk. *A handshake?* Jameson's mind turned the possibilities over, examining them from every angle. *Not that. So what's the opposite of a handshake?*

The night the tree house restoration was completed, Jameson found himself alone with Avery in one of the towers, looking out over the Hawthorne estate.

"I've been thinking," she said.

Jameson smiled. "Thinking is a good look for you, Heiress."

She put her hand on the tower wall behind him—almost, but not quite pinning him in. "About the Game."

Jameson knew her—and the look in her eyes. "It *was* fun, wasn't it?"

"It was," Avery agreed. "It always is when we play." His gaze was drawn to her mouth, the slight curve of her smile. "You told me once," she continued, "that your grandfather's games weren't designed to make you extraordinary—"

"But to show us," Jameson murmured, "that we already were."

"Do you believe it now?" Avery asked him. "That you are *extraordinary*?" The way she said the word made him feel like he was, like he always had been.

Like winning might never be enough, but *he* was. Together, they were.

"I do," Jameson told her.

Avery brought her fingertips to the edge of his mouth, then traced it lightly over the edge of his jaw. "Ask me again what I've been thinking about."

Jameson narrowed his eyes. "What exactly have you been thinking about, Heiress?"

"It doesn't seem fair, does it?" Avery said with a quirk of her lips. "That only the rich and powerful get the chance to play the Game?"

Jameson's own lips turned upward. "Not fair at all."

"What if there was another game?" Avery asked.

"Not hidden," Jameson murmured. "Not secret. Not just for the rich or powerful."

"And what if we designed it?" Avery said, her voice electric. "Every year."

Jameson loved playing—but *designing* a game? Making the puzzles? Showing other people what they were capable of?

"Cash prize," Avery told him. "A big one."

"The game would have to be complicated," he told Avery. "Intricate. Perfectly designed."

She grinned. "I'm going to be pretty busy with the foundation," she told him. "But everyone needs a hobby."

He knew that she knew—this wasn't going to be just a hobby for him. "The Grandest Game," he murmured. "That's what you should call it."

"What *we* will call it," Avery replied.

And in that moment, staring at her, imagining this future with her, Jameson knew: He was going to tell her everything. If he'd learned one thing from the Game he'd played—and won—it was that he *could* trust himself to tell her. He was more than hunger, more than want, more than drive, more than what Tobias Hawthorne had raised him to be.

And he wanted to be *more* with her.

"I went out that night," he said, his voice hushed and liquid, "and I came back at dawn, smelling of ash and fire." The memories were right there—as vivid as they'd always been. Jameson reached forward to take Avery's hand in his. He pressed her fingers to the place where his collarbone dipped, right at the base of his neck. "I had a cut *here*."

Avery's fingers curled slightly, stroking skin that hadn't scarred. "I remember."

He wondered if she could feel the pounding of his pulse. Was he imagining that he could feel her heartbeat? Feel *her*?

There are some things, he thought, *that shouldn't be said out loud.*

On the floor of the tower, there was a box—a game one of them must have left up here way back when. *Scrabble.* Jameson knelt and took out the board.

"Are you sure?" Avery murmured.

He was—achingly sure, so sure that he could taste it. This wasn't a mystery that either of them could risk trying to solve. They'd make their own mysteries instead, their own Game. But he didn't want a damn thing standing between the two of them in the meantime.

Trusting her. Trusting himself. It was all the same.

So Jameson spelled out his secret, the truth he'd discovered that night in Prague, what he'd written down on that scroll for the Proprietor. Four words. An *H*. The word *is*. The letters *v* and *e*.

Avery took in the message on the Scrabble board and stared at him.

ALICE HAWTHORNE IS ALIVE.

SIX YEARS, TEN MONTHS, AND THREE WEEKS AGO

"When you're old enough, when you're ready, be warned: There is *nothing* frivolous about the way a Hawthorne man loves."

Jameson thought suddenly of the grandmother he'd never even met, the woman who'd died before he was born.

"Men like us love only once," the old man said quietly. "Fully. Wholeheartedly. It's all-consuming and eternal. All these years your grandmother has been gone..." Tobias Hawthorne's eyes closed. "And there hasn't been anyone else. There can't and won't be. Because when you love a woman or a man or anyone the way we love, there is no going back."

That felt like a warning more than a promise.

"Anything less, and you'll destroy her. And if she is the one..." The old man looked first at Jameson, then at Grayson, then back at Jameson again. "Someday, she'll destroy you."

He didn't make that sound like a bad thing.

"What would she have thought of us?" Jameson asked the question on impulse, but he didn't regret it. "Our grandmother?"

"You're still works in progress," the old man replied. "Let's save my Alice's judgment for when you're done."

EPILOGUE

EVE

The day that Vincent Blake died—the day Eve found him dead of a second heart attack less than five months after the first—she called nine-one-one. She dealt with the authorities and with the body, and then, that night, she hid herself away in the bowels of the Blake mansion and turned on the television. Numb.

He was my family, and he's dead. He's gone. And I'm alone. On the television screen, Avery wasn't alone. *She* was being interviewed for the whole world to see.

"I'm here today with Avery Grambs. Heiress. Philanthropist. World changer—and at only nineteen years old. Avery, tell us, what is it like to be in your position at such a young age?"

Each breath burning in her chest, Eve listened to Avery's reply to that question and the back and forth that followed between the Hawthorne heiress and one of the world's most beloved media moguls.

"Wouldn't watch that if I were you."

Eve turned to Slate, feeling too hollow to be annoyed. "You're not me," she said flatly. "You work for me."

"I keep you alive."

"As of a few hours ago, I have an entire security team for that," Eve replied. "Inherited, along with everything else."

Slate said nothing. He was irritating that way. Eve turned her attention back to the screen—to Avery.

"Why, having been left one of the largest fortunes in the world, would you give almost all of it away?" the interviewer was asking. "Are you a saint?"

"Might as well be," Eve muttered. "To them." *The Hawthornes.*

"If I were a saint," Avery said on screen, "do you really think I would have kept *two billion dollars* for myself? Do you understand how much money that is?"

Eve did. *Seven times more than Vincent Blake's fortune. Mine, now.* That difference in magnitude didn't matter to Eve. When you'd grown up with nothing, an empire was an empire. All Avery had over her—really—was the Hawthornes.

Eve tried not to think about Grayson, but not thinking about Grayson Hawthorne was harder some days than others.

Today was one of the days when it was very hard.

"Seriously," Slate said beside her. "Turn it off."

Eve almost did, but then Avery said something on screen that stopped her in her tracks.

"Tobias Hawthorne wasn't a good man, but he had a human side. He loved puzzles and riddles and games. Every Saturday morning, he would present his grandsons with a challenge..."

His grandsons, Eve thought bitterly. *But not his granddaughter.* She should have grown up at Hawthorne House. The dead billionaire had known about her. She was his only son's only child. *She* was the one who'd been betrayed—not the other way around.

All she'd ever done was try to take care of herself.

"If there's one thing that the Hawthornes have taught me," Avery said on screen, "it's that I like a challenge. I love to *play*."

"Do you?" Eve murmured, staring bullets at the happy, happy girl who'd stolen the life that should have been hers. "Do you really?"

"Every year," Avery—*perfect, beloved, brilliant Avery*—said, "I'll be hosting a contest with substantial, life-changing prize money. Some years, the game will be open to the general public. Others... well, maybe you'll find yourself on the receiving end of the world's most exclusive invitation."

Avery, in the spotlight.

Avery, calling the shots.

"This game. These puzzles. They'll be of your making?" the interviewer asked.

Avery, smiling. "I'll have help."

Those words—more than any other part of this interview—were blades to Eve's heart. Because she didn't have help. Besides Toby, who loved *Avery* as a daughter, besides Slate, who half despised her, she had no one.

All the money in the world, and still, she had no one.

On the screen, Avery was being asked when the first game would start. She was holding up a gold card. "The game starts right now."

Eve turned off the television. She closed her eyes, just for a moment, then turned to Slate. Avery wasn't the only one who liked a challenge. She wasn't the only one who liked to play.

Vincent Blake was dead. He was *gone*. Eve wasn't bound by his honor anymore. She wasn't bound by *anything*. "I have a job for you," she told Slate.

"Whatever you're thinking," he advised her, "don't."

"Do it," she told him, "and I'll give you one of my seals, make you one of my heirs."

Slate's expression was never easy to read. He wasn't easy at all. She liked that about him.

"What do you want me to do?" Slate asked.

"I need you to help me get a little one-on-one chat," she told him, "with Grayson's little sister."

"Gigi?" Slate's eyes narrowed at her. That she'd gotten any emotional reaction out of him at all was . . . unusual.

"No." Eve shook her head. "The other one." The one who reminded her of Grayson. "I think it's about time that Savannah Grayson and I had a discussion about her father."

Eve imagined herself back at thc chessboard, across from Avery. *No one is* letting *me win this time*, she thought. Avery had her game now.

And Eve had hers.

ACKNOWLEDGMENTS

Expanding the world of the Inheritance Games series and getting to spend more time with these characters has brought me so much joy, so I want to start by thanking every single reader whose passion for these characters has given me the opportunity to think big and continue writing in this world that I love so much.

To everyone at Little, Brown Books for Young Readers, thank you, thank you, thank you for everything you have done to get these books into so many hands. I am constantly in awe of this team's brilliance and creativity; I feel like the luckiest author in the world to have such a powerhouse team behind me, doing everything they can to get books into readers' hands.

Thanks especially to my editor, Lisa Yoskowitz, who is a joy to work with and such an incredible advocate for me as an author and for these books. Lisa came up with title for this one, and her keen editorial insights helped me take it from a draft that I liked to a book that I LOVE. Some of my favorite moments in this book came about based on Lisa's suggestions, and it's hard to overstate how comforting it is as an author to work with an editor whose intuitions, insights, and feedback make me feel like I can shoot for the stars every time, because I know that together, we'll get there.

So much goes in to making a book; the words on the page are just the beginning. My publishing team, led by the amazing Megan Tingley and Jackie Engel, is so incredibly good at their jobs that some mornings I just wake up thinking "HOW ARE THEY SO GOOD?" I am incredibly grateful to everyone at Little, Brown who helped bring this book to life and get it into readers' hands, including Marisa Finkelstein, Andy Ball, Caitlyn Averett, Alex Houdeshell, Virginia Lawther, Becky Munich, Jess Mercado, Cheryl Lew, Kelly Moran, Shawn Foster, Danielle Cantarella, Claire Gamble, Leah CollinsLipsett, Celeste Gordon, Anna Herling, Katie Tucker, Karen Torres, Cara Nesi, Janelle DeLuise, Hannah Koerner, Lisa Cahn, Victoria Stapleton, and Christie Michel. Special thanks go out to cover designer Karina Granda and artist Katt Phatt for the absolutely gorgeous cover, and to Emilie Polster, Bill Grace, and Savannah Kennelly for their amazing efforts to find fun ways to bring Inheritance Games fans together and build anticipation for this book—and everything that comes next!

Thank you also to everyone who helped copyedit or proofread this book. As it turns out, the more books you write set in the same fictional universe, the more there is to look out for, and I am grateful to Erin Slonaker, Jody Corbett, Su Wu, Marisa Finkelstein (again!), and Lisa Yoskowitz (again!) for their attention to detail and helping me keep the whole Inheritance Games universe in order!

To my agent, Elizabeth Harding, thank you so much for guiding and championing my career for nearly twenty years now. Having you in my corner means the world to me! Thank you also to Sarah Perillo, who has sold foreign and translation rights into a mind-boggling thirty countries so far, and to Holly Frederick for her work toward bringing the Inheritance Games to the screen. Thanks also to the rest of my amazing team at Curtis Brown, including Eliza Johnson, Eliza Leung, Madeline Tavis, Jahlila Stamp, and Michaela Glover.

Thank you to Rachel Vincent, who sat across from me at Panera once a week while I was writing this book and got me through the highs and the lows that go along with the writing process. And thank you also, Rachel, for being willing to listen to ALL THE SECRETS about what's to come in the world of the Inheritance Games and for being such a brilliant, supportive, amazing, and genuinely kind friend. I don't know what I would do without you!

The Brothers Hawthorne was the first one I wrote from scratch after leaving my day job as a college professor, and I owe a huge debt of gratitude to my family for helping me through that transition. To my boys, my parents, and my husband—thank you!

The games continue in

THE GRANDEST GAME